HATE

Her Monsters Book Two

K.A. KNIGHT

CONTENTS

Hate (Her Monsters Book Two)

This is a work of fiction. Any resemblance to places, events or real people are entirely coincidental.

Edited By Jess from Elemental Editing and Proofreading.
Formatted by Kaila Duff .
Cover design by Rabbit Hole Designs.

Dedication

*To the woman who thinks I write too much darkness
and told me to write more positivity and less death.
This one is for you.*

P.S. I killed you in this book too...

Author's Note

Warning:
There are no heroes in this story, only monsters. Enter at your own risk...

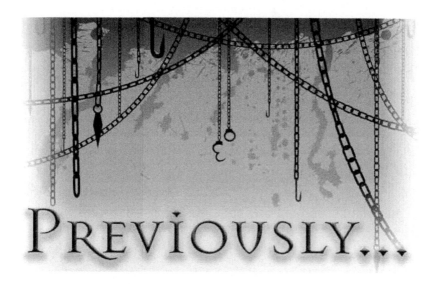

PREVIOUSLY...

I tried to include a recap, but so much happened in *Rage*..so here is the basic gist.

Dawn was murdered. She came back. She met a god who turned out to be her mate. Killed and shifted into the skin of many people. Went shopping and had lots of kinky sex while falling in love. Met another of her mates, a fallen, he's a bit nuts that one. Dreamed of a dragon who is also her mate. Woke up an ancient minotaur who killed witches and bad guys to try and get to her only to be captured.

The dragon goes in search of her and meets three cooky witches along the way. Starts a fight with a sat nav and is genuinely clueless.

Meanwhile, Dawn gets kidnapped and breaks free. Kicking ass and taking names as she tries to figure out what they are doing to human females. She finds a scientist who tells her the big bad, The Others, pay them to do it. To bring out latent, supernatural blood in humans.

Griffin turns up, they escape. They meet at his house with Nos and make some plans and have more sex. Some people are tortured, some killed, until they finally meet Victoria, AKA Victor, who her shitty ex husband was stealing from. Victoria takes down her husband and rings Dawn to meet her there.

Dawn shows up with her mates and they kill the bastard. But then, oh no! The bad guys turn up and kidnap her! She wakes up and meets an asshat called Veyo who works for the council. She pissed him off in her usual Dawn style and is dragged to a cell with a beast...Dume.

Aska stands dramatically on a hill and swears his revenge. See? Now you are mostly caught up.

Grab the wine, and maybe your vibrator. It's about to get a whole lot darker...

Chapter I

Dawn

I must have fallen asleep because I wake with a scream trapped in my throat, Tim's words echoing in my head, and the horrible, sadistic look on his face right before he killed me.

"You. Are. Mine."

I swallow them back like razors, he was wrong. I don't know why I'm dreaming of him now, maybe it's because I finally got my revenge and now, with him gone, all that's left where there was once revenge is an aching pain and bad memories crowding my head. I was never his and I will never belong to someone like that again, it's different with my mates. They don't want to own me, they want to love and protect me.

"Forever, Little Monster. You will never get away from me."

Oh, Nos, I hope you keep your promise. I miss my horned god already, miss that smile. Those white eyes and his sweetness...the hard way he used to hold me. Push me to my limit and keep me there, forcing my body and heart to accept everything. He was there when I first woke up into my undead life, he was my constant, and now he isn't here. I feel it keenly...I wish that when I open my eyes, I'd find him sitting cross-legged before me, his animalistic face tilted as he watches me...

But I don't.

Chains ring out, slithering across the floor, so I lift my head. I can't see much, it's dark, not the inky grey of night but utter blackness. The sight of death, the end, and in it hides a minotaur.

Everything must have been too much, my body shutting down not long after being thrown in here, but now I'm awake. Awake and aware I'm trapped with a mythological predator. So what do I do? I sit up and cross my legs, tipping my head, wishing I could see into the dark.

Then, suddenly, I can, my eyes light up white, bright as the moon's rays like when Nos is changed...he did say mates can possess some of each other's powers, and my eyes have turned white before...is that what's happening now? I'm learning what I am and what I'm capable of as I go, and it seems my mates are as well.

I wonder if I will grow wings like my moody fallen...or scales like my dragon if I ever meet him.

Aska.

How will he find me now? He said he was close...will he give up? Will I ever feel his lips on mine for real like I did in that dream place we met? Only time will tell, but right now I have more to deal with than missing my monsters.

I'm trapped in here with one, after all.

"Minotaur," I call out, my voice steady. He hasn't hurt me yet and I'm tired of being afraid. I've faced down too much to let it take hold of me. Instead, I'm steady...and curious. Like when I met Nos.

A rumble comes from the corner where even my eyes can't pierce the black veil surrounding it.

"Hello?" I try again, and this time a louder rumble sounds from the dark.

I slump, almost giving up, but then it moves. Not *it*, him. Too fast for me to track, he breaks free of the shadows. Towering above me is a monster from my childhood storybooks. Horns protrude from his head, a golden nose ring hangs from his snout, and his legs are splayed and end in hooves. A tail whips the ground behind him. His fur is dark, almost black, and intersected with old scars. He's huge, almost touching the top of our cell, his body wide and big like, well...a bull. He's what nightmares are made of, yet I'm not scared. No, something else starts within me, a tug low in my belly, pulling me to him.

Calling me.

I stare at him and he stares right back, his eyes flicking almost red like flames as he takes me in. He moves again, so quickly he becomes a blur, and then he's so close I can smell him...like fire and ash. He smells delicious.

Getting to my feet, I realise my head barely reaches his chest, and I have to tilt my chin back to meet his eyes, a smile playing around my lips. I've met enough monsters now to know this one is something powerful...something special.

"Are you afraid of the dark, *Draya*?" he asks, his voice like the crashing of two rocks, the clang of shields in war. Blood and pain almost wrap around us from his deep, dark timber. I don't know what *draya* means, but the way he says it sounds almost like a prayer. He circles me, the slinking of his chains following him as I stand still, letting him. I don't even move my head. He doesn't scare me, no...I want him.

Lust blooms through me, covering the dull ache in my stomach, one that started when I was taken from my other mates. It calls to me, cooing for me to reach out. To touch him, to taste that darkness and pain...and the hate buried inside him. Swathed around every fiber of his being. To find out whether the darkness and animal lingering around me is as strong and as powerful as he feels.

"No, I live in the dark," I reply, and lick my lips. "I was born in the dark. I died in the dark and I was reborn into it. I'm a monster, just like you. No, I don't fear the dark... I crave it," I answer honestly, and a breath blows across my neck, making the hair stand on end. I can feel him behind me, almost close enough to touch. Goosebumps rise from the proximity, my breathing speeding up as my heart races.

"Are you afraid of me?" he whispers. The dark rumbling should send fear through me, but instead I shiver in need. His voice is obviously created to inspire fear, but to me it sounds seductive.

A dare.

A challenge.

And if there is one thing I've learned about myself since waking up as this new person, it's that I always rise to a challenge, and nothing or nobody will ever make me feel weak, like prey, again.

Because I'm not, I'm as much of a predator as this creature. Just in a smaller package. I turn to face him then and move closer until we're touching. He sucks in a breath, smoke curling from his muzzle to me, but he leans down so his face is almost level with mine.

"If you wanted to play who is the biggest monster, you only had to ask, beast man." Standing on my tiptoes, I dart my tongue out and lick his nose ring. "I will gladly play."

CHAPTER 2

ASKA

My dragon takes over and I let him.

I feel the echo of my mate's pain, her scream in my head covering the distance between us through our bond, and a roar of agony fills my animal at being helpless, at being so far away while she suffers.

I leave my car on the road as I smash my way through the woods, following her scent. More animal than man, no rational thinking, only the need to hold my mate. To see that she is safe and to destroy the souls of those who dared touch what is mine. I break through the witches' protective circle like its paper.

I. Am. A. King.

They dare hurt her?

They think they have seen power and pain, death and bloodshed, but they haven't seen anything yet. I will burn this world apart until I find her, I will bathe in their souls and hear their screams.

My animal and I agree with that.

The once sunny forest turns dark with the spirits and powers leaving my gaping mouth. It blots out the sun, wrapping around the trees and ground like a mist. All noise stops as every animal cowers, feeling my immense power.

I reach the place she was last and circle, her scent, her soul more prominent in this location. She was here for a while, as were others, and then they left...but not of their own accord.

Tire tracks lead through the mud, as does the dragging of feet. But only one set.

Who was with her? Where are they now?

Just as I think that, I see a flash to my right, bright white cutting through the darkness. I turn my massive head, snout open and rows of teeth flashing in warning at any who comes too close. My purple eyes shine through my own blackness, like lasers seeking out a target. Anyone to take out my frustrations on.

My spine ripples as my spikes come out, my scales locking down like armour. Another flash comes, this time near one of my wings on my left. Spinning in a circle, I lash out with my tail when I hear movement, and a grunt follows.

"Fucking dragons, what the fuck next?" comes a snarl, followed by a snort and the flapping of wings.

"Fallen, remember why we are here," someone growls from the trees, and I find a horned man—if you could call him that—standing there surrounded by animals.

The wings freeze and a grumble comes before another man joins the first, his hair down to his shoulders, his eyes flashing black, and his feathery wings spread out behind him like a warning. He glares at me, arms crossed and face snarling.

A fallen?

A forest man...only one I know exists in this country.

But what does a forest god of old and a fallen have in common?

My animal takes back over, overriding all rational thought. He doesn't care who they are, just that they are not her. My mate...Dawn. He roars and flaps his wings, taking us up and flattening the grass and flowers around us. His mouth opens, ready to suck out their souls and kill them.

CHAPTER 3

DUME

She grins at me, and she is so close I can almost touch her. Does she know who I am? Does she know what she is to me? The witches left me here to rot, they stopped coming in after I let my animal maul two of their people, and then out of the blue the door opened...and in came my mate. Tumbling into a graceful heap where she proceeded to pass out. I watched her the whole time, protecting her, my animal wanting to roar at having found her, but I wouldn't let him, she needed her rest.

She is a tiny thing. I was sure during the time she slept and I watched that she would be terrified of me. Such a little body with long, golden hair the likes of the kings and queens of old. Her beauty unmatched throughout the ages, her eyes huge and blue and I wanted to see them again, craved those long lashes to open so those orbs could once again lock on me. Her body is curvy, and I ache to reach out and map each dip and flare.

But no, she was not terrified of me like I thought. What irony, I had thought, to give a monster like me a tiny mate who wouldn't be able to fight. Yet here she stands, toe to toe with my animal. A feat no one else has ever managed...and lived. Those eyes as blue as the water near my home, unwaveringly focused on me. Her red, rosy lips pulled up in a smile that has my cock rock-hard even in this form.

She might be small, but she is a warrior.

I can tell as much by her bravery to face down a monster like me, her courage outweighing any fear she may have. I inhale hard, I don't smell any at all. No, something else. Something sweet. It wraps around me, drifting from her body, and settles into my bones. Its roots spreading through my veins, pulling an echoing call from deep within my soul.

It isn't her who steps away or cowers, it is me.

"What magic are you pulling?" I roar, moving until my back hits the cell wall. Never again will I be trapped, not even by the woman who is to be my mate. No magic will force me to servitude, not again. Whatever she is doing, it won't work.

"Magic?" she echoes, tilting her head and watching me as she strolls closer, uncaring that more and more smoke drifts from my snout as my anxiety spirals. I can almost feel the magical chains dragging me back to my pit. How much of a fool was I, thinking I could trust another being? She will betray me, they always do.

"Witch," I hiss. Surprisingly enough, my animal is...calm. Settled almost, wanting to curl up around her and purr. It is my human half which is suspicious, always is and always will be. Mate or not.

"No, try again." She laughs like we are playing a game, finding amusement in seeing me scared of her.

"I can feel it," I snap, and my hooves clank against the floor in agitation.

"Can you?" she purrs, stepping closer and laying her head on my chest. Her eyes widen. "I can taste the racing of your heart, is it you who fears me?"

"I fear no one," I snarl at her. "I do not want to be trapped by a pretty face again."

Her expression softens then as she searches my eyes, an understanding entering them, but how could anyone understand what I have been through? "Me either," she whispers. "I promise you, minotaur, I'm not doing magic. I don't think I even have any, not like that," she vows, and it echoes around—truth.

"Dume," I rush out. "My name is Dume."

"Dume." She rolls it around on her tongue before a smile curves her lips. "What are you feeling that has you spooked?"

"My heart is racing, head fuzzy...I, erm, my cock is hard. I want you, so badly with an inhuman need," I admit.

"It isn't magic, minotaur." She laughs, her eyes bright with amusement, lips stretched in a grin.

"No?" I rasp.

"No, it's lust, Dume. Good, old-fashioned lust. You want to fuck me. No magic here." She winks.

CHAPTER 4

GRIFFIN

The dragon swoops right for us. A motherfucking dragon. With solid black scales, spikes running down its back, and bright purple irises. Rolling my eyes, I look at Nos. "We don't have time for this shit, we need to find her."

Panic flutters through me, fuck, only I get to touch her—well, Nos and I. She's ours, I might not have always liked it, but she had grown on me...more than that. She had grown to be my everything, an unexpected, perfect storm rocking my world and tearing it apart.

And now she's gone. They took her.

When we had woken up from whatever spell the witches hit us with, she was gone, as were they. I took to the sky immediately, ignoring the aftereffects of the magic, and followed their trail, except it went cold. But I know who they are.

At least one of them is on the council.

Our own leaders took Dawn...why?

I don't have time for questions, I need to get her back. I know better than anyone what they are capable of and I refuse to let them hurt another woman I love. Refuse to watch another die while I'm unable to help.

I use that weakness, I channel it with my panic and turn it into hate. Rage. I aim it at the dragon and take to the air to meet him. I hear Nos sigh, and then suddenly, the world freezes.

My eyes widen as I'm stuck mid-air, locked in place. I see Nos stroll between us on the ground, his hands held out on either side and eyes bright white. Is this him? What else is the forest god capable of?

He holds us in place effortlessly, anger on his face. "This is not helping," he screams, and birds take flight and a howl of wolves goes up, the wildlife echoing his pain. He was with Dawn longer than I was and I could see their love, even though I hated it and was jealous. This must be killing him, not that I'll ever admit that to him.

He looks to the dragon with narrowed eyes. "I do not know who you are, but we mean you no harm. We are searching for our mate, she was taken from here and we are trying to find a trail. A lead. Anything to get her back."

The dragon blinks and then a voice blasts through our minds. Fuck, that's why everyone hates dragons. They can get into your head and past your defenses without you even realising it.

Mate? What's her name?

Nos tilts his head and I see a small smile there. "I have a feeling you already know, dragon."

HER NAME!

"Dawn, her name is Dawn and she is ours. We are going to get her back."

The hold on us breaks and we both fall to the ground around the forest god's feet as he stands there like he's at worship. The dragon melts, shifting in a swirl of purple and black until a man stands in its place.

Pastel purple hair, short and messy on the top, crowns his head.

His eyes are black, the colour seeming to swirl. He's tall, fucker is even taller than me and bigger. Like a tree trunk. He holds his head up, his chin tilted back like only those fucking rich pricks who sit on thrones can. Daring us to defy him as he takes us both in. In dragon form or not, he's powerful, I can feel that. I hope he isn't an enemy, but if he is, I will kill him. Whatever it takes to get our girl back and then I'll never let her go again.

Fighting or not, she is mine.

"Dawn," he rasps, voice hoarse. "She is mine."

CHAPTER 5

NOS

Interesting. I knew my little monster would call more mates. She is too powerful not to, she needs them to help balance her, there can be no power without grounding. However, even I did not expect the power of the dragon she has called. To call him forth...the power she holds is incredible.

But none of it matters if we don't get her back. "Then we can't fight between ourselves. She is gone, and the longer we take to find her the more damage they will do to her. We do not know what they want, but when I find them, I plan to find out."

"Then kill them," the dragon snaps, eyes flaring purple for a moment.

I incline my head and a smile breaks out across his face. "Can't say I'm surprised she has more mates, but you were both not what I was expecting."

"Well, whoop-de-fucking-doo," Griffin snarls and looks at me.

"He can sleep on the sofa, I'm not sharing my room. Now stop making pleasantries and let's get her back."

Used to the fallen's grumpy nature by now, and knowing the only one who can make him smile and not kill everything is our mate, I look to them both deciding I need to take charge. Something I don't enjoy. I like my solitude, my forest, and knowing if something happens to people it isn't because of me, but for her I will. Someone needs to ensure they don't kill each other and that individual looks to be me, especially if the daggers Griffin is glaring at the dragon are any indication. I even catch his eyes leaking black as he strokes his blades.

I narrow my eyes at him and he rolls his, but he drops his hand as the dragon starts to stride away, into the forest. Sighing, I call out to him, "Wrong way. Why don't you follow us?"

He turns and with a lift of his chin, indicates for us to go first. I do, stepping through the forest like I have walked it a million times, which I have. The trees move out of my way and the plants welcome me, all making my journey easier, but I hear growling and swearing behind me and turn to see the dragon struggling over roots and branches, a disgusted sneer on his lips as he glances around before suddenly stopping, his head tilted to the side.

Griffin snorts and storms past me, smashing through the trees without a care. "Do we need a fucking leash for the dragon?" he snaps.

"Be nice," I warn, and he snarls at me, spinning, his wings flaring out and smacking the trees on either side of us. In his eyes I see the madness from which he hides, one so deep and integral it is a part of him, but I do not fear it. Neither does Dawn, it simply makes Griffin who he is.

"Nice? Fucking nice?" he shouts, stepping closer, mist coating him and wrapping around his form, darkening the forest. The animals go silent, sensing a predator.

"Guys," the dragon calls out, but we ignore him.

"Yes, nice," I grind out. "I don't like it as much as you, but we are going to need all the help we can find to get Dawn back...that is what you want, correct?"

At the mention of her name, he growls, grabbing my throat and slamming me back into the tree. With a flick of my power, I send him sailing through the air, where he smashes through branches and underbrush before he suddenly materialises in front of me again. His eyes are nothing but darkness now, all the blue is gone. I remember how my mate likes him like this, how she can handle it, tame him almost...I cannot. And I can't kill him, which only leaves talking to him.

"Other mates!" the dragon calls louder, but we don't break our stare down, knowing if I do, he will strike. He wants an excuse to attack, he is looking for a weakness. He won't get it from me.

"We have no choice, Griffin. We work together, we will go back to your place and reach out to everyone to see if they know anything and then make a plan. We are getting our fucking mate back," I snap, his attitude and anger rubbing off on me.

Uncaring about the enraged and slightly mad fallen, the dragon steps between us. "There is a dead body over there, if you didn't know."

It makes Griffin laugh suddenly, the sound slightly manic. "Hell yes we do, that's what happens when you fuck with our mate."

It breaks the tension between us, and I relax as Griffin's wings disappear and his eyes bleed back to normal. He claps me on the back as he passes me and follows the dragon, who yet again is going the wrong way. Aren't dragons supposed to have a good sense of direction? "Let's get her then."

Sighing, I send a thought out to my mate, hoping she can hear it.

Little Monster, it will be a miracle if we don't all kill ourselves before we find you, we need you...without you we are falling apart already...please, little one, come home.

CHAPTER 6

UNKNOWN ONE

I stir, unable to help myself. Something pulls at me. I felt something similar before, but it was weaker, miles away. Almost a world away. I ignored it and went back to sleep, back to my magical slumber we all agreed to when we took our position, sleeping away the ages until we are called forth to serve...and rule.

But this time, I can't. I can't ignore it, the pull. It's filled with pain and rips through the magic and layers of sleep shrouding me like a blanket. Stabbing into my brain and echoing in the prison of my head. It's female, her mind reaching for mine even across the many miles separating us. I see flashes of what is happening, stabs of electricity moving through her to me. Men in black, flickers of corridors, and then darkness...just the scream remaining.

Screaming for me, even though she does not know me.

I sit up with a roar, my body bolt upright in my tomb, my eyes sealed shut and body weak from years of resting. But not for long. It's unnatural for me to be awake, it will cause ripples. Problems.

None of it matters.

Not the years of control I learned, not the power I gathered and wielded like a sword. Not my place.

My name.

My position.

Only her.

CHAPTER 7

UNKNOWN TWO

My head droops uselessly against my chest, my once long hair cut and matted and greasy, hanging in shorn lumps across my oily and dirty face.

Pain is my constant, it is all I know.

My mouth is so dry, I feel my lips crack and bleed.

My body feels like a husk, all the water, all the liquid gone until I am nothing but a starving skeleton of what I once was.

That is what they want.

To deprive me of the very thing I need most and watch as I crumble into nothing but a monster for them to control. It's the only way they can control me. Make me what they want me to be. I don't know how long I have been here, but they should know one thing about me—I do nothing I do not want to.

This world has seen my anger before, the tales and stories told even today. So many names and so many works of fiction are based on me...and these men think starving me will make me break? How wrong they are. I will prove that to them before I rip their bodies apart and spike their heads to decorate my house.

I hear the door open once again, just as it does every day like clockwork. I no longer visibly react, not even to lift my weary head. Something is tossed inside, a someone, I should say. And then the door slams shut once again, trapping them in here with me.

I can't help it, I sniff, inhaling the aromatic fragrance of their essence. The very thing I need. Next, I hear their heart slamming so hard in their chest from fear I'm surprised they haven't died from it.

Human bodies are so frail, after all.

They breathe slowly to remain quiet and they don't move, thinking it will save them. But I can hear every tiny inhale, each exhale, and every slight movement of their body. The blood thundering through their veins, calling to me.

Madness encroaches the recesses of my mind, a darkness I have given into more than once twisting around me until I finally lift my head and spot the tiny human. The living blood bag is kneeling against the door with her legs pulled to her fluttering chest. Her lips quiver and her eyes overflow as she stares at me.

My nose twitches and my mouth parts to reveal my huge fangs, which is what finally breaks her.

She screams, howls, and cries, battering her fists against the metal door to escape me and I laugh, throwing my head back and letting it flow from me.

They won't break me today, or even tomorrow.

It was a good try though.

I let them hear my mocking guffaw, even as my arms are pulled up and chained, my legs spread and shackled to the walls.

Blood.

It coats the air, calling to me, telling me its story. How it could make me feel better, make my strength return, quench this never-ending thirst which was imposed on me many millenniums ago.

No one can.

CHAPTER 8

DAWN

"How long have you been here?" I ask, changing the subject when Dume just stares at me. If a minotaur could look shocked, I think that would be his expression right now.

With nothing else to do but sit and wait for that fucking Veyo to come back so I can kill them and escape, I make myself comfortable on the floor, sitting cross-legged and watching as the bull man walks around me, almost pacing.

"A few days. Witches trapped me while I was travelling," he almost roars, the floor actually shaking with the force and his hooves making a clanking noise as he moves.

"Travelling to where?" I question pleasantly. Again, I should probably be more afraid trapped in here with a clearly angry minotaur, but instead I'm fighting off my attraction, the lust that's drawing me to him. I've only felt like this with my mates, so why now? Is it magic like he said? It's not like I know much about it, so it could be, or is it something else?

He turns to face me and copies my position, sitting down surprisingly gracefully for such a big man. "To find someone," is all he says. "Why are you here?"

"That's the question, isn't it?" I muse. "I was hunting someone. I guess they didn't like us prying, it led me to these people and what they're doing here."

"Which is?" he presses.

The door opens and we both shoot to our feet. The three guards wearing solid black stream inside, so I part my legs and brace myself. Their faces and the crackle of electricity from their weapons unleashes something in me.

Something more than rage...hate.

When the door shuts behind them and they grin at us, I turn my head slowly to look at Dume, flashing him an evil grin. "They are mine."

Even my voice doesn't sound like me—it's darker, filled with anger and need. Need for their blood and pain. I let it take hold and when one of them steps towards me, his baton aimed in my direction, I move with a scream that would rival the minotaur himself. I'm almost a blur, moving so fast that one second I'm in front of him and the next I'm behind him. I hear their panicked yells, but it all fades away until nothing but darkness surrounds me.

Leaping onto his back, I yank his head to the side and rip out his throat. I feel the moment my teeth break through his flesh, the spurt of his blood hitting my tongue. Laughing, I jump down and watch as he swings around, arms flapping as he tries to stop the bleeding.

I grin, feeling blood trickle from my lips and onto my chest, making it heave. Each drop is like a boost of energy shot straight into me. I turn my undoubtedly black eyes to the other men who are staring at me in fear.

"What the fuck?" one of them screams.

"What is she?" the other yells back.

"Your death." I laugh and then throw myself at them. One of the guards manages to dodge my attack, so I tumble to the ground with the other beneath me. A natural instinct takes hold like before, not to feed this time, but to kill. Curling my hands like claws, I stab his chest over and over again. My now sharp nails slice like knives as they cut through skin and bone. Blood sprays everywhere as I continue to stab and slash, even when he's unmoving.

Stilling, I lift my head, noting the room smells like blood and fear, and it sends a shiver through me. I need more.

"*Draya*," comes a warning.

I spin and watch the last man race towards me. My eyes catch on Dume's chain and I grab it, jumping to meet the guard and wrap it around his neck. His weapon drops to the floor with an audible thud as he starts to choke, his hands grabbing at the metal, trying to pull it away. His eyes bulge, his veins prominent now and his face starts to turn red. His mouth opens in a silent scream and suddenly, I need to feed with such ferocity that a snarl escapes me before I seal my lips to his.

I let his now skeletal corpse drop to the floor, then I meet Dume's eyes in the dark which are red and locked on mine. Raising my black nails to my mouth, I lick the blood trickling down my hands, staining them. "Tastes like fear," I purr.

Nos and I experimented with blood. I learned that night I could feed from it. His was so powerful it bowed my spine, but this is lesser and tastes like a cheap imitation. I growl in frustration, needing more, needing power. My body aches, every cell screaming for it.

I set my eyes on the minotaur and he huffs out smoke as I prowl closer. "I'm hungry, bull," I tell him, and this time he doesn't back away. "I need to feed, that wasn't enough. They weakened me, I need it." I stop before him. "Dume," I purr, "I need you."

Before he can protest, though I don't think he would from his sharp inhale, I strike.

I throw myself towards him with that same blurring speed, but my monster must be able to see me because he catches me. Wrapping my legs around his waist, I inch up his body until I can bind my arms around his neck and stare into those red eyes.

"*Draya*," he rumbles, but I don't think he means to warn me away.

"I need to feed, Dume. I need your blood, I need your power. I ache for it," I whisper, as I lick his nose ring again.

Something in the minotaur snaps, I can feel it, how close to the surface his true animal side is. Compared with Nos and Griffin, who can almost act human, this monster seems to be struggling to even string sentences together. He's primal, raw, and has my pussy wet.

He turns and slams me into the cell wall, his strength showing as he holds me there with one hand. "Mate," he snarls, without a single sign of his human side. No, this isn't Dume. This is the minotaur.

Mate?

Could it be?

My need clouds my mind again, pushing away rational thought, and I let out a whimper, my neck arching to try and reach him. "Need?" he growls.

I nod.

"Mate need?" he repeats, smashing me back into the wall, the force of it making me gasp even as I bow up into his touch, wanting more.

"Yesss, my bull, mate needs," I purr, rubbing my body against his, the fur surprisingly soft, like a feather caressing my skin. It only heightens my desire and I cry out, arching for him again like a cat.

Smoke curls from his nose as his red eyes watch me, then he tilts his head, and with one big paw drags my head to his exposed neck. "Feed."

"With pleasure."

I lay a gentle kiss on his fur before I feel my teeth sharpen, very much like my nails. I dig them into his skin, but they aren't sharp enough to pierce his fur. Grumbling, I gnaw his neck like a dog and he grunts, but not in pain. Snarling now, so close to what I need but so far away, I rip and tear, trying to get to it but it's no use.

I cry out and he pulls me away, looking at my face. "Blood?" he rumbles.

"Or power," I correct, licking my lips, tasting the guard's blood still lingering there.

He tilts his head like I've seen animals do and his face shifts for a moment. I watch, entranced, as the lower half of his face turns human. The golden nose ring is still in place, and his eyes are still red, but he has a human nose and lips and cheeks. His horns curl from his head, but where there was once fur, there is now hair.

He looks like he's caught partway between a shift. How is that possible? I don't have time to question it, though, because his animal is done talking. He might look human now, but he very much is not.

He seals his lips to mine, obviously seeing what I did to the guards, and I groan. He tastes like fire and metal. I suck like I usually do to feed and his power curls into me like the smoke from his nose. It shoots straight to my heart, making it skip a beat before settling into my belly and smouldering. The more I pull, the stronger the fire grows, almost burning me alive. I want more.

It makes me sloppy, the kiss raw as I accidentally cut his tongue with my teeth. He roars and pushes closer as I lap at the seeping blood, and another shot of power shoots through me. It's stronger, more unfiltered, and heads straight to my clit where a throbbing begins, matching the thump of his heart.

We are locked together, my mouth fused to his as I feed and I know, with a hundred percent certainty no matter how much I take, I could never drain him.

It's a freeing thought, not having to worry about pulling away, pulling back before I kill someone. Whatever that other side of me is, the one that kept me alive and pulled me back from death, revels in it. Smashing closer and taking as much as I can, I feel it flow through me, filling me to the brim until, with a cry, I explode.

The orgasm rips through me, called by his power and blood, and I feel like I leave my body with the force of it. When I come back down, I'm panting, and my head is curled into his furry neck as I cuddle closer.

"Thank you," I whisper, and he rumbles again.

"Anything for my mate."

I grin, I can't help it. I should have seen it before, worked it out, but I blame being held prisoner for the distraction. There is a thread, a pull, a call, whatever you want to call it, between us, like the ones I have with Nos and Griffin, each so different but very much the same.

I am his.

He is mine.

My eyes start to shut again, the power overload and orgasm making me tired. I'm still healing, recharging from the fight with the guards and everything that's happened. I let out a yawn and my minotaur turns, putting his back to the wall and sliding down until he sits with his legs outstretched.

He almost purrs as I settle in his lap. I'm tiny in comparison to him. Like a little doll. He wraps his arms around me, his fur keeping me warm as I rest my head against his beating hearts—he has two?—and close my eyes, my lips still coated with his blood and the guards' bodies still in our cell.

It's the best night's sleep I've ever had.

CHAPTER 9

NOS

The only thing I see when we enter the fallen's house is the picture of my little monster. Everything else is unchanged, but that picture draws me until I am stroking her face.

"I'm coming, Little Monster, then we will kill them all."

The dragon barges in, pushing me out of the way, and I shake my head and step back, allowing him to see. He freezes at the image, staring at Dawn's perfect face. For once I see something other than pride and disdain written across his features. I see hope and pain. No matter what we think of each other, we are all brought together by fate or love.

Destined to share our lives together, our paths entwined because of her. Our mate.

"We have to find a way to work together or we are all doomed. Not for us, but for her. She needs us, she doesn't always realise it. She will never ask for help, she is too strong, too wild, but she needs us. To ground her, to keep the pain at bay. To help figure out who she is and what she is capable of. If we can't do that you might as well walk away from her now."

The dragon looks at me then, his lips turned down, and I carry on, "Because I never will. I will never walk away from her. Never abandon her or leave her. Even if I was following her into hell itself, into my own death, I would still follow. Know this, dragon, you might be a mythical creature, but so am I. There is nothing I wouldn't do for my mate, nothing I wouldn't be, nothing I wouldn't destroy."

He watches me, his eyes filled with understanding, the type you only get after living a hard, long life filled without happiness or love. Dawn is that. A bright spot, a hope for a better life...one filled with love and happiness...and yes, blood and power.

"You think I would not?" he asks, his voice low and almost quiet. I don't think he even realises he is still touching the picture of her face. "I have been waiting for her my entire life, forest god. Where other dragons fought and trained for prestige and power, I did it for the idea that one day, I would have someone to protect. When they put that crown on my head and bowed to me, asking me to lead them, I turned away and left. Because I knew, out here, in this world somewhere, was my true purpose. It was not a crown or being a leader, it was something greater." He looks back at the picture.

"Her, I was waiting for her before I even knew it. So know this, forest god—you say there is nothing you wouldn't do, I say there is everything I *would* do. I will burn this world to the ground until I find her, the skies will rain blood and souls. I will never stop, never waver until I have her back. We can work together, but only because I know it will help lead me to her quicker." Then, he turns away and strides upstairs as if he owns the house.

Griffin snorts, leaning back against the wall while sharpening a blade. He was so still and quiet that if I wasn't looking, I wouldn't have seen him. "And you guys thought I was the asshole mate."

"You still are." I grin.

He looks up and smirks. "Yes, but she loves it. I can't wait to see her knock him down a peg or two."

"You just like watching her fight, you get off on it."

"And you don't?" He laughs, putting his blade away. "He is right, though, we need to work together. Doesn't mean I won't try to kill him...or you for that matter."

"Then she will kill you, remember?" I grin, knowing I have him.

He grumbles, tugging at his hair for a moment, his eyes losing their colour as if he is far away. "Fucking woman, spoiling all my fun. His dragon head would look good above my fireplace. Next she will be telling me I can't kill sheep."

Just then the dragon comes tramping back downstairs. "Do we have a plan?"

Griffin and I share a look and the fallen waves his blade at me as if to say *I can kill him if you want*. I shake my head slightly and look back at the arrogant creature. "Not yet, let's make one."

"Very well, does this...abode have a TV? I like to watch Jeremy Kyle, it helps me think."

CHAPTER 10

DUME

"How did you change your face?"

The voice stirs me awake. I can't remember the last time I fell asleep in an enemy lair. I have just been resting, eyes open in case they came in, but with my mate wrapped up in my arms I must have drifted off.

Careless of me when I have such a treasure to protect. I will do better. Cracking my eyes open, I see my face is back to that of my animal, and the truth is I don't know how I changed it. The chains and magic surrounding them should prevent me from doing so, but something about my mate's plea, her hunger and need, pushed me to break through that, for just a moment, to be able to change my face for her. I can still feel her lingering touch, the brush of her petal soft lips against mine.

The ravenous way she devoured me, making me shiver.

"Your need, our bond broke through the magic," is all I say, and she nods, accepting my answer without question. It makes me wonder what my mate is and what she knows of magic and witches and the rest of this world we are in. "It's the chains, they trap me."

She looks at them, head tilting to the side and eyes flashing black for a moment. I try to remember the supernaturals I have encountered who had black eyes, but I come up short. "What are you, *Draya*?"

"Skinwalker, I am told." She huffs when I just continue to stare. "Short version, my ex-husband murdered me and left me for dead, then I pulled myself from the ground and woke up like this...able to change my face and body, super strong, super hearing."

"Skinwalkers are rare...wait, ex-husband?" I almost roar.

She pats my chest. "Yeah, don't worry, I killed and buried him." I blink at her and she grins, making me huff out a laugh.

"You don't talk a lot..." She trails off.

"Habit." Her eyebrows raise so I force myself to carry on speaking, trying to break through years of conditioning. "My old queen," I snarl, "didn't want my conversation, she thought me nothing but an animal and as such I should act like one."

Her eyes narrow, and jealousy flares through the mate bond for a moment, so I stroke her head, patting her awkwardly. "Not to fear, *Draya*, I killed her." She settles a bit then.

"Queen?" she finally prompts.

"A false queen, a human who, with the help of witches, gained power. She married a king and became the leader. Under her reign, she entrapped many supernatural species and used them for horrible purposes such as entertainment and science."

"You as well?" she queries, anger in her sensual voice.

"No, I was made. A result of magic and experiments. My whole race was made for her. To be the animal she craved, the minotaurs of the great maze sent to protect something that we didn't even know...but when she saw me—" I grind my teeth and a soft hand lands on where my cheek would be and strokes. I look down into those eyes and soften, the words tumbling out. "When she saw me, she wanted me, and what the queen desired she took. I was taken from my people and made into her slave. One day I displeased her, so she threw me into the arena to fight for amusement. I won and became a famed fighter, so she had no choice but to share me with the people, fighting for their entertainment. Slaughtering many, some I would call friends. It changed me. I let my animal take over more and more, unable to stand it. One day we tried to escape and she took my shift away. All I am left with is this and my human form."

"What was your other shift?" she inquires curiously, no fear or disgust in her voice even after what I just shared.

"Something beyond human imagination, something made of black magic and anger...but so strong." I shake my head.

"How did you kill her?" Dawn asks, leaning closer again, comforting me even when I did not know I needed it.

"She thought she could tame me, was so sure of her witch pets' control...she was wrong. She often brought me to her bed chamber, a punishment for me and her dying husband next door, who was forced to listen. She knew I hated her, hated touching her. I had no choice, she would often bring another of my kind and threaten them unless I did. I began to realise it was pointless, so I waited and watched, looking for her weakness."

"What was it?"

"Me, the thing she feared most. The Beast of Cornacadia, the monster she created. She dreaded what she had made so she tried to keep me close, but in the end all it did was kill her. She had handed me my swords the day before, pried from the dead hands of a brother of mine, it was the turning point..."

Memories flash in my mind and suddenly Dawn is there, her hands on my face, head against mine. "I can see them," she whispers. I try to pull away, but she holds me there. "You don't have to talk, show me."

"*Draya.*" I cover her hands. "The memories are dark and ugly."

"I can do dark and ugly. If you haven't noticed, bull man, I thrive on it. Show me, let me see you, my minotaur."

I search her eyes before closing my own and opening my mind to her. I fight the need to roar and pull away, old habits dying hard. I have to remind myself she wouldn't hurt me, she is my mate, again and again. She must hear.

"Oh, my minotaur, I would never hurt you, I see your struggle." Her voice is sad. "I promise you, on my life, I will never harm or betray you. I don't know how I became this or what brought us together, but neither of us will ever be alone again."

Her voice whispers through my head, calming my bull, a feat no other has ever managed. He curls around her, protecting her, loving her, and I know...this goddess was made for me. I may not be worthy of her, but I will strive to be. If what she wants is to see the darkest, most depraved parts of me, she can. I will split myself open and let the memories tumble out so she can bathe in them if that is what she wants.

"Beast," the queen greets, turning from the mirror where her hair is being coiffed. With a wave, she dismisses the young witch helping her get ready. Tilting her chin up, she stands, her skirts moving around her like water, and strolls towards me, the crown on her head held there by magic. "I did not call you."

"I am not an animal you can just call for," I snarl, voice rumbling with my bull who is huffing and digging his hooves in my mind, wanting to be unleashed upon this woman.

"Oh, but you are." She grins, still not seeing my true intent, her boldness and pride blinding her to the truth, the hate that her people feel for her. "You will always be mine, my beast, and when I die I will have you entombed with me. Serving me forever." She trails her fingertip down my body, heading to my crotch, and I snap.

My bull comes to the forefront of my mind, forcing himself out. He has been chained long enough, and his hatred only rivals mine.

With a roar, I change, faster than she has ever seen. She is too close, too trusting that she had me controlled. Her pride and fear will be her downfall. My horns gouge her as I flick them, tossing my head about. She is thrown around like a ragdoll until she falls to the once white silk of her bed with a pained scream. The blood slowly leaks from her many wounds onto the mattress, staining the silk crimson. Before the witches can arrive and heal her, I take up my swords she keeps in here and cross them at her neck.

"I am no one's pet. I am the Beast of Cornacadia, a legend. A myth. The monster of the labyrinth and yours no longer. History will not remember you. You will be nothing but a bad memory for me. All this power, and at the end you die alone and weak. Nothing but a pathetic human," I growl, turning my face back to human so she can see the hate there.

I hear the witches coming, the incantations on their lips. I know what this will mean for me, but I'll gladly take any punishment of death they offer, it is worth it to free me of this human monster. She holds a bloodied, weak hand up to me, eyes terrified and reeking of fear and her own mortality.

Humans are so breakable. She thought she was more than that, but it's time I remind her where she belongs.

"My beast," she pleads.

"Never yours," I roar and slice, her head rolls from the bed and towards the door, eyes open wide, mouth parted on a silent cry. The runes on my swords flash, covered in the queen's blood as I let out a triumphant roar. It fills the night sky, floating down to the supernaturals I had freed not five minutes before from the cells under the arena. They will carry my story, they will be alive, even if I am not. And that is enough.

I turn to face the golden double doors, swords held at the ready. If I die here today, I die like a warrior. How I wish I had my other shift so I could decimate them, but I will fight until I can't fight any longer. Never again will I be trapped, chained to another person. My soul and swords theirs to control.

The doors smash open with magic, the witches pouring in with their black hoods up, powers ready in their hands. The high priestess steps forward, the queen's head rolling to her feet, and her head tilts back, the hood falling down to reveal her withered face as she lets out *a cry of grief. Her beloved, very human daughter is dead...at my hands.*

Magic smashes into me from all sides, incantations filling the room. With a roar I charge, even though the odds aren't good. I'd rather die now than later. I manage to kill a few, but they are too strong, their magic wrapping around me like chains and dragging me to the ground.

Before everything goes black, I see the high priestess's bright, cold blue eyes before me. "You will suffer for your actions, beast."

"I woke up chained, which seems to be a recurring theme in my life." I pause. "I was searching for you, the witches found me first, and when I woke up I was here."

"I'm sorry, Dume." She grins at me. "Want me to help kill them?"

A laugh tumbles free, a sound so foreign to me that I freeze. "You are bloodthirsty."

"One of my better qualities, I assure you," she purrs. "We were confused. My other mate, Nos, could smell witches, and when we contacted a few others they all smelled something different. We figured out they were working together, we just don't know why. Women are disappearing and now I'm beginning to think the council is behind it."

"The witches will work for whoever pays the best, or if it means they can hurt supernaturals. They hate them with a passion, they think they are above us, think their power was bestowed by gods and we are nothing but nightmares gone wrong."

"Well, they are going to love me." She beams. "My bull, I'll free you, and together we will figure out what's going on and stop them. Humans are being taken as well, I saw them and the labs set up in the basement to try and bring out supernatural qualities in them." She frowns as I growl.

"That sounds like the experiments they used to work back when I was free, always trying to find better, badder monsters to control."

"We need to find out what's going on and stop them before there is no one left to fight them. I haven't been in this world long, but I know about people who crave power, they won't stop here," she mutters.

"How do we stop them?" I frown. "I am chained and we are locked up."

She grins then, and if she wasn't my mate, I might even be a little scared of that smirk, instead my cock pulses, making itself known. Just then the door opens and we both jump to our feet. I try to push her behind me, but she crosses her arms and strolls around me with a shit-eating grin aimed at the eagle waiting there.

"Veyo," she greets. "I would like to thank you for your lovely hospitality."

"I'm glad you have enjoyed your stay, skinwalker. Are you ready to talk like civilised people now or shall I lock you back up again?"

CHAPTER II

ASKA

"The test shows that Will is...not the father!" I lean closer with wide eyes as the woman jumps up from the seat and starts attacking an older woman as a shocked man watches on and the crowd cheers. "This show is something else," I whisper, shaking my head. "Are humans really like this? Do parents not claim their young? You must be tested? Are they fighting to the death? What are the rules?" I wonder out loud.

"This is helping him think?" comes a snarky response from the fallen in the corner who, whenever I look over, keeps pulling blades from more places and showing me them in a threat. What an amusing man he is.

I am in a bad mood, though, mainly because I got here too late and my dragon wants to kill people. Right now he is pacing around in the cage in my head, snarling at me and blowing darkness. I really need to feed him, to keep him calm enough so we can think of a plan to get our mate back.

Our mate.

I knew she would have others, she was too strong not to, so I don't care about that as long as they are honourable men. These men...I guess they will do. One is clearly insane with a strange blade obsession and a wall covered in other images, the other watches us both, cataloguing everything. He is powerful, but also soft. I guess it will be up to me to save our mate.

"I'm hungry," I tell them, looking over. "I require sustenance or I will end up ripping the souls from everyone and eating them instead."

"Fucking hell," Griffin snaps and leans forward. "Fine, your fucking majesty, we will feed you, and then when we come back you will help us get our mate." Each word is spit like it hurts to say.

"Thank you, I appreciate the title as well, but I am no longer a king. Sir will suffice." I nod at the fallen, and he throws himself forward with a snarl, but he's thrown backwards into the wall by the forest god who points at both of us.

"Behave," he warns, his voice filling the room like a banshee roar.

I frown. "I am confused, why is he angry?"

The forest god rubs his head as if it pains him. "Why me?"

We file out of the house and I stare at the metal contraption which is lower than the one Jean Claude provided for me. "We will not all fit in that."

"Then fucking fly, you dragon prick." Griffin throws his hand in the air and clicks something, then lights flash and a beep sounds. I start to change to protect us before the forest god stops me with a look and opens the back door.

"Get in, dragon."

I snort. "I ride in the front." I open the other door and try to cram myself in—my knees are up by my head, which is bent due to the low angle.

I grumble as the car rumbles to life and we take off into the city. I reach out and start pressing buttons on the dash, music blares out, changing every second as I flick between things. Griffin starts to slap my hand away, so I slap him back, and I hear Nos sigh in the backseat.

"Little Monster, can I kill them?" he mutters, before he raises his voice. "Children, stop, or there is no food for anyone, and when we get Dawn back I will tell her."

A forest god telling our mate on a dragon and a fallen. How amusing.

WE END up at a place where the fallen explains they make burgers, whatever that means. I am led inside, and there are children everywhere, screaming and running around in maddening circles as parents ignore them.

"Sheep," I mutter.

"Finally, something we agree on," Griffin mumbles, and then shows his teeth to a little human girl who stops before him. She grins at him and he huffs and pushes past her, but she follows after the fallen.

He leads us over to a white machine. "Order here," he snaps at me, and crosses his arms, glaring at the child who stares back.

I look at the contraption and clear my throat. "I require food, meat."

Nothing happens, so I try again in a louder voice. "Meat."

Frowning, I look at the fallen, but he is still glaring at the child. "Squire, I require meat, lots of it, please." I tack on the last part, remembering my manners. The fallen sighs and presses something, and I nearly jump back as what looks like items of food scroll down the screen.

"Meat, I require meat!" I yell at the machine, but all it does is blink, scrolling through a list of items, something called a salad. "Confusing device, give me meat!" I roar, shaking the machine and ranting.

When I am done, I look over to see four humans in funny little hats gaping at me from behind a counter, and then a child starts to cry and it is followed up by more and more of them.

"Someone get the man some meat," the fallen drawls, "before he has a tantrum and kills everyone."

The servers jump into action, and in under a minute a plastic tray is offered to me with shaking hands piled high with meat. "Many thanks, squire."

"Y-You're welcome," he stutters. "How would you like to pay?"

I blink at him and then smile. "Fallen, pay the man," I call, and then turn away, finding a table away from as many people as I can. All the adults glare at us openly, but the children have finished crying now. I have to squeeze myself into a slippery seat, then I rip into the meat. "Delicious, so much better than a chargrilled goat," I mutter.

Nos sits opposite me, snacking on something that looks like leaves. He places a tray of the same before me and then Griffin who slips in beside him.

"Eat it, it's good for you," Nos instructs us, his eyes on the fallen. Griffin throws it in the bin, while I simply throw mine at the fallen who snarls and narrows his eyes on me.

I go back to eating, but notice a small human near my table looking at my food with big eyes. I lean my head down and growl, my dragon mostly in charge now. He squeals and runs away. "Dragons don't share food," I mutter.

"Fucking hell, only I could get stuck with a tree lover and dumb shit over there," Griffin grouses.

"You are dumb." I sniff, lifting my head.

"Brilliant, dragon, truly brilliant come back, did your momma teach you that?"

"My mother tried to eat me." I frown.

"What a way to kill a conversation." Griffin laughs.

"I did not kill anything, yet, but I will gladly. Starting with you," I snarl.

Nos leans forward. "No killing each other over food, remember why we are all here and together."

"Dawn." I nod.

"Fucking mate of mine." Griffin rolls his eyes and I narrow mine on him. "Don't worry, I only tried to kill her once," he retorts, and that is how we end up getting kicked out of what Griffin called a fast food place as I try to murder him for hurting my mate.

CHAPTER 12

GRIFFIN

The dragon almost made me crash my car on the way home, and when we get back to my house, he plops himself on the sofa and goes back to watching the shitty sheep's show. Nos and I share a look and he sighs, then he stands in front of the TV, blocking the dragon's view.

"We need a plan and to start finding Dawn, anything could be happening to her right now."

His words hit us all and the dragon finally gets serious. "I will change and rip the souls from everyone in the city until we find her."

"Your plan is rubbish, no wonder dragons are almost extinct," I scoff, and spin in my chair, turning off the TV. "Now, here is what we are actually going to do. We go to Victor, get all the information on The Others we can, then we put an alert out to all other supes. Nos, contact your people again, see if they have anything else for us. We suspect the council, yes? Well, I have a way in, I am their good little servant, after all, so I'll check that out."

"What will I do?" the dragon asks, watching us.

I share a look with Nos as if to say, *can I lock this prick up in my basement?* I can already feel the darkness swirling unchecked in my brain from being away from Dawn. At least while she was here I could take it out on her and she helped keep it in check, but now it flows through me and I never know what it's going to do next.

Nos sighs and sits down. "We need to get serious. We all know the council is behind this. I will do as you suggested as well as stay outside of the chambers of the council in case anything goes wrong with you. You find her and get her out, Griffin..."

"I hear a but coming," I prompt, clenching my fingers into my palm to push back memories of the last time I lost someone to the council.

"But we need someone who can take the council down. Yes, we could kill them and then we would all be executed, including Dawn. If they are truly behind this, they aren't doing it with sanction from the sleeping council. I suggest we involve them, let the councils fight between themselves and that is when we extract Dawn."

"You know she's going to want revenge. If you haven't noticed, she's a little bloodthirsty, our mate." I grin, remembering her covered in blood and grinning at me. What a woman, and to think I tried to fight it, fight her.

"That comes after." Nos nods.

"Then that is what I do," the dragon adds, and we both look at him. "I know some witches I can trust, they will find the location of the sleeping council."

"Which has been hidden for thousands of years," I point out, but he ignores me.

"And instruct them on what is happening and make them come here to deal with their own council's disobedience," he finishes. "It will not be easy, but you're right, if it is the council it is the only way to stop them."

"It has been coming for a long time," I mutter, and they both look at me. "Oh come on, we all know the council is corrupt and full of assholes. All they want is power, they don't care how they get it. We wanna fuck the system, then let's do it. I will be your biggest supporter."

"Griffin!" he shouts, eyes flared in panic as they grab him. He fights them, but it's no use, there are too many. From the smoke comes a man in a suit. "Run! Take her!" he screams helplessly, his eyes on me as I hesitate, and the man in the suit smirks.

"Grab that one, bring him to me, oh, and the female."

"No!" I yell, grasping Gabriel's fallen sword and rushing the man.

Pushing away the memories, I cut my palms with my nails, focusing on the flash of pain and my own blood to fight the madness, clinging to that little bit of sanity I have. "Are we doing this?" I look around at them both. "For her?"

The dragon lifts his head stubbornly. "Whatever it takes. They are nothing but old men sitting in chairs in their castle."

Nos inclines his head. "If they have taken my little monster, they die. I will send word to those I have spoken to that we have a suspect for the disappearances and let them know to be ready. The council falling will cause uproar and a scramble for power. We need that sleeping council to stop an all-out war between the races."

"War is always on the horizon." The dragon sighs. "You are right, we can't fight all the races though. We put the sleeping council in place before extracting our mate. Fallen, can you protect her in there?"

I grin then. "Have you ever met her? She doesn't need my protection, they will need it from her."

CHAPTER 13

UNKNOWN ONE

My resting place is sealed with the strongest magic on Earth to protect us from those who mean us harm. A last defence while we slumber. I can't break it, so I simply bypass it.

"Sire?" comes a trembling voice, as the servant flattens himself onto the cold, stone floor where our sleeping bodies are housed and protected beyond anything else in this world. He must have been the one tasked with watching us on this day, ensuring our bodies remained secured and our surroundings cleaned. He lowers his face, unable to look at me as I float through the cracks and fill the room like black smoke. I know what he will see—nothing but bright red eyes flaring in the dark. A nightmare beyond anything this world is accustomed to.

And I am awake again.

"Sire?" he whispers, undoubtedly feeling my malice. "Y-You are not to be awake for another two hundred years."

"I am aware," I reply, my voice floating around the room, making him shiver and compress himself further.

"Sire, would you like me to fetch Master Xaph?" he inquires with a whimper.

Of course it is that winged bastard who is awake and in charge right now, the only one of us whom I hate. Not that we care for each other, we are simply together due to power and position, but that goddamned angel and I have always butted heads. Probably due to what we are, it is ingrained into us to detest one another. He will not take this lightly, he will see this as a slight against his power.

I sigh at the discussions that are to come, aching to race into the world and locate the female whose call awoke me, but this must come first.

"Go," I order, and he scrambles up, still bowed and not looking at me he goes to fetch the angel.

I reform myself as I wait, holding out my arms to watch as they fade from black mist to a corporeal body. Cracking my neck, I confirm I am all there, my golden and black armour in place— another thing the angel hates about me. He thinks gold should be his colour and red mine.

I walk across the floor on bare feet, passing the burial areas where the others are still sleeping, and settle into the throne. Throwing one leg over the golden arm, I lean back and wait, preparing myself for the imminent argument.

I wonder idly what year it is. I keep up to date for the most part with the knowledge funnelled to us, but the last time I was truly awake and in charge, the Romans were in power. They were quite amusing, so much anger. I did like the Vikings best though, easily feeding from their battles. So much hate and rage, not to mention blood. I almost shiver at the memory of how much power I syphoned from them.

The angel felt otherwise, and where I tried to start wars, he attempted to stop them. You see, the world can be nothing without balance, just as an angel sits on this throne, so do I.

A demon, one of war and pain. Not just any demon.

The demon.

Most supernaturals are created through their bloodlines and reproducing, but I wasn't. I was simply here one day when this world was first created. Called by the need for balance. I have walked through the ages, seen it all, always alone. Constantly feared, the very ground burning under my feet, and the stories of my power spread and were repeated, sometimes in different names.

My favourite is that of the ruler of the underworld. Though the pictures of me were eerily close sometimes—my own fault, I find amusement in scaring the humans of this world.

I go by many names.

Lucifer.

El Diablo.

Hell Spawn.

Evil.

The Snake.

What will she call me?

CHAPTER 14

UNKNOWN TWO

"*Papa!*" comes my little girl's scream. I jerk up in bed. Antoinette is awake by my side and staring at me with fear in her dark brown eyes. Her curly brown hair is up in rollers and askew from sleep. Yanking away the covers, I grab my gun and stumble from our farmhouse in just my sleepwear.

"Ella!" I shout, gazing around at the dark night. Our cows are asleep in the field, as are the sheep. The trees are moving with the breeze, and I shiver from the cold mountain air. The darkness seems somehow stronger tonight, the mountains behind us casting shadows along our land. Something is out there, something evil, I can feel it. I felt it once before, in war, but this is so much more, and my little girl is out here somewhere. "Princess, where are you?" I yell, loading my gun as the mud squelches under my bare feet. To the right are the fields and crops, and I search them as far as I can see, but nothing moves out there. To the left is the barn, the candle burning in front of the fogged windows. I narrow my eyes on it, stepping closer.

The barn doors fly open then smash closed with the breeze, and I notice the light in it then. Racing towards the structure, I slip in the mud before scrambling back to my feet, then I freeze when a high-pitched scream comes from inside, so filled with pain that I don't know what to do for a moment.

The horses whinny in fear as well, a predator is in there...so is Ella, I know it. Moving forward, I raise my gun and check behind the doors. The light is from the very end, so I move as quickly as I can past the stables and horses, which are rearing with screams.

"Ella!" I shout again.

A laugh cuts through the barn, the eerie sound raising the hairs on the back of my neck, and then I see it. A little, pale hand is stretched out on the hay, covered in blood, still clutching the figurine I made for her yesterday from hair and buttons.

"Ella?" I cry, stepping around the wooden partitions to see my little girl.

Dropping the gun, I fall to my knees with a grief filled scream, clutching her broken body to me. Her face is pale, her eyes open and unseeing. I have seen enough death in my time while fighting the war to know what it is. Blood saturates her nightgown, her little legs covered in mud, her once pale blonde hair streaked with her death.

"Ella, princess," I cry, tears flowing down my cheeks as I hug her to me. She is so cold, she always hated being cold. "No, no, no."

A laugh comes again, the light flickering overhead, and I still, something...whatever, whoever is still here and watching me. I slide my hand across the hay to reach for my gun just as the barn doors fly open behind me.

"Ella?" Antoinette shouts, and my eyes fly wide open.

No!

I jerk in my chains, a scream of grief caught in my throat. I am trapped in my own mind, the madness taking hold. I can see the cell, feel the cold, pain, and thirst, but my head is still hearing that laugh. The one that haunts me even today.

The thirst is too much. I've gone too long without feeding, and my injured mind is breaking. Caught between the past and present, filled with pain, hate, and grief. My memories flash by like a slideshow of horror.

All the evil I committed, all that I allowed to be perpetuated, reminds me that maybe I deserve this. I am the monster of legends, though most get my origin wrong. I did lose my wife, that is correct, but it was long before I became the monster I am today.

Blood splatters my armour as I rip away the man's head with my fangs, crying out with glee as I raise it up before me like a trophy, another to add to my spikes. The castle looms behind me, an army before me marching straight towards their death—me.

Panting, I force my eyes wider to keep myself in the present. I can feel my fragile state of mind. This is what they want. Me, weak and broken, until I am nothing but the creature of the night they can use to kill and leave a trail of bloodshed.

I have done that. I told myself I would never again fight for a cause I didn't believe in. I would withdraw from this world, be nothing but a tale. But here I am, caught in the middle once again.

The cell door opens and another girl is shoved inside. Snarling, I lunge at them in my chains, but all the men in black do is laugh and slam the door shut. The girl's sobs fill the air as I force myself to be still.

To not give in.

Not now.

CHAPTER 15

DAWN

I crack my neck and grin, but go like a good girl. I don't attack them now, I need information first. Information they have. I look to Dume and wink. "Be good, bull. I'll be back."

He roars and strains to try and get to me, his animal no doubt angry about me leaving him, but I have to if I have any hope of setting him free and my bull deserves freedom.

He roars again, but the cell door shuts and cuts it off. Huh, must be soundproofed. Veyo glances back at the door then to me with a question in his eyes I choose to ignore. He starts to walk, so I fall in next to him, ignoring the guards trooping behind us.

I'm led past more and more cell doors, and I wonder what they are keeping down here, but I hold my mouth shut, trying to play nice and let them think I've learned my lesson. The idiot obviously believes it because he struts taller, like a fucking peacock prancing.

"Where were the men who were with me?" I inquire politely as we walk. I can see him watching me out of the corner of his eye, wondering if I will attack him.

"I don't know, we did not need them so we left them there."

I relax a little at that, knowing Nos and Griffin are safe. I keep my mouth closed as we turn the corner and ascend some stairs into a formal sitting room. He sits down and surveys me. I sit also, relaxing like I belong here and don't have a care in the world. He doesn't scare me, I can feel his power and it's low. No, he is nothing more than a pawn.

"You intrigue me, skinwalker. There hasn't been one of you for centuries, so why now? I can't help but wonder," he questions, and I'm betting he doesn't usually ruminate a lot.

I shrug and his eyes flare for a moment before he fluffs like a bird. "I bet you're curious why we took you."

"Not really."

His eyes narrow, so I grin.

"I'm assuming for some nefarious purpose, though you clearly want to tell me, so please do." Okay, not so good at this good girl act.

A laugh comes from the door, and I turn my head to see a man standing there, leaning against the frame. He is older looking, holding a black cane with a golden eagle head on the top, although I think it's more of a statement than out of need. His hair is grey and pushed back, his eyes sharp and yellow...but I can feel his power. This isn't a man to be fucked with, and I'm betting he's the one in charge. "She's smart, this one."

He moves through the room and Veyo jumps to his feet, bowing his head, so I know I was right. The man sits heavily on the sofa and stares at me. I stare right back. He might be powerful, but he's still a man. "I am Amos, the great eagle, and who are you?"

Huh, so he's an eagle shifter like Veyo. Didn't they say an eagle sat on the council? It only confirms that the council is behind the disappearances. My question is still why? What can they gain from experimenting on humans and stealing females of different races?

"Dawn," I reply. He raises his eyebrows as if prompting me to carry on, so naturally, I do. "Fucker upper of men, the great killer of assholes who think they rule the world because of power and money."

"I see," he says with disdain.

"So, Assmos, I'm going to be honest—"

"Amos," he corrects, and I nod.

"Of course, Assmos. I get the humans. Even if it's fucked up, you are trying to make more supernaturals. I don't know your reasoning, but why kidnap women from different races? You didn't think they would talk to each other, but they did and they are hunting for the perpetrator. Though they don't seem to know to look at their own ruling body."

"It is Amos," he repeats with a frown, clutching his cane harder like he's imagining smacking me with it. "But yes, I suppose I owe you somewhat of an explanation. First, Dawn, how did you become a skinwalker?"

I debate my options, but I honestly don't really know much, so I don't see the harm in telling him. "I was murdered and buried, I was on death's door when I...just didn't die. I woke up and crawled from the grave and became what I am now."

"The thing is, Dawn, our bloodlines are weakening. Each time another is born, their blood is diluted from interhuman breeding and supernaturals losing their powers. Humans are becoming the dominant species with the original gods gone, while more and more are born with latent blood running through their veins...waiting to be activated. Essentially, we are speaking of a whole army's worth of supernaturals trapped in a sheep's body. I think that happened to you."

I grit my teeth as he carries on, what a prick.

"When you woke in the ground, so close to death, you had a choice. Yes, I see it in your eyes, you remember the moment. You chose life, you chose to keep fighting, and in doing so your body changed to keep you alive, your very cells evolving until you became what you are now. But those awakened do not always have the traditional blood of their ancestors, they are adapting. Whether it be the environment or human blood, some are stronger, their powers untold...like you."

I do remember the moment he's talking about, where I chose rage instead of peace. I chose to come back for revenge, to hurt those who hurt me. It was then the pain started and I changed—he's right.

"And others?"

"Others are subspecies, not human and not enough to be one of us. Abominations."

I snort. "Wow, monsters snubbing other monsters, and here I thought only humans were such assholes."

"Whether you like it or not, Dawn, we are evolving, we must keep the lines as pure as we can."

I lean forward. "That's not all, is it? To me it sounds like a last-ditch effort. You said your numbers are dwindling, the humans are dominant, and I don't think you like that. I believe you are trying to build an army...but for what? To take over? To make those you deem worthy in charge again? It would be chaos, humans will always come out on top. We are better off sticking to the shadows, we are monsters, after all."

He sighs. "I can see you don't understand yet, you will, maybe with a bit of effort and pain, you will see what we are trying to do is for the best of us all." He stands, still clutching his cane.

"Doubt it, but please try. I do enjoy a bit of torture, really gets my blood going if you know what I mean." I wink and he turns away, then he stops before Veyo.

"Break her, I want her obedient, I have plans for her," he instructs, and sweeps from the room.

Veyo calls out, and guards with the glowing medallions—witch magic—step into the room. Getting to my feet, I crack my neck and let my monster out to play—my eyes bleeding black, my claws extending, and strength surging through me. It comes easier and easier each time. He was an asshole, but he's right, we are changing.

I'm becoming...more than just a skinwalker. I can feel it, the power growing within, wrapping me in its arms...the question is, what will I become and what are his plans for me?

I have a feeling Veyo doesn't want to share that kind of information, even if he knew. No, he was ordered to break me, and he will try.

I will kill them, rip their faces from their bodies and wear them as I laugh. "Come on, boys, let's play."

Veyo nods and they rush me in a wave. They are stronger than humans, the magic of the witches running through them, making them almost as strong as me. Almost.

I throw myself at them, taking them down. I rip out one's throat with my nails. I take the other's own energy weapon from him and use my strength to stab it into his chest. He jolts and shakes with a scream as he's locked in an endless cycle of electrocution.

Someone smashes theirs into my back, and I lurch before spinning with a howl and gutting them. More and more come at me, and I fight and slash, taking down as many as I can. I know I won't win, but I don't give a fuck. I'm going to hurt them, show them they might be able to subdue me, but they will never break me.

Tim couldn't.

Death couldn't.

These magicked up bitches can't.

They start to overpower me and I end up on the floor, still hacking and kicking, but soon I have to curl up to protect myself, their boots and magic too much. Veyo cackles and I glare. Fuck these pricks and their agenda.

Refusing to let them see me hurt, I laugh, spitting my blood in their faces as they rain down punches and kicks on my curled up body. I continue to laugh until a boot slams down on my head, knocking me out.

CHAPTER 16

ASK A

"See you soon, dragon." Nos shakes my hand and I return the gesture. Maybe they aren't so bad after all, they do seem to love Dawn, that we can agree on at least.

"Try not to die before you bring us that council, dickhead," Griffin orders, and I snort at him, sweeping my leg out to kick his sofa on purpose as I turn. I hear him swear, making me smirk as I head outside and straight into the road that leads to the forest behind his house. I follow his directions so I can find a secluded place to change and return to my car. I need information. I have to go back to the witches and pay yet again. I wonder what they will ask for this time.

I will pay it, they can have all my gold and treasure if it means keeping my mate safe. I refuse to consider what is happening to her right now, I can't without losing it. I will, however, try to contact her tonight through our link before I leave the witches' safety net. Even if it's just for a moment to see for myself that she is okay.

I head to the very edge of the street and walk until I find a cove of trees. Stepping inside, I make a nest out of leaves and fallen branches and settle to try and contact her. It's dangerous out in the open, but I have to try.

Animals still, sensing me nearby. The forest smells crisp and of magic, old magic, undoubtedly from the forest god my mate has claimed. This is his land, after all, and I can sense the fae here and there as well, and a recent trail to the left of me a couple of miles away. I map the land in my head, letting my dragon out to see and sense any threats. When we find nothing, I settle back down again and try to force myself to relax.

The branches crack with each shift of my body, and I wish I could make an actual nest. My dragon is restless, and just when I am about to give up, I finally slip into a troubled slumber, my soul reaching across the miles between us, searching for her...

"Dawn?" I call out, my voice loud and echoing.

We are back at the lake of my homeland, the one I often escaped to when I thought about the heavy weight of leadership and my need to break free from traditions and my own people. Everything is hazy, white, and too perfect to be real, but the trees are the same.

The identical rock where I used to lay after flying, dipping, and diving in the water is situated where it should be. I used to leap off the cliff over there when I was just five until I could do it myself. It was tradition. No one could be a dragon who couldn't fly—it should be instinctive, they said. So they threw their children off cliffs and hoped for the best, but I didn't wait for that to happen. I did it alone. They called me fearless even back then. My wings sprouted on the first go, but they were too big for me and I crashed into the water.

But I kept trying and trying until I could flap before crashing, and then hover...and then fly. It was ungraceful, but I was the youngest dragon ever to fly, and when I shifted at fourteen for the first time, they found it wasn't the only non-traditional thing about me.

Heading to the water line, I wait, wondering if she is coming. She might not be asleep, I can think of all the horrible reasons why, but I push them away, forcing myself to relax and watch the water lap against the shore. I will wait. If she doesn't turn up in a few hours, then I will head back to my body and find the witches.

I sit and linger, and just when I am about to give up hope and try to wake myself, I feel her. Leaping to my feet, I spin to see her standing behind me in a golden flowing gown, her blonde hair in loose waves around her shoulders.

"Dawn!" I gasp and rush to her, and she meets me halfway.

I scoop her into my arms and bring my lips to hers. She returns the kiss with equal fervour, but she pulls back. "We don't have long, my dragon, where are you?"

"Where are you?" I countered.

"I don't know, the council is involved though—men named Amos and Veyo. Another of my mates is here." She sighs.

"Are you hurt?" I ask.

She hesitates and I roar, so she strokes my face. "Nothing that can't heal. I can look after myself, dragon."

"I have met your other mates, Nos and Griffin...first, can I kill the fallen?" I grumble.

She giggles, her eyes alight, then it fades. "He has that effect on everyone. Are they okay? Are they searching for me?"

"They are, we all are. We have a plan, my love, do not fear. We will get you," I vow.

"Good, don't rush, I have a plan of my own. This is what we were hunting, we need to stop it. That comes before my freedom. I can do much from the inside." She strokes my face then. "Oh, how I wish I could touch you in real life."

I rest my forehead against hers. "Soon." I kiss her again, wishing I could feel her in my arms, feel that she is safe. She is the treasure I always sought. "Griffin will be joining you, playing the good servant, work with him. Nos is calling all the allies. Is there anything you need me to tell them?"

She exhales heavily. "That it's the council, and they are trying to make an army with human mutations and by stealing women. I just don't know how or if they are all involved. It's clear they think they are doing the right thing though. It won't be easy to stop them, they have witches and human hunters somehow working with them. Maybe chase down those leads, cut them off at the source."

I nod, my mate is clever. "I will tell them."

"T-Tell Nos I miss him. Tell Griffin not to kill too many people." She snickers.

"And me, mate?" I growl.

"Dragon, I better see you soon," she purrs, kissing me again, and I lose myself in her for a moment before pulling away. "Then you can take me to this place for real."

I don't tell her I can never return here, not without risking everything I ran from, not without risking her. Something I will never do. Dragons are merciless, unfeeling, proud assholes—I should know, I am one. Only I feel for her. More than I ever thought possible.

Dawn.

Her eyes go far away for a moment. "Stay safe, my dragon."

"Dawn," I call, but she fades out of my arms. I try to hold her, but it is like trying to grasp the wind.

I roar into my dreamscape as it crumbles around me, and I wake up in my nest with that same roar.

My dragon breaks free, uprooting the trees we were using for shelter as we shoot into the sky, filled with determination. She is counting on me, she made her wishes known. I will find the sleeping council and I will bring them there. Then we will be together.

Finally.

CHAPTER 17

DUME

I roar and jerk from the magic in the chains from the moment my mate leaves my sight, my bull taking over. He wants her back, wants her touch and kisses, the gentle way she stroked his fur. He craves it, can't settle without it, never mind the fact she might be in danger. It sends him over the edge, into a rage I have never seen before. Not even when *she* was alive. He was angry then but logical. Now? He is nothing more than a monster.

They must hear him or have been waiting for the unknown to be removed, because not thirty minutes after she is taken, the door opens, and a huddle of witches is blocking the light. Their hoods are up, concealing their faces, and the black material has a life of its own, moving when they move and never revealing what they seek to hide.

They step into the cell in unison. It is possible some were alive when I was, especially if they were dark witches and worked with blood magic and necromancy, but I haven't seen any I recognise. Either way, they hate me. It is bred into them, I am the monster from their tales, the one who killed their queen and ended many of their lines. They even have a name for it, I heard it once—the great black death. So many witches died, and so many powers were lost to my sword and vengeance...now, here, their ancestors stand. Dark hate shines in their eyes and magic coats their hands as they face me, ready to exact vengeance for their lost.

I grin at them with a snarl. Bring it, I need to let out this aggression before Dawn is brought back anyway. They can be my bull's playthings, a way to occupy his hate and mind as we wait for the return of our mate. I see the whirling of the light conjuring in their hands as they step farther into the cell and spread out in a half circle, their hands nearly joined, startling my bull as they begin to chant.

Fucking witches and their magic. Without it they are nothing... weaker than humans, and they know it. They rely on it, inspire fear and loyalty with it even as they present their hubris as their strength, but I know it and I don't fear them. I have felt the touch of their magic and now the touch of my mate, and nothing or no one will entrap me again. She needs me, I need her.

They will die for trying to get between us.

I hear the stone behind me crack with the force of my determination and strength, giving the chains a little leeway. My bull snorts as they stop chanting for a moment, their energy permeating the air as they watch us strain to get to them. I throw my head back and roar, letting it shake the room, the force of it sending a gust of power towards them. They tumble to the floor like broken dolls as I feel the change come over my body, just like when Dawn needed it, only this time we are changing to full bull, the animal taking over completely. I feel myself become pushed to the back of his consciousness, I let him happen. He needs the bloodshed and violence more than me.

When our head is lowered, I have nothing human left, and I let them see that in my red eyes. My horns seem to grow and reach for them, my hooves smashing into the stone floor and ringing out like a fighting bell. My bull is daring them to come closer, to hit us.

They do.

Magic is flung at me from all angles, but something strange happens...some of it bounces off. Some of it sinks into my fur and skin and muscle below, making us bellow in pain, but some of it seems to be repelled, hitting my fur and then rebounding back to the caster, striking them instead. I don't have time to ponder that, because we are moving. They got sloppy with their casting, relying on their magic to take me down, and now they are close.

Too close, within my range. It will be their deaths.

I ram forward, impaling two on my horns, tossing my head around and ripping their insides. I feel their blood coating my head and face and my bull snorts and charges, tossing them aside. Ignoring their screams and the scent of their deaths on the air, we aim for the others. One of the smart ones backs away and starts throwing magic, but I use her sisters as a shield and it hits them. She yells and bangs on the door, trying to open it as we roar and rip our way through their masses.

The cell lights up with their magic and the sound of screams. Blood, piss, and shit coat the air as they realise they willingly walked themselves into a trap with death. A beast, one that is carelessly shredding them to pieces.

They don't stand a chance. My bull snorts in pleasure as I split one of their stomachs open and they shriek and fall under my hooves. I smash one's head, feeling it squelch under me. Pausing, chest heaving, and smoke curling from my nose, I look around at the bodies littering the cell. Some of them are trying to heal themselves, one of them is attempting to crawl to the door with no legs, and there is one still untouched. Her hands are still pressed to the door, her face against it as she sobs as if not looking at the monster, at me, will make me not real.

"Please, please, no, please, oh great mother, hear my pleas.

Protect me with your bright, guiding light," she begs, her voice cracking and small, like a child.

"Your prayers won't save you," I tell her, voice garbled, but she hears me.

She whimpers, pressing closer to the door, repeating the prayer again and again, louder and louder as she hears me drawing closer. The chain stops me before I can reach her and my bull roars in anger, wanting her blood, wanting her cries of fear. She came here to hurt us, kill us, stop us from protecting our mate. She must die.

"Oh, little witch..." I laugh, the sound like a roar and she whimpers, flattening herself against her only exit. "Come out and playyyyy."

"Our bright mother, darkness unbound, come upon me," she cries.

My bull recedes slightly, letting me change our mouth and face back so I can talk. "Little witch," I rasp in a human voice, and she shivers like she fears that more than my animal, interesting. "Your great mother has deserted you. You are weak, shivering in terror. At least your coven went to death with pride, facing their fear while you whimper and hide. What would they think of you now?" I laugh, spreading my arms to encompass her dead people. Some are still sucking in stuttering breaths to try and stay alive.

"Moo-ther, please, save me from this certain death," she whispers.

"Oh, bright mother," I mock, stepping forward as far as I can to reach her, my arm outstretched and brushing her hood. "Save me!" I cry and then chuckle. "She didn't save your coven, she didn't even save your vile, fucking demented ancestors as I ripped through them and left them to choke on their blood."

She stops talking, breathing heavily now, and I sense her fear retreat slightly, morphing to anger. Ah, yes, that's what we want. So I carry on, throwing out barbs at her people and she turns with a cry, her hand held outright, flinging the last of her magic at me as she steps forward. We watch as the bright blue and black orb hits my chest and then seems to melt into the floor. Her mouth flops open, her eyes wide as she watches me.

"But how? That was death magic, I threw my own life into it...you couldn't..."

I don't care how, only that she is close enough to reach now. Close enough to kill. I grab her as she screams for mercy and tear her in two, throwing the parts to the side, then I just stand there amongst the bloodshed and death and wait for my mate.

My bull needs to let something else out now, something much, much stronger and much more deadly—lust. All that hate and blood lust is turning into pure desire, until our body flicks between animal and human as we roar in need for our mate.

Dawn.

CHAPTER 18

I leave my house and the forest god there as I mount my motorcycle and pull from my drive, heading down a familiar road to the place I hate most on this Earth. I have tried so hard to gain my freedom, even though I'm their fucking pet, to have my own space and life...yet here I am, willingly riding back into their masses. To become their assassin, their servant, to do with whatever they want.

For her, always for her.

I can feel the madness clawing at the edge of my mind, brought by my need for her, my mate, and my lingering fear of going back. I haven't stayed willingly in their presence since the night I lost everything, since I was forced to watch...no, I can't go there. Not now, otherwise I'll give into that madness and just go in there, kill all those fucking bastards, and rip Dawn away, which isn't a bad plan apart from the fact we will be hunted for the rest of our lives.

No, I can't do that to her.

She had a shitty enough human life with that piece of shit she killed and buried in the woods. She deserves a better second chance. I almost snort at that. A better second chance...with me? We both know I'm the craziest motherfucker out there, so close to losing it and giving into that blackness inside me like a poison, which seems to be out of control without her here to push it back and revel in it. She deserves better than me, I know that, but I'm not letting her go.

If they have touched her, hurt her...my mind flashes black for a moment and I look down at my hands on the handlebars to see them leaking black mist. No, I push it away. I can't afford to lose it, not here, not with her so close. I will have to play their game, the perfect little servant, and get close to her. Find her, protect her.

She trusted me, gave her life to me...told me I would never be alone again.

It's time I prove neither will she. I'll always come for her. She's the reason I keep going instead of giving in, she is the reason I'm walking into the viper's nest, willing to take any pain, any punishment or humiliation they deem worthy. She was right, we need each other.

I need her.

She keeps me sane—well, as sane as can be—and makes me want to fight. To keep living, to feel her with me. To feel her soul wrapped around me, her body entwined with mine. I ache with the need to touch her, the pull stronger than ever before. To hold her, fuck her, claim her, and make her mine.

I didn't have nearly enough time with her to prove I can be more than a sour, angry brute, but someone she could care about...I daren't say love. I don't deserve it, nor do I have it to give. My heart is blackened and cold, but she helped it beat again and now I will never go back.

What a fool I was, thinking I could resist her. She shook up my world and I miss the madness she brought. Her smiling face flashes through my mind as she squared up to me, toe to toe, unafraid even in my bitterness and hate. My mate is something, that's for sure, and unlike the others I know she can survive whatever they throw at her, but what will she evolve into to survive it?

I became this bitter, winged monster flying above the world but never touching it, held apart...my mate, Dawn...*Vasculo,* will she embrace the pain and let it fuel her or will she withdraw?

I don't want to find out, so I gun it, speeding up as I wind down the road through the forest that leads to the council and to her. My Harley purrs between my legs. It's as close to flying as I can get without spreading my wings and taking to the sky, but they don't appreciate it when I turn up like that. It usually ends with a lecture or a punishment, saying I'm flaunting the gifts I was given from my angel father and the horrible twistedness of my nature—not that they care when they use them for their own gain, but that's something else altogether.

I can feel Nos in the forest, there is a link between us now, connected from Dawn. It feels strange not to be alone in my head, but not unpleasant, but I will never tell that fucking tree hugger. He's at least better than that snobby fucking dragon, who thinks he is better than all of us. He reminds me of everything I hate, those bastards who sit on the throne and give orders. I wanted to kill him, had come very close to doing so, sneaking up behind him when he hadn't noticed, but Nos had stopped me. One simple word on his lips was a reminder.

Dawn.

Would she forgive me? I doubt it, since a mate is more than a choice. As much as I hate it, it's fate. He is as much hers as I am, doesn't mean I won't try to kill the smug fucking bastard. My only consolation is that my wings are better. His look like fucking bat wings, while mine are soft and feathered. She seemed to enjoy them last time, my cock buried inside her as I wrapped them around her while we plummeted.

I groan, shifting as I turn, trying to ignore my now hard cock. I really shouldn't think of my mate's pussy when driving. I might crash and then I would scratch up my bike. It took me years to save up enough to buy it and customise it how I wanted.

I wonder if I could get Dawn one once this is all over, then she can ride beside me...no, I want her in front or behind me, wrapped around me, clinging to me as I speed across the world. Not alone anymore.

I pull up to the gates and wait for them to open and let me in. They don't for at least five minutes as I idle there, and I instantly know what kind of mood the council is in—a testing one. They are wondering what I want. I wasn't called, so they are showing me their power by making me wait.

Fucking bastards. I push back the darkness and madness, which is whispering for me to kill them all...not yet.

Finally, the gate swings open, admitting me to the sprawling manner. I pull around the fountain and park my bike out front. A little rebellion, but I know it will annoy them, disrupting their splendour and outward show of money and power. Standing back, I lean against my bike, knowing if I head inside they will punish me. Instead, I must wait outside like a dog called home, and often for hours. Once they left me out here for a full day even after ringing me to come back for a briefing. The fuckers. I used the time to debate all the ways I could kill them, and when I got bored I started flying loops around their fountain and doing target practice. It's safe to say they never made me wait that long again.

They are quick for once, probably due to their curiosity of why I'm here. The door opens, and standing there is the council's bitch. I stand tall and brush past him without a word, heading inside.

"Stop!" he calls, but I'm done with formalities. They are testing my patience and I can feel myself itching to rain holy fucking madness down on them. They can rip my damn wings off again, see if I give a shit, the smug assholes.

I barge through the marble reception area, ignoring the winding steps that lead upstairs, and instead head right to the waiting room. They won't see me straightaway, but I'll be damned if I sit there taking shit from that lackey. I head through the double doors and take a seat on the elaborate chesterfield sofas, purposely putting my dirty boots up on the spotless gold and glass coffee table between them.

I snort at the paintings in the room, all depicting battles the council members have won. There is one in the middle opposite me of the moment they took down the angel operation—the angel who gave life to me. They show him in chains on the floor as they lord over him, with children hiding behind the council like they're their saviours. Fuckers, they don't see themselves for what they really are. Us children were taken from one life of servitude to another, at least with the angel we knew what he wanted and he cared for us. We were his holy children, his reason for living, the council? To them we are nothing but disposable blades, something they wish to squash and mould into their own personal killers and most did. They gave themselves over, acting as nothing more than an assassin, no emotions or regret. No dreams of the future, just a blade to be wielded. Not me, I made a deal with the devil to save the one I loved and look where it got me...

Right under their boot and she's dead. But now I have something else to live for, to fight for, and I'm back where I started, on a disadvantage under their boot. The only difference this time is that I'm smart enough to not let them know it. Or let them use it against me.

The door opens to reveal Veyo. He takes in my boots and narrows his eyes in displeasure, but he knows to pick his battles with me. "We weren't expecting you, fallen, they did not call."

I don't reply and he stands taller.

"If you wish to see them, you will have to wait, they are very busy people and do not come when called like you, dog," he spits.

I raise my eyebrow, my eyes undoubtedly melting into shadows as I try to rein in my anger. He huffs at my lack of response and turns his pompous ass around and leaves me there. Closing my eyes, I lean back and wait to be seen. I need to make them think I'm coming home, that I miss this place, and that I want to serve and be with my kind, but I can't lay it on too thick or they will know I'm lying. It's a fine balance between being an asshole and a servant.

I let my mind drift as I wait, trying to sit still, but there's that pull again, that one to Dawn. She's close, I can feel her, and I want to storm through the corridors, demanding to see her and killing those in my way. My fists clench at my sides as I fight off the madness and need.

Instead I sink into it, unable to resist as it wraps around me, drawn by where I am, my memories crowding my head, screams tugging at my consciousness. Mine and hers, and I roar and fight it, but it's no use, it's too strong, and without Dawn here I plunge into that pit, into the darkness...

"Griff, run!" comes her scream as she's dragged away from me, her human arms frail as she beats at their armour to try and get to me, her brown hair whipping in the air, out of place. I idly think she would hate that. I stand there, my arms held on either side as she's dragged kicking and screaming down the aisle to be thrown before their seats.

I follow behind her, rushing to her side. I push myself in front of her, my wings and arms spread wide, their golden chairs towering over me. "You promised! We have a deal!" I shout helplessly.

I look to my brothers, those who were raised with me for help. I search their faces, all blending together where they stand shackled around the neck like pets. But there is nothing left of them, they are blank soldiers waiting for orders. I stare at the council with a plea, anger coating my voice. "We had a deal!" Is it not enough that they took and killed my father, now they want to kill my human mother? Grief flashes through me. I made a deal, they have to honour it! My life for hers, she would be safe. I didn't care if it would cost me, that I would be theirs to do with what they wanted. All my life I have been owned, hidden like a dirty secret, but behind closed doors...my human mother loved me.

I was the only one kept with her, allowed to be raised as my father looked on, stoic and calm, but with us he was so much more —loving, caring, a family. Now that is all gone. She grips my back and cries for me to run, even now worried for me, her human body weak and not enough to stand before them.

I see it in their eyes, in their faces as they watch me in disgust. They never intended to keep their end of the deal.

"This is a lesson to those who think they can betray us, who are above the rules...this experiment, this abomination, pleads for a human, for us to save her because only we can, but she's nothing. A sheep, her purpose fulfilled. We can't condone what happened, but we will not turn our backs on these children, these fallen...we will take them and train them, give them a purpose, but that purpose does not need a family, a mother. You are an experiment, a weapon, that is all." He watches me as he speaks, and I want to scream as my arms are taken by forces stronger than me and I'm dragged before the beings in the seats and my mother. She reaches for me, crying, her blue eyes filled with so much pain and grief. "They do not require love or a mother, do not let them fool you, they feel nothing...just another illusion to gain sympathy. It speaks of a deal, as if we would make a deal with such an atrocity. Today I will show you how we will keep those new soldiers in line, with pain!" Some of the crowd cheers, but I don't look away from my mother's eyes as I feel my wings lifted up straight, and something cold pressed against the joint where it meets my back. What will they do to me? To her...

My eyes snap open, dragged from the memory at the sudden sound in the quiet. There is a fallen standing in the doorway, watching me, his eyes empty and dead. His wings are pulled in tight behind him, and he's a sickish grey colour, his body not as strong as mine but lithe and thin. He's taller though, he reminds me of those depictions of death in storybooks sheep love so much, even has the ugly fucking smile to cover it.

"Fallen," he greets, his voice cool and emotionless. The fucking bastards. I never could muster that, always too much swimming around inside me. How they can serve these assholes with no emotions, I will never understand. Do they not want freedom, want to feast on their pain and blood for what they did? No, they are happy being servants.

"Brother." I nod and he hisses.

"I am not your brother, fallen." His voice whispers through the air. I try not to let the sting show as it sinks in, but even among my own kind I'm looked down on, disowned for the madness and emotions, for being stripped of my wings, something I had no control over. I survived but they all think I shouldn't have, that it made me into...well, a fucking monster.

They aren't wrong, but the part of me that's still human aches at the thought of the people I was once family with, the children I grew up with, turning their back on me. I was never close with them, but they were all I had. They were jealous back then of what I had, but now? Now they would kill me given the order or choice. For simply surviving.

"What do you want?" I finally ask.

"To see why you are here. Is it to finally beg for forgiveness and meet death like a warrior?" he whispers, his voice filling the room with power, no doubt a gift from his angel father, the fuckers. He steps into the room then, so I sit up, my boots ringing out as they hit the floor, my hands loose at my sides, waiting. It wouldn't be the first time they have attacked me, tried to kill me. The council calls it a test, saying if I don't survive them, I have no worth, but if I do then I am of use.

"Or maybe to grovel at their feet, to try and become one of us? It will never happen," he carries on, circling around the room, feathers ruffling. "You are too mad, we see it in your eyes, in your actions. You are uncontrolled, a force for sure, powerful thanks to your father, but your soul? It's as black as your eyes, too far gone to be saved. You will never be one of us, one of those who serves, you are nothing but an experiment gone wrong, too human to be a warrior, too mad to be sane..."

"And what does that make you?" I snap, getting to my feet to face him. "You are an experiment, *brother,* just as human and angel as me. You forget where you come from. You think licking their boots makes you more holy? More worthy? It makes you a fool, one not strong enough to fight."

He hisses again, his eyes bleeding into gold for a moment, another thing that makes me stand out. "We never loved, not like you. You craved the human, the one who birthed you, you held her close with your human sentiment. You let it blind you. We are the force the council uses, chooses to save and keep, and you...you are nothing more than an outcast that, in their mighty power, they deemed too sad to kill. One day they will and I will do it, and we will rejoice for the scourge is gone. They should have killed you that day, like they killed that human you loved and that angel."

I snap, the madness taking hold. I've lost so much, faced so much pain and grief, and with my mother's screams resounding in my ears and Dawn too far away to touch and drag close and keep safe, I let it all out...unleashed like the animal, the beast he accuses me of being.

He doesn't even see me moving, he doesn't expect it. He is too formal, too emotionless to see how hate and anger can guide you. It makes me reckless and unpredictable and he doesn't know how to fight me. I grab him around the throat and my wings burst from my back as I drag him into the air and slam him back against the wall, next to the painting of our captors. His eyes widen slightly, his breath quickening for a moment, the only sign of fear he will share, to do otherwise would be to dishonor his father, his council.

I know they were treated worse than me back then. Their fathers didn't love them, just what they stood for, a chance to train warriors. A lot of them were tough, hard, evil even, but I can't help that or change it. I will not let them sully my father's or mother's names in my presence. They might have been raised by monsters, but they chose to work for them, they chose their path and now they have to live with it.

He fights my hold, but I'm too strong, the veins bulging in my arms with the strength of gripping him. He stops struggling and just stares at me. "What will you do now, fallen? Kill me? You do and they will torture you and rip your wings away again, you over-value yourself, you are nothing but a toy to them."

"And you are nothing but a blade," I counter, leaning closer and letting him see the madness he thinks he knows, he has no idea. "You think they would really care if I kill you? There are hundreds of others just like you, waiting to step into your spot. You are noth-ing, disposable."

A throat clears and we both turn our heads to see Veyo standing there with a dirty expression on his face. "That painting is very expensive. Wings away, fallen, they are ready to see you." He sighs and waits until I release the man who drops to the floor before jumping to his feet, his arms crossed behind his back like a good soldier. I float to the floor, my wings going away as soon as I land and push them both back.

It's about time. Now, let's trick the council.

CHAPTER 19

NOS

I watch them both go with a sigh on my lips. How I wish my little monster was here, but we will get her back soon and this infighting will stop. They wouldn't dare bicker with her here. I lock up behind them and leave the key before walking into the forest, shedding my clothes as I change, my hands catching on the trees as I pass by, absorbing their knowledge and strength.

I feel the change wash through me, like letting out a breath as I move through the forest. I am to collect allies and wait near the council in case anything goes wrong, which tests my patience. I can feel my little monster, and to not be with her is a torture unto itself.

As I amble, I let out a call to the animals and creatures that linger in the forest under my protection. I hear their howls and songs of answer, and the stirring of the dark creatures that slumber here undisturbed under my protection, awakening as they feel my need. I called a few of my friends before I left and spoke to them.

They were suspicious at first, not believing the council was behind it, but we all know the council has its own agenda, and these beings will stand with me if it turns out to be true. I also spoke to Victoria, who is scouring the city for any sign of The Others, as they called them, and she will report back to me. Additionally, she put the city on lockdown, so nothing moves without her knowing. Her last words were a warning—get Dawn back or she would. It seems my little mate is collecting friends as she goes.

Powerful friends.

I reach across the vast forest and send a whisper to the fae, knowing they want their people back too. If the council did this, they are going to face an army of angry supernaturals, all mixed and united because of them. All I care about, however, is getting my little monster back. She needs me and I need her.

Being apart from her after all my years of searching is painful, but she is strong, and if anyone can make it through, it is her. They do not know who they have taken or they would have let her be. It is very much like shaking a hornet's nest, they will get stuck and not know what to expect from her. Even I don't as her mate.

She is powerful, that is for sure, and unpredictable like the fallen, but there is something more there, waiting, like a hunting wolf. And I will be there when it is unleashed, standing at her side as I was always meant to. Until then, I will rally an army for her.

Wolves join my sides, eagles and owls float in the air, the rabbits hop closer, and snakes and bugs assemble us as I go, until I look back and I see the forest moving with the force of the animals. An army trails after me, ready to follow my call. I protect them, they protect me, everything is a balance in this world. I am the God of the Forest and they have taken my mate, they will see my wrath before this is through.

They will taste my power and bow before it, huddled in their thrones as they realise their mistake. I have stayed out of politics and wars, but no longer, they have taken the one thing I will always fight for and they don't even comprehend it...

I can feel our bond, our souls linked across the miles. She smiles at me, waiting patiently for me to come and get her, but my mate doesn't need rescuing, I can feel it. She has a plan, a purpose. I will have to wait and be ready, because now I can see it all. She needs me to ground her, to keep her safe as she fulfils her goal.

For now she needs her fallen...and a minotaur? Interesting. I send my birds forward, cooing in their mind to get into the compound and watch her and keep me updated. Ravens, eagles, and so many more rush forward in a flap of wings that sounds like gunshots through the forest.

Far across the world I feel a darkness coming, reaching for her, and I know. I just know, my mate has called something old, even older than me and more wild...untamed. I have to have faith in her and fate, that she will never call what she can't control.

I put my hope into that, otherwise I will have to try and kill him. It's a good job we have a fallen and a dragon on our side to help, because mate or not, if he hurts her, we will watch him scream in agony as we rip him to pieces in front of her. This world doesn't even realise that monsters are uniting around them, that the darkest and strongest of us all follow one tiny woman, called by my mate's power and purpose.

A natural disaster, that's what she is. Strong, powerful, untrained, and wild, and we are just swept along with her. My little monster, determined to right the wrongs and save or damn us all, it's in her hands...

I'm here, Little Monster, feel me. I am always here with you, just look inside.

CHAPTER 20

LUCIFER

Xaph sweeps into the room with a roll of thunder from Heaven and his holy father. His white wings flare in anger, his golden halo floating above him, spinning faster with his fury. He wears his white robes tied with golden leaves, his feet clad in sandals. His blue eyes lock on me with hatred upon where I sit in his chair. He slams the door shut, his light fighting my darkness in the chamber, clashing in the middle of the room as we both fling our power at each other. A test, as always, to see who is stronger.

"What are you doing?" he screams, stepping forward, and for a moment my darkness retreats a bit, but with a mental flick I shoot it out and it hits him, throwing back his golden power until it curls into him with a pained groan. He likes to think his light is the strongest, but everyone knows darkness always wins. It's where people seek power and conduct rituals, letting out their fantasies and energy. It's where they find solace in warm blankets, their hate, anger, love, and hope all coming together. It's where they hide.

Light has only one thing to offer, shining on you...spotlighting everything.

No, darkness will always win. I will always win, and it's about time the angel realised that. I never cared to prove it before, never needed to. I could do this job with my eyes closed, but now...now I have something I need...I want.

Her.

It gives me a purpose, something to use, and there is nothing more dangerous than a demon with a mission. He must see it, because he falters for a moment, unused to me pushing back as much. His eyes flicker nervously, wondering what hell I will bring down on Earth and the humans he cares so much for.

They pray to me for redemption and him to save them...he is worried I will walk among them, killing and seeking bloodshed, bathing in the pain and death. Maybe I will, but first I will find her. I will find my mate, the one who called me from my slumber. If it is a trick, I will wipe this world clean of sinners and saints alike. If it is not...it's unknown, something I have never faced before. I have nothing to offer in the way of love or kindness, my heart is as black as my forms and power, unbeaten for thousands of years. I live in hate and darkness with betrayal and lies wrapped around me. She will hate me, but I don't care, I will take her anyway. She will be mine, to do with as I wish, chained to me for eternity, forced to burn with me—a cruel outcome, but I cannot stop it now. It is fate, it is destined...she is meant to be mine.

"Xaph," I greet conversationally.

He straightens his back, lifts his chin, and steps closer, showing he is unafraid. I smirk, we both know that's a lie, for there is nothing the angel fears more than me. One day I will be his downfall. We have been locked in this game for thousands of years, light versus dark. I do not know who will win, but it was my only entertainment until now, the only creature who could stand against me.

"Demon," he replies, refusing to call me anything else, even after all these years. He hates that I have a seat on the council, but this world needs balance and light and dark to lead. If I did not, it would fall into chaos. "Why are you awake?" he demands, his holy power ringing with truth and calling the same forth from me, but I snort at the simple trick he tries to wield on me. He should know by now I keep things close to my chest, never to be used against me. Lies are my usual and my power comes from secrets, those whispered into the night, both mine and theirs.

"Why not? I was tired of sleeping." I grin, flicking my fingers and setting the torches in here alight, pretending to examine my nails as he glares at me. His holy righteousness takes over as he steps closer yet again, his wings still spread like a declaration.

"You should not have been able to break the spells holding you," he states. It's not a question, so I don't answer and he carries on, his voice growing angrier with each word. "It is my turn to rule and yours to sleep, this is out of place, you will upset the rules of nature and our world. You cannot be awake, demon, it is not right!" he finishes on a scream.

I turn my head, not my body, no doubt looking disjointed, and stare him down. "Is that right? I do enjoy the chaos of breaking the rules," I purr, my voice wrapping around him like a tightening leash, probing for chinks in his armour. That's the thing with being so good, so angelic, there is always a part of you, a dark little voice that wants to break the rules, who craves the chaos and wrongness I bring. I exploit it now.

My darkness curls through those cracks, those doubts, and pushes them, the voice in his mind urging him to give in. I see him battling his beliefs, his nature, as I thread my power through him like a puppet, showing him just how strong I am. How powerful. How I could have this whole world on their knees before me as I walk through their worship of fear and death.

"Demon, stop!" he orders, his voice shooting out like bullets, but I just laugh, still relaxing on the throne. This is almost like the time he tried to perform an exorcism on me. I grow bored though and pull back, it was enough, a warning. He is breathing heavily, his sweat covering his brow as I sit there unbothered. "Why are you awake?" he asks again, his voice shaken now that he is aware of just how formidable I am. I wonder what he would think if he knew I could possess him.

Tilting my head, I watch him as I decide what to share. "Not for you, or your seat. Do not worry, angel, I do not crave your power or the love of your people. I have a different purpose, it will take me away from you."

"You are not to leave this place! This is our duty!" he retorts.

"I do what I wish, do not test me again, angel," I warn, my tone exploding like a volcano and he flinches.

"We have had enough of your reign, of your unruly behaviour. You represent our people, you are a leader now, vowed to protect and guide our populace. A hundred years awake, five hundred asleep, that is how we work! You cannot break tradition or your vows on a whim!" he protests, but just then we are interrupted by the servant. He scurries into the room and throws himself on the floor between us.

"Yes?" we both say at the same time, and the angel cuts me a glare as I grin.

"M-Masters," he offers worriedly to not offend us, I do have a tendency to kill them. Once we had to replace him nine times in one week, that was a good time. "There has been a disturbance."

"A disturbance?" Xaph repeats with a frown, and I shrug at him, already bored with this conversation.

"Yes, master. Unrest, unbalance," he explains quickly.

"Someone is trying to rise above their station?" I muse and Xaph frowns.

"Maybe, do you know anything else?" he inquires, addressing the servant.

"It is to the south, master, towards the dragons' homes. There is a crack forming, they are breaking back through into the world."

"What? Why?" Xaph fumes as I grin, I did say I enjoy chaos, after all.

"Well, it looks like you have your hands full, angel, I will be on my way," I comment before standing, and he turns to me with a heavenly glare.

"You will do no such thing. We must determine why you are awake, and as a leader you are duty bound to investigate this disturbance, which does not mean killing them! Or have you forgotten your blood oath, snake?"

Damn oaths, I hate them, pesky bastards to break. Last time I tried I sunk Atlantis, fun times.

I sit back down, smoke curling around me as the chair burns under my anger. He does not understand. My duty is no longer to this world or the people under us, but to finding her, to claiming her before she is snatched away. If they knew I had a mate, that she was out there...they would do whatever it took to take her and make her theirs, to control me. She is my one weakness and she is left alone in the world, unprotected as I face an infuriated agent of God.

Chapter 21

Vampire

I can't remember my name or birthplace. Or even my life before this. How long have I been trapped here? I can't tell, it is all a blur, a foggy memory I can't grasp. The thirst rips holes in my mind and lets in the darkness until I'm half mad. My memories, my past, flickers through my head, a horror show that weakens me further, my own mind turning against me until I am howling both internally and externally.

I leap to my feet and whirl, my gun held in my hand, but I am too late. Antoinette screams as I watch a creature rip into her neck. Blood arcs out, hitting the door and floor, seeping through the hay and wood, staining it forever with her life force. I race forward, firing again and again at the creature, which jerks and laughs as my gun clicks that it is empty.

With a scream trapped in my throat, I watch my wife's dying body crumple to the ground as the creature spins to face me, its fangs flashing in the night, its chin covered in my wife's and child's blood as it taunts me.

"Do you want to die with them?" it questions, its voice strange, rasping around the fangs I can't help but stare at. We have all heard the stories, believing them to be nothing more than tales to scare children, but before me stands a creature from myth...mocking my pain and loss as my wife and child's bodies lie broken around us.

I grab my shells with shaking hands and try to reload the gun, but my eyes keep going back to Antoinette to see her gaze locked on me as tears roll down her beautiful face, her neck still pumping blood onto the floor. The creature laughs again and is suddenly before me. It knocks the gun out of my hand, and I watch it tumble to the ground out of reach. Dragging my eyes from my lost weapon, I meet the bottomless pits of the creature before me. I stare at it helplessly, my eyes defiant. I will not flinch in the face of death, my time was up many a year ago, only luck has kept me alive to this day. To see my dearest bear our child, watch her grow, and now watch her fall. Oh, this world is cruel. It is my time to go, I will join them on the other side.

"Kill me, creature, and I will rejoin them once again. I do not fear death, I have seen it on the battlefields," I snarl, my head tilted back, arms straight and back proud. A soldier in the face of a nightmare.

It laughs once again, its eyes flashing in the night as the light goes out and plunges us into darkness. "No, my pet, I think I will do something much worse to you..."

A noise brings me back from the edge, a mocking laugh like the one in my memories, following me into the present. I hang there, limp in their chains, my mind shattered and falling apart, my body dying, crumbling into itself like a skeleton. My bones are brittle, my skin like parchment paper, tearing and old. My fangs throb, and my mouth is dry and screaming with a thirst so strong I have never faced anything like it before. I had tried to stop once, to sustain myself on animal blood, but this...this is so much more.

I am nothing beyond the thirst coursing through my body.

I let it fill me, guide me, make me until I am feral. I thought I was strong enough to face this, to die with dignity and not give in to their wants and demands, but this thirst is stronger than I could have ever imagined, and it will not let me just waste away. It will pull me back, kicking and screaming, and I know once I taste blood, I will be nothing more than that ravenous monster who killed those I held most dear and made me into what I am.

A monster.

I will bathe in blood with bodies drained around me until I come back to myself and the regret settles in, but in the haze, the red covering me at the moment, I don't care. I would consume every single human in this city if it would quench this...this need.

The sound comes again, closer this time, and I recognise it through the blood gushing in my ears. Boots are heading this way, the tell-tale smack of the soles the only sound other than the human's cries they throw in here. I know this time I will give in. They will throw me a blood bag, a human, and I will drain them, not stopping at just one, becoming their ravenous killer.

I brace myself, trying to stop my breathing, but I will still scent their fear, their blood, no matter what I do. It will not stop, I need to feed, it's a craving so strong my head falls back and I let out a scream of grief and pain at becoming this monster. Reduced to a killer...

The door opens and I don't allow myself to look, maybe I can fight it off. I hear it slam shut again, but there are no cries or movement, and that is what has my head jerking up and then the smell hits me.

The fragrance, goodness, I could bathe in it. Wrap it around myself like armour and wear it into war. It smells like blood, sex, and the fields where I grew up. I suck in lungfuls of it and it settles that thirst, covering it for a moment so I can have some form of rational thought, but just for a moment. A stolen moment of sanity, all because of how she smells.

Then I see her. The red fades from my vision and my eyes work again, resting on the goddess, the general of war lying before me. A face that men would race into battle for, that they would follow to the ends of the gallows, to death itself. A beauty like I have never seen through any of the ages I have lived. One that sends a punch straight through me and restarts my shrivelled, hungry heart.

Her hair, long and blonde and the colour of wheat in harvest, is wrapped around her like a coiled snake. Her face is pressed to the cool cement and I'm jealous of it for touching her. Her skin is pale, covered in specks of blood, and I inhale again, noting it's not hers. Her eyes are shut, black lashes resting along her cheek, her body curvy and slightly short, but oh so tempting. I can scent her blood, though, recent as well, and as I watch her body stitches itself back together from many, many wounds. What did they do to her?

A flash of hate and rage surges through me and I wrench on the chains.

Who is she? Another prisoner, a monster like me they are trying to break? What is she? I have never smelled something so delicious in all my life, and just like that my hunger roars to the forefront of my mind again. It makes me yank on the chains, my fangs snapping down as I try to reach her, to sink my incisors into her and taste that delicious blood, drain her dry and bathe in it.

She stirs for a moment, her head turning the other way as if to escape me. I glance at the guard they left in here, the one I injured, to see him still pale and asleep, but alive for now. A noise has my eyes dragging back to her, but she is no longer lying down.

She is staring right back at me, her black eyes peeking through golden hair as she crouches on the tiles like an animal, staring straight at my hunger with one of her own. What does she hunger for? I have the insane urge to ask and give her whatever it is.

Scratching sounds, and I glance down to see her long, black nails dragging along the floor as she watches me like prey, waiting to pounce for any wrong move I make. I stare right back, noticing the jumping pulse in her throat, feeling it calling to me, imagining the noise she would make as her blood squirted into my mouth.

I jerk forward, automatically reaching for it, and she pounces. Her body flies through the air like a blur and I fall backwards with the impact, still swinging from the chains that hold me. I snap forward, trying to bite her, but she grabs my head in her hands, her small, delicate fingers spread across my cheeks as her red, rosy mouth slants and comes down on mine. It's enough to make me freeze, and then suddenly I'm opening wide, like an old habit, an instinct I didn't know I had and she's there...I taste her, her need, her hunger.

I feed her.

She pulls, not physically, but her kiss tugs at my energy, the very essence that animates me, sucking it from my mouth like a drink through a straw, again and again, drawing it from deep inside me and absorbing it into herself. Her claws cut into my face slightly, and the scent of my blood only makes her wilder. A whimper comes from her throat as she tries to get closer, to find a better angle on me.

It's like she is draining the madness, the thirst from me with each pull of her lips on mine, taking it into herself and making it hers with a hungry sounding moan. Her hands splay on my face as she leaps onto my body, wrapping her legs around me to keep me still as she drinks and drinks. I gladly submit with every pull of her rosy, delicious lips as I start to feel normal. She's warm, oh so warm, and her body is smashed against mine. With each ounce of blood thirst draining from my being, I realise another one is roaring forward.

Lust.

My cock tents my ripped, dirty pants, aching and pointing towards her. Each draw of her mouth makes it jerk and my balls swell like she is sucking me down. I groan into her kiss, rolling against her pussy which is pressed tightly to my stomach, her legs constrict around me like a snake wrapping around its meal. I would happily give it all to her, she can have it.

She can drain me dry, kill me, take all my energy. Everything that I am. She can devour it.

I don't know why, but she can. I feel a thread, a small, thin one linking me to her and that pull, the one I thought was madness, is back, low in my gut...drawing me to her. Her mouth locks tight onto mine, no longer just feeding now, but sucking me down, each one a line straight to my cock until I am panting as lust roars through me stronger than I have ever felt before.

The taste of her wipes me clean, rebuilding me into something else...something hers. I feel it. Her call now rings through my head, reaching for me in the dark, in the blood lust, her black tipped hand encircling my own bloodstained hands as she pulls me free from the clinging fog and back into myself.

I'm thrusting against her, rutting like an animal, my cock jerking and precum leaking as she presses closer, rocking against me, her pussy rubbing back and forth through the ruined dress she is wearing. My hands ball into fists as I ache to reach for her, to rip the dress away and sink into her wet heat, feel her surrounding me fully, owning me, her pussy tight as I drive into her again and again as she feeds, her name on my lips...

I roar as I come, my cock jerking in my pants and spilling my seed there. She moans, rocking against me, licking at my lips before trailing them across my cheek to the cuts there and lapping at my blood. I groan, my eyes shutting as I shudder in pleasure.

I feel her stop and move away, so my eyelids snap back open and meet two bright blue orbs, no longer black as she blinks at me with a strange little smile on her face as she meets my gaze without fear or judgement, just an almost lax, lazy pleasure.

"Who are you?" I whisper, voice hoarse from disuse.

CHAPTER 22

DAWN

"Name's Dawn, hot stuff, yours?" I reply, still wrapped around the man. It was like a haze. I woke up on the floor in yet another fucking cell after they beat me and tried to break me and I saw him there, hanging from the ceiling, waiting for me.

I couldn't help myself, I needed a taste. I felt his power even though his body is almost skeletal. I could taste it and I wanted more. I remember leaping at him, wrapping around him, and draining. I can see it has taken its toll on his already lean and dying frame.

He has a face I can tell is super attractive even if it's gaunt and frail at the moment. His dark eyes are almost sunken into his skull, his eyebrows brown and his hair the same colour, long past his shoulders like you used to see in paintings and pictures of times long past. Yet now it hangs lifeless and lacklustre, flat and bedraggled, cut in patches. His body feels frail like he will crumble to dust at any minute and float away, and for some reason that would make me sad. Very fucking sad.

His giant fangs hang over his lips, protruding from his face, it must be painful. Is he a vampire? If so, it doesn't look like he's fed, is that what he needs? Bad Dawn, he's hungry and you fed from him. It's a wonder he didn't just strike and bite me, not that I would really mind.

The thought sends a shiver of thrill through me, straight to my wet, aching pussy which is still pressed to his hard cock. Even in the state he is in, he is still stiff and wanting against me, pushing close, seeking out my heat, and I have the insane urge to fuck him, but I don't.

Yet.

He freezes, his eyes confused for a moment as he seems to be drifting away. "I don't know," he mumbles with the hint of an accent on his raspy words, a cadence to them that tells me this isn't his first language,.and I want to know what is. I want to know this man, this vampire. Why? Is he yet another monster I'm calling to me like Nos proposed? Or is this a temporary feeling from the feeding?

I feel weird being wrapped around him now, so I drop to the floor and we both let out a whimper at the lost contact, making me freeze and stare at him...what is he to me? "You don't know your name?" I ask.

He nods, his eyes going far away. "My mind...is fracturing from the lack of blood. I can't remember some things, but others I can see in excruciating detail...like..." He sucks in a breath and I fall back with a cry, my hands going to my head which feels like it's in a vice as images rip through it...memories that aren't mine. They imprint there as I fall to my knees, tears falling unchecked down my face. I can feel my body, feel the sobs escaping me at the pain in those recollections, but I can't stop it...it's too much, too powerful...

"No, no," I chant, then I scream as my head is ripped to the side and fangs sink into my neck. I kick and yell, fighting, but the crea-

ture is too strong. My gaze lands on my baby girl as my life is drained from me. When my eyes begin to close and the darkness takes hold, I send up a prayer that the next life will be kinder to me, that I don't lose my love and fate is not as cruel...

Then nothing but darkness encompasses me. I swim in it like a sea, paddling in nothingness. I have no body, only a consciousness, just floating, merely existing. No pain or grief, nothing but warmth. I sink into it, accepting its welcoming embrace, but just as I do, I am ripped away.

I feel a jerk of a pain then the sensation of choking. I can't open my eyes, but I know I'm not dead, yet I'm not alive. I'm still caught in the dark, but the pain, God, the pain. It races through me, burning everything away like lava through my veins. Erupting, destroying, and breaking, and in its path something new blooms, something darker...stronger...a monster.

I scream both in the dark and in reality, the sound inhuman, and then something cool hits my lips, dripping down my throat. I drink it down, swallowing again and again, feeling each drop hit my stomach like water putting out the blaze, and only when there is none left do I stop, the fire burning low, still there, never gone, but simply subdued...ready to return at any time.

A thirst.

"No!" comes a scream, and I'm thrown backwards from the memory, into my own head, my fingers on the cool, stone floor, my chest heaving as I suck in desperate breaths, my tears still falling as I look up slowly to meet his eyes.

They were his memories...of how he became a vampire.

"Wh-Who did that to you?" I whisper brokenly. I felt his pain, his utter grief. He wanted to die, welcomed it...had lost something so precious, but his own life, his own choice to die was ripped away from him and in its place he became this—a vampire controlled by thirst. God, the thirst. I couldn't imagine it, it's so much worse than mine, a pain unlike any I have ever felt, control-ling him, guiding him. To fight that for so long...the strength he must have. I shake my head and wipe the tears away as I gaze at him.

I have seen the darkness in his mind. I know him. He thinks he doesn't know himself, he has no name, no memory of his identity, but I know him. I do, right here and now, I know it. He's mine, my destiny, meant to be here. Like I am meant to be. His human life was cruel, his vampire life not much better from what I can gather, but it led him here...

To me.

"You don't want to see that, see what *she* made me." He spits the word 'she,' his distaste clear.

"I can see it already, I don't need your memories for that," I point out, reining in my breathing as I sit up and scrub my face clean. He looks away, not meeting my eyes, his hair hanging like a curtain before me as he shudders and sucks in breaths, muttering under his breath. Words, phrases I can't understand, to push back the memories, I think. I leave him to it. He exposed himself without meaning to, and one of the hardest moments of his life was shown like a video to me, a stranger. I'll let him rebuild and pull himself back together. It's not like I'm going anywhere, so I sit back and wait.

I TRIED to release his chains, but I couldn't. I also tried to feed him, but he wouldn't let me. After I saw his memories, he isn't even looking at me, his head hanging in shame. I'm leaning back against the wall, watching him.

I think he's worried about what I think of him, that I'll be disgusted at what I saw. He doesn't understand I was awed. Many would have given into that fire before now and ceased to exist or become nothing but death, yet I found peace and lust in his arms, not mortality. He doesn't know himself, doesn't see himself. That's hard, I imagine, when you can't remember bits of your life or even your name. Maybe that's a good thing, a fresh start for him. With me. It's clear he isn't comfortable with what he is, maybe even hates it. I can't imagine going through life like that, perhaps I can help him. He helped me, after all. I know now how easily he could have killed me, I left my throat vulnerable, but he didn't, he let me feed, heal, using his energy.

My eyes flicker to the other man in the room, the guard. He's on death's door, I can feel it. Sense it. "Want me to kill him or are we keeping him as a pet?" I muse.

He gazes at me then, seemingly more put together. Less...fragile and fractured, even though those are not the words I would use to describe the warrior, the fighter before me. "Do what you want with him," he mutters, his voice hoarse and cracking. He needs to feed but he won't. He looks away again, and I ache to see those eyes. I debate what to do and finally sigh as I slump against the wall, stretching out my legs, not staring at him but at my feet.

"I was murdered," I start, blowing out a breath. "By my husband, ex," I correct, knowing my mates hate it when I refer to him in the present tense. "He was not someone I chose, I was a fool. I was charmed by his money and face, and I didn't see the monster hiding below until it was too late. I needed to get out, but I couldn't. He made me his little pet and I caved, sinking into myself. Doing everything he asked just to not feel the pain of his anger. I looked at myself in the mirror and didn't recognise who stared back." I raise my eyes then, unwilling to be ashamed about what I survived. "I endured it, waiting, becoming what I had to be to get through every single fucking day, and do you know what I became? He raped me, killed me, and buried my body, but I still wouldn't fucking die. Too stubborn and filled with the need for vengeance, I rose back up into what I am now. I don't know whether the pain, death, or need for his blood changed me. I don't care, I'm not ashamed of the monster I am. I've seen those human monsters, and they are so much worse than us. They hide behind masks, being cruel and craving pain and control. We are monsters from circumstance, with no choice..."

He meets my eyes then, watching me curiously.

"We become what we had to in order to survive. I'm not sorry about that. I'm not sorry I enjoy blood and pain and death. I'm not even sorry I want to kill, to bathe in blood and sex. I want to feed, I want to watch you sink those fangs into me as I take you into my body. I won't apologise for what I am."

He sucks in a breath at my declaration, his pupils blown as his fangs elongate.

"Don't ever feel ashamed about what you are. Our lives were ripped away from us and replaced with this darkness, this new cruel and dark world, but I refuse to be a fucking victim ever again. You are a warrior, a fighter, so goddamn strong. Don't break now, I can see you cracking, embrace that darkness. Show the world who you are, and I promise you that you won't ever walk alone again. I'm here, we're here, others like us. Survivors, fighters, we are damaged and reassembled stronger than before to become the monster of our own stories, not the hero. I don't need a fucking hero, I need a partner. You, you need to feed, get your strength back. If you remember who you are, good, if not, start again. You are resilient enough. Don't let them break you, use it. Use that hate, that pain and rage. Make it yours."

He licks his cracked lips, watching me now. "I remember snippets...the things I did...they should horrify me, but they don't. I revelled in blood, spiked heads, and hung them as decorations as warnings to my enemies. I ripped through thousands of soldiers like paper and laughed as blood rained from the trees..."

I inhale sharply at that, not in disgust...but need. Fuck, like I said, I'm messed up.

"I don't fear what I am, but what I was...I fear that I don't care. Does that make sense?"

I nod. "Of course, but fear has no place in our world. In private? Yes. But we are survivors, and right now we're in a cell and we need to get out. Make them pay for what they have done. After...after we can worry about everything else."

"Okay," he replies calmly, lifting his head. I can see him now, how he will be, so strong with his head tilted back in defiance, blood in his wake as he walks through death and laughs. The image makes me shiver and clench my legs together. He reminds me very much of the films about Dracula I used to watch as a kid, so formidable, and the spiked head thing? Was he a rip-off or were they? Or maybe the stories of Vlad the Impaler are just a mixture of legends, I can't be sure. Did they base those stories on the vampire before me? It makes me wonder how old he is and just how powerful he will be...

"For that, you need to feed," I remind him. Deciding to circumvent his argument, I sharpen my nails and slash them across my wrist so blood wells. The ruby red is stark against my pale skin, and I watch him with mild interest as it drips down my arm, the cut deep and wide, and then I look up at the vampire to see him straining to get to me. That's better.

"Feed," I demand, and get to my feet. "I need you. Let me save you the way you saved me."

CHAPTER 23

ASK A

I fly to my car, change back into my human form, and get back in, starting the engine and heading back the way I came—to the witches. I wonder what I will owe them now, but it is worth it to save my mate. I would do it and worse.

A buzzing comes and I realise my phone is ringing, so I snatch it from the passenger seat as it goes off, making me grumble. I spot the many notifications as it starts to ring, Jean Paul's name coming up. I swipe to accept it.

"Hello?" I call, driving as I do.

I can hear him speaking in a tiny voice, so I glance down at the phone. "Fucking machines hate me. *I can't hear you, speak up!*" I scream, and I hear miniature laughter. Pulling over, I put it to my ear to hear him still laughing.

"Sire, press the speaker button." I move the phone away and examine it, pushing buttons while I swear until I finally hear him speaking loudly.

"Magic." I sigh. "Jean Paul, is everything okay?"

"Yes, sire, I wanted to check on you. Have you found your mate?" he asks, and I sigh.

"Not yet, there are some complications, nothing I can't handle. How is everything there?"

"All fine, sire..." He trails off, and I can hear something in his voice which makes me grip the wheel tighter.

"Jean Paul," I command.

"I didn't want to tell you...I have heard some rumours, a rumbling if you will," he hedges and sighs. "There has been another dragon sighting, not far from the town you stopped in for the night."

"You think he is coming for me?" I frown. Why would a dragon be here? We don't leave the realm...well, they don't.

"I don't know, sire, I couldn't say. He was last spotted there about fifty minutes from the boat you went to and hasn't been seen since. Would you like me to send you the location?"

"Yes," I reply distractedly.

"Very good. Good luck, sire, ring me if you need anything else." I hang up and toss the phone away. A dragon here...now? It's too big of a coincidence, it has to be for me. I can't lead them to Dawn, so as much as I hate it, I will have to see what he wants before I find the sleeping council.

I pull back onto the road, rolling down my window and roaring at someone as they honk their horn and flip me off. They soon drive away, speeding no doubt. Sheep.

I restart my journey back to the witches. I will stop after and find the dragon. I just hope it doesn't take too long and that my mate doesn't need me in the meantime. I am feeling antsy to meet her in reality now.

I FIND their location with ease this time, not needing the little phone magician to direct me, thank God. It does take a few hours though, and when I step back onto the ship, I shiver at the feeling that passes over me. Something, or someone, is here. I debate waiting until they leave, but Dawn needs me, so I go inside anyway. Luckily, it leads me to where they are.

I stop when I see them. All three witches turn to face me, but that isn't what makes my blood cold, it is the men...or more aptly ghosts, standing behind them.

Ghosts are usually sad, mopey bastards left in this world after a tragic death, or when someone still clings to the living, they stay here, stuck between worlds. Over time they seem to fade unless they feed on power, then they can even move objects and that's how rumours of hauntings come around, some even possess people...but these? These don't look like any ghosts I have ever seen. Of course I haven't seen many, they are miserable bastards and keep mostly to their selves, but these men? These ghosts?

They are something different...I can sense their power, their age from here, and when their gazes focus on me, my dragon roars to the forefront of my mind to try and protect me from their unnaturalness. I can feel it now, the witches' power flowing through them, keeping them here and strong and almost human.

If it wasn't for the slightly grey pallor of their skin, and the mist seeming to surround them, I wouldn't even know what they were. Loxley steps forward first. "Dragon, did we not give you what you seek?"

My eyes track the three male ghosts. One is really tall with a long, unkempt brown beard, bright green eyes, an old-style hat on his head, and a leather vest and jeans. He almost looks like a cowboy. The second is smaller and leaner, wearing what looks like a tux and a top hat, his lips curled up in a sneer, his eyes showing such rage and hate. The third? He appears normal, but his eyes...I shiver from the look, the intelligence, and just what I see there, as if I stare too long I might not come back out alive. He is wearing jeans and a shirt, and his brown hair is swept back to reveal a boyish face. He is almost unforgettable and disarming, but I know better.

Chloe is next, watching me closely. "Dragon, you seek something else now, something much more dangerous..."

"He does," Mercy concludes. I watch the ghosts encircle them.

The cowboy stands with Mercy, the brown-haired, normal one with Chloe, and the sneering one with Loxley.

"We told you one day you would meet our men, but this is sooner than expected, yet you need them, don't you?" Loxley inquires, her eyes far away as her hand goes out to stroke the man at her side, but he slaps it away and grabs her neck, dragging her closer. She sucks in a breath, wearing a grin on her face as he controls her movements.

"What does he seek, sisters?" Mercy whispers, coming to circle around me, her cowboy trailing after her. The cold gust of wind from him nearly knocks me back, so I snarl and he laughs, stepping away.

"I need the sleeping council's location," I declare, wanting to be gone from this place as quickly as I can. These men are not natural or sane, I can feel it. The hate they carry fuels them, yet the witches seem to thrive on it.

"That will cost you," Chloe tells me, leaning against her man who wraps his arm around her, watching me closely.

"I will pay it, whatever it is," I reply straightaway, knowing I will do anything for Dawn.

They glance at each other and have some form of silent communication before all looking at me and speaking at the same time. "You are powerful, the cost is high. Let our men feed on you and we will get you the location."

"Witches," I hiss, and they ignore me.

"Not enough to drain you or make you weak, a taste is all," Mercy clarifies.

"That means they will be able to track me anywhere in the world, forever," I counter, and they grin, knowing that. I debate my options, but what choice do I have? I need that location. They must sense my hesitation though.

"They will not harm you, dragon, they are loyal to us, but we need to be paid. Finding the location will not be easy for them."

"Them?" I repeat, confused, and Loxley nods.

"They will find it. Only the dead can walk among the sleeping court and survive."

Grinding my teeth, I jerk my head in a nod. "Fine, one may feed before, the others after I have my information."

The witches grin. "Accepted."

Chloe turns to her man and strokes his face lovingly. "Edward, my love, feed."

The one in the tux snarls and jerks, but Loxley leans back against him and he settles down even as he glares, watching Edward coming towards me with malicious intent, his eyes alive and filled with hunger as he takes me in and the power pouring from me. It is against a dragon's nature to share it, to share our power or let another take it or feed from it. It means we are weak, exposed, but I have no choice.

For her, I remind myself.

He steps close enough for me to feel the ice-cold touch of his form, and I have to refrain from ripping him to pieces. He flashes me a grin as if he knows my thoughts.

"This will hurt," he informs me, seemingly happy about that before his hands dart out and grip either side of my face.

I growl as the chill penetrates my cheeks and glides into my blood, freezing the vessels and making me sluggish as it pumps through my body. He closes his eyes with a groan, his face lax in pleasure as the warmth leaks from me to him, my heat replaced by ice inside me.

"Enough," I snarl, ripping his hands away after a few minutes. He laughs, stepping back with a stumble, drunk from the power.

"So powerful," he whispers with wide eyes. "So filled with it, I could eat it all up."

The other two step forward, but I narrow my gaze, my body shifting slightly until I'm larger, my scales starting to cover my arms. "Enough, dragon," Loxley shouts, and looks at the ghosts. "Go, find the location."

The man in the tux grips her chin harshly and kisses her. She moans and leans against him, and then suddenly he is gone, and I glance around to see the others do the same. I relax slightly when they leave and cross my arms, glaring at the witches who watch me curiously.

"Why do you need the sleeping council?" Chloe asks inquisitively.

"Enough, I have paid your price, you will not get my secrets from me," I growl, and they titter with laughter.

"Oh, dragon, we could rip them from you if we wanted to, but we don't. You are a friend. Did you not notice we stopped our men from stealing your soul and warmth to survive on? A little appreciation, dragon, or we will start to think we are not friends after all," Mercy warns.

I grind my teeth, but I still need them, so I have to play nice. "Fine, thank you." Each word is like glass on my tongue.

"Better." Loxley grins. "I'm guessing it has something to do with his mate. Did you find her?"

"Not yet," I offer and they nod.

"Soon, she has a destiny after all," they murmur in unison. I shift, feeling annoyed and wanting to be on the road. The sooner I leave, the sooner I can find Dawn.

The witches must notice because they step closer and all focus turns to me. Their eyes hold far too much knowledge, they see too much, and it makes me wonder what they see when they look at me.

Never mind, I don't have time, I have to get that location.

"They will be back soon, dragon, but do not be in so much haste. Are you so ready to throw your life away?" Mercy questions.

"The sleeping council is a secret for a reason. They are our most powerful brethren, well, apart from the gods. They intentionally live in solace, because they are too strong to be around us. They will kill you with nothing but a thought for going before them. What will they do to your mate? Tread carefully," Loxley adds.

"They are locked away for a reason, dragon, do you really wish to disturb that?" Chloe challenges.

I want to say no. Dragons survive because we are smart, and this, this isn't smart, but I am learning love makes you do crazy things.

For her I would do all the crazy, stupid things it takes to keep her with me.

CHAPTER 24

DAWN

H e watches me with feral, hungry eyes as I step closer, not teasing him. He needs this, I need this. My breathing picks up, my heart hammering in my chest as I willingly walk towards the hungry vamp, towards the predator, but instead of fear, lust fills me. I'm almost moaning, imagining him sinking those fangs into my flesh. He sniffs the air like an animal and growls, the chains creaking as he strains to get to me.

"You smell like life, like sex and blood," he rumbles, the words muffled and rough from his fangs as need courses through him. His tongue darts out and licks his incisors, his eyes locked on the blood on my arm. Stepping nearer, I flinch at his sudden lunge then laugh.

"Feed," I order, and press my arm to his mouth. He groans, lapping at the blood. His tongue is rough and wet, making me shiver as I visualise it buried in my pussy, blood dripping down me from his many fang wounds.

My eyes almost shut from the feeling. His are hooded as he licks my arm, tracing around the wound, his tongue tugging at the edges, making me moan at the flash of pain and the sexual way he does it. His eyes meet mine and then suddenly, he strikes. I jolt and scream in ecstasy as he sinks his fangs into me.

He rips through my skin, and the flash of discomfort fades into pleasure like I have never felt before—so hot and sudden. I fall forward into him and he catches me, wrapping me in his deadly embrace as he carries on drinking. I rub myself against him like a cat as I close my eyes, my pussy clamping down on air, my own cream dripping down my thighs. With each draw of his mouth, it feels like he's sucking on my clit and I can't stand it, it's too good, too much pleasure. He pulls back and licks the cut, watching me as he strikes, this time not feeding, just biting.

I scream yet again, the pain making me wild. He watches my reaction with my blood coating his lips and chin. "Dirty little thing, you like my fangs," he murmurs, and I nod breathlessly.

"Yesss, do it again," I demand, gripping his hair which seems fuller, but before I can concentrate on what my blood has done to him, he attacks. Tearing into the skin at my elbow, he throws me into an orgasm from the force of his bite, leaving me spiralling in pleasure and pain.

I jerk against him before going limp. He holds me up as he licks the bites and heals them, but the blood still covers my arms and legs, except I don't care. I cuddle into his chest and he holds me there, cooing words in French that I have no ability to understand.

"Fucking hell," I whisper, my pussy still fluttering with after-shocks. It was one of those orgasms that rips through you, leaving you weak and tired after, but also strangely renewed. My legs are still jelly, so I let him hold me up until a noise has both our heads whipping around.

I spot the injured guard finally waking up. The vamp snarls, his fangs flashing as he grips me tighter. When the guard spots me in his embrace, he starts to laugh, the sound bitter and rattling.

"I knew you would break," he murmurs, his skin pale, close to death.

The vamp holding me snarls as the guard chuckles, jerking in the chains as a plan forms in my head. "Let me go," I whisper, and turn my head to lay a soft kiss on his bloody mouth. He groans, his fangs slicing my lip as he grabs my head and controls the kiss. I feel my fresh blood mix on our tongues, making us move against each other as the cut heals until I finally pull back, breathing heavily again.

I step away, turning to face the guard with an evil grin. "I'm glad you're here," I coo and crouch in front of him, stroking his face, ignoring the vamp's possessive growl. "You are going to help us, aren't you?"

He frowns at me. "You're fucking crazy, you will die down here."

"You're right," I agree and he starts to laugh again. "Partially. I am crazy, but I'm afraid it will be you doing the dying." I yank him to me, and he screams as I start to laugh, the sound echoed by the vampire behind me.

I cover his mouth with mine as that power, the one keeping me alive, reaches out and latches on to him. He cries into my mouth, his body shuddering with the end of his fight, but he soon slumps and I jerk my head back, slurping the last of his power and shivering. Fuck, that was good.

I turn with a gasp, my mouth curving with the power flowing through me. Usually I change straightaway and I feel it coursing through me now, so surely I can send it back as well?

I drop to the floor, my body forgotten as I use all my power and turn it inwards, stopping the change. It halts, and as I push harder, sweat breaks out on my brow until slowly, ever so slowly, it starts to recede. When it's done, I can still feel it there, waiting to be used, but I can function and I'm still in my own body. The whole plan depended on that.

I open my eyes and they lock with the vamp's to see him watching me curiously. "Don't worry, I'm getting us out of here. Be patient, hot stuff."

I rise to my feet gracefully, power flowing through me as I start to stroll towards him, but I hear the door open and turn to face them instead. I grin at the guards there as they gape at me. "Hello, boys, thanks for the vacation spot, though I wouldn't recommend the service."

Eyes narrowed, they step towards me, so I wave my vampire goodbye and he blows me a kiss. Only then do I realise just how much my blood has affected him and it makes me stare for a second.

I was right, he is breathtaking, like a warrior of old. His face filled out, his body strong and muscular, skin golden and gleaming, eyes alight as he watches me be dragged away. He looks powerful and oh so fucking formidable that I debate killing the fools holding me and heading straight back to him to finish what we started, but no, I have a plan.

So I let them haul me out. They whisper amongst themselves about what to do with me, all of them worried how their masters will react when they realise I'm healed and untouched. I whistle and hang in their grip, kicking my legs gently in the breeze, looking around at the walls.

"Who's your decorator down here? 'Cause it's very depressing. You could do with a splash of colour instead of all the grey and brick...maybe red." I turn my head, grinning at them then, letting my eyes go black as I lick my lips. I watch the pulse of the one I'm staring at jump in his throat. "How about the red in your veins, boy?" I start to laugh as he gapes at me, horrified.

"Assmos wants her back in with the bull, said something about getting what they need..." one of them looks me up and down. "Another way."

They drag me away faster now and throw me back into a

familiar cell. I spin when the door shuts and stare at my bull. "Hi, honey, did you miss me?" I look around then, my eyebrows rising at the dead bodies everywhere. "I see you did some redecorating, love what you've done, very macabre."

"You were gone," he snarls, completely bull now, no hint of my gentle, confused Dume.

"Oh, are we back to playing?" I coo, sauntering towards him, his chains slinking across the floor as he steps further into the dark corner. "I do enjoy our games and I have a whole lot of energy to burn, what do you say, my bull?"

"On your knees," he snaps, and I see a hint of Dume peeking through now as they both comprehend I'm more than fine. I'm fucking thriving despite being kept prisoner.

After all, you can never keep a bad girl down.

CHAPTER 25

GRIFFIN

I follow the lackey like the good little dog they called me, and I wonder for a moment where he will lead me. The dungeons? The tower? The sitting room? But no, I should have guessed, everything with these people is a game, a way to lord power and use others' weaknesses. I know this path, I was dragged this way many times before and thrown before them in their throne room...where she died.

Each step closer has the madness spinning faster and faster, searching for a way out, imagining Dawn in there waiting for me like my mother was, seeing her die. Fisting my hands, I try to slow my breathing before it bursts from me and I do something stupid like slay them. I have to be smart, I have to be in control for once. For her I have to accept their form of torture and I have to be stronger than I have ever been before.

"Oh, my little Griffin, don't you listen to them. Your emotions, your love for me does not make you or your father weak, it makes you

impossibly stronger. You're stronger than they or even you know, because they only fight since they are ordered to, but you, my boy? You fight because you have to, because you have people expecting you, needing you. Fighting for love, not respect, will always win. You will always triumph, Griffin. They think it a weakness, show them it is the exact opposite. Use it, let it fuel you." She smiles softly at me, her human eyes filled with love even as tears trail from my angel eyes, like my father's. She rubs the wet cloth across my face, dabbing away the blood from the fight.

We are not permitted to fight outside of training, but I was cornered in the bathroom by five other kids, kids like me. They attacked me, ganged up on me. I fought as hard as I could, wanting to prove to my father and to them I was strong enough, but they just laughed. They called me weak, told me my human whore of a mother made me worthless. It infuriated me, I saw red, and when I came to, they were all crawling away with disgusted sneers on their faces. I watched them go, my muscles shaking, and only when I was alone did I break down. That's where she found me, and like always she picked me up, dusted me off, and loved me.

How can they think she's nothing? How can they think this, her loving me and me loving her, is nothing more than normal? I find myself asking her that, and she sighs softly, her nose crinkling like it always does when she is thinking, her brow furrowing and her blue eyes sad.

"It is jealousy, my love," she whispers, gripping my shoulders with all her strength, which is admittedly not much. Her human body is frail, but her spirit is stronger than any person I have ever met, angel or otherwise. "Their mothers, well, they aren't like me. They don't understand why you get to have me, why you get to be loved and they aren't. They see you with me and your father and they envy it. You have to understand that. Because to understand someone's motives and emotions is to understand them, and then and only then will you know what the right thing to do is. Trust your

heart, Griff, you have the biggest one I have ever seen. It will never lead you wrong."

"Fallen," the lackey snaps, and I realise I've stopped just before the grand double doors. The grandiose entrance is another game for them, used to intimidate and show their wealth and power, but I'm starting to learn some of the strongest of our kind do not need tricks to amass fear and love—it's simply just them.

Gritting my teeth, I step up next to him and he leans closer. "Worthless dog," he spits, and then pushes the door open, striding inside with his head held high like he owns the place, even though he's nothing more than a servant. When they are bored with him, they will toss him away like they do everything else.

I know the drill by now, so I wait, not wanting to give them an excuse to punish me. He strolls down the empty aisle of chairs. There is no court or ceremony today, so the space is empty save for the council members who sit at the end of the way too fucking long room filled with candelabras, chandeliers, and golden chairs like they are kings of old.

Pretentious bastards.

Veyo sweeps into a low bow, almost scraping the floor. "My lords and ladies, our esteemed council, may I present, as your humble servant, the fallen they call Griffin." He stands and turns, and everyone does the same to see me standing at the door.

I hesitate. If I cross over this threshold, I'm giving them power over me even if they don't know it. I'm giving them everything, my very life...for her.

It's worth it, after all, like my mother said, if I'm not fighting for love...what am I fighting for? I step through the doorway, my head held high, and storm down the aisle towards them. They get no theatrics from me, and they don't expect me to beg and scrape, they know me too well, know that I hate them, so if I started to act otherwise they would suspect me as a mole or a spy straightaway. No, I need to play this right.

This time my fight is with words and intelligence, not my swords and wings.

I don't bow. Instead, I tilt my head back, letting my eyes run across all five council members.

To the left and in the first seat is the least powerful of all the council. At only four hundred years old, the vampire, Harald, is practically a baby, but he's known for his mean streak and made his way to the council by carving a bloody path to the position and clambering for power.

Next to him is the second least powerful, an incubus named Derrin. No one knows where he originally comes from, but I know better than to get on his bad side. He can be kind when he needs to be, but don't let that angelic smile and charm fool you, he's one mean bastard. They have to be to sit on the council.

In the middle is Amos, the head of the council and the man who ordered my mother's and father's deaths. His eyes gleam in triumph as he watches me, thinking he has finally broken me, finally got what he wanted. He is the worst of them all. The others pity me, see me as amusement, a servant, but Amos? He wants to crush me, rebuild me in his image, and own me as his own personal fucking dog. He plays games the way others breathe, his every word a move on the chessboard, and I just stepped onto the checker opposite him.

Next to him is Gina, a shifter, and the only female to sit on the council, but she is the biggest snake of them all. She spies for the men, using her sexuality and charm to get what she needs. I'm pretty sure she's fucking both Amos and Derrin. Her icy eyes lock on me in hunger, not for my body but for the secrets I hold and the surrender she wants from me. She is one ice-cold bitch.

On the very right is the last member of the council. No one knows what or who he is. All we have is a name—Titus. There are rumours that he was sent from the sleeping council as their spy, and it could be true. No one can get close enough to him to even know his true name or what he is or capable of. His seat was empty up until about six hundred years ago when he suddenly appeared and took the chair overnight. The council did not explain why, but you could see they were unhappy about it. Even now he's leaning to the side, reclined and relaxed, watching everything happen with sharp eyes while distancing himself from the council pigs...he appears almost angry. Well, me fucking too. He catches me staring, and his lips turn down in a frown for a moment as he takes me in before he blanks his face into one of disinterest, and then leans back like he doesn't have a care in the world.

Amos speaks first, as always. "Fallen, this is a highly unusual occurrence. We did not call for your...services, did we?" His tone is mocking as he looks at the others who shake their heads, all the while knowing they didn't. Dramatic bunch of bitches, all of them. "I didn't think so, so tell me, fallen, why are you here?"

This is where it either goes really right or really fucking wrong. I need to make them believe I want to be part of this again without them thinking it's a trick or laying it on too thick. With a sneer, I start, but make sure to drop my eyes just a fraction to seem somewhat respectful. "You asked me once to stay here, to be closer to the council. I'm tired of the sheep, tired of the stupid fucking hunts I'm sent on. I'm tired," I admit, and let some of my true frustration leak into my voice. "Tired of sitting on the fence, of not being in either world. I—" I rip open my old wounds, my own fears of never being good enough, and hand it to them on a platter, knowing they will use it against me, but she's worth it. "I want to be part of this world, I want to belong, to have a family and a home again."

That's the key to making them believe, to show them I still hate them but they are the lesser of two evils...to make them think they have finally broken me. My hands are clenched into fists from being so close to vengeance, yet giving my fucking enemies everything they want.

One of them laughs, I can't tell who. "Took him long enough, fucking experiment."

I grind my teeth, wanting to lash out, but I control the urge...just.

"If you truly feel that way, boy, you are, of course, welcome here, but we need to trust you, depend on you, so we need your obedience. Prove that to us," Amos declares, sounding sincere, but I can see the glee in his eyes.

I know what he wants, the only thing I never gave him, gave them—my loyalty...my servitude. They want to see me on my knees before them, showing everyone that their power is beyond measure, that they can control everybody, even the fallen who evaded their clutches for years. That I'm finally theirs to do with what they wish.

Sucking in a breath, I force myself to fall to my knees in the same place my mother was slain. I kneel before the people who wielded the sword. I hate them, I knew it before, but this...this rage towards them is morphing into a hatred so strong I can barely contain it.

I want to see them dead and bathe in the ashes of their demise. I want their blood coating my wings and hands knowing I finally got my revenge. I want their screams, I want their weaknesses, but I can't. Because my mate comes first.

Save her, then together we can kill them, because these smug bastards are as corrupt as they come, that much is clear, and I'm not letting them get away with it anymore.

They killed my father.

Murdered my mother.

Stripped me of my wings.

I survived it all, but what I can't survive is them taking my mate from me, thinking she's disposable, that she is theirs to bend to their whims.

They will pay for it.

I will unleash the madness they created in me, becoming their worst fucking enemy. They won't see it coming, thinking they can control everyone and everything, but for now I bite my tongue and lower my head, staring lasers into the floor as my knees hit the marble with an audible boom.

To them it's the sound of my defeat, to me it's the beat of my war drum. This is the beginning of their end. Either they'll die or I'll die trying. I can imagine it now, my mate at my side, striding through the fight with blood covering her as she tears them to pieces. The very person they took, locked up and thought to use, bringing them to their knees. They will kneel before us, before her, see her strength and what real power looks like...and real loyalty.

I can feel their glee, their absolute confidence they are too powerful to touch, but that's the problem with being at the top, there is only one way to go—down.

"I am whatever you wish me to be," I growl out, true anger in my tone, I can't fake that.

They leave me like that, letting everyone see, allowing me to stew in my hatred, another game, another test. I pass it, I don't move, I don't lash out, I let them believe they have finally tamed me. Tamed the madness they created.

"You are on your knees, fallen, but I don't know if we can trust you. You have been vocal in your disdain for the council and our people, your people. You are too mad, like a wild animal, how do we ensure you do not attack us, turn on us?" Amos challenges, always the smart one.

I raise my gaze, which is shimmering with the mist of my madness. "You don't. Prove to your people how strong you are by controlling me. The mad fallen, the strongest of his kind under your orders, it will send them a message. It's a chance to prove your powers and inspire fear and loyalty again."

"Again?" Derrin repeats, narrowing his eyes.

"Our people are loyal!" Amos snaps, leaning forward. "They know of our great powers, that we lead them for their best future."

"Do they?" I taunt bitterly, and my lips tip up in a mocking smirk as Amos's eyes narrow on me. "You have me out there, among the sheep, doing whatever I want, and they see that. They think that makes you weak, that you can't control your own servants."

"He's right," Titus chimes in, and then covers a yawn.

"Put him in the barracks, have the other...experiments watch him. If he steps out of line, let them punish him, they hate him enough. We can use him like a lap dog. String him in chains in here for the next ball, let them see our fallen decoration, a mere toy for us, someone so powerful worshipping at our feet," Gina adds, watching me with that same snake-like expression, ready to strike.

"Hmm, that does have its merits. Veyo, for now take him to the barracks, let the others keep a close eye on him. If he so much as looks at them wrong, they are allowed to punish him as they see fit," Amos calls, and looks at me with an evil grin on his face. "You can be their whipping boy, fallen. Let's see how that stubbornness keeps you alive now. Get used to being on your knees, you will be living like this now."

I grit my teeth, not responding because I'll say something that will blow my cover, until finally, they dismiss me. I get to my feet and follow Veyo from the room, his mocking laughter wrapping around me as he leads me through the servants' corridor, out of the back of the mansion, and across the lawn to the barracks hidden behind a maze of flowers—they can't have such hideous creatures and servants be seen, after all.

I prepare myself for what's to come, this won't be easy. They will use any excuse to hurt me, punish me, but I will endure it. For her. For her I would survive anything. I'm led through the flowers to the hidden building there. It looks like an army barracks with an assault course and a training area for the nephilim out back, it even has a gym building attached. Inside is a long room filled with beds where they sleep. They aren't given rooms or possessions, just the essentials. They don't need anything else as servants. It chafes against me, how everything is controlled. The nephilim have no life, they are just here for the council's use.

Yet they don't care, they covet the attention, proud of what they are and who they fight for. I wonder if they know the true depth of the corruption?

The door is yanked open. I would expect noise, rowdiness, laughing, and teasing since that's what the sheep are like, but it's deadly silent as we step through. They are here though, some sleeping, some cleaning, some reading...they are all just waiting. Like good little servants, they make no noise, waiting to be called to duty.

They turn my way when the door slams shut, every golden eye locking on me, and suddenly there's an uproar as their anger...their hate is thrown my way. They slowly get to their feet and Veyo turns to me with a laugh. "Hope you are ready for a world of pain, fallen."

"I was born into it," I snap back, standing tall, Dawn's face flashing in my mind.

You better be fucking ready for me, Vasculo, because I'm coming...if they don't kill me first.

CHAPTER 26

DAWN

"Well?" I whisper, trailing my fingers across his chest, watching the muscles jump from my touch. I love how my mates react to me, how easy it is to tease them...to push them.

"I said on your knees, *Draya*," he orders, as more and more of Dume peeks through even as his voice is still a bossy growl, which sends a shot of lust surging through me. I love his animal side.

Grinning, I drop to my knees, my head tilting back to watch him as I run my finger down his body to the chains that hold him. I want all of him and they are in the way. I want to see his human body, to touch him, taste him, and from the hunger on his face, so does he. He growls in frustration, tugging at the restraints.

Annoyed and still turned on from the vamp's bites, I focus all my attention on those chains, and suddenly I know what to do. I wrap my hands around one and close my eyes, pushing all that power into it. I hear it crack and then it drops away from him. I turn, eyes still closed, and grip the other. It takes more power, but I feel it fall away finally and I blink open my eyes, a secret smile on my face. "Change, I want you," I whisper hungrily.

"How did you—" He shakes his head, staring at the chains and then me as he seems to realise he can change back. He groans and does so, the fur and hooves sinking into his body as gold tinged skin appears, stretching across his huge frame. I find myself missing his bull, but when his hard cock smacks against his stomach, I lick my lips, distracted from it.

My eyes run across his body, noting the scars and mottled flesh that indicate he's a warrior. He still wears the nose ring and the golden band on his arm, and his hair is wavy and cut short. He's massive and imposing, and the sight of him standing over me in the dark, muscles bulging, and eyes filled with a hunger so strong it sends a current through me, has me rocking on my feet, seeking pressure.

He glances away for a moment. "I am scarred, *Draya*, not worthy of touching you, but—"

I snarl, reaching out and grasping his cock. He gasps, his eyes jerking to me, and I purposely keep my eyes on his as I lean forward and lick the head of his cock, making him moan, watching him watch me with hopeful eyes. Pulling away, I stroke him with my hands. "I say who is worthy of touching me, Dume, don't ever think otherwise. Each scar shows me exactly how hard you fought to be here, to be at my side now. They show me the battles you won, how strong you really are, and I can't wait to have all that power and fury inside me where you belong."

I get to my feet, my hand still circling his cock though I can't quite close my grip around it. He is thick and long, bigger than even my other mates, but everything about my bull is huge—cock, power, and animal.

His hips jerk forward. "*Draya*," he whispers in wonder, even as he stands taller under my words.

"You are a warrior, Dume. Own it, fucking make it yours, and then they can never use it against you. I want you so fucking much and I can see you don't believe it. I am not your queen, bull. I won't use you, I won't hurt you...unless you want me to." I wink and he snorts. I grip his hand and drag it up my thigh to my panties to show him how drenched I am. "Look how wet you make me. This isn't a trick, Dume, this is fucking. Plain and simple. We want each other, and life is way too short to question and second-guess and worry about others and judgement. All that matters is that I found you, the most phenomenal creature I've ever seen, scars and all, so, my bull, what do you say?"

"*Draya*," he whispers, his voice rough as he searches my face and then he groans, his hand moving against me. "I shouldn't, I've been burned before, but-but I want you too much, it feels right, you feel too good."

Grinning, I lean closer and lick his nose ring, flicking it while plastering myself against his chest as he strokes along my panty covered pussy like he can't help himself. "I'll burn you, bull, but you'll like it."

He snaps. I see the moment he gives into his need and I almost jump in happiness. I know he's scared of being tricked again, but he must feel how real this is. You can't fake this kind of attraction, this kind of bond, but if I need to remind him every day for the next hundred years, I will.

He is mine and it's about time he proved it.

He grabs me roughly and throws me back into the cell wall. I grin as I wrap my legs around his waist. "Yes, that's it, show me everything, let me feel your strength."

He growls and steam curls from his nose, making me rub against him. His eyes flash red and I moan as his hands grip me tighter, hoisting me higher up the wall as he rips my dress away and tears off my panties, tossing them to the floor.

"You will be bare for me, for anytime I want you," he rumbles, glaring at me. "Understood, *Draya*?"

"Ooh, possessive, I like it. As long as you do the same, my bull," I tease, rubbing my wet pussy against his hard cock.

He roars right in my face, and in one smooth move he slams inside me, no teasing or hesitation as he takes what he wants and I love it. I relish the possessive way he holds me, the strength coiled in his body that he uses to bring me pleasure just as easily as he brought death to the witches lying in pieces around us.

"Yes!" I cry out, lifting my hips to meet his brutal, raw thrusts as he hammers into me again and again. The pain blends with pleasure until I'm calling out random words, those red eyes locked on my face and drinking in my pleasure.

He wrings it from me with each jerk of his hips, hitting that spot inside me that has my eyes nearly crossing as I lose myself to him, my nails cutting strips down his back as I try to draw him closer. He growls with it, a particularly brutal thrust accompanying the sound, making me cry out and arch my chest into him, begging for more, wanting everything my monster has to offer.

I want to bathe in his lust and anger, feel his claws ripping into me as my blood drips down our bodies as we fuck...as we mate.

He pulls out of me and throws me to the floor. I flip onto my knees and crawl towards him as he kneels and drags me to him. His cock finds my wet pussy and slips back inside as he falls to his back, dragging me down until I'm spread above him, straddling his giant body. He's too big. He grasps my hips again, and the smell of my blood hits the air. He sniffs and roars when he scents it, my bull becoming unleashed.

I sink down on his cock, rocking myself, but I'm unable to get much leverage until he starts to lift and drop me, my clit hitting his pelvis and sending bolts of pleasure through me until I'm suddenly crying out, my pussy clenching around his cock as I jerk above him, the orgasm dragged from my very toes. Wave after wave rolls through me, but he doesn't stop, no, he fucks me through it, demanding more.

I can feel blood dripping from the punctures on my hips, rolling down my thighs, the ruby red liquid matching his eyes. "Dume," I whimper, my pussy still clenching with aftershocks.

His name on my lips makes him grunt, and then suddenly we are moving again, but this time I'm on my knees with his hand on my back pushing me down as he enters me from behind. This feels right, primal, and fucking animalistic as he forces my thighs open for him and he fucks me roughly from behind. My nipples drag across the floor, the flash of pain adding another layer to my pleasure.

Being with him is perfect as his animal takes me from behind until everything else fades, and I can almost feel the sand under me from his maze where he belongs, the moon shining down on us as the minotaur claims his mate.

I feel his cock grow inside me, thickening and becoming impossibly longer, and his breathing picks up, harsher now, less human—I know he's changed. He doesn't let me look, keeping my head down, but I want to see, I want to touch, so I rip myself away and roll over. He rears back, his red, animal eyes staring down at me, his horns curling from his head, scarred like the rest of him. He's not quite minotaur, not quite human. Fur covers his forearms and some of his human legs, but his cock is all animal as is the gleam in his eyes and the slight lengthening of his face. He looks like a monster from a nightmare and I fucking love it.

He growls, a low bass as his head tilts down like bulls I've seen, but he doesn't attack me, no, he grabs my hips and yanks me to him, my legs pressed against his wide chest as he slams back inside me, filling me and stretching me so much it edges on pain.

Smoke drifts from his nose, wrapping around us, seeming to caress my skin as he fucks me, makes me his, our blood and minds mixing, the high like no other. I watch those red orbs, they keep me afloat as pleasure explodes from every corner of my body with a screech, leaving me unable to move or think, but he still carries on, powering into me again and again like a man possessed.

"Mine," he snarls, over and over.

Moaning, I arch up and roll my nipples. "Yours," I agree.

"Mine!" he snarls, and I cry out as he slaps my clit with his hand again and again as he drives into me until I'm thrown over the precipice. I come with a scream, clamping around him as he roars my name for everyone to hear.

Gasping, I collapse back to the floor and he rolls until he's on his back, then he drags me onto his chest where I sprawl, my ear to his chest, listening to his heart race in time with mine.

I feel him shift beneath me, his animal retreating with a purr until he encircles his very human arms around me. "*Draya*, where did they take you?" he asks worriedly, dropping a kiss on my hair which makes me smile.

Stroking his pecs, I lift my head and prop my chin on his chest, watching him and the muscles playing in his torso. He truly is beautiful in a rugged, rip you to pieces way that makes me a walking, talking ball of need. "They were trying to break me. He wants me for something, but I don't know what yet," I muse, and then I proceed to tell him about Amos and Veyo. He growls and draws me closer, so I pat his chest. "I'm fine, they can't break me. People have been trying their whole lives, and it won't work now."

"*Draya.*" He shakes his head, watching me with the softest expression I've ever seen on him. "What happened after?"

"They dragged me to another cell and threw me in with a vampire, I think it was to break us both. They thought he would feed and become their minion, depending on them for food and scaring me in the process." I snort and he grins.

"I take it that didn't work?" he inquires, his hand massaging the base of my spine. I groan in bliss as my eyes flutter closed for a moment as he works out the knots there. "*Draya.*" He huffs out a laugh and I blink.

"Don't distract me then, hot stuff," I tease, and then become serious. "No, I spoke to him. He's like us. A prisoner, Dume." I suck in a breath, remembering what I saw. "I saw into his mind. God, the way he was made—no one should have to suffer that, but he did. He's old and very powerful. We can help each other, I have a plan."

"And what's that?" he murmurs, watching me closely, so I tell him what I thought we could do and he starts to laugh, a grin covering his face. "You are a genius, *Draya*, they aren't going to know what's hit them."

"They will learn not to fuck with a skinwalker ever again," I retort, offering him a matching grin.

I lay my head back on his chest and he carries on the rumbling purr, relaxing me so much I nearly fall asleep until a thought hits me. "Dume, once we are free, where will you go?" I question sleepily, the blackness of slumber trying to claim me, but I fight to stay awake, to hear his answer.

"Wherever you go, my goddess," he whispers, and kisses my head. "Sleep, I will watch over you."

CHAPTER 27

NOS

I wait and watch.

I see Griffin arrive. He goes in and doesn't come back out, which could either be good or bad, I can't tell yet. But I can't worry about him also, I need to focus on my part of the plan. My only concern is getting my mate back alive and well.

They have her.

It's simple.

Crouching down, I tilt my head and watch the wolves' alpha creep closer. He plops down by my feet, his bright blue eyes watching me with too much intelligence. Others think they are just animals, but they are so much more, and they have all answered my call. Reaching out, I stroke his fur. "My friend, send your pack far and wide, carry my message on the winds to the wolves. We need them, tell them I request them, they are to meet me here in three days' time when the moon is high, come in animal form. I have found their missing pack members."

The wolf inclines his head, turns tail, and breaks into a run, heading into the forest. I turn back to watch the house, seeing the usual guards patrolling the property. I scan the area wondering where they are keeping her. It must be behind the building or below it, but I have to trust Griffin to find her. However, I am prepared in case I feel her fear or pain. I am ready to go in. To throw a curveball into their plans and gain their attention so they leave her alone.

They want powerful supernaturals, that much is obvious.

Women too.

I will give them whatever they need to help her. I will show them my true capabilities. They thought they genuflected when they approached me about that final seat on the council, thought they could control me, but they were wrong. They are nothing, just an inconvenience, and I could kill them before they even raised their powers.

They are nothing more than toddlers throwing their toys from the pen, and it's time to remind them who the true adults are around here.

A whisper comes from above as if held on the wind. The elementals have heard my call, so have the fae. Now, I am just waiting for everyone else. They are all missing people, women, and the more I searched and put out a call, the more I realised had actually been taken.

They were all angry, wanting them back, wanting to know who and why. I am offering them that for purely selfish reasons because I need them. I can kill the council, but the uproar would be astonishing. No, I need the supernatural world behind me to keep my mate alive and safe, so when we do kill them and stop whatever plans they have in motion, we are free to leave and know that our world won't fall apart—that's another reason we need the sleeping council. They need to step in and take over. I have no desire to lead. I want my mate, that is all.

I breathe in softly, urging myself to have patience which is hard when I know my mate is in there, so close but just out of reach. No, we have to do this right. So I settle down into a cross-legged position on the forest floor and wait with my animals around me, awaiting the order.

I am the God of the Forest, after all, and they will protect my mate as if she was me. I tilt my head and send in my birds out, seeing if they can find her location and get eyes on her, I need to see her. I need to see if she is okay.

They forget what else I am, though, a god of death. I will remind them. It's time they remember why myths and horror stories were created around me. I feel the shift coming on, my third shift, one so horrifying humans fight at the sight, their minds breaking, even as my mate plastered herself to me.

Little one, whatever you are doing, know I am here. Here waiting for my love, we will be together again soon. Until then, give them hell.

CHAPTER 28

GRIFFIN

As soon as the door shuts, they come for me. I don't bother trying to fight back, it would only get me punished and thrown out. No, I need to be here, so I stand there with my head tilted back, eyes defiant as they converge on me.

"Fucking human lover," one spits, as his fist connects with my jaw, snapping my head around. Spitting my blood onto his boots, I turn back to face the front, a cocky little smile on my lips.

"You are nothing!" one roars, as he stabs me with the point of his wing. I grunt in pain as he pulls it free, my blood clinging to his black feathers.

They surround me, beating, kicking, and punching. Trying to break me, to beat me down. I try to remain on my feet, but there are too many bodies and too many attacks coming from all angles. I fall to my knees then to my side, still smiling even as one eye swells shut and one eardrum explodes so I can't hear their taunts and insults.

My body tries to heal itself as it breaks and bleeds, but there is too much trauma, and as soon as it starts to heal me, they inflict the same injury again. It's a never-ending circle of agony. Their faces contort in hate, true hate, as all that emotionlessness dissipates, and they become an army joined in their hatred for me.

The fallen, the mad one. I see their lips forming insults, and they fling them at me like their fists, their golden eyes glaring with angelic indignation.

It's fucked up, but with each punch, each kick, each broken bone, and blood drop, I start to feel better...more human. As if I'm finally being punished for being born. The pain helps me feel like I can move on...like I'm more. Stronger, because I know now they can't break my body. They simply can't. I can survive whatever they throw my way. My madness swirls in my mind, making me laugh even as they crack my ribs.

I will heal.

Get Dawn.

Kill them all.

I repeat it again and again as my eyes blacken and my madness cries at me to get up, to rip them to pieces, and wear their blood like a badge of honour. I can't see or hear now, and my blood burns with madness and pain. My body is one big wound, every bone is broken, and every organ is bleeding. I should be dead, but my body won't allow it.

They know it, and it only infuriates them more. I can't even die properly. Eventually the attacks stop and they leave me on the floor, like trash. I let my mind wander as I feel my body start to heal, my muscles stitching back together, my bones mending and popping. It's sluggish, since there are so many injuries, and it takes a while. While I wait, I think of Dawn, and the way her blonde hair would fall into her face, that little smile she used to give me that told me she knew something I didn't. That utter trust she had in me even when I didn't trust myself. She was always so strong, knowing what she wanted and unashamed to act on her thoughts.

Even that night in the basement when I was vile to her, she

simply laughed. Or the night I dropped her from the sky, testing her, she had accepted it, trusting me more than anyone else ever had. To her I wasn't nothing, not an experiment, not a mistake or trash...I was hers. She wanted me.

I still tested her, touching her and expecting her to cringe away, but instead I found the truth in her body—she really did want me. And when she looked at me, those eyes filled with need and kindness, I knew. I knew I would never leave her side, I would change fate, and not let the past dictate my future. I won't lose her like I lost my mother, I'll fight death itself to claim her back.

She is mine.

I can't wait to watch her grow in this world, to see the true power she has hiding in that tiny, curvy body explode out and rain down on these fucked up people. They will regret taking her, she will make sure of it, and I'll be by her side watching as she kills them.

Imagining her eyes black, her body covered in blood, has me hard. It's a strange fucking time to be sporting an erection, but that's just another factor with my mate. I want her all the time, but when I see her fighting? When I see her covered in blood and power? I want to grab her, throw her onto the nearest surface, and bury myself in her sweet little pussy as she screams my name and fights me.

My eyes pop, making me grunt, and then they open. They ache and the light is bright, causing me to wince as I flip over and get to my knees before pushing to my feet. I waver for a moment before blowing out a breath and straightening to my full height. I give the other men a haughty look. A dare to try it again. A man can only be pushed so far and they keep on pushing that same button.

"Where's my bed?"

I'm PRETENDING to sleep with my arms under my head and eyes

closed where I lie on the ground. Apparently a mad bastard like me, a traitor, doesn't get a bed. I get a square of flooring, but at least I don't have to make it military neat like the others.

I've been here almost a day now and I'm feeling the itch, the one that's always telling me to kill people, but now it's telling me to find my mate, so with a sigh I get up and approach the head nephilim, who is sharpening his blade on his bed near the door. All of the ones here are waiting for orders while some are on patrol, some on other duties, and some are out on missions.

I stop near him and he pretends to ignore me, but his eyes flicker up to assess the threat before going back to watch the rhythmic movement of the stone against the metal.

"Give me something to do," I snap.

He carries on ignoring me, so I narrow my eyes and grab his sword, cutting my hand on it. We both watch the blood mar the steel. "You want to punish me, fine, put me on a shit detail but use me. I'm fucking bored of watching you dicks wank each other off over who's the furthest up the council's arse."

He jumps to his feet, his sword going to my throat as his nostrils flare. Oh, angel boy didn't like that one bit. But then a strange smile melts onto his face. "You want a job? Fine." He jerks his head to the left. "Follow me." He doesn't take me out the front door, but the one at the end, which opens to reveal stairs that lead down. Without bothering to grab a light he descends the stone steps, and I follow after him, my eyes adjusting to let me see.

It leads down to an underground corridor with cobwebs and old, melted candles on the wall. He strides away from me and I trail after him, taking my time just to piss him off so when he gets to the other end, he has to wait for me, his face crinkling in annoyance.

"Your face might freeze like that if you're lucky," I drawl, and with a snarl he turns, yanks open the metal gate behind him, and storms through. Laughing, I follow him and find another set of stairs, which open up into what I'm guessing are the dungeons.

That gets my attention, and the thread that pulls me to Dawn seems to be tighter. She's down here somewhere.

The nephilim stops in a long corridor filled with cells. "Behind you to the left is a janitor cupboard, you are on clean up duty. You can play bitch to the prisoners, make sure they don't kill themselves and they get fed." With that he walks away, leaving me here, but it's the perfect job.

It means I can search for Dawn without being caught. I start straightaway, but over six hours later I realise just how big the dungeons are. The series of corridors make up a maze with thousands of cells. Other than the other poor bastards working down here, I can't find her. I'm exhausted after all the fighting and healing, so I head back. I'll get an early start tomorrow and find her.

I SPEND the next two days on meal and clean up duty, my eyes searching every cell for my mate until on the third day, I find her. I wrench open the cell door, ready to clean up the bodies they ordered me to. It chafes at me, so I'm annoyed when I storm inside only to freeze.

My heart slams in my chest, my eyes wide as hope flows through me. My mind settles instantly, the irritation melting away to something darker, something so much stronger. "*Vasculo*," I whisper.

She lifts her head, blinking open her eyes, and when she sees me a smile curves her lips, like she had no doubt I would find her. Those blue depths lock onto me as she gracefully leaps to her feet and struts towards me. My eyes drop to her body, not just to satisfy my lust, but to see if she's okay. There is blood here and there, but I don't notice any wounds. That doesn't mean there weren't any, she could have healed.

Then the smell hits me.

Blood, sex...and fur?

I bristle and my eyes shoot behind her. I blame my excitement at finding her for not noticing the big fucking man leaning back against the wall, watching me with blazing red eyes.

I snarl, "Who the fuck are you?"

Dawn rolls her eyes and stops before me, tilting her head back to gaze up at me. "Really, cutie, that's the first thing you're going to say to me? Not even a hello kiss?" she purrs, running her black tipped nails down my chest and making me shiver as my cock hardens further, jerking in my pants to try and reach her.

"Who is that?" I snap, glaring at him...not that she cares. "Did he hurt you?" I demand, searching her eyes, but she giggles and shakes her head.

"Only in the way I like. I missed you," she tells me, and I melt for a moment before shooting another look at the man. I tug her behind me and cross my arms as I glare at him. I know she fucked him, I can tell, and the possessive way he gets to his feet and steps towards me only confirms it. Hurt and jealousy surges through me. While I was being beaten, almost dying, she was fucking someone else?

I can't tell what he is, but he's massive, like a walking, talking tree trunk with a golden nose ring. What a prick. I hate him instantly, and not just because he has muscles where I didn't know you could have them.

"Who are you?" the man asks, his voice thick and growly.

"Her fucking mate, tree trunk, who are you?" I fire back.

"Her mate, it's minotaur to you," he retorts, stepping closer to try and intimidate me.

I let my madness come out as I whirl to see Dawn grinning at me like this is the best news in the world.

"How many goddamn mates do you have?" I yell, throwing my hands in the air. "Is it not bad enough I have to deal with that snobby dragon?"

"Wait, Aska?" she exclaims excitedly, and I narrow my eyes, my hand darting out and gripping her throat harshly. She moans, her eyes flaring in lust.

"No fucking more," I warn.

I'm flying through the air before I even know what's happened. Turning, I land on my feet, pulling my blades as I glare at the minotaur who's now standing defensively in front of my mate like I would ever hurt her. He feels like she needs protecting from me, it makes me see red.

She is mine.

With a snarl I launch myself at him, and he meets me halfway across the cell as we tumble around in a blur of limbs, trying to hurt each other. All this time I've been looking for her, worried about her, and here she is shacking up with a fucking minotaur in the dungeon like it's a love den. It infuriates me and I take it out on the tree trunk. I stab and slash, the scent of his blood filling the air, my mist wrapping around me as I flap my wings to keep us airborne.

He starts to change, his face melting to that of an animal, and his whole body ripples and thickens, which I didn't think was possible. Suddenly, as quickly as it started, it stops. We are frozen in the way Nos stopped me before, floating in the air. I roll my eyes to see an angry-looking Dawn glaring at us. She flicks her head and we are pushed back from each other and thrown into the cell wall with a grunt, stuck there as she crosses her arms and watches us with black eyes.

Her hair floats around her as her power fills the room, leaking from her body. Her chest heaves with her emotions, but it only draws my gaze to her breasts as I imagine fucking her here, fucking the anger out of her and letting the minotaur watch so he knows whom she belongs to.

"Boys," she snaps in a bored tone, "if you aren't getting all that aggression out on me, it's not worth it. Now stop fighting each other before I kick both your asses."

"You could try, *Vasculo*." I grin. "I might even enjoy it."

"Might? We both know you would." She laughs as she strolls

towards us, effortlessly holding a fallen and a four hundred pound minotaur pinned to the wall like bugs. Her hand trails across my crotch and then the wall to the minotaur. She looks up at him with a secretive smile, one that's different from the one she saves for me. I don't know why that settles me a bit.

"This is Griffin, another of my mates. He can be a bit possessive and quick to anger, but he is a good man," she tells him like I'm not here. I snort at the 'good man' comment and she winks at me. "And when he's not, when he's bad, I love it even more."

"*Vasculo*," I warn, and she steps back.

"Now, do you promise not to attack each other again? Only then will I let you down." She frowns.

"I promise, *Draya*," the minotaur vows—the kiss ass.

"Maybe," I mutter, and she laughs, waving her hand, and we both drop to the floor. I notice the minotaur stumbles while I do not.

Striding across the room, I block him as he heads to her. I tilt her head back and press my thumb to her throat as I circle it, without pressure this time. "Dawn," I murmur, and her eyes light up as she leans into me. "I missed you."

"Of course you did, angel." She grins. "I've been having some fun here."

I look around at the bodies piled in the corner. "I can tell." I smirk. "Want to have some more?"

"What did you have in mind?" she purrs, and my eyes drop to her lips. I groan and step back before throwing the minotaur a glare.

"We'll be back. Stay here and try not to charge anyone, good bull," I taunt, then grabbing both of her hands, I hold them behind me like she's a prisoner and drag her from the cell, shutting it on the enraged snarl of the bull inside, which makes me laugh even as Dawn shakes her head.

"Be nice," she chides.

Backing her into the cell door, I slam her hands above her,

keeping her restrained as I lean in, letting her see the need and anger in my eyes. "You don't like me nice, *Vasculo*."

Her breathing picks up and her mouth parts slightly as she rubs against me. "Then be mean to me, I've missed you."

Growling, I throw her over my shoulder, spanking her as I storm down the corridor. I kick open the door to the bathroom then throw her inside and shut it behind me, locking it as I rip off my shirt and toss it away. She watches me hungrily as I flick open my jeans. "You want mean?" I snap.

She nods, almost moaning. "Yes, Griffin, I want the madness I see in your eyes. Show me how much you missed me."

Before she can draw in another breath, I throw her against the toilet stall wall. Gripping her throat, I drag her farther up the wood, and she wraps her legs around my waist, grinding against me as I grip her cruelly.

Her breasts brush over my chest, making me groan as I stare at her pouting lips, imagining them wrapped around my already hard cock as I take her here for everyone to hear.

"Griffin," she whispers, eyes alight with lust as I squeeze tighter, causing her breath to catch in her throat and her hips to jerk against mine.

She likes me when I'm nice, but she loves it when I'm mean.

"Do you want me, *Vasculo*?" I murmur seductively, leaning towards her as I lick her lips. "Do you want me fucking you, my cock inside you? Reminding you who you belong to?"

"I don't belong to anyone," she snarls, fighting in my grasp.

I slam her back into the wood and pin her there with an angry glare. "You belong to me just as much as I belong to you."

"Fuck you," she spits, growling and twisting.

"No, I'm going to fuck you," I taunt, as I shove up her dress and line up, driving into her tight pussy.

She moans, stilling her fighting as she squeezes around me, whimpering, her eyes fluttering closed.

"Good girl," I coo, kissing her mouth.

I dominate it, and use my body and mouth to prove to her that she does, in fact, belong to me. She kisses me in return, nipping at my lips as I pull out of her clinging heat and drive back inside, forcing her to take me as I fuck her against the wood stall.

She groans before yanking her mouth away, watching me with bruised lips. "Griffin." She pants my name, making me grunt as I grip her tighter and start to move faster.

"You are mine," I snarl as I drive into her again and again. "Not his, not theirs, not right now, you are just mine and I can do whatever I want to you and you will like it, won't you, baby?"

"Yes," she moans, her head tipping back to expose her throat. "I can take it."

Pulling out of her, I throw her into the sink, and she grunts when she hits it. I step behind her and kick open her legs before gripping her hair and yanking her head back. I force her to watch me in the mirror, my wings spread out behind me, knowing she likes to see them. She moans and wiggles to push back against me as I keep her there.

Sliding my hand down her back, I play with her wet pussy, watching as a flush covers her face and chest. I dip my fingers inside her, twisting and curling them as she moans, then I fuck her with them before pulling my digits free from her tight channel.

Tracing them across her ass, I slip a finger inside her tight back hole. She groans, watching me in the mirror as I force her to take me. I'm aware we could be caught at any minute, but I'm not fucking her fast, I'm reclaiming her. Let them catch us, I will kill them and fuck her above their corpses.

She pushes back, wanting more, her black eyes locked on my every move, ready to take whatever I offer. My crazy little mate loves my madness, so I paint it across her skin, I fuck it into her and let it claim her as surely as I do.

I force it into her ass, adding two more fingers. She whimpers in pain and pleasure, arching back as I run my other hand down her throat. I tug down her dress until I can see her breasts, the tight rosebud nipples so bright and perfect against her pale skin.

Fuck, she's stunning.

I grab her throat again harshly as I narrow my eyes on her in the mirror, still fucking her ass with my fingers. "Say it, say who you belong to."

"No." She laughs breathlessly.

I twist my fingers and she moans, so I do it again and again, making sure it hurts her, but I feel her cream dripping down her thighs and my hand anyway—my mate likes the pain. My cock jerks from that, and I'm two seconds away from pushing her down and fucking her ass until she screams that she's mine...in fact...

Shoving her head down, I grip her ass with my hand and slap it a few times to see it pinken with my marks. She gasps my name, asking for more, but I pull my fingers free, and with my cock still wet from her pussy, slam into her ass, forcing past her muscles.

She screams, writhing against me, but I keep her pinned there as I drag my cock out and force it back in, over and over as I continue to smack her. "You are mine, say it."

"No," she snaps, pushing her ass back to meet my thrusts. My dirty little girl is wet as hell, her pink, raw pussy dripping for me, her clit engorged and begging for my touch. She won't get it, I'll force her to come from the pain of my cock in her ass until she admits it.

"You do, look at you, begging for my cock in your ass. You'll take me however you get it and you know it. That makes you mine, Dawn." Licking along her spine, I leave a trail of stinging bites. "Your body, your mind, your soul, and even your dark little heart. It's all mine."

"Please," she begs, her eyes wild, blood dripping from her lip where she bit it. Reaching down, I brush a droplet away tenderly and she whimpers. My touch is a sharp contrast with the harsh way I'm fucking her, getting all my rage, hate, and love out on, I mean in, her.

"Please what?" I snarl, my wings blocking the room behind us. In the mirror I look like an angel of death here to steal her soul, but it's the other way around. This former little human has my soul wrapped around her finger. I will always come for her, wherever she is, her fucked up angel.

"I need to come so badly," she implores without shame as she fucks herself on my dick like a good little girl. "I want to feel you filling up my ass."

Growling, I grip her hips tightly and drive into her repeatedly. She moans in one long string of curses, her ass tightening around me as she explodes. Roaring, I yank my cock out of her ass, not giving her what she desires because she didn't say what I wanted. Instead, I aim my cock at her red ass cheeks.

I splatter my cum across her ass, watching as it splashes there like a warning. The minotaur will be able to smell it and that makes me grin as I watch it drip down her cheeks to her pussy, mingling with her cream. Using my other hand as she lies there gasping, I cup some of the cum and stick my fingers in her pussy, pushing it deep inside her. I do it several times, and she cries out my name and begins to press back to meet me again, wanting more.

"Yours, yours, yours," she chants.

"Good girl," I murmur, dropping to my knees. Uncaring about my cum dripping from her pussy, I drag it to my face and lap at her wet heat.

Licking up her wet center, I taste my saltiness and her sweetness, making me groan as I circle her clit before pressing my tongue inside her. She pushes back into my face, forcing me deeper, her pussy clamping on my tongue.

Humming, I do it again and again, licking and pressing her clit with quick flicks of my tongue before dipping it inside her. Before I know it, she's coming on my face, her pussy clenching down on my tongue, trying to keep it inside her as she falls forward from the force of her release.

Sitting back, I watch her raw, cream and cum covered pussy as she pants. Her legs are jelly and not offering much stability. She turns and slips to the floor in front of me, her breasts high and tight, nipples hard, mouth red, eyes wide and hazy from pleasure. Dawn looks so fucking beautiful, even more stunning knowing my cum is spread across her pussy and ass.

She reaches over and grips my chin, forcing my gaze to hers. "I missed you, but you need to learn how to share, my love, or at least not kill them," she murmurs in a playful tone, and then turns serious. "I am yours, Griffin, that's true, but you don't own me, you can't. I promised myself that wouldn't happen ever again."

"I promised never to love again," I blurt out, and then my eyes widen in horror as hers soften, searching mine.

"Your mother?" she asks, and I nod. "Oh, baby, I'm sorry, but I will never leave you, not like that. We are forever, Griffin, so stop trying to fight it."

"My mother would have loved you. She was a fighter too, even until the very end. Her loyalty got her killed, Dawn, and I fear it will be your downfall as well." I turn my face away, not wanting her to see the fear there, but she grabs it and draws it back. Her eyes are on fire and alive with purpose, determination, and something beyond even us...destiny.

"I will always be loyal. I will never walk away, even when the path is filled with obstacles, Griffin. We are together now, no one can stop that." She leans closer and kisses me so softly and sweetly, I feel a crack in my twisted black heart, a shard of light shining in. Pulling away, she rests her forehead against mine. "When you're ready, I would love to hear about her, about the woman who raised the man I love."

"*Vasculo.*" I suck in a breath and she grins.

"Don't tell me the big, bad angel fears love?"

"Yes, don't you?" I whisper.

"Yes, it terrifies me, but that fear lessens when I look in your eyes, every time you reach for me, and every time you hold me tight. It's my greatest fear and biggest hope," she divulges and then sighs. "I guess we should talk about the main thing here though—what's next?"

I nod, drawing her closer, needing to feel her in my arms. "We have a plan."

"So do I." She laughs and pulls back to see my face. "Tell me yours, and I'll tell you mine."

"Dirty girl," I tease, and she snorts.

I can feel the madness settling at her proximity and it allows me to breathe easier. I outline our idea and she frowns. "How did you get in anyway? Did you kill everyone?" she inquires, and it makes me sit taller that she thinks so much of me.

"I wish," I grumble. "I had to return and beg to be let back in, told them I wanted to be part of it, the other nephilim were not happy."

She must read between the lines because her eyes flare black. "They hurt you?"

"Nothing I can't handle," I snap.

"They. Hurt. You?" she says slowly, and I can see her changing before my eyes. My cock hardens instantly, my madness rising to meet her.

"They tried," I admit, and she snarls, leaping to her feet and storming towards the door. Chuckling, I jump up and wrap her in my arms, stopping her progress as she fights and kicks to get free, ranting about all the horrible things she's going to do to them for hurting me.

It makes me grin uncontrollably, knowing she cares that much about what happens to me, but I try to hide it as I bury my face in her hair. She's so angry it's like holding a wild animal in my grip. "Dawn," I growl, and she stills. "It's okay, we will make them pay, but not yet. Now, what was your plan?" I question, trying to bring her back before she goes out there and kills everyone. I know she would.

She huffs.

"If you tell me, I can find Nos outside and tell him, who can then tell Aska," I offer, and their names make her slump.

"Fine, but I'm killing them," she warns, and I nod, dropping a kiss on her shoulder.

"Of course, my little demon," I agree. "Your plan?"

She turns in my embrace, a grin flirting at her lips, and I know whatever it is, it's going to be crazy, my favourite type.

CHAPTER 29

DUME

Draya returns with the fallen. He looks smug and she is grinning in satisfaction. They smell like sex and blood, and I debate charging him, but I remember what happened last time, so I stop myself. Instead, I lean back against the wall and cross my arms, my jaw locked as she leans up and kisses his cheek.

"Better get back to work, cutie. I'll be here waiting." He nods, throwing me a venomous look before cupping her cheeks and kissing each eyelid softly. His face changes when he does, going from angry to...almost soft. It lessens my fury towards him, he clearly loves my mate.

"Be bad," he orders.

"Wouldn't that be good?" She laughs and he grins at her.

"No, good is boring, you, *Vasculo*, are bad." He kisses her again, and with one last glare at me, he turns and leaves, slamming the door behind him.

Dawn spins my way and saunters closer, unbothered by my crossed arms and angry face. I'm jealous, a feeling I'm not used to.

She drapes herself on me and I have no choice but to hold her before she falls. "*Draya*," I rumble as she grins up at me.

"Missed me, big guy?" she teases, watching me closely. "'Cause I think you did. Is that why you look like you want to murder everyone or fuck me but can't decide?"

I narrow my eyes on her and she pouts a little. "Not going to talk to me?"

"I can smell him on you," I growl, my body vibrating with the need to grab her harder, throw her down, and claim her again.

"Yeah? Then why don't you replace his scent with yours?" she purrs, stroking down my chest to my hard cock.

I grind my teeth and look away, trying to breathe through the urge to change and take her. The way I am feeling, I can't control it, and I don't want to hurt her. Suddenly, a burst of pain flashes through me and I look down to see her teeth buried around my nipple as she stares up at me.

Giggling, she pulls back, licking her lips as I watch the blood from her teeth trickle down my chest. "Play with me."

My chest is heaving, vibrating with my imminent change as I watch her step backwards, her eyes black as she runs her hands down her body, making me watch. "*Draya*," I warn, my voice an animal bass as my bull comes forward, wanting to punish our mate.

"He fucked me real good," she taunts, and it breaks me.

My animal bursts free with a roar. In a blur, she is pinned to the floor with us on top of her in a minute, he rips open her thighs as she laughs and slams home. She yells, arching up into us as he hammers into her again and again.

"Yes!" She groans and pulls her dress down as he growls, claiming her. He tears her apart and reforms her around his length. I feel our balls draw up and she whimpers as he pulls free, and with one pump of his hand he covers her chest in our cum.

He lets me back to the forefront of our mind with a satisfied growl after sniffing her to ensure she smells like us. I watch her below me, her chest flushed and heaving, my cum dripping down her heavy breasts and tight, hard nipples. Her thighs are pink and bruised from my hands, with a trickle of blood sliding down her porcelain skin from our rough treatment, and I feel guilty instantly, but she doesn't seem to care. She grins up at me, her eyes hazy as she traces her hand through our cum and down her body to her pussy.

Sitting back, I watch her spread her legs wider and, with her eyes on me, she starts to play with herself. A rumble starts in my chest as I watch her fingers spread her glistening pink folds and dip inside. She moans loudly, her pussy dripping with cream.

"More," I demand, wanting to watch her come.

She whimpers, biting down on her lip as her legs start to shake, her fingers blurring as they push in and out of her channel, her thumb rubbing her clit furiously until, with a cry, her whole body seizes up.

Groaning, I watch as she pulls her fingers from her pussy. They are wet with her release, so I lean down and suck them clean, making her gasp and start to laugh. "Feel better?" she teases.

"Yes," I admit with no shame.

"Brilliant, so next time one of you is jealous, I just need to let you come on my tits." She grins and I growl.

I help her clean up using the water that drips in the corner and then back into her dress before pulling her into my arms and holding her tight. She sighs and buries her head in my chest before telling me the plan her other mates have. They sound smart, and I am hopeful they are honourable, good men and I don't have to kill any of them.

Because I am never letting her go.

Chapter 30

Lucifer

The angel drawls on and on about procedure and politics and the proper position and reaction for a council member such as myself. His righteous bullshit nearly makes me gag as he paces back and forth where I'm sprawled on the throne. The more he talks, the angrier he gets, until his halo is smoking and his hands are glowing.

I wonder idly how much I could push him.

He turns to me with golden flames burning in his eyes as he swells with power, stepping closer. "Are you even listening to me, Serpent?"

I've had enough. Before he can continue, I get up, appear before him, and snap his neck. The crack is audible in the room and I watch with unrestrained glee as he falls to the stone steps like a broken ragdoll. I kick his body down them and sit back on the throne. "Ah, that's better, nice and quiet."

"Master."

Oh yes. I look to find the servant glancing from me to the

angel's body in shock. I wave it away. "Don't worry about him, bring me a drink, a stiff one. All those references to goodness and righteousness have me wanting to throw up."

He gasps, but with another look at the angel's corpse he scurries away. Sighing, I close my eyes, wondering how long it will—

Blinding light flashes and I lazily slit open a lid, already grinning at the furious angel as he gets to his feet and cracks his broken neck. "I have told you not to do that, now where was I?"

Groaning, I throw my arm over my face. "One day you will stay dead."

"And one day you will burn in hell!" he screams.

"Been there, done that, got the pictures to remember it. They really know how to have the best parties there," I remark, and I can actually feel his anger.

"Let's go find the dragon, then you may go back to sleep," he suggests slowly.

Just then the servant returns with my drink, and when he sees the angel he falls to his knees in reverence. "Master," he exclaims in glee, as I watch my drink clatter to the floor with a frown, but the liquid slowly makes its way to the angel and covers his feet, making him grimace and step back. He stares at me with narrowed eyes. "Dragon, now."

"Go," I retort, waving my hand before clicking my fingers. Hades, my hellhound, appears and I scratch his smoking black fur. "Who's a good boy? Oh, who missed daddy?" I coo, and he barks in excitement, the floor burning under his paws. His eyes are as red as flames, his body almost skeletal.

"No pets," the angel snaps.

"We keep you, and I'm betting you're not toilet trained," I fire back, ignoring him again as I stroke Hades.

"Serpent—"

"Angel, go and deal with your dragons, but I will not be joining you. They are old fools. They have power, but no drive to use it, though I do like the way they burn people. It's quite the sight to behold." I grin, sitting back.

Hades sniffs around the angel and he throws him a dirty look before stepping away. "I am not leaving you here, we need to put you back to sleep—"

I let my power leak out, filling the room with darkness until he can't see. "I am not going to sleep!" I roar, and then pull it back until I'm sitting casually on the throne again. "Now go before I tire of you."

Just then, Hades cocks his leg up and pisses all over the angel's leg. It starts to smoke, his legs burning as he watches in disgust, then he turns that sneer on me. "Mark my words, Serpent, this will bring nothing but evil and bad to the world. You will ruin the balance and create chaos."

"A little chaos is good." I shrug.

"You are playing with fire, demon, I hope you know that," he counters, and then with a haughty lift of his chin, strides away, with bits of hellhound piss trailing behind him.

How dignified.

"Good boy," I praise with a grin, and Hades barks. "Let's go, we have someone to find." Standing, I smirk at the servant who is still pressed to the floor and then disappear into the beyond, ready to search the world for the woman who woke me from my sleep.

Let's hope she realises what she called forth, because she isn't getting away from me now. She can't hide from me either in this world or the next.

CHAPTER 31

ASKA

The ghosts return a few hours later, but before they will give me the location of the sleeping council, they demand I feed one of them, claiming they used a lot of energy. It is just as horrible as the first time, so I am in a bad mood after.

"Tell me," I snap, when the angry ghost steps back to his witch, tiring of these games.

"They are north, as far north as you can go. In the old mountains, Rejek, you have heard of this, yes?" one of them asks.

I nod, Rejek. Fuck, no wonder they are never disturbed. That place is said to be the resting ground of such evil that even stepping foot onto the black mountain will kill you. But if that is where I must go, I will.

"How do I get inside?" I inquire.

"There is a cave near the top and one at the back. The whole mountain is their home, but beware, there are traps and tricks, more than you could imagine, dragon. Now for the final part of your payment."

I grit my teeth and hold out my hand, letting the last one feed. I feel weak after and stumble before forcing myself upright. I will not let them see me unsteady, or they will use it against me, maybe attack and take the rest of my powers. "Thank you. I shall take my leave now." I bow and turn to go, but Loxley's voice calls out, stopping me.

"Beware. You will find what you seek, but you will unearth more than you wanted." With that cryptic piece of information, I depart their ship, leaving them to their ghost men and shivering as their stares follow me until I'm back in the car.

Rejek.

I will travel as far as I can in the car and then I'll have to fly the rest of the way, stopping when I can to rest. It should take about two days as long as nothing goes wrong. Then I remember the dragon.

Punching the steering wheel, I let out my frustration. I do not have time for them, my mate needs me, but I know I can't lead him back to her if he is looking for me. I wonder why, though, why now?

But I know my answer. They didn't know where I was, and now they have felt me awaken...let's hope they don't want me to return, I would hate to have to kill the messenger when so few of us still exist.

I travel north to where they felt the dragon. There wasn't an exact location, so I pull into a rest stop and get out, letting my senses stretch as wide as I can. Scales form on my arms, my eyes turning into those of my dragon as I search for the familiar sensation of my kin. Closing my eyes, I push further, seeking any hints.

Part of me wishes that I won't find anything. I need to get to Rejek and then back to my mate. I have been waiting so long to actually meet her, and now she is in danger and I am not there, so every protective and possessive instinct I have is surfacing.

But then I feel something. It's faint, almost non-existent, but there, that flame in my mind's eye that burns bright like a dragon's. Sighing, I open my eyes. This dragon better have a good reason for breaking through the barrier right now and pulling my attention away from the only thing that matters—my mate. Otherwise, I will rip out his soul and eat it.

My dragon almost purrs at that, wrapping itself around me, stretching under my skin, wanting to be released to let out some frustration at not having our mate yet. He's a possessive, impatient creature.

Growling, I rip the door from the car to get in, but overestimate my anger at the distraction from my real mission, and the now warped piece of metal goes flying. I watch as it tumbles over another car, the plump woman sitting inside it staring with her eyes wide until it comes to a stop on the other side of the road.

Slowly, she turns to me, her face pale and shocked as she ever so slowly reaches out and locks her door. I hear the audible click and actually snort. She saw me rip a door from its hinges and she thinks a lock will stop me?

Sometimes I wonder if they really are severely lacking in intelligence.

Climbing into the car, I cringe a little at the missing door, but start the engine and head to where I felt the dragon. As I pass the human still watching me, I allow my eyes to change to the bright purple of my dragon, and I watch in glee as she faints, her head hitting the wheel and letting out an almighty beep of her horn.

Feeling petty but better, I drive through the winding country roads. The air is getting colder, and I feel it on my face through the gaping hole in my car and it actually makes me feel better about driving. It feels more like flying, especially when I put my foot down on the pedal and we shoot forward.

Whooping, I swerve and drive like I am flying through the air, finding joy in the little moments in life, after all, what else can I do? It is these little experiences that I will remember, that will encourage me to keep fighting another day, something I have learned over the last hundred or so years.

A noise, a siren, echoes around the hills I am driving through, and when I glance through my mirror, I spot a car speeding up until it is behind me. Two serious-looking humans stare at me from the front seat. I notice the writing and curse—the human police. I pull over and get out, unfolding my frame, and wait for them.

They climb out of the car and head my way, looking around my vehicle until they spot the missing door. The one holding a notepad pushes up the thin glasses perched on his crooked nose and gapes at the car then me.

"Sir, do you know how fast you were going and that you are, erm, missing a door?" he questions, his voice high and confused.

"I am decorating." I shrug.

"The car?" he presses, his eyebrow rising.

"Yes, it's called fashion," I retort, mimicking human terms I have heard before.

He shares a look with his partner, his eyes narrowing. "Sir, can we have your license, and can you please take a seat in our car?"

"I don't have time for this!" I snap. "I have a dragon to find and then probably kill, then I have to go to the cold, cursed, mystical mountain to find the sleeping court so they can deal with their subjects so I may retrieve my mate and have lots of sex." I throw my hands in the air.

They both step back, holding their hands out. The one with the glasses watches me as he raises a radio. "Car 418 to control, we found the escaped crazy, standby for more details, we may need backup and sedatives. He is completely loopy." He then looks at me with a patient smile on his face. "Sir, come with me, we'll get you back to the hospital down the road, okay? Maybe there's a dragon there?"

"No, the dragon is that way!" I jerk my head over my shoulder with a frown.

They share another look and then he pulls a black baton from his side. "Come with us. Don't resist, make this easy for yourself, kid, they can help you. You must be missing your medication about now, hmm?"

"Medication...kid? Did. You. Just. Call. Me. Kid?" I roar.

"Sir!"

I don't have time for this. Striding towards them, I punch one square in his face. He falls to the ground, his eyes closed and face pale, blood running from his nose. Jerking, I hiss as electricity races through me. I look down and raise my eyebrow at the black object sticking in my chest. A wire connects it to the other officer.

"That was stupid," I tell him, and then using the wire I drag him to me. He yelps and tries to get away, but I smash his face down on his car and let him drop to the tarmac.

Frowning now, I gaze around, knowing I can't leave them here. So I hoist one over each shoulder, head to their boot, and open it. I put them inside and lock it. There, that's better.

"Car 418, check in, how did the capture of the patient go?" comes through their little radio in the car.

Picking it up, I press lots of buttons. "This is car 418, we have been knocked unconscious." There, that was nice of me.

A crackle sounds, then barked, panicked talking from multiple people. "418 is down, I repeat, officers down!"

Whistling, I head back to my car and slide in before I set off again.

I drive for over two hours. I have to stop twice more to pinpoint the dragon's location, and each time it seems to be weaker until, when I halt a third time, I can't feel it. Sighing, I head to where I last felt it and pull over, having to shift on the side of the road to fly over the trees and up to the top of the hill. Circling in the clouds, I notice an unmoving dark form on the side of the hill. It's too big to be a human or a bear, so it must be the dragon. Shifting as I land, I walk towards it on human legs, but the smell reaches me first, making me growl.

Death.

Then blood.

There was a fight, and it's clear now that the dragon lost.

Jumping down the ledge it is on, I glower at the scene before me. One of its wings is bent and hanging over the rocks. It is covered in blood and talon marks. The face is curled inwards, even in death, and its skin is black like burnt coal. Bloody gashes are carved across its body. Its tail is broken off, the end missing. That, more than anything, tells me this was another dragon's doing.

This dragon fought with another then fled to die? It doesn't make sense. Crouching down closer, I try to search for anything I have missed. The talon marks are long and wide, so it was a full-fledged dragon, a powerful one too. Widening my senses, I search for any threats, but I don't even find the trace of another animal nearby.

So, did this happen in Klasfor and then he broke through to escape into these lands? He was probably afraid the dragon would come and finish him off, but it looks like his wounds did before the other one could.

It makes this easier. This was a lost challenge, that is all, even though it is strange to find the body here.

I have no choice though, I have to perform last rites. Unlike the fairy tales based on dragons and shifters, we don't shift back to human flesh when we die, instead the human body stays trapped inside. We die as we fight, either in dragon or human form. But we can't be buried as dragons, and to ensure we pass over to Valhem where our gold and wildest desires await, we must have last rites executed. To not do so is a grave insult, reserved only for outcasts and the disowned.

I don't have the proper tools here, not the blessed knife and bowl, but I will have to improvise. To walk away without performing them would not sit well with me, even if this dragon is unknown to me. I was once their king, and that drive to protect them does not simply fade, it is ingrained into me.

Pulling out the knife I stole from the angry fallen, I slice along my palm and walk around as much of the body as I can, letting droplets of my blood drop onto the body.

"*Incremento dislesi,* I, Askaliarian of Klasfor, King of the Great

Dragons, release your spirit. *Relsa spirto*, continue your journey, rider of the skies." After I speak the ritual words, I step back, watching the blood start to sizzle as it melts through the thick outer shell of the dragon. Where it does, I spot the pinkened skin of the human inside start to emerge. It takes a few minutes for the dragon to melt away, and with it, the dragon's spirit is released, which is now at rest and allowed to move on.

All it leaves behind is the human body. A lot of dragons believe that because we are born in dragon form and spend a lot of our early years stuck in that shape, it is our true form and the human side is our shift. I think we are born of both, which is why we bury the human body or burn it.

Crouching, I turn the corpse slowly to see the face, and when I do, I sigh. I knew him. His short, shaggy dark hair is familiar, as is the royal slope of his nose. He was a mere boy when I left. He used to follow me around the palace, trying to fly, always wanting to shadow me. I often showed him attention. It is sad he is dead. He was strong and proud, everything a dragon should be. That pride is probably what cost him his life. Picking up his body, I hold him delicately as I jump back to the top of the hill. I lie him down and trace my finger over his face. "Sleep now, my friend, your ride is through. I will meet you in the next life."

Changing my hands back, I dig through the ground with my talons until I have a grave. It's a good spot, high in the clouds where he liked to fly, and it won't be disturbed. It is also where he fought his last fight. A noble dragon, laid to rest.

Shifting my hands back to human so I do not disturb or harm his body, I lay him in the grave and cover him in soil, patting it down until it is secure before sitting back on my haunches. I stare sadly down at the grave. It is a reminder of how long I have been gone. He was grown, a true dragon. I wonder what else has changed.

I shouldn't think about it, that is not my home now, I left for a reason.

For her, before I even knew she existed, and now she needs me. They do not. I whisper goodbye before shifting and launching back into the sky. It is time to head to Rejek and the sleeping council.

They will come with me, I will give them no choice.

They will fear me, because with the way I am feeling now...they dare not refuse me.

CHAPTER 32

DAWN

"So the vampire doesn't have a name?" Dume asks, lovingly stroking down my back.

"He either doesn't remember it or isn't choosing to, who knows, I might have to pick one because I can't keep calling him vamp," I muse.

Dume appears to be thinking, his hand stilling on my back. "What about Jair?"

"Jair?" I repeat in confusion, and he peers down at me, his eyes flashing red.

"It means to eat death, it is what they used to call the vampires when they were forced to feed on the dead and dying competitors in the fighting rings when I was a prisoner. They were quite literally eating death to survive," he explains.

"Jair." I let it flow from my tongue. "I like it, I will ask him."

Just then we hear footsteps heading our way, so I leap to my feet and look at the chains and groan. They are obviously pissed at me for killing a guard and are still trying to break me and the vampire. They are coming to drag me away again, and I have to convince Dume to pretend to be chained. If they knew he wasn't, they might hurt or even kill him. He does it begrudgingly, his nostrils flaring and his eyes narrowing as I wink and saunter towards the guards.

"Let's go, boys, another fun day of torture ahead!"

One of them glowers at me and grips my upper arm, dragging me out and slamming the door behind me. "Ooh, rough, I like it, make it hurt, daddy."

He thrusts me away in disgust, and I laugh as I tumble into another guard. "No? What about sir? Does that make you hard when you watch them scream and bleed?"

They ignore me then, tugging me back down a familiar path, only this time I keep my eye out for Griffin, but he is nowhere in sight. I hope he's okay. If any of those winged fuckers hurt him, I'll eat their souls and wear their bodies like a dress as I fuck up their friends.

The door is opened, and I'm tossed inside before they shut and lock it and walk away. Turning with a grin, I wink at the vamp who is waiting for me. He watches me with hungry eyes, still suspended in his chains. They have taken the guard's body away, but blood covers most of the room. "Hello, sexy, miss me?" I tease.

"Dawn," he rumbles, his lips around my name making me shiver. His fangs flash in the dark and I lick my lips, remembering how good his bite felt.

Running my finger across the wall, I saunter around the chamber, keeping out of his reach as his eyes track me, his body not moving an inch. "Another fun day of torture for us both, but I have something to run past you first." I stop and look at him for a moment. He says nothing, not a big talker, this one, but that's fine.

"I don't know if you don't remember your name or you simply

don't want to use it, so what about Jair?" I suggest. "Apparently it means to eat death, apt, no? I like it."

"Jair?" he rasps, his eyes far away for a moment. "I have had many names. My human one died with that body, the one they called me as I decimated kingdoms and armies no longer holds meaning, and the one they called me after only reminds me of their hate...Jair. I like it, it comes from you, my fresh start. My saviour and future, Jair. I am Jair."

"Jair, it suits you," I reply and step closer, running my finger down his face. He leans into the touch, his eyes closing, his fangs hanging over his lower lip as I trace around them before pricking my finger on one. He groans as I gasp, blood forming on the tip. Eyes flicking open, he watches me hungrily as I press it to his mouth.

He sucks it between his lips, his eyes on me as he laps at my blood, drinking it from my finger. The draw seems to link to my clit which starts to throb in time with each pull of his mouth. Panting, I watch him with lust filled eyes, wanting that mouth on my pussy. Imagining the threat of his teeth as he did that to my clit...

"Jair," I whisper breathlessly.

He pops my finger from his mouth, and his eyes bleed to black as his lips tip up in a snarl. It sends a shot of lust and fear through me. This is a feral man, I love it.

I step back, and his growl increases until his arms suddenly dart forward. The chains creak and then snap, the manacles still around each wrist. He moves fast, lunging at me.

Grabbing me, he tosses me onto the floor and follows me down, blanketing my body as he wrenches open my thighs. He presses his hard cock to my pussy as he twists my head to expose my throat. Snarling my name, he sinks his fangs into my throbbing vein, making me scream and buck beneath him as he starts to feed.

Each draw of my blood has me rubbing against his cock, wanting him buried inside me, both fangs and cock. He must get the hint because he glides his cock across my wet pussy, teasing me as it bumps my clit and makes me moan. He groans, ripping his mouth away and looking at me. His eyes are still black and my blood covers his lips and chin.

"Yes," I growl, gripping his hair and dragging him down. He comes willingly as I cover his lips with mine, licking my blood from his mouth.

He kisses me hard, our teeth clashing as our tongues duel. The kiss is frantic and hungry, and he tears his mouth away, panting before he leans down and laps at the blood trickling from his bite. He kisses down my chest, crawling lower until he's between my legs.

Holy fuck, yes.

"Eat me, Jair," I demand.

He yanks my thighs farther apart and stares at my wet pussy, his tongue darting out and tracing across his plump lower lip. I groan, fuck, that's hot. Especially with his fangs still hanging down, he looks like he could kill me and I would gladly let him. I would die happy with his cock buried in me, his fangs draining me of my blood.

Shit, it makes me wetter imagining him doing that. Once upon a time, I would have cringed at these thoughts, at crossing that line between pain, pleasure, and death and playing with it...but now? I crave it, I want it. I want him to try and kill me, to bring me untold pleasure as he does.

He lies between my thighs, his long, lean fingers tracing through my wetness, and his eyes meet mine as he sucks his fingers into his mouth. Jair closes his eyes for a moment as he moans my name. "You taste like death," he whispers.

Fuck.

Reaching down, I clutch his hair, dragging him towards my pussy and making him laugh. "Now," I demand.

The first touch of his tongue against my slick folds has me bucking, pushing my pussy to his face. His hands dig into my thighs, keeping me still for his attention. I'm at his mercy and it only makes me needier. I'm so close to coming already, all it would take is...

Yes.

His tongue dives into my pussy before pulling out and flicking my clit over and over again. Some men tease, play, but he doesn't. He demands my pleasure, forcing it from my body as his fingers dive into my channel, stretching me, pressing against those nerves inside.

Grinding against him, I watch him desperately, my eyes wild, breath panting. My whole body tingles, and I try to resist the rising heat, but I can't. I'm so close, so close...

He turns his head and bites my thigh, making me scream in release. It comes over me so suddenly, the pain making it so much stronger, my back actually bows. Rearing up over me, he grabs my legs, throws them around his waist as he lines up his cock, and pushes inside my still clenching pussy.

Wrapping my arms around his shoulders, I drag him back down, turning my head to offer him my neck. He laps at my vein as he drives into me again and again, his cock slightly curved so it hits that point inside me. It's brutal, raw, and dirty.

It's fucking.

It's claiming.

His cock is almost cold, and the sensation of that icy caress inside my molten heat causes me to cry out and clench around him again, wanting it. Wanting to feel that ice-cold touch everywhere.

"Bite me," I beg, wrapping my legs higher around him, making him slip farther in until he's bumping my cervix. That touch of pain, coupled with him dragging along my nerves has me climbing back up to another release, and I want to reach it with his fangs buried in me as he drains me dry.

"Jair, bite me!" I scream.

He growls, pushing my face down as he buried his fangs in me once more, the flash of pain melting to red-hot pleasure that tracks down my throat, to my chest, and then meets his ice-cold desire building in my belly, twining together. The heat and ice leaves me with nothing but a hole for him, keeping me locked in that sensation as it flows through me repeatedly until suddenly, it explodes in a firework of ice and lava, sweeping me away as something clicks into place.

A bond.

My eyes fly wide, he's my mate!

His teeth leave my neck as he grunts, burying his face there as I feel his cum fill me, his hips stopping. Panting, we lie there, wrapped in each other's arms with blood dripping from my neck, cum from my pussy, and a smile curving my lips.

Leaning up on his arms, he stares down at me with a smile as he pushes my sweaty hair away from my neck and gently cups my cheek. His touch is so opposite to how he just fucked me.

"Well, I didn't expect that," he remarks, and I swallow, my throat dry.

"Me neither," I reply, my voice hoarse. I feel a bit weak from the blood loss and my thighs are shaking still, but it was worth it. "We are mates," I mutter, as much for me as him.

"I felt it, I felt you click into place. That part of me that had always been missing, like when air comes back into the room or when you feed and it just feels right. Your edges match mine perfectly, sealing me, rebuilding me to make me whole again. I have been waiting all my life for this, for you. My heart once belonged to another. It's damaged and used, but it's yours, as is my soul. They always belonged to you."

"And it will always be theirs as well. Your daughter and wife. I will never replace them. It's not a competition, you can still love them and me. I'll share that space with them, I want to see them in your memories, see how they made you into the man I met here."

"Dawn." His eyes mist and he sighs, resting his head against mine. "That was a lifetime ago. Sometimes I feel like it happened to someone else, but thank you."

His eyes go to the blood, which is dripping slowly from my neck, and he winces. "Sorry, let me heal that."

I stop him with a hand on his face. "Wait, will it scar?"

"It will if I don't heal it," he answers, confused.

"Then leave it, I'll wear it proudly."

I feel his cock jerk inside me, making us both groan as he gets hard again. Digging my feet into his ass, I start to rock against him and he meets my movements with shallow, slow thrusts. Our eyes remain locked in shared pain and need.

Both of us have suffered, both of us have died and were reborn into something else...

Both of us found each other in the dark.

"I will always find you," he whispers.

The fucking turns into something else, something softer. Emerging from all that need, anger, and blood lust is something beautiful and strong.

Us.

WITH NOTHING ELSE TO DO, we sit and talk. He wraps me in his arms and tells me stories of all the places he's seen and people he's met over the years. He builds me kingdoms and palaces from words, winding the tales around me until I feel like I'm there.

Each one of my mates offers me something different, a strength, a weakness, a chance to be better. To build and grow. And each time I'm in their arms, it feels perfect, special. It doesn't feel the same or get old, it always feels right. And if Griffin or Nos or Dume or Aska walked in right now, I would be just as excited to see them.

I know this won't be uneventful forever, there will be jealousy and fights, but we can handle it. We can handle anything together. In a way, being locked up down here with nothing but my thoughts to occupy me has given me a chance to really look inside myself.

With no ex to hunt, I've stopped for a time, taking a break, and it makes me realise just how much I've grown to care for all of them —even Jair, whom I just met. They all have a piece of me. It's a dark and damaged piece, but it's me. I know we have enemies on all sides and life will never be easy. We are going to have to fight each and every day, but when the aftermath comes in such a sexy, depraved package like my mates, can I really complain?

Besides, wasn't that what I was doing as a human? Only back then I had no one to fight by my side, to watch my back, to care if I lived or died.

Now I have five creatures who care. Who will always be there, who will never hurt me—unless I want them to—who will never abandon me, or deem me not good enough.

It's mating, it's forever, and I'm beginning to see just how amazing that is. The rage I once felt melts to something softer, brighter almost, with shades of grey thrown in.

Being good isn't the best thing a person can be, and it depends on whom you surround yourself with. If you live in the light, but you live alone, is living and loving in the dark really such a wrong thing?

I don't think so.

We hear it then, the booted feet heading our way, and it pops our bubble of happiness. Sighing, I look up at Jair. "Time to play again. Next time I see you, we are putting the plan into place. It's time to show them exactly what kind of monsters they have kept locked up."

He grins with an evil look in his eyes, and I know I have the same one. Monsters recognise one another, after all. "Until then, my rising moon, make them hurt." He kisses me soundly before helping me to my feet. Stepping back, he pretends to be chained as I wait in front of the door, hoping they won't look too closely at him.

The door swings outward and five guards stand there sneering at me. "Well, hello again," I purr. "I'm afraid we got a little bored and decided to have some fun, hope that's okay?"

"Grab her, Amos wants to talk to her," one orders.

"Oooh, Assmos? Why didn't you say so, let's go." Winking back at Jair, I push through the guards, whistling as I start to saunter away, feeling them gape after me.

I hear the cell door slam shut then they soon catch up with me. One grabs my arm, but after Jair's loving touch, I find myself hating their hands on me, so doing as Jair prompted, I rip out his throat with my nails.

Stepping over the body, I carry on walking. "Don't touch me."

They yell and get mad, but don't try to guide me again. Instead, two walk behind and two stride in front as my hand steadily drips blood behind me like a Hansel and Gretel trail.

Let's see what the great and powerful Assmos wants now. I hope he has cake this time. I'm famished after all the fucking and blood drinking. I wonder if I told him that I wouldn't kill any more guards if he would get me some?

See? I can be a good prisoner, assface, now cake please?

I doubt it, might be worth a try though.

CHAPTER 33

GRIFFIN

Sliding the tray through the hole in the cell door, I snatch my hand back as a stone claw comes through and seizes it. Grumbling, I throw the now empty trolley into the storage cupboard. Why the fuck am I being a maid again? Oh, that's right, my mate has a plan.

I should have just grabbed her and got her out of here when I had the chance, but she distracted me with her logic and boobs and now I'm stuck serving all the crazy fucking monsters and criminals the council keeps down here. It's taken me over a day to do my section and exhaustion is settling in, so I head back to the nephilim sleeping quarters. Some of them are already asleep, one even has a knife in his grasp as he snores.

The fucking psychos, and people think I'm crazy, it's no surprise when I grew up with these nut jobs.

I head to the back of the room, past the beds, and find a corner I can put my back to. I need sleep, but I'm not trusting them not to attack me when I'm weak. Sliding down the wall, I press my spine against the cold brick and pull out two blades, one in each hand, and close my eyes.

I know I need sleep, I need to be rested and strong for whatever my mate has planned, but shutting my eyes is like sleeping in a viper's nest and sends a shot of adrenaline through me as I wait for them to attack...but then nothing happens.

I start to relax, sighing as my body unlocks from its defensive position, and I slump tiredly as the adrenaline drains away. The cold from the floor seeps through my wrinkled clothes, making me shiver. The air is stale and smells like you would expect with over forty men asleep in here—bad. I focus on everything else, trying to get my mind to settle. I anchor myself in the moment, what can I smell, feel, and hear...

Eventually I relax enough so I start to feel myself drift off to sleep. I sleep half awake, keeping my ears open for any attacks, but the room is quiet other than the rhythmic ticking of a clock.

"Mum," I call, my fist propped under my chin as I watch the hands on the clock move slowly. "Where is he? He promised to be here by five, but it's now half past. He's always late! He promised this time, promised me!"

I hear her sigh. "I don't know, sometimes I wonder if he cares," she whispers quietly, and I know I shouldn't have heard that, but sometimes she forgets I don't have human hearing. I turn my head, spotting her worrying her bottom lip as she looks at the clock herself before seeming to shake it off and perk up. "I don't know, baby, he probably got held up working—"

"Like always, we see him less and less, does-does he even love us anymore?" I ask, my bottom lip wobbling uncontrollably as tears fill my eyes. "Is it me? Something I did? Am I not good enough? Is that why he doesn't love us? I can be better! I swear!"

She rushes over and drops to her knees before me, cupping my face as her human eyes fill with sadness and anger even though her voice is soft. "Shush, baby, no. You know he loves you very much, sometimes he just gets distracted with work is all. Everyone has their downfalls, Griff, but we love them for it even more because those imperfections make them real. You are an amazing son, the best he could have ever asked for, so don't ever question that again!" She squeezes my cheeks harder then, forcing my lips to create a fish face, and she smiles in return, like the sunshine through a cloud. "There, how can anyone not love that squishy little face?"

"Mum!" I protest, pulling away softly, remembering my own strength versus hers and not wanting to hurt her.

She laughs but drops her hands, clasping my own on my lap. "He loves us, baby, don't ever question that, he just doesn't know how to show it. He's not like us."

"Soft? Weak?" I say, throwing back the words of the other kids.

"Strong," she corrects in a stern voice. "It takes true strength to love, Griffin, true strength to admit someone is your weakness and let them in anyway. Only the strongest of us love, because to love is to give someone the keys to hurt you."

"What...what if they hurt you?" I question, looking away from her eyes, tracing the wrinkled hands clutching mine. Her body is getting weaker by the day. Dad—Gabriel—says it's because she's getting old. I asked him if I would, and he said he didn't know, that we would have to see.

"Then they hurt you. That hurt shows you just how deeply you cared. And in that hurt you find your true strength, you find the will to carry on, and eventually you will discover that sometimes heart-break is the best thing to happen to you because it teaches you lessons and only makes you wiser for the next time. Don't be afraid to love, Griffin, it's scary, unpredictable, and imperfect, but it's also beautiful, life affirming, and the reason we live. We search our whole lives to love someone, and when you find them you hold on tight and don't let go. You love everything about them, every quirk, every flaw, every failure because it shows you who they really are, that they love you enough to show you them."

"Do you love me?" I query, trying to understand what she's

saying. It doesn't add up to the cruel names the other kids call me for caring, for loving. Or even the clinical, almost cruel way my father describes the necessity for companionship.

"With all my heart. You are my miracle, Griffin. The reason I keep on living, the reason I fight all those bastards out there, and sometimes even your father. I love you more than this human heart can hold." She presses her hand against her heart and then mine, listening as it beats along with hers. "You have such a capacity for love, my boy, don't throw that away. Be strong. This world will try to tear you down, don't let it."

She smiles then, it's beautiful and imperfect like she describes. Her teeth are slightly crooked, her lips hanging higher on one side, but it's familiar and the one she gives me every night and every morning. It reminds me of home, of love, and I am finally beginning to understand what she means.

"Mum—" She starts to fade away and I jerk, my hands reaching out to grab her as she disappears into mist, the smile on her face turning sad.

"Be strong, baby, trust yourself," she whispers.

"Mum!" I scream.

A hand covers my mouth and I jolt awake, realising I had fallen into a deep sleep. Fuck. My eyes connect with those of the two nephilim above me. They seem familiar somehow, but I don't have time to connect the dots because they are hauling me to my feet. I fight back, slashing out with my knives, and I hear one grunt as I hit my target, but then a black bag is placed over my head and I'm disoriented. I'm guided from the room and I feel cold air hit my body as we head outside.

I stop fighting, saving my strength for whatever they have planned. They are silent and I feel the gravel give way to grass under my feet. Suddenly I'm jerked around and my face is smashed into something strong and rough. A tree? Maybe. My hands are tugged around the wide trunk and I growl, slashing with my knives again, but a grunt escapes me when they break both wrists, my knives falling to the ground with an audible thud. My hands are tied, the razor wire cutting into my injured wrists which I can feel trying to knit back together. They step away then, and I can hear their ragged breathing from somewhere behind me.

Grinding my teeth, I tug on the razor wire. It's tight, but I could cut through my wrists if need be to escape, except I don't know how long it would take for it to heal and I would be weak from blood loss. Plus, what would I do? I can't hurt them back, the council would have me killed. It would give them proof that I'm the mad dog they call me.

No, I need to be strong. I've survived worse, I can survive this. As long as they don't kill me, I can survive it. I repeat it again and again, forcing my mind to toughen up and push all thoughts of my mate away. She makes me feel weak, and I can't afford that now, not if I'm to get through this and back to her side where I belong.

They don't remove the bag, so I can't even see them, instead I close my eyes and focus on my other senses. I can smell them, the scent of wings and the metal they are carrying. I can feel their anger and hatred brushing along my back with the force of it. I hear them shifting, their boots crushing twigs even as they try to stay silent, but they can't stop their breathing or the pounding of their hearts.

"Well, isn't this fun," I deadpan. "Do trees make you hard or something?"

"You fucking abomination," one of them spits, his voice low.

"I've heard that before, you guys need new insults, it just sounds like a pet name now," I taunt. I don't know why, maybe it's a habit. I won't show them my fear, I'll force their hand, mess with their plans. They don't get to see my weaknesses, only Dawn does.

"Do you remember us?" the other one questions, his voice breaking like he can't speak, and that's when it hits me. I know why they are familiar.

I go quiet and the one with the deeper voice laughs. "Oh, I think he does, so he knows why we are here...revenge."

"I was a kid, I had anger issues and you guys were assholes," I snap.

I remember them, and he's right, they want revenge. They had been saying shit about my mum for days, spreading rumours, calling her a whore, weak, a sheep. They made the mistake of saying it to my face the day I had a fight with my dad over slapping my mum. It was their blunder.

As much as I like to believe the darkness, the madness hiding inside me was created the day they took my wings, I know differently deep down. I was born with it. I've always had it. Yes, they brought it out that day, but it appeared one other day before. That day with these two. I had waited for them, attacked them. The one with the ruined voice? I ripped out his throat with my bare hands and put it around my neck like a trophy. Later, I handed it to my mum as a way of telling her they couldn't hurt her anymore with their words. The other? Let's just say it's a good job we can't have kids, because there's no way he ever could now.

Afterwards, my mother had been horrified, and that's when I realised I had done something bad. Something really messed up, something only a monster would do. She looked at me differently after that, as if she finally understood I wasn't human but something else, something capable of killing and hurting in ways she couldn't imagine. Oh, she still loved me, but it was tinged with fear. I hated them for making our last moments filled with that. I blame these assholes for it. Maybe I would have been triggered some other way, maybe I wouldn't have. All I know is they are the reason I became scared of myself, of what hides within. I buried it deeply after that, never letting it show, becoming perfectly in control, cold even. It was easier if I didn't feel, because then I couldn't react. I saw the sadness in my mother's eyes as I became more and more like my father, but I did it for her. To protect her from me.

"I didn't know any better," I growl. "I was a kid, we were all kids. Plus you totally had it coming. Tell me, how's the cockless life going?"

One of them growls, and I hear the other nephilim holding him back. "You are nothing but a feral animal," the one with the ruined throat tells me. "Do you know how they break feral animals?"

"If they can't tame them, they kill them," the other one continues, "but before that comes a whole lot of pain. We are going to tame you, Griffin, but I really hope we can't. I have been dreaming about killing you since I was thirteen."

"All I'm hearing is that you have dirty wet dreams about me. Kind of weird," I tease.

"I hope that humour helps you survive this," he growls.

Something thick, barbed, and sharp slices across my back. It tears through my shirt and skin as pain flashes through me in white-hot heat. A groan slips out from the suddenness of the attack, but then I bite down to stop any more sounds from escaping.

Weakness is strength.

Pain is living.

I can do this.

The lash comes again and again, and they leave different stints between the hits so I can't predict them. I only hear the slither as it slices through the air, heading for my unprotected back which is already on fire. My body stiffens at the sound, making the pain worse. I feel the skin trying to stitch back together again, but there are too many wounds, so it's slow going. I feel blood coating me, dripping down my back to my trousers and to the ground below. Like a sacrifice to the earth.

They laugh as I writhe in agony, a scream trapped in my throat. Unwillingly, my mind reaches for Dawn, needing to feel her loving touch for just a moment. It was the wrong thing to do as she fills my mind instantly, gasping in pain. She feels the next lash and the lash after that, I try to push her out to block her off, but she won't leave.

Her anger and hatred fills my head, her utter helplessness at not being here to kill them. I feel it, the need to bathe in their blood, to stop the pain they are inflicting on something she has claimed...something she loves.

It gives me strength, her love guides me, and I try to make my mental voice as strong as possible.

Calm down, Vasculo, this is just a bit of foreplay. See you soon.

Then I push her from my mind and block it off so she can't come back, so that she doesn't have to witness this humiliation, to see the weakness of her mate and let the pain rip through her. No, this is mine to deal with.

And she reminded me of one thing—we are not victims.

Not anymore.

I'm stronger now, because of her. Fuck this and fuck them.

I let her anger twine with mine, and it fills me up, blocking out the pain with icy tendrils of utter madness. It reaches for me, telling me I can make it stop, that it can help me.

Fuck this. The madness takes over and I let it. I hide in it like a child huddling in the dark, crying for his mum. Pain flows through me and I realise I've ripped my wrists open on the wire, but I am free. Blood flows quickly from my body and I instantly feel light-headed, but I ignore it as I tear away the bag and turn with a snarl to see the two fallen.

My wrists blaze in agony as they stitch together, but I don't give them the time I need, no, I move, uncaring about the pain or the damage. All that fills me is the hate I feel for these men.

They unlocked this madness when we were kids, and now they will feel the full wrath of it. I will kill them like I should have back then, without mercy or tenderness. They are dead men walking.

The one with the messed-up throat and a vicious-looking scar marring it tries to turn and run, no doubt remembering what I did last time and seeing his death in my eyes now.

He dies first.

Grabbing him mid-leap, I break his neck and then rip his head from his body. Using it like a weapon, I throw it at the other nephilim who is also now trying to run. It hits him in the back and sends him to the ground.

I stroll towards him, picking up the whip laced with barbed

wire as I go. My shirt is falling from me in tatters, so I pull it off and let it fall to the grass, the night air stinging the healing cuts on my back, but it only makes me stronger.

I let the whip trail along the earth, hissing over the leaves until I stand above the man. He freezes, locked there like prey smelling a predator. I guess he does. All his life he was taught to be the perfect weapon, the perfect slave. It makes them unable to think for themselves, unable to react quickly enough.

It makes them easy targets.

Lifting the whip into the air, I let him hear it coming, enhancing his fear which permeates the air, and then I bring it down again and again, faster and faster. Droplets of blood and chunks of skin spray as I shred his back. When I stop, my chest is heaving, and I loosely hold the whip in my hand which drips with blood, hair, and skin, and the nephilim is unmoving beneath me.

His back looks like mauled meat, but I don't want him to heal, so lifting his head I rip it off and toss it with the other, leaving them there. Slowly, my madness pulls back with a laugh in my head and I stumble.

Pain hits me and my head spins. During the heat of the moment it had disappeared, but it comes back full force and I drop to my knees on the grass, my body contorting as I try to keep in my screams. Fuck.

My eyes blur as it heals slowly. I feel each cut, each rip stitching back together, and all I can do is crouch here in pain, knowing someone could find me at any moment and I would be sentenced to death. I know what this means—my demise. If they find the bodies, the council will hang me, and it won't be my wings they take this time, but my life.

Dawn.

She flashes through my mind, she needs me. I can't leave her. *Think, Griffin, think!*

"Well, that was impressive," comes a drawl, and I leap to my feet, spinning to see whoever is there. I crouch in a defensive stance. I won't let them take me alive, I'll escape and come back for her.

Titus.

He leans against the tree I was tied to, his face impassive, but there is a smile in his eyes as he watches me. He runs his gaze across the bodies and then back to me. "Well, well, well, fallen. I've got to admit, I didn't expect you to have it in you."

"I—" I fumble with words, fuck. I can't kill him, they will launch an investigation and then I will be killed for sure, but how do I get out of this?

Escape is my only option, but I'm weak and still healing, so I won't get far. I'm at his mercy and he knows it. He sighs before standing up and stepping towards me, ignoring my growl.

"Don't worry. I'll tell them I caught these two trying to leave and killed them." He glances at the back of the nephilim I used the whip on and rolls his eyes. "Not before punishing them, of course."

I stare at him in shock and confusion, but distrust winds through me. The only reason he would help me, lie to his own people about this, was if he needed something, and I don't think I could afford the price, but what other option do I have?

"Why are you helping me?" I snap, my voice lined with pain. My energy is waning now and I stumble forward. I need to rest, not stand here arguing, but I have to know why. He notices and looks around before moving closer, his arm held out to help me, but I push him away and straighten of my own accord.

"Come with me," is all he says, and then he starts to walk. Titus stops at the edge of the trees and looks back, waiting for me. I hesitate, but what choice do I have? Maybe he's leading me to my death, maybe not, but unless I magically heal and can escape him, I have no other option.

I step towards him and his lips turn up slightly. He waits until I reach his side. My eyes narrowed, I threaten, "Try to kill me or betray me and I will rip out your heart and feed it to the monsters in your dungeons."

"Noted." He laughs. "Come, I am not here to harm you, fallen."

"My name is Griffin," I snarl, and he tilts his head to the side.

"As you wish, Griffin, come." Then he turns and winds through the trees and I follow.

HE LEADS me through the forest, and just when I think he's going to turn around and laugh and kill me, he bends down and pulls open a trap door hidden there. He glances back up at me for a moment before dropping into the dark.

This is a bad idea.

But I descend down there anyway. It's black, utterly black for a moment before I hear the strike of a match, and then he illuminates the tunnel with a candle. He passes it to me before climbing back up and shutting the hatch. He takes the candle back and then heads down the passageway without talking.

I follow behind him at a safe distance, noticing the cobwebs on the curved walls which are brick and, unlike the dungeon, there are no claw or escape marks. So what is this place...and where does it lead to?

"Where are we going?" I ask, my voice loud in the quiet. He doesn't answer me but keeps on walking, our boots splashing in the small puddles of water floating at the bottom of the tunnel.

We walk for another five minutes before it starts to curve upwards, then it ends in stairs. Titus places the candle on a holder there and blows it out. At the top of the steps is a square of light escaping through cracks of a thin door frame.

He uses it to climb the stairs and waits for me there, letting me decide what to do. I don't trust him, that's for sure, but I can't go back, so the only way I can possibly go is forward. I follow him up the stairs and wait behind him as he unlocks the door, swings it open, and steps through.

I follow again and look around in shock. Where the hell are we?

It has to be in the council's mansion, but I've never seen this room before, and if they were trying to show off power this would be a good chamber to do so. It's lined with gold. Gold frames house various watercolours of supernaturals in their forms. Golden lamps sit on a mahogany desk in the corner with the lights on. A golden chandelier hangs with what I can only guess are real diamonds.

Everything is gold.

It's so fucking over the top.

There are two emerald green sofas pushed together in a L-shape underneath a gold, ornate mirror on the left wall with a small table between them. Titus heads to a bar in the other corner, pours two tumblers of amber liquid, and strolls my way. He presses one into my hand before sitting on the sofa, his legs crossed.

Testing him, I throw myself down on the other one, making sure to cover it in blood and sweat, and then I put my dirty, mud-caked boots on the table and cross them at the ankles. Sipping the liquid, I watch him. He doesn't even flinch or frown, he doesn't care. That, more than anything, tells me he's different from the other council members, but why? And why help me?

"Where are we?" I inquire. I struggle not to move around as my back starts to itch with the healing. He sips his drink before placing it on his knee and letting his head fall to the back of the sofa, his eyes closing as he sighs.

"A safe place away from prying eyes. It's cut into the walls, and only the original council knew about this. They used it as a hideout, a safe room, and to spy on people," he explains.

"How did they spy?" I press, deciding I might as well get information out of him while he's talking. It's rare for him to be speaking, never mind to offer anything.

"Through that mirror, it shows the private council chambers where meetings are held," he replies without looking at me.

"So why bring me here? Why tell me that? These secrets are dangerous."

"So are you." He shrugs.

"Who are you?" I question. He's a mystery, he knows about the rooms and tunnels not even the council does. He's powerful yet doesn't show off, and I'm not sure Titus is even his real name.

Most importantly, is he friend or foe?

"A friend," he offers.

"I don't have any," I growl back, but then that's a lie, isn't it? Dawn flashes through my mind, as does Nos.

"Fine, I'm not an enemy, Griffin, so stop looking for ulterior motives." He exhales wearily.

"No one helps someone without a reason, especially not council members, so what's your reason, Titus? What's your story? Where did you come from?" I counter, throwing back my drink and letting the glass drop to the table with a thud.

He sits up, sipping his drink and watching me. "Knowledge is power, haven't you ever heard that?"

"Yes, so, what, you're going to use this against me?"

"No, I don't need to. But I needed you alive, for now at least," he admits.

"At least that's the fucking truth. Fine, what for?"

"You'll see." He grins. "To answer your question, Titus is my name...now. It wasn't always, I had another given to me by the man who made me."

He nods then.

"Yes, like you. We have more in common than you could ever imagine, Griffin. I know everyone wonders what I am, but the truth is I am not one thing. I am so much more, a mix, a powerful one. I'm here because it is where I need to be, because I have things that need to be done. And you come into that plan, Griffin."

"You were made? How? By who?" I ask, interested now. I feel my strength slowly returning, and every minute that passes relaxes me. He's not here to attack me. I might not understand his reasons, but that's clear.

"By a human many, many years ago. He created me out of fear and need, but I wasn't the original, I was simply the first that went well. I didn't try to kill him and had my own mind and soul, which is a tricky thing to create. But he bore me out of hate, Griffin, and fear and hate are strong emotions. It made me into a cold monster, as did the way I was brought up. I wasn't a child, no, I was born into a man's body and thrust into a world of pain and war. So let me assure you, I understand what it means to be called an abomination, an experiment. They will never know that I am one as well, but just think..." He grins. "A monster, a fucking experimentation on their own council, the thing they fear and hate most. Brilliant, isn't it? Anyway, we have to stick together, so believe me when I say I mean you no harm."

He turns his wrist then, looking at his watch and sighing. He drains the glass and adds it to the table with mine as he stands and tugs his shirt back into place, it doesn't dare defy him. I sit watching him. "Council meeting time. Why don't you stay? You might find it...illuminating." He winks and then heads to a painting on the other wall. "Oh, and Griffin? Don't worry about those men, they are nothing. You? You have a destiny." He opens the painting, steps out, and closes it again with a click.

The room is silent, and I debate his words before standing and peering through the mirror he said was a spying aid. It must be a two-way mirror, but only able to be seen one way? Smart, really. I wonder who made this. He said the original council...the sleeping council? Why would they need to spy on their own officials? Unless they trust them as little as the rest of us do.

Like Titus mentioned, it shows the inside of the council chambers. The four walls are soundproof, so no one can hear in, and the giant golden door is locked from the inside, so I've never even glimpsed it before, but I can tell from the table. A massive, wooden, ornate piece takes up the middle of the room with six throne-like chairs spread around it.

There isn't much else in the room except for a fire which is lit and a small serving area in one corner with yet another bar. Leaning against the wall, I watch as the door opens and the council files in. The last one is Amos, who sits at the head of one end of the table, while Titus takes the other, surprising me.

"Meeting is called to order. Does anyone have any issues to discuss?" Amos calls, sitting back in his chair like a king. I almost snort, but I don't know if they can hear me, so I stay silent, watching instead, collecting intel.

"Not an issue, just informing everyone I had to dispatch two of your little loyal servants, they tried to escape and then attack me when I caught them. I punished one and then killed them both. Their bodies are currently decorating the east woods," Titus says in a bored voice.

I see Amos jerk, his face darkening in anger. "You do not have the power to dispatch any of my spies without first consulting me."

"You are not in charge yet, Amos. We are all entitled to punish our servants if we feel they are disrespectful, unless you feel you are better or deserving of more power than the rest of the council?" Titus challenges, a grin playing on his lips, knowing he has backed the man into a corner.

"Titus is correct. If they were escaping, then they are useless to us. Moving on," Derrin declares, his eyes looking at the clock on the wall.

"I have been hearing rumours," Greta starts, and Amos rolls his eyes, "of missing supernaturals. Has anyone else?"

"Of course, we hear it all the time, nothing more than made-up stories. They have probably run off." Amos waves it away, but she leans forward.

"I do not think so. I trust these sources, and I do not think we should dismiss this so easily. We already have people questioning our leadership, so I think we should make a stand, show them why we lead and figure out what is happening among our own people."

Fuck, I wasn't expecting that, and it tells me two things. One, Amos is a part of this but not all of the council is. I analyse their faces, trying to note those who appear to be in agreement, but it's hard, they have all had hundreds of years at perfecting their poker faces.

"Understood, we will monitor, and if the situation gets worse we will, of course, figure it out," Amos concedes before looking around. "Any other issues?"

"There has been movement from the dragons. A source of mine informs me one broke through the gate and has since disappeared. I will continue to keep my eyes and ears open to ensure this was not a random occurrence," Derrin offers.

"Dragons," Greta scoffs. "They wouldn't step foot here, they think it is beneath them."

"There have been rumblings," Titus interjects, tracing his hand across the wood in thought. "At Rejek."

Rejek?

The...the old mountain? I frown at that. I thought it was dead, cursed ground where no one walked. Why would it be rumbling with activity and why would they be monitoring a dead mountain?

Amos glowers with contemplation in his eyes. "Indeed? How much...rumbling?"

"Abnormal amounts," Titus responds, seeming happy about this news.

"I will send a message to confirm everything is okay," Amos replies, distracted. "I will do that at once, we don't need them interfering."

"Why? Hiding something?" Titus retorts, and Amos narrows his eyes.

"It is for the best of us all. You are too young to remember the last time they walked among us, it was chaos. There was so much death, and half the council was killed as an example and replaced," Amos snaps, standing and pressing his fists onto the table.

"Indeed?" Titus mocks. "Maybe that wouldn't be a bad thing."

The others look back and forth between them, but it's clear these two butting heads isn't an unusual occurrence.

"I am confident you do not want that to happen, Titus, and that if they did come here, they would agree with every decision I've made, which has nothing but the betterment of our people and their interests at heart. Now, if you will excuse me, the meeting is adjourned."

Amos turns and leaves the room, walking swiftly while the others talk amongst themselves as they exit, but Titus stays behind, turning his head and staring at me through the mirror like he can truly see me. I have so many questions, and that look only gives me more.

Whose side is Titus on?

His own? Ours? It's clear it's not Amos's.

So if all of the council members are not in on this, then I need to find out which members are before we kill them. My job just got a whole lot harder.

CHAPTER 34

ASKA

W hen I cannot drive any longer, I take to the sky, flying the remaining distance to Rejek. I text Jean Paul and Nos beforehand to let them know where I am going. I hear back from neither, but then again, I am impatient and only give them thirty seconds.

I soar over the frozen tundra, mountains, and fields. Civilization is left behind as I head to the very peak of the country, an unforgotten corner too dangerous for humans and most supernaturals. It doesn't help that the mountain is believed to be cursed, which I suppose makes sense as a council location. They are the oldest of us, after all. One is awake at all times to rule over the others and step in only in dire circumstances. They are relics of lost years...yet now we need them. More than ever.

Let's hope they don't kill me on sight.

The flight takes over two hours before I see the first stirrings of the mountain. The air starts to get thick and cloudy until I can barely see in front of my face, and I am forced to glide lower, almost touching a frozen lake surrounded by trees. Even then it is foggy, an unnatural fog. I feel it passing over me, judging me for what I am.

A security measure, no doubt.

I soar above it and over the trees, and then a black shape comes in to view ahead. I turn that direction, knowing it must be the mountain. I can feel the old magic there, pushing me away, warning me to leave.

It forms through the clouds and fog, stretching so far into the sky I can't see the tip of it. Flattening my wings, I push higher and higher, climbing through the clouds until I reach the peak, which is an open top, giving me a clear view downwards into the base of the mountain that is far, far down.

It's a volcano.

A dormant one, clearly, and I can feel the net over the top to protect the opening from attack. To keep things in...or out? I'm not sure, but I can't get in that way, so I tuck in my wings and dive, flying around each side as I try to find an entrance.

I have to circle three more times and open my mind, pushing out my powers to search the thick, black rock until I locate the opening the ghosts mentioned. A concealed entrance sits at the base behind it, hidden by the edge of the cliff it stands on. If you didn't have the power or knowledge of how to look, you wouldn't find it. They really were not taking any chances.

I set down on the edge of the cliff and change back, lifting my head as I reach for Dawn.

I will be there soon, hold on.

Let's hope the sleeping council doesn't try to kill me. It would be horrible to explain to my mate why we have the whole supernatural world hunting us down if I murder them.

Sucking in the cold air one more time, I head into the carved black doorway. I feel a boundary pass over me instantly and I drop to my knees in agony. I can't breathe, can't see, or even hear. I lose track of everything, and I seem to be spinning, but I could be wrong. Heat starts at the soles of my feet and travels through my body like lava erupting from my head.

The sensation surges repeatedly until I am screaming. At least I think I am, it's hard to tell. But I am a dragon and this is fire. I let the change flow through me, and the cool feeling of the souls trapped in my dragon sooth the burn until I flick open my eyes, my tail dancing behind me as my mouth expands to eat whoever did that to me...

But there is no one there.

Surely that couldn't be a deterrent to get out? If so, what else will be lingering the closer I get...that one nearly killed me as it is. And Griffin said I was antisocial, these guys take it to a whole new level. Forcing the change when I realise I won't fit through the path that seems to lead up through the caldera, I let my bare human feet meet the sharp rocks, which instantly cut into them. My blood puddles on the black, shiny stone for a moment before being absorbed, like the rock itself is tasting me.

I shiver, I can't wait to get out of here. A bad feeling pushes through me at being here, my dragon roaring to flee. Who and what exactly is on the sleeping council? I wish I had asked.

But I push forward, knowing Griffin will never let me live it down if I come back empty-handed or abscond from the mountain. He will be all, 'oh big, bad dragon got scared? Poor baby,' and then I will have to gut him, and that will really put a damper on my relationship with Dawn.

Muttering to myself, I head farther into the volcano. I insult Griffin and his stupid wings, which are more decorative that functional—I mean, come on...feathers? He can't even kill anyone with them! Next I start on his stupid, pretty face, the crazy bastard.

My muttering only stops when the rocks on either side of me give way and open up into a giant hole in the volcano. Okay then. Standing on the edge, I look around for stairs or a path, but there isn't one, there is just blackness below me in a chasm, and darkness above me.

And I thought Griffin wasn't very hospitable.

Leaping forward, I change mid-air, catching the upstream and flapping my wings to carry me upwards. I'm hoping that's where they are, they wouldn't be down, right? Who knows, this whole place is a maze.

I spot another open cave near the top, which seems a lot taller than the outside, undoubtedly with more magic. I have to change mid-flight and throw myself forward to get into the cave. Rolling to my feet, I come face-to-face with a small man wearing a drab, grey tunic tied at the top with short brown hair. His eyes are wide and alarmed. In his hand is a jug, and I sniff to smell whisky.

"Hello," I greet, and he squeaks like a mouse and takes off back into the cave, his feet slapping against the rock. I hear the squeal slowly grow quieter and quieter until it disappears.

Well, that was odd.

Shrugging, I follow after him at a normal pace, wondering if he has gone to warn the sleeping council or whoever is awake. They felt me enter, I know it, unless they were distracted. Wait, do they actually sleep? What if they are asleep right now and he panicked because they didn't feel my arrival?

The tunnel curves around and down a bit, with carved stone stairs that assist in my descent, until it opens up into what looks like a throne room where two angry-looking supernaturals are standing with the small man hiding behind them and pointing towards me.

They both turn my way. One's eyes flash gold, while the other grins, even as mist swirls around him.

"Hello, do you have any appointments available to speak to the council?" I inquire, and then almost cringe at that. Who storms into a volcano, which is cursed and protected by magic, hunting a sleeping council to save their mate, and then is that polite?

"I mean, I need to see the sleeping council!" I demand, and raise my chin.

"Well, well, a dragon, how interesting. How did you get past the guards, I wonder?" the one with the black eyes muses, stepping by the infuriated man who is glaring at me as if I have burned down his home and then asked him to cook me dinner.

"It was easy, I am a king, after all." I sniff.

His lips quirk up again. He's taller than me, skinnier though, but has some bulk. The power that is leaking from him is staggering and his face, though just as beautiful as my own, has an edge to it—it's too perfect. Too sharp, too many angles. His eyes are dark, and his eyebrows slope down even as he smirks. I can almost see the outline of a giant monster behind him in the mist that swirls around him.

What is he?

"Not something you have ever encountered before, dragon, I can assure you," he answers, addressing my thought, and I startle.

"Serpent, this is not protocol! That—this is disturbing, unruly, and against all our laws! We must kill him!" the other man yells, but the first, Serpent, ignores him and tilts his head, watching me closely as a dog comes to his side...if dogs measure to your chest and look like the spawn of evil. Yet the man pets its head like a treasured toy without one ounce of fear on his face.

"I do not fear what I created. Come, dragon, step inside, tell us why you are here."

"You step too far, Serpent! You crave chaos and now look where this has brought us—" The other man's voice cuts off in a gargle as the serpent whirls and rips out his throat, throwing it to the servant like a trophy. He then turns back to me.

"There, that will keep him quiet for a while, he does talk too much." He turns and heads up a dais I didn't see before and sits on a throne, throwing his legs carelessly over it as his...pet sits at his feet, its red eyes glaring at me.

I step into the room, the rock solid under my feet. The ceiling is massive here, reaching high up with floating lanterns. To the right are inscriptions along the floor, almost flaring with magic. The servant is standing there, still holding the throat as he looks from it to the other man and back again.

"M-Master, I—what shall I do with this?" he asks, fear coating his tone as he lifts up the other man's trachea.

"Whatever you would like to do with it. Bring us something to drink," the serpent calls, and waves him away, his eyes locked on me with interest. "So, dragon, why are you here? Not many would be able to find us, never mind get through our barriers. You had to know this would be a death sentence, so tell me why?"

"For my mate," I tell him, stepping farther into the room. The hound snarls and I still.

"Ahh, love." He spits the word 'love' like it's a falsehood, and I raise an eyebrow. "Or maybe just lust. Free piece of advice, dragon, love is a lie, always trust lust." He pats the hound. "So, your mate, what does she or he have to do with you seeking us out?"

"She, she's in danger—"

"How marvellous, why should we care?" he interrupts, and I force back my growl. I can't be a 'rich prick,' as Griffin said, around this man, he could kill me with a blink of an eye. I can feel it. Even a dragon knows when they are beat, and this man is some-thing...old. Ancient, dark, and powerful, maybe even a god.

"Because that danger is your council," I offer instead.

He blinks. I've shocked him, I can tell. "Those pompous assholes, what have they done now?"

It's my turn to blink, he doesn't like them? "They are kidnap-ping female supernaturals and experimenting on them, humans too. It is starting to get noticed. Human police are involved and now hunters are working with the council," I summarise quickly.

He leaps to his feet with a roar, the room filling with darkness that seems to suffocate me. I have trouble breathing and fall to my knees, and when it finally clears, I get a look at the true monster I am dealing with and it steals my breath once again.

If he doesn't kill us, he might just be the key to saving Dawn.

He stands before me, no longer a man, his curved horns touching the ceiling. His eyes are black, and in them I see roaring flames. His mouth is wide and filled with rows and rows of sharp teeth like a shark. His face is skeletal but covered in flesh, and he has no eyebrows, but his hair remains the same. His body is wider than even my dragon's, his arms bigger than my human body. He is covered in nothing but a black piece of cloth over his manly bits, and swirls of red cover his skin, lighting up like I saw a volcano do once while it was erupting. It looks like the flames of hell are trapped inside his body.

He is a true monster and my dragon grins in approval.

"They are stealing women?" he booms, and I hear a noise. Turning, I see the other man getting to his feet, rubbing his throat. He glances up and gawks at the serpent who, with a giant fist, punches the other man straight through the wall. He looks back at me. "I felt pain, it woke me up, the flashes of a woman. She was being kidnapped."

My eyes fly wide, he could mean any woman, he could...but my gut tells me he doesn't. "Blonde hair? Body to die for?"

His eyes narrow. "I did not see." His voice is so deep, like the shifting of rocks, that I feel blood start to drip from my ears. He finally calms down enough to change back. I watch this monstrous form melt, and then he is before me again with determination on his face.

"I was going to find her, she intrigued me. If they have taken her, they will answer to me. Come, dragon, let us free your mate and find out what the council is truly doing. I might even let you help me kill them." He walks past me, the hound on his heels which I swear sticks his tongue out at me.

"She doesn't need rescuing, she can rescue herself, she is strong, really strong. The problem is she will kill all of them. I didn't want you to come after her."

That stops him, and he turns his head, a grin on his face. "Your mate sounds like fun. I can't guarantee I won't kill her, but I would make it quick. Now, are you coming or do you want the angel to resurrect again and kill you?"

Fuck, what have I unleashed on the world?

Chapter 35

Nos

I feel her need, it calls to me. Echoing through my head and heart. The urge to rush to my mate's side is so strong I actually step from the forest. My little monster wants for nothing, yet here she is. Needing me, needing to feed and to fuck and I am not there. I have trust in the fallen, but she is my everything and I am done waiting on the side lines.

I did not become the fabled Cernunnos to hide amongst the trees when the soul I have been waiting for since birth is in need. Turning my head to meet the eyes of the animals waiting for orders, I send the whispers into their head. Giving them instructions on what to do. I have two plans in place.

Give me a minute, I am good.

Give me an hour, I am amazing.

Give me days? I am unstoppable. I could raze this world to the ground and walk amongst the ashes until I found her.

One way or another, the next time I walk free from that house it will either be with my mate or dead. Once they know their roles, I turn back to the house. The early morning light is warming the world, cutting through the dark where humans believe monsters hide.

But monsters don't just work in the dark, no, they live in the light. Amongst you, hiding in plain sight. I am done hiding. Dawn is mine and I am getting her back. I stood by and did nothing once, and all that was left was the empty husks of the people I once cared about.

If I have to become that monster, the one the world fears, to save my mate, then I will. I will gladly feast on their fears as I kill them. I promised myself never again, but when your mate's life hangs in the balance, nothing matters. Not fear of yourself, not promises. Just her.

The world is silent, an eerie stillness as if it is holding its breath for what I will do. I know there is something special about my little monster, something destined, and it seems I am part of that destiny now. Actions have consequences and I can feel the fates' keen eyes locked on me, waiting, wondering.

Maybe this is the reason for my creation, mystics are made for a purpose. The old gods were made to create the races, others were built for a pivotal point in history, but me? I have been waiting...waiting for now?

Dawn is my reason. I will do my duties by the fates and pray they let me live through it to spend a lifetime or two with my mate.

I step from the forest, ready for what is thrown my way. My decision is made, I will pay whatever the consequence may be. As long as my moments are by her side, nothing else matters.

I feel it then, the warm brush of the fates, they whisper to me of destinies and prophecies before blowing away with the wind, and I know I have made the right choice. I am meant to be here, as is Dawn...for what purpose?

We will find out together.

The gravel crunches under my feet as I head to the front gates and wait. Legs spread and head tilted back, I feel the brush of their magic as they try to assess who and what I am. I allow it and I feel them pull back instantly. Shock reverberates through the air.

The gates open like I knew they would, they would not dare deny me access. They once asked me to sit on the council, but being a mystic meant I had no one to represent, and it would have been wrong of me. It did not stop them from trying, and I ultimately walked away and never looked back...so for me to be here?

They are scared of what it means.

I can feel it, taste it on the breeze as I walk up the drive, past the water feature. I sense the bond connected to Dawn pointing downwards, but I do not head there instantly, it would only begin a war. No, for now I will play the political game.

I also feel Griffin, he's angry and in pain, the norm for the fallen.

I brush along his mind and I sense him look up in shock and confusion, but I simply pull back and leap up the steps as the front door to the council house opens. There, standing in the doorway, is Amos, head of the council. He is ruffled, I can tell it immediately. His suit is wrinkled, his cane is held tightly in his right hand, and his eyes are narrowed and lips thin.

"Cernunnos, to what do we owe this pleasure?" He sniffs, probing for information, but I flare out my power and push him back. He stumbles from the force, his face flashing in anger before he smooths it and lifts his chin defiantly. I will not get away with that again, to snub his question was simply etiquette and a proof of power, but to attack him again would suggest I am an enemy and the council would be within their rights to kill me on sight.

The dance of politics begins.

"I simply wished to visit our council and offer my assistance in the case of the missing females," I rumble, bowing my head slightly to show that I still see him as the leader. "You are looking into it, are you not?"

"Well, I am afraid that is private council business—"

"Of course, I ask merely because others have been coming to me with their worries. May I come in?" I inquire with a small smile.

I watch as he tries to come up with a retort, a way to block my entrance, but he can't. I am here with help, and though we both know it hides ulterior motives, he can't call me out for it without breaking etiquette and suggesting I am a spy, which would give me cause to challenge his leadership. His throne is balanced on shaky ground, he needs no more shaking to topple him from it and he recognises that.

Stepping back, he allows me to pass and I stop in the entryway, looking around at the obvious grandeur they are projecting. "I see you have redecorated, it could do with some more nature in my opinion, it would make you seem less..." I look over my shoulder at him, allowing my eyes to flash white, a simple slight. "Dead inside."

His face scrunches up, and I can actually see his eagle feathers ruffling as I turn away. Without being invited, I head to the lounge on the right, making myself at home as I wander around the room. Picking up artefacts and mementoes from history. I hear him follow me, his power washing through the room in a petty display. If only he knew that his tiny drop of power did not even match me on my weakest days, I wonder if he would try to kill me now or later.

Later is my guess, while I was sleeping.

Those kinds of assassinations and subterfuge are the council's game, everything is done behind your back. They smile to your face while their servants plunge the dagger there. "Care to share why you are here and not playing god in your little forest?" he sneers.

"I have already informed you, I had people come to me with concerns on how the council was handling the missing women. I wanted to offer my services as you seem to be struggling," I drawl, and then turning around, I throw myself onto the sofa, taking a note from Griffin's book, making sure to put my dirty boots up on the pristine white sofa. "As always my service is open for our esteemed leaders."

"How touching, but it is not needed." He sniffs, still standing in the doorway.

"No? Well, I will stay for a few days just to ensure that, if you don't mind. Unless you have something to hide?"

I see his cheeks bulge as he grinds his teeth. "The council hides nothing and to speculate that we are is treason."

"No speculation, just ensuring," I clarify, and then rise so quickly he jerks back. "Do not worry, I remember my way around. I don't need an escort."

"Do not think because you are a mystic," he spits, "that it means you get special favour. We are in charge, not you, false god."

Stepping closer, I peer down at him, letting him feel my power. "Then lead, your people are waiting for answers. I suggest you give it to them before there is unrest. It wouldn't be good for your life expectancy, I assume."

Sweeping past him, I start to whistle as I explore the house. I can feel his rage thundering through the walls. He does not like having me here, which means he does have something to hide other than my mate—the question is, what?

I spend the next few hours mapping the house before finding a spare guest room, already made up for when people such as myself stop by. It is on the third floor—I picked the chamber farthest from the council members in the west wing to conceal what I am truly doing. Slinking into the white fur rug before the golden mantle, I cross my legs and place my hands on my knees as I close my eyes.

Letting my mind clear, ignoring the tug in my lower belly urging me to find our mate, I spread out my senses, searching for disturbances or any magic to find what they are hiding.

The dungeons are blocked, as I expected, otherwise they wouldn't be able to contain the monsters of our world down there. The first floor is empty, so I keep going, but every floor I find is vacant bar the magic of the supernaturals here. The council no doubt feels me, but how can they question what I am doing?

They can't.

Tipping up my lips, I expand my senses across the grounds. I find more nephilim out back in what looks like a bunk house. Sweeping past that I keep going, searching, pushing my power until sweat breaks out on my brow.

Just when I am about to pull back, I feel something. The edge of something...power. Stretching out my tendrils, I poke them and they react, swirling with dangerous black magic. It is shielding something, something big at the edge of the property. A building. I glimpse a silver door built into the ground before I am blocked.

It's strong...and ancient. So old that I can't break through the shrouding. What is locked behind that door? And why is it protected with wards that I haven't seen used in over a decade? Does it have something to do with my mate? Or the missing women?

The more I find, the more questions I have.

What is the council doing...and how are we entangled in this web?

CHAPTER 36

DAWN

I'm not led to the sitting room where we met last time, no, this time I'm dragged outside. I gulp in the fresh air, shivering under the midmorning sun as it heats my skin. I have missed this, missed being free. You don't realise the toll of being locked in a dark, damp dungeon until you come up for air. There can be no darkness without light to shade it, and it seems even as I thrive in the dark...I still crave the light.

I'm dragged across the grass, past a pool which looks so inviting. I stifle the urge to push Veyo, the asshole, into the blue water, only just. We move around some bushes and past a training ground. I almost stumble there, because standing in the middle of a circle of what looks like other nephilim is Griffin.

His head is back, his eyes bright and angry. That face I crave is locked in a snarl, his body bulging with power as his wings flare out behind him. He looks like heaven and hell in one sexy package, and I almost say fuck the mission and instead fuck him there and then.

He must feel me because his head turns, those bright eyes locking on me with such intensity that I shiver. I see the questions —where am I going? What's happening? —but I can't answer him. Veyo tugs me again, his hand wrapped around my upper arm. Griffin spares him a glance, but then looks down at his grip on me and I see the change come over him.

The madness enters his gaze, filling it up with black smoke as he transforms into a monster before my very eyes. One intent on getting to his mate. Fuck! As much as I would love to see him rip this man to pieces, I need to speak to Assmos and find out everything.

We have to play this smart for once, not let our killer instinct lead, as hard as it is for both of us.

So, I do the only thing I can think of to do. I turn and punch Veyo in his smug fucking face. He howls as he falls back, and I see all the other nephilim turn my way, I wink over my shoulder at them, especially Griffin. "Handsy bastard. Didn't even buy me a drink first."

Turning back, I glare down at Veyo who's crouching and clutching his broken nose. I let my eyes bleed black for a moment. "Touch me again and I will rip off that arm and feed it to the monsters below, understood?"

He doesn't answer, too busy howling and spitting curse words. Bending down before him, I pull his hand from his nose, making sure it hurts. I lean forward and lick the blood from his nose and he shivers in revulsion, lurching backwards to fall on his ass. Licking my lips, I watch him. "You taste like fear."

He leaps to his feet as I laugh, and his hand comes out to smack me, but I warned him. Grabbing it, I snap his wrist and fling him away. We all watch him sail into a tree with a thump. He's on his feet in a second, eyes blazing yellow and face almost shivering with the need to transform.

"Come on, bird boy," I taunt.

I watch as the change starts to sweep through him, but then a voice cuts through the air, stilling everyone. "Enough!"

We all turn to see Amos standing at the edge of the grass glaring, he turns his eyes to Veyo and snaps his fingers. Veyo screams as he falls to his knees, his hands gripping his head like a vice, his face contorted in agony. Amos stares at him as the man shrieks and writhes until, finally, he clicks his fingers again and Veyo falls to the side panting, as tears roll down his face. "You do not attack our guest, do not change ever again unless instructed to. Understand?"

"Yes, master," Veyo whispers, loud enough for us all to hear.

I glance over at Griffin and give him a slight nod to let him know I'm okay, and he deflates a little, the madness retreating, just in time for Amos to look at me. "Apologies, Dawn, that was some nasty business. Shall we?" He gestures his arm behind him as he looks over at Griffin and the nephilim. "Shouldn't you be at work?"

They quickly launch into the sky, while some rush back to training, but not Griffin, he glares at Amos as I saunter over and walk past the council member. They have a stare down and I see Amos starting to step towards my mate. "Assmoss? Shall we? Torture can't wait all day."

He looks at me instantly and seems to forget about Griffin, which lets me relax. "Amos, Dawn, do not make me tell you again," he cautions, his tone smacking me with power like a whip.

"Sure thing, Assmos," I reply, and turn and saunter away, whistling to myself. This is the most action and fun I've seen in a few days. He throws his power at me again, but I just keep walking without a clue where we are going, just happy to be outside.

Eventually he catches up and steers me in the direction he wants me to go. We seem to walk for at least two miles until I feel like we are almost off the property itself. He also doesn't look ruffled like I imagined he would outside in the real world, in fact he is very light on his feet and makes short work of the walk to whatever evil scheme he has planned for me now.

We head through the trees and the pine riddled back garden until he stops in what looks like the middle of nowhere. As far as I can see, there are only trees in each direction, I can't even see the house from here. But then I feel it.

Power.

Pure, strong...and dark power.

It tastes like blood and sex, fills me up, crooning of massacres and orgies. My kind of power. It seems to be shimmering in this area, contained, but what is it from...or whom?

He watches me, is this a test? Am I about to get ambushed and killed? Why do men in my life keep trying to kill me in forests? How unoriginal. "Do you feel it?" he asks, breaking the silence.

"That big old burst of dark power surrounding us? Hard to miss it, Assmos." I laugh.

"Where is it?" he questions, his eyes narrowed. One of these times he's going to lose it, I can tell.

I search the area with my eyes but can't see anything, so I start to walk around it in slow circles, waiting for something. I pass over a spot that sends a shiver up my spine, the hair on my body standing on end. So I stop there. When I lift my hand, I notice the goosebumps raised on my arms and know I must be close.

My fingers seem to shimmer for a moment, so I wiggle them around, watching the play of light, like a bubble is surrounding them, prisms of colours playing across my pale skin. "It's here."

"What is?" he barks, growing impatient.

Muttering about how his name matches his personality, I crouch down to where the power seems to be strongest and close my eyes, looking with more than my physical sight like Nos does. If I have some of his powers, I might be able to use it...

I concentrate hard, focusing on the spot below my hand, peeling back the power. Opening my eyes, my jaw drops as I spot the silver door built into the ground like a bunker entrance. It wasn't there before, so it was cloaked?

"The power is concealing it from us," I tell him.

"Good, let's go inside," Amos orders, and strides over to stand behind me, waiting for me to open it.

In films this is where the girl always dies. I should turn away and run, but honestly I'm not scared. I can handle anything and I'm curious what the head of the council feels like he has to hide out here in the woods with spells. It must be something bad, and bad attracts me.

Fuck those dumb bitches in movies, I'm the villain and nobody is killing me.

Grabbing the handle, I pull it open, and the hiss of air comes out smelling like blood hidden beneath antiseptic. It swings open sideways, banging against the forest floor. Inside, I see stairs leading downwards with silver railings on either side and the lights hospitals use guiding me down.

I have a feeling he's waiting for me to beg, waiting for me to be afraid. So I do the opposite. With a wink at him, I throw myself down the stairs, rolling to my feet at the bottom. It's a smooth grey, almost plastic material down here, with a long corridor lit all the way down, leading away before splitting off into a junction.

Not creepy at all.

Amos takes his time coming down the stairs, the dramatic bitch, and when he reaches the bottom, he places his cane on the floor with a loud bang. I only arch my eyebrow and lean against the wall. "What's this? Your sex dungeon? 'Cause I gotta tell you, you just don't do it for me, sorry, but I do like a good sex swing."

"You are vile," he spits.

"Aww, thank you," I retort, touching my hand to my chest before wiping my face clean. "Let's get on with whatever you have planned."

With a huff he starts to stalk forward, guiding me down the unnecessarily long hallway. At the end we turn left, and I hear a scream. A very human scream.

A female human scream.

It echoes through the walls, making me shiver from the bone

deep terror in that one sound. Amos doesn't seem surprised and carries on walking, rounding another corner into yet again another long corridor. This one has a door at the end, and as we walk, the grey wall falls away to a glass window into a large room.

A lab.

There are four gurneys in a row along the back white wall with machines waiting next to them. An EKG machine, defibrillators, tubes, and wires decorate the space. Along the back wall are cupboards, which are built into the wall, with more underneath holding microscopes and other equipment that I don't even know the name for. When I see what's on the other side of the room, I freeze in place.

It's a fucking surgical unit.

And there is a woman lying on the table with a man in a white coat bent over her. His hands are covered in blood as he digs them into her chest. His hair is blonde and cut short, pushed back and perfectly styled. His eyes are a muddy brown with flecks of gold. He's tall and muscular, very attractive actually, but the cool, calm, almost serene expression on his face as he rips open the screaming woman makes me shiver in revulsion.

"What the fuck is this?" I snarl.

It reminds me of the experiments I found in that warehouse basement, but much more extreme, and the poor woman is screaming in agony. Her face is covered in sweat and blood, her once blonde hair is dyed pink with it, and her body is stark naked and exposed to everyone. Tears roll from her eyes as she slams her head from side to side.

"Ah-ha," I hear him mutter, and then there is a sickening ripping noise and the woman collapses on the table, unmoving. His hands pull from her chest, and I watch as he lifts her heart free and walks over to the bench and grabs a needle. My eyes flicker back to the woman as her head lolls to the side, her eyes empty and locked on where we are standing. A lone tear trails down through the blood on her face. Her whole chest is torn open, like something tried to get out...or in.

I stare into those grey orbs as horror and anger fill me until my eyes bleed to black, and I look at the man responsible. He presses the needle into the heart and lifts the plunger, and her blood fills it before he places them both side by side on a black board on the table. There are what appear to be runes and other objects placed around it.

"What the fuck is this shit, Assmos? I get the whole kidnapping women to make better supernaturals..." I turn then. "But I thought you were trying to breed them. That's not it, is it? Or at least not just that?"

"No, that is part of the agenda. Most involved know of it and agree. They want stronger bloodlines and mixing ancient or powerful beings with pure bloods was a brilliant idea, but in case it did not work, we needed another way of ensuring our races live on. That we live on, the dominant species."

"To take over the fucking world, yeah, I've heard that on every bad hero movie...but what is he doing? The experiments on humans? Pushing them to their limits to bring out latent genes...it's more than that. That looks like black magic or some shit, I can almost feel it in the air."

"It is in a way, I cannot tell you any more, Dawn. Not yet, not until you understand why. You are important, your power is indescribable, and with you, with your blood, we could create something so powerful it would be unstoppable." He turns to me, looking hopeful, like he thinks I'll really be onboard with this shit. "We are dying, Dawn. This is the only way. Surely you see everything I do is for the good of our people? Your people now, you are one of us."

"The hunters?" I query, grasping for information now that he's talking, trying to put the pieces of the puzzle together.

"Easy, they need money. I simply posed as a rich human disgusted in finding out the world is filled with monsters. They think they are hunting them for us and that I use the witches to help contain it. They are willing to turn a blind eye to most things for money, so easy to corrupt." He shakes his head.

"The witches?" I press.

"They want what I do, power. More reach, to rule again. To be the people behind the crown." He shrugs.

"I-I still don't get it, what is he doing? Who is he?"

"Do you remember how I said you had a choice? How many people have latent blood in them? What if we could change that? What if we could, at will, make them like us? Not as strong of course, but everyone needs soldiers and servants." He peers at me then, his eyes alight with purpose. "What if we could change humans to be like us? I don't mean change them like vampires, but change their actual genetic structure until they are all monsters? We could pick the brightest, the strongest—"

"The richest," I snap.

"Exactly, make them us. We would have no one against us, this world would be ours for the taking." He grins. "Don't you see, Dawn, we could play god? Make our own army!"

"And who would be left to fight? No one should play god, humans serve a purpose, leave them to it, we are better hiding in the dark," I whisper. "Look at what we do to those we deem weaker than us. How can you really think we are right to rule this earth? We kill everything we touch! Corrupt it and use it, draining it."

"Dawn." He sighs in disappointment, looking back at the man who is making notes as he watches the heart. I watch it too, and it slowly starts to beat again, to pump as we stare. "You wanted to know, this is the truth."

"You are breeding supernaturals with ancient, powerful beings against their will and changing humans with torture...and magic and science? Does that about cover it?"

"Yes, I am creating a whole new world, Dawn. One where we no longer have to hide, one where our power, our hungers and needs, are seen as normal, not wrong. They have had their time, now it is ours, and you are either with us or against us. I can use you either way," he growls.

"How?" I whisper, watching as the man picks up the now beating heart and stalks back over to the woman. With delicate hands, he presses the heart back into her chest and steps back, blood dripping from his fingers to the white floor.

Nothing happens at first, then slowly, ever so slowly, the bones rebreak and bend, the skin knitting together over the cavern until nothing remains but a corpse. Then her chest lifts with a breath, and I watch as she blinks those once empty grey eyes. They bleed to purple for a moment before she blinks again, her head turning to look at the ceiling. Her skin seems to smooth, her hair growing rapidly until it hangs from the table.

"You are changing her into a monster."

"We are remaking her, Dawn, and you? You were the very first," he offers.

"What do you mean? You said my genes changed when I chose to fight, to live, not to die," I recall, feeling lost, and for once very unsure of what to do. What's happening here is atrocious, even for monsters this...this evil is so wrong.

The woman sits up, her back arching, tits swaying with the movement, and her head turns from side to side like a robot. What is she now? She was a human with hopes, dreams, fears, love...a home. Probably a family and now? Now she is whatever they want her to be. Nothing more than an experiment, something to control. Her eyes are vacant...still dead.

"You see, we can't create a soul. For now he has been struggling to get them to function like us. They are simply vessels, servants very similar to my nephilim, but you?" He turns, eyes blazing with something, and I step back, knowing I'm not going to like whatever he's going to say.

"All your life, Dawn, have you not felt different? Like some-thing is missing? Just out of your reach? You were the very first, he did not work for me then, he was doing it in secret, trying different things. A lot of them died. You weren't made in a lab, no, he found your mother when she was pregnant and low on money. Money opens a lot of doors, it did with her. She let him run tests on her baby. She thought he was trying to find a cure to an autoimmune disease, but really he injected pure power and magic into the embryo. Into you. He watched her, and when you were born human, he thought he had failed so he left you alone. Just another sheep. We all felt it that night, the night your power was unlocked. He did as well and sought you out. But we couldn't find you until, suddenly, you came to us. Now here you are, our very best. The only one to ever survive, you are proof this works. You are the future."

"I-I'm not like her!" I almost scream.

"No, you are better. A living, breathing, thinking, soul-filled creature. You have so much potential, so much untapped power... the things you could be, Dawn! Think of it! The things we could do together, and using the same process with you, we could fill our courts again. Make more supernaturals than humans! We would be unstoppable."

"You made me a monster," I state, my voice dead.

"We made you better, stronger, you are immortal! We made you more than you could have ever been as a human." He spreads his hands in front of himself like it's simple.

"You made me a monster!" I scream, my heart cracking. Everything I thought I knew about myself is crumbling around me and pouring from my mouth.

All the rage, the pain...the hate. Filling me up and exploding from my mouth. How dare they play god. How fucking dare they make me into this! They have no right. They claim to be doing it for the better good, but everything comes down to power. They want more, they want to rule, and they don't care who they hurt along the way. They are changing things that should never be changed. It enrages me until I can't stop.

All this time, I thought everything I had survived, lived

through, was for a reason. So I could be reborn and find my mates, that I had a purpose. A destiny. Instead I was a madman's creation in a bid for power. I am corrupt, an experiment, nothing more than wrong. The world falls from beneath my feet and I do what any monster does when threatened—attack.

The scream changes, warps into a war cry so loud and powerful the window shatters next to me. Shards float and my hand flings out, palm flat, stopping them until they hang suspended between us. Amos watches me in shock and pride.

"See? See what we made you? Just think of everything we could do together!" he yells as wind whips around the room, unnatural wind. It lifts me from the floor as my eyes light up white, lasering around the space.

Amos steps back, fear entering his expression for the monster he created. "Dawn, stop this," he orders. "Stop it now!"

It whips faster and faster, fuelled by everything. I see flashes of Tim's mocking smile as he beats me. I see my human body dying, my hands clawing through mud and dirt until I suck in lungfuls of air. I watch the human girl die again and again, I watch Griffin's eyes as he explains his past. I see it all. All the suffering these men have caused because they thought they could play god.

"I am ordering you! Stop this now, you are ours to control!" he shouts over the wind.

It was the wrong thing to say. I fling out my hand and the shards turn like daggers and fly towards him. They slice him, cutting into flesh, carving him for me. He screams, ducking and covering his head as his blood drips to the floor.

He created a monster, one he thought he could control. He was wrong. I'm a monster, that's for sure, but he will never use me. Never control me. I will kill them all for what they have done to me, to every woman down here...to every single human and monster alike.

But then I see the good. Nos, his warm smile and white eyes as he watches me with pride, his hand outstretched to me as he calls me. "Little Monster."

Griffin swoops about me, feathers curling around to warm me, his mind brushing mine. I see Aska roar as his dragon soars through the air. I see a black shape zooming towards me on the night. I see Jair striding through the glass and madness, his eyes only for me.

Yes, I was made.

Yes, they might have created me, but they are not responsible for me. I am, me alone. I make my own choices, my own destiny, and they are mine. Not this man, not this madness and hate. I am not something wrong, I am not evil.

I am Dawn.

Skinwalker.

Mate.

Draya.

Vasculo.

Neriso.

Little Monster.

I am all that and more, and it's time I showed them what they created.

CHAPTER 37

DAWN

I drop my arm, letting the wind die as I pull the power back within me. The glass falls to the floor with a shattering jingle as my feet touch the ground.

Amos clambers up to stand, his expression outraged, the cuts on his face and body healing as his power hits me. I throw mine back at him, meeting him halfway. We are evenly matched...in fact, I think I'm stronger. I step forward, pushing him back with each step. "I am not yours to order about. I will stop what you're doing here. It's evil and wrong. I will stop you."

He laughs even as he is pushed backwards. "If I am evil, then what are you?"

"Evil's worst enemy. You have no idea what you created, and you are scared of that. You don't know what I'm capable of, I can hear it. You should be scared, because when I'm done, nothing of your precious council will stand. You will be dust, forgotten to the ages while the humans rule, and everything you hate most will still be alive while you are nothing more than a bad dream."

I'm concentrating on Amos so hard, I don't hear him until it's too late. A sharp prick comes at my neck, and I swirl to see the man from the lab backing away with a needle held in his hand.

"As I was saying, Dawn, you are ours, with or without your permission. We need you and we will use you," Amos sneers behind me, his voice warping halfway through until it's slower and deeper, disjointed, and wrong.

No, wait, that's me.

I stumble to the side, my head fuzzy and my eyes going dark as my ears ring. "What have you done to me?" I ask, but it comes out garbled.

I fall to my knees and then to my side, the blackness claiming me as I fight it.

No!

But it's no use. I'm gone.

I WAKE up cold and naked.

Why always naked? Can't the evil bastards just let me have clothes? Not that I have modesty, but my mates will kill anyone who sees me like this, and these fuckers are mine, not theirs. Cracking open my eyes, I blink at the bright light above me, groaning as I turn my head to the side. My whole body aches like I drank way too much and passed out. Whatever that drug was, it was really powerful.

I'm in the lab, strapped to one of the metal tables. When I look down, I see bindings on each ankle, over my middle, and shackling both wrists. It seems they aren't taking any risks this time.

Lifting my head hurts, so I lay it back down and wait. They must have something planned. They wouldn't just leave me here if what they said is true—I'm too valuable, as disgusting as that thought is. My mind focuses on what he said. Is that why my mother left? She knew there was something wrong with me? What about Tim...did he sense it too?

These thoughts get me nowhere, so I push them away and focus on my body, feeling the drug slowly ebb away until there's a crunch of glass. Raising my head, I see Amos come through the door and walk over to me. He looks down at me sadly, as if I disappointed him. Asshole.

"We do not need your permission, you have outlived your usefulness, we can get what we want by force." He sighs then, almost sadly. "You could have been so powerful, it's a shame."

Amos wants to leave me here. And I know it's to die. I have outlasted my purpose. Well, fuck being smart, fuck being good.

It's time I let my monster out to play.

He turns away. Growling, I yank on the bindings, thrashing as I try to get to him, but he leaves the room, and about a minute later I hear the bunker door slam. The silence is eerie down here. I look around the room, but I don't spot the guy who injected me or the woman. It's empty except me.

I relax my head onto the table and wait, letting my strength return as the drug leaves my system so I'm ready for what's to come. It takes hours before someone arrives. It's stupid of them, because the drug is fully out of my system by now and I'm back to full strength and pissed as hell.

It's not the same blond-haired man from before, it's four guys. I sniff the air, trying to discern what they are. One smells human, the other smells like magic, and the other two smell...wrong. That's when I realise those two? They are replicas of the other two.

They made clones?

What the fuck is this place and how has the council gotten away with this shit?

They head my way and I strike. Power flows from me as I scream and launch myself at them, snapping the bindings like they were paper. The lights explode in a shower of sparks, plunging us into darkness. I can see them just fine though, but they don't see me until it's too late.

I tackle the first one to the floor, just moving on instinct now. Snarling, I bite, ripping through his cheek and spitting it away. He screams in agony, trying to push me away, but I'm too strong.

The whole time all I see is those women.

I see the one from in here.

I see the ones I saved, and what might have happened to them.

Their images fill me so completely there is no room for anything else. Just hate. Blood fills my mouth as I dig my claws into his chest, tearing it to shreds before slashing his throat. Blood spurts in an arc, covering me and dripping into my eyes.

"Where is she?" someone screams.

I hear them stumbling around the room and almost falling, attempting to escape. They can't get away from me. Rising to my feet, I leap over one of the gurneys and crouch on all fours before one of the men. His hands are outstretched in the dark, his eyes wide and darting around wildly, his mouth trembling.

I laugh and he shrieks, trying to run away. I land on his back as he hits the floor, and I waste no time ripping his head off and tossing it at the man just about to reach the door. He goes down, falling over it, and shakily picks it up, feeling along the bloodied skull.

I know the moment he realises what it is. His face goes pale and he faints, smacking back into the floor with a crunch. Turning away, I spot the other man just as a red flashing light flickers on above, tingeing everything. The man stumbles back in horror, his mouth opening and closing, and I can taste his fear. I watch as he pisses himself, the wetness covering the front of his trousers and trickling down onto the floor as he cries.

I know I must look monstrous. As I stroll towards him, I catch a glimpse of myself in the shattered glass and laugh. My hair is crimson with blood and my face is covered in it. I look like something out of a horror movie. My eyes are black and white, mixing together in each pupil like the night sky. I have fangs hanging over my lower lip and smoke is trailing from my nose.

"Beware the monster that hides within this small blonde, she will eat you whole." I laugh, and he falls back with a scream, his back smacking into the ground as he lets out a pained yelp.

I pounce, landing above him on all fours, sniffing along his neck. "You smell like fear," I rumble, voice low and velvety. Licking a path up his sweaty neck, I chuckle in his ear. "You taste like it. Tell me, I bet those girls cried. I bet they pleaded and begged, trying to reach your heart. What does the inside of your cold, dead heart look like? Why don't we find out?"

With a snarl, I dig my hands into his chest, prying it open. He screams wordlessly, tears rolling down his cheeks as I crack open his ribs and pry his heart from his chest. Holding it up, I look down at him and frown. "Huh, not black, shame."

A noise has me spinning to see the other man now awake, crawling backwards on the floor. Grinning, I drop the heart to the ground with a squelch that makes him gag. I bring my fingers to my lips and lick the blood from it as he watches.

He tastes like metal and fear, delicious.

"Oh God, oh God, oh God," the man chants as he freezes.

"Not a god, not yet, little human," I purr, and I crawl to him, my body swaying slowly until I reach his feet and sit up, watching him. "Are you scared of dying?"

"Y-Yes," he sobs.

"Did you fear anything when you tried to play God yourself? Did you fear the consequences, fear what you were becoming? Did you feel anything at all?" I whisper, digging my nails into his ankle, cutting through skin and making him scream. "Focus, little human, I grow bored."

"I-I was just doing as I was told," he whispers, and I snarl, snapping my teeth at him.

"I fucking hate that excuse. Do you not have a mind? If they told you to leap from a cliff, would you? And as you crashed to the rocks at the bottom say that it was ordered? No! You wouldn't! You chose this, do not blame others. You made the choice to hurt those women, to disrupt nature. For power and money. Tell me, how do those things feel now? Do they protect you? You see, I will. I will protect those women, every woman who has been hurt. Hurt by men like you who think they are nothing more than a fucking uterus, nothing more than something weaker than them. We are stronger than you will ever know, not always physically, but mentally? Fuck yes, we put up with assholes like you and rise above it. Every day, women out there pick up their pieces from cheating spouses and abusive partners, neglecting people they trust. Women are the strongest thing on this planet, and you will all see that soon. They will see that. For I am the monster who fights for them, for those who can't, and you? You are simply a weak little man, therefore in your logic, I can hurt you."

He shakes his head mutely.

"Nothing to say? Guess you aren't that smart after all," I purr.

Tired of this game, I end it. Something stretches inside me, something calling for me to use it, to be let out, so I do. I watch curiously as purple mist flows towards the man from my mouth, wrapping around him. He screams and fights beneath me and then suddenly stops, his strings cut. The purple rises from his body, something bright and swirling held within it.

Is-Is that his soul?

It stays there for a moment, and then it's gone, as is the purple magic. What the hell was that?

I fall back, breathing heavily as the change recedes. Maybe Amos was right, maybe I am stronger than I know, with things hiding inside me. What else am I capable of? No. No, he's wrong. I can control it...right?

Looking around, I get to my feet and leave the lab, heading into the hallway on bare feet. Amos must know by now, and I doubt he thinks I'm dead. Fine. He wants this to be over? I will end this.

First things first, I need to free my monsters.

CHAPTER 38

ASKA

I follow the...demon...outside and we stop at the base of the mountain as he tips his head back and grins, sucking in air. "How are we getting there?" I snap, interrupting his moment.

His dark eyes turn to me, and even I feel fear looking into them. It's like staring at death. The dark abyss of his gaze is so empty and cold, that loneliness, hate, and fear flow through me just from a glance.

"Hop, of course. I couldn't do it inside, but I can beyond the boundaries."

"Hop?" I repeat, confused, and then look down at my legs, wondering how only using one will get us there faster.

"This is going to get annoying. Hop, dragon." His voice grows louder at the end, as if I wasn't supposed to hear the first part. "As in hop across time and space."

"Ah, well, I drove here and I need the treasures from my car." I huff.

"Driving...you want me to drive with you?" He seems to be

searching his mind for what that is and then his eyes lock back on me. "You came to the sleeping court to fetch someone to...drive us back? Are you a chauffeur?"

Growling, I let my power raise and he waves it away. "Fine, let us hop to my car, and I can call someone to collect it. I can't just leave it, it has everything for my mate."

That gets his attention and he sighs. "Fine, then we hop to the council."

He doesn't warn me before black smoke encases me. I snarl as the world seems to spin and my ears ring. I have the sense of movement, but I can't see anything. Finally, the smoke retracts and I look around in shock to see we are next to my car. The snake is leaning against it, watching me impatiently.

"Come on, dragon, I have things to do. Slow me down and I will leave you here for Xaph to kill," he snaps.

"He could try." I sniff, making him laugh.

"Maybe I won't leave you, you're funny," he remarks.

Ignoring him, I get into the driver's seat and grab my phone, dialling Jean Paul's number. Just as he is answering, I let out a less than dragonly scream as the snake pops into existence in my passenger seat.

"Sir?" Jean Paul panics.

Glaring at the laughing man, I turn back to the conversation, clearing my throat and lowering my voice. "Sorry, I am here."

"Smooth," the snake scoffs.

"Can you please pick up my vehicle from the location on this device and bring it to the city? I will meet you there," I rumble.

"Of course, how are you getting there, sir?" he queries, typing away in the background, not asking anything else.

"I am travelling with someone," I inform him, and then lower my voice, almost whispering, "Lucifer."

"You are traveling with who, sir?" Jean Paul asks.

Smiling at the snake, I turn away and cover the phone. "I'm pretty sure he's Lucifer," I mumble.

"Sorry, I can't hear you, sir. Are you on speaker again?"

"Lucifer, as in Satan!" I scream, and then look over at said man who is watching me from the passenger seat with an eyebrow arched and a grin curling his lips.

"I prefer Snake or 'Oh Dark and Powerful One,' but please, continue," he comments.

"I will see you soon," I say to a laughing Jean Paul as I hang up. "We may hop now."

His face darkens for a moment, wiped clean of amusement, and the car fills with the same black smoke, his red eyes flaming through it, the only thing I can see. "Do not order me, dragon, you will not like what happens." Then, his eyes blink back to normal and the smoke embraces me. "Shall we?" he offers politely.

And they say I'm crazy.

CHAPTER 39

DAWN

I drop to my knees as pain washes through me. I'm finally changing, using that power. That face, that skin I stole that's been waiting to be used flows over my body until I'm panting with my head pressed to the floor.

Taking some deep breaths, I push to my feet and grab the closest large, broken mirror shard, checking out my new skin. Good, I look like a guy, I even have his uniform on. That will help me get into the dungeons. Throwing the shard away, I stroll down the corridor as murderous intent fills me. The council wants to play God? I'm going to show them just how wrong they are.

Sauntering down the passageway, I pause at the bottom of the stairs to the underground laboratory, taking in the two nephilim standing guard at the top near the open doorway.

I don't have time for this shit. I need to get to my mates, free the monsters, and kill the council before they can experiment on any other poor defenceless women. But nephilim won't be as easy to kill as humans, so I guess it's time to put my power, my strength, to the test.

Rolling my eyes, I grab the wall dramatically, panting and looking pained. "Help, please, she's escaping!" I yell, and then pretend to be dragged backwards with a scream.

Hiding behind the wall, I wait as I hear them storming down the stairs. *Come on, you winged bastards.* I wait with bated breath as they pass my hiding spot. Stepping out, I block their exit with a smirk.

They glance back and then look around in confusion. "Where is she?"

"Right here, boys. Now, tell me, if your dad was an angel and your mom was a human...does that make you only half asshole?" I ponder, tapping my chin. They glance at each other in bewilderment before searching around again. "Wow, well, you clearly didn't get their brains. Fuck it, let's just fight, shall we?"

They reach for the knives at their hips but hesitate, still confused about why a human guard is attacking them. Really, if this is the council's protection, then this whole mission will be a cakewalk and I'll be back to having orgies with my mates before I know it.

Transforming my eyes, I let them flash black to see if that will do the trick, but the stupid winged bastards just stare...and Griffin thought sheep were stupid, just wait until I use this against him. Fuck it.

I lunge at them to get the ball rolling, but the new swinging appendage between my legs pushes me off balance and I stumble into the first nephilim. He pushes me away, frowning, and pulls his blade as his friend rushes off into the bunker to undoubtedly search for me.

"Bloody penis getting in the way, can I ask you how you fight with it? Do you tuck it to the side? What about your balls?" I question seriously, reaching into my black pants and pushing my temporary cock to the side. Hmm, not too small actually, congrats to the guy.

"Why are you still talking?" he rumbles, looking very uncomfortable.

"Blade! They are all dead!" comes the yell from the other nephilim, and the one in front of me looks down at me—ah, he's finally getting it.

"I tried to tell you, also...Blade? Really? How fucking cliché." I laugh, leaning against him. "Oh, Blade, please don't kill me," I mock, my deep male voice breaking as I try to talk in a higher pitch.

Before he can push me away again, I grab the knife in his hand and bury it in his stomach. "Ironic, Blade dies by a blade," I sneer, as I twist it in deeper. He groans, blood pooling around my hands as he falls backwards. But his wings shoot out and his eyes flash gold. Whoops, angel boy is mad.

Well, so the fuck am I.

Grabbing the blade, I leap into the air using the human's strength, and imbed it in his eye, driving it into that golden orb. "Take that, you winged bastard," I mutter as I drop to the floor and roll, getting to my feet. I watch as the nephilim falls to his knees before tumbling forward to the ground, the blade pushed deeper with a sickening squelch by the force of the fall.

I yelp as I'm smashed into the wall and a hand goes around my throat, cutting off my air supply. The other nephilim pins me there as he snarls at me, his eyes glowing with that same golden hue. "Skinwalker," he hisses.

"You...are...smarter...than...the...other...one," I wheeze, bringing my knee up and connecting it with his cock and balls. He drops me to the floor as he falls backwards with a pained howl. "Still weak though."

He recovers quicker than I thought he would and lunges for me. I duck under his hands and snatch some glass from the floor, cutting my palms, and I slash upwards. Sliding out from between his legs, I spin and throw myself onto his back, then he starts bucking and slamming me into the walls.

His wings take us higher as he smashes me into the ceiling, trying to dislodge me. Grunting from the impact, I wrap my legs tighter around him and use the glass like a weapon. I stab at him, at every inch I can get, again and again, until suddenly we drop to the floor. Groaning, I roll from his body and get to my feet, panting as I glance down to see his eyes open and wide as he gapes down at the glass embedded right into his chest. Blood pumps out quicker than it can heal. Crouching down, I grab the glass and twist it, narrowing my eyes at him. "This is for Griffin."

His eyes flare at that as I wrench out the glass, letting the blood spurt and drain from his body. I watch him die, a sick satisfaction filling me. Standing, I drop the glass to the floor and step over their bodies. I'm just about to leave when a thought hits me. Looking back, I spot all the wasted blood and a grin stretches across my lips.

Dipping my finger in the crimson liquid, I start to write on the wall, leaving the council a warning. Let them feel the same fear I did, that all these women did. For once they are the prey, and I want them to know it.

I'm coming for you.

Whistling, I make my way back across the property. It takes as long as it originally did to get here with Amos, but something strange happens. A wolf emerges from within the darkness of the trees like it was waiting for me. But it's no normal wolf, it's huge, as big as me standing in this male's skin. Its eyes are a bright, abnormal blue, like the stars are caught in its eyes. Something about it stops me and I stare, it stares right back. Its fur is a deep black with streaks of grey lighting it, and what look like silver hoops hang from its left ear, three of them. The symbol on its head makes me stare—

an upside-down crescent moon that seems to glow silver with specks of white around it. What is this wolf?

My heart slams in my chest, my body unable to move, to walk away. What the fuck is happening? Its muzzle opens in a snarl as its head lowers.

Narrowing my eyes, I flash my teeth at him.

"Don't start, doggy, I know a forest god who will kick your ass," I warn, pointing my finger at him. He snarls and snaps at me, so I smack his muzzle. "No, bad wolf, no eating."

He whimpers, a whine catching in his throat as he puts his teeth away and lowers his head before dropping to his belly and rolling over. I snort, bend down, and rub his fur there. "That's a good little wild wolf, yes it is, who's a good boy? Yes, you are. Now go, eat the council for all I care."

Standing, I start back through the forest but the hair on the back of my neck rises again, so I look over my shoulder to see the wolf trotting behind me. "No! No wolf pets, Griffin will kill me!" I groan and it stops and sits down, giving me those wide eyes. "God fucking damn it. Fine, but I swear if you piss in the house he'll try to kill you!" Turning around, I rub my hair in frustration. The stupid mutt better be potty trained, how the fuck am I supposed to explain to my mates that we adopted a wolf? Is it not bad enough I'm coming back with a new vampire and a minotaur?

Grumbling to myself, I head back through the training grounds which are empty, pretending that I'm supposed to be here. If I do and anyone sees me, they might not question it. Fake it till you make it. The wolf lopes after me happily, his tongue lolled out to the side.

I use the entrance Veyo pulled me through and easily find the steps down to the dungeon, then I take a deep breath. I willingly go back down there to the monsters that are waiting.

The wolf follows me as I pass the many, many cells, trying to remember all the twists and turns that will lead me back to Dume, but my power starts to falter. I've been wearing this skin for a while, not to mention I stored it and it feels like it's stretched too tight, like it might snap.

A groan leaves my lips as I stumble into the wall, breathing heavily as sweat beads on my brow, and when I try to step forward, needing to get to Dume before I change in the hallway, I tumble to the ground.

Back bowing, hands scratching at the cement, I stop the scream in my throat as the change takes me by surprise. When it's done and I'm back to being Dawn, I hear a snarl and look up, spotting the wolf. Fuck. He watches me in confusion, sneaking closer, and I freeze, wondering if it's going to try and eat me again. But then he whines, and his tongue comes out, licking my face.

"Good boy," I coo, rubbing his neck.

"What the fuck, *Vasculo*, is that a fucking wolf?" Griffin yells, and I turn to see him with an apron on and two trays held in each hand as he gawks at me.

"I can explain...are you wearing an apron?" I ask, cocking my head to the side. "Cute. Will you wear one at home and nothing else?"

He drops the trays to the ground and the wolf bounds over and starts to lick up the food as Griffin rips the apron away, his expression transforming into one of anger, his eyes flashing with that familiar madness that has my thighs clenching. He storms my way and yanks me to my feet, pressing his hand to my throat. "What the fuck were you doing up there? Where did he take you?"

"Oh, just out for a creepy stroll through the woods."

Griffin roars, pushing me away and staring down at my wolf friend who is snarling and biting at his leg, trying to pull him away from me. Griffin looks up at me with an expression as if to say 'see?' before pushing him away and growling at the wolf.

"He doesn't understand, he thinks you were attacking me." I huff and get to my knees, stroking the wolf. "Did big bad Griffin scare you? He's all bark and no bite, sweetie."

"I'll fucking bite you! Look what it did to me!" he yells, and I look back to see blood seeping through his pants, the material ripped along his leg.

I scoot closer, placing myself between them as Griffin glares down at the wolf who is now snarling at the fallen. Pressing my hand against the wound, I kiss around it. "Is that better? My big bad fallen, look at your wound," I coo, and when I glance up, he sniffs and crosses his arms. Hiding my smile, I kiss my way up his body until I dot them across his chin. "Did the wolf hurt you, my love? Need me to make it better?" I whisper huskily.

"Yes," he snaps and then sighs, melting under my touch. "You're not keeping the wolf."

"Yes, I am." I grin, kissing along his face until I reach his mouth.

"Fuck," he mutters, knowing I always get my way.

CHAPTER 40

MAGNUS

I watch the blonde female they call Dawn press herself against the large male and a snarl escapes my muzzle, my wolf feeling possessive. He wants her attention again, those hands stroking through our fur until we purr like a pup. Embarrassment shoots through me at how easily she controlled my animal, making us nothing more than an oversized dog rolling onto his back for scratches.

I have been trapped in this body for so long, trapped in my wolf, but she called to me. Brought something out in me. I had been lost to the animal side, giving myself over to it knowing I would never be free, and then I felt her all those moons ago.

When I found her in that forest with that god, I had watched from the shadows, more wolf than man, wondering who she was, what she was, and why she pulled me to race across Earth to find her. I didn't show myself to her, I observed and waited from afar, each day my mind returning more and more until I was simply a man in a wolf's body.

But then she was taken. I had sprinted through the forest along-side the vehicle and watched as they brought her here, a howl of agony and grief leaving my maw. I feared I would never see her again, so when I felt her move outside, I took the chance. But it wasn't her, it was a man.

That tug was still there, however, that calling, unwilling to let me turn away until I watched her turn back to the blonde I had been tracking. It filled my wolf with joy, he had known all along it was her, I didn't. She can shift like us, but with faces. I wonder what else she can do. I want to ask, I want to reach out.

I want her to touch skin, not fur, but I can't.

I can't even reach for her mind. She might as well be a million miles away, and when she looks over at me, I know all she sees is a wolf. Not a man. Fine, if this is all it can be, if this is the closest I can get, so be it. I will walk through this life by her side as her pet wolf, it's better than receding back to that dark, dead place as my wolf takes over.

Maybe one day I will find a way to reverse the magic that keeps me trapped like this and I could be at her side as a man. But that would require a miracle, a touch of destiny. The fates told me once I would never walk this Earth again until I learned how to love, how to care and not destroy.

But that is what I am, it is why I was born. To destroy. I was raised to prevent that, to keep me under control—not that it worked. They feared me, feared what I could do. The gods who raised me, they tried to entrap me. The first two attempts failed, but I grew complacent, believing I was stronger than them and they won. They locked me in this form, so far under the earth that I could never harm anyone. It is said I will lead the end of this world and kill the gods.

They feared what had not even happened yet, and for that I was cast aside. Magic entrapped me, but one day a woman appeared to me. She told me I would be free, but what I did was my choice. I could complete the prophecy, killing this world, or I could save it.

She spoke of love.

Love. Who could love a monster like myself?

Even the gods feared me, no, no one will ever love me. But before my death or theirs, I will ensure this woman is safe. I don't know why it is important, but I have to. My wolf is unable to take a step away from her.

She turns to look at me then, those eyes flashing black and for a moment. For just a moment I believe that just maybe the fate wasn't wrong. But then she turns away again, bestowing a kiss on the male and I growl in anger.

Fate was wrong, I am nothing more than a destroyer and this woman will not be able to stop me, she will burn with them all.

CHAPTER 41

GRIFFIN

Throwing a glare at the wolf, I look back down at a grinning Dawn. "Fine, if he pisses anywhere, he's dead."

"Thank you." She grins, kissing me again.

Groaning, I grip the back of her head and kiss her harder. She gasps into my mouth, plastering herself closer, while I ignore the growling wolf as I back her into the closest wall. I was so worried when I saw her with Veyo and Amos, but here she is. I need to ask what happened, but I can't rip my mouth away. I do, however, run my lips down her cheek and shoulder to her arm where he gripped her. She sighs as I kiss the red mark better and then meet her gaze. "I will kill him," I vow, meaning it.

He can torture me, try to break me, I don't care. Touch my mate? They are dead men walking, they just don't know it yet.

"Fine." She pouts, her eyes lighting up. "I get to kill everyone else."

"Bloodthirsty little thing." I grin and she kisses me, her lips moving against mine, making me ache for more.

"You know it," she whispers against my mouth. "Tell me, fallen, are you still serving?"

"Serving?" I echo with a frown, confused, and she giggles.

"Yes, because I could do with a service." She wiggles her eyebrows, making me groan.

"That was terrible," I mutter, but my cock jerks in my pants as I pin her to the wall.

"Fine, fuck me, fallen. Right here and now, make me feel alive. Prove to me that I'm more than what they say," she demands, almost begging. What the fuck did they do to her?

Madness surges through me, and my movements become jerky as I grab her and hoist her up the wall. She wraps her legs around me, her eyes locked on mine with a need so strong it makes me falter for a moment. I know it's reflected back in my gaze. As much as I hate it, I need her more than air.

Always do, always will.

"They almost got me this time," she admits. "Almost killed me."

"What a fucking waste of a perfect body that would be," I growl darkly, and she laughs even as she kicks me.

"Asshole."

"Always." I nod seriously, my lips curving into a smirk as I reach between us and cup her pussy through the too big trousers she's wearing from her transformation. "You want to feel alive, *Vasculo*?"

"Yes," she pants, shamelessly rubbing herself against me.

I grip her harder, making her groan. "Admit it."

"Admit what?" she inquires in confusion, but my madness is driving me now, from being away from her, from seeing her with others. It's jealousy. I'm jealous and feeling mean.

She can handle it, she can always handle me.

Pressing my arm across her throat, I hold her like that as I rip away the trousers, leaving her pussy bare for me as I snarl, "That you are mine. You want to fuck a beast? You want your new toy, your minotaur?"

She grins lazily, pressing herself harder against my arm.

"You should remember, *Vasculo,*" I purr, leaning closer. "I'm the biggest monster of them all, not because of what I can change into...but because I could really hurt you. I could kill you and you would love it, you would let me."

She moans, rubbing herself against me as I yank one of her legs higher and undo my trousers, palming my cock as I keep her there, whispering vile, almost hateful words to her. My madness seeps from me, taking over my mind until all I see is the council.

The ones who killed my parents.

The nephilim who betrayed me, who tortured me.

I see it all in her place, and she accepts it, her body pliant against me. Taking all that anger and hate inside of her and aching for more, she takes my madness and twirls it with hers.

"Wouldn't you? You would let me kill you, here and now with my cock buried in you," I growl.

"Yes," she wheezes, pushing against me, daring me to.

Pressing my cock against her soaking pussy, I slam inside her. She screams, thrashing against me, so I slam her back into the wall with more force as I pull out and thrust back in, fighting the tightness of her pussy as it tries to cling to me.

"More," she demands, as I lift my arm a bit for her to breathe. Her eyes are wild, leaking black, white, and is that purple? Like a galaxy in those orbs, all mine. All those powers are useless against me as I fuck her, reminding her that she might be theirs, but she is also mine.

"Griffin," she moans, lifting her hips to meet my brutal thrusts.

There is nothing better than being buried in my mate, this is as close to heaven as I will ever be.

Us monsters thrive in the dark, but here, between us, is only light. Our love fights off the madness, her body and mind taking it from me and giving me some sanity in return. She sees my pain, my need through the hate I'm feeling, and gives herself freely.

Groaning, I press my hand to the wall by her head. Her eyes are closed as she moves, rolling against me, but something makes me look to the left, and when I do my eyebrows raise. The wolf is there watching us, its eyes locked on our joined bodies and it doesn't look pleased. I falter for a moment, weirded out, but he huffs and with a snap at me, turns his back and watches the hallway like he's protecting us.

Dawn kicks my ass, urging me on, and I turn back to her to see her grinning, obviously catching my interaction with her new pet. Gripping her hip, I drive into her again and again, our breathing mixing in the quiet hallway. My need is too strong, I can't stop. I want it to hurt, but she likes the pain.

It makes her scream as I fuck her until I don't want to hurt her anymore. I want to love her. I see her eyes through the darkness in my mind and reach down, rubbing her clit as she gasps and shakes through an orgasm. I fuck her through it, needing to imprint myself on her.

Needing her to remember me even when she's with the others.

She moans my name, her pussy clenching around my cock as my balls draw up, but I try to hold off, to make this last. We can both feel the impending end coming, knowing something is going to happen and this could be our last time together. I need her to remember this, remember me if something transpires.

But I can't, she pushes down, grinding on my cock, and I come with a yell, filling her pussy with my cum as she grins at me, still panting. "Fuck."

"We just did that," she teases as I lean against her. She wraps her arms around me, holding me close, always knowing what I need without me having to ask. We should move before we are caught, but I don't want to and neither does she.

"What happened?" I question.

She sighs and tells me everything. My anger fills me again, but she stops me from going off and killing everyone. "We will get them, just not yet. What about the council, what did you learn?"

"Titus is up to something, he tried to befriend me," I divulge.

"Can we trust him?" she queries, and I look away.

"I don't know," I mutter. I've trusted the wrong people before.

"Fine, then we trust no one, figure out who is part of it, who I can kill." The dark expression on her face calls to my madness and sends a bolt of lust straight to my hardening cock that's still inside her.

"I will go back up and find out for us. There is a gathering tomorrow."

"A gathering?" She frowns.

"The full council will be there as well as some of their subjects," I clarify, and I see her mind turning before a smile graces her lips.

"Then that's when we do it. Go to the council, figure out as much as you can. I'll set everyone free and we'll meet you at the meeting in the morning. Will you be able to get to Nos as well?"

"I can try, he's here." I sigh.

"He's here?" she asks, her face lighting up, and I growl, making her roll her eyes. "Calm down, Griff."

"Yeah, the crazy bastard walked through the front door like he owned the place," I tell her.

"Good, get him there too. I'll try and contact Aska again and see where he is, and I'll bring some others as well."

"How many are there?" I inquire, pulling away and dropping her to her feet.

"Oh, just a few friends," she says ominously, sighing when she realises her trousers are ruined. She pulls down the shirt, which barely covers her ass, making me smirk.

"I'll see you tomorrow. We will end this and then we are free," she declares, leaning up to kiss me. "Then we can start our lives."

"If I accidentally kill the dragon, how mad would you be?" I call after her as she turns away and starts to leave.

"Very," she retorts, and then pats her leg to call the wolf who happily trots to her side, rubbing along her hip. "I would bring him back and let him kick your ass."

"Then you would kiss it better." I laugh, although that doesn't sound too bad.

"Griffin, don't test me on this," she warns, her voice filling the hallway with power, making me snarl. My wings fly out behind me as I meet her head-on.

"Do not test me either, *Vasculo*," I growl.

She grins, the crazy bitch is loving our fight. "I just might one day, to see what you do."

"It might get you killed," I reply, and she sighs wistfully.

"That would be fun, but until then be good. Well, as good as you can be." She turns away and saunters off with her massive wolf at her side. I watch her go with a smile playing on my lips.

One day, we'll probably end up killing each other. Wouldn't that be fun?

CHAPTER 42

JAIR

I wait and wait some more. I keep feeling the thread between Dawn and me stretching farther and farther until suddenly, it stops. She stops. Then comes pain and anger. It flows through her to me and I roar with it, gnashing my teeth as I beat the cell door.

It feels like it lasts an eternity, but when it's over I'm gulping in air as I wait for her. But she doesn't come. I feel her drawing closer. Where is she? I try to rip the door from the cement, but it's too strong, magically bound, so I can't. Instead I pace my cell, counting the steps to stop myself from going mad. She is strong, she doesn't need my protection, but I just found her. We don't know each other very well yet, but she is already locked into my soul like the missing piece, so to lose her now?

No, I can't think of that.

Just then the cell door opens, revealing my mate. A very large wolf stands behind her, its eyes narrowed on me as he pushes past her and enters first, sniffing me before circling. "New pet?" I ask, raising my eyebrows.

She smells of blood and sex, and I have to rearrange my hard cock in my trousers and ignore the urge to throw her against the nearest wall and have her. "Something like that." She shrugs and then her eyes darken. "It's time."

"What happened?" I demand, closing the distance and ignoring the wolf that snaps at me to grab her and bring her into my arms. Feeling her solidly against me settles all that panic and worry.

"They tried to kill me. It seems I've outlived my purpose. They are having a meeting tomorrow, everyone will be there. We are going to crash it." She grins, and it's an evil smile that has me groaning.

"But first I need to shower and then we need to build my army." She winks and turns away, but stops at the cell door to glance back at me. "Coming?"

"Always." I incline my head. Army? What army?

I FOLLOW AFTER MY MATE, the wolf at my side, as she wanders down the corridor before stopping at a scarred door and heading inside. She looks back at the wolf. "Guard the door, won't you?" she asks in a sweet voice. He lowers his head in a strange nod before turning and sitting right in front of the door.

I step inside and shut it behind me, pondering over the strange animal. He acts like a person...is he a werewolf? No, he felt...raw, animalistic, and powerful. So what is he? But all my questions disappear as Dawn starts to undress.

Her eyes light up as she watches me, pulling up her dress and tossing it aside, leaving her bare before me. She grins naughtily like she knows my exact thoughts and turns, sauntering into a shower stall. A moment later, I hear the water flick on and close my eyes in pain.

I imagine the water tracing down her curves the way I wish my hands could. But she has been through a lot, and I don't think she even realises that she doesn't just need sexual intimacy, but comfort as well. I do not believe she knows how to ask for it, my poor little mate. It tells me a lot about her. She has been hurt before for asking, for needing. One pained soul recognises it in another. Shedding my own tattered clothes, I head into the stall. She turns with a triumphant smile on her face as her wet hands reach for me.

"Turn around," I tell her softly.

She blinks but does as bid, her voice low and purring. "Want to play like that?" she teases, sticking her luscious arse out at me. I have to fist my hands and count backwards from thirty to stop myself from taking her up on her offer as she wiggles at me.

No, this is about her needs, not mine.

I can feel it pushing at me, she needs to feel cared for. Cherished, loved...wanted. Whatever they did shook her to her very core, left her reeling and unsure. We are heading into battle, into a war, and she needs to be her usual strong, confident self. But in here, with me, she can be weak. I will always look after her.

A warrior knows pain, a general feels it. I will take it inside myself and add it to my own.

Sliding my hands across her curves, I wrap my arms around her stomach and press my head to her shoulder. "Let it out."

"What?" She laughs, pushing back with her arse to brush my hard cock. "You need help freeing it?"

"No, my little blood lover, you need to let it out. I don't know what happened, I will not ask. You need to be strong, I know that. But to be strong, sometimes you need to be weak. So do it. Here and now, in my arms. Do what you need to, I will hold you through it and help put you back together again. No sex, Dawn, just the offer of someone to stand with you through it."

She goes quiet, her body stiffening. "I'm fine."

"No, you're not. And that's okay, you don't have to be this sexy, strong monster all the time, my love. You hate and rage so much because you care, because you feel so deeply, but that is a sword. It cuts both ways and right now you are bleeding from those wounds, let us seal them shut. Together."

She turns in my arms and I let her. Her blonde hair is pushed back and slick. Water rolls down her face, clinging to her lashes, her eyes wet with unshed tears as she searches my gaze. "I'm scared," she admits in a low voice.

"Of what?" I query softly, holding her closer.

"O-Of being weak. Of letting people back in...of not being enough." She blinks then, swallowing hard. "Of becoming what they made me, not this...I can control myself if I want to. But they are saying my power will keep growing, how will I control it? What if it controls me and I hurt someone I love?"

"My love." I sigh, dropping my forehead to hers and looking deep in her eyes. "Your mates will never let that happen, you know that, as do I. I see it in your head, they will be there. Anchoring you always." I smack my hand across my chest. "I will be with you to the death. I would follow you over that cliff, into battle, or worse. We will support each other. You never have to worry, we will be there."

"But how do you know?" she challenges, desperate.

"Know that you won't become a puppet of power? You are too strong, too stubborn. You wouldn't let it, but when you feel weak. When you are scared or the power gets to be too much, pass it to us, Dawn. Look into your mind, look at those threads to your other mates, waiting there for anything you need. Let us aid you, let us help you absorb it. I think that's why you have so many powerful mates, Dawn, because you will be the most powerful of us all, and that power will need an outlet. You've got more than one. You have us, feel it. Look at what love you have brought to the darkest of us.

Lighting us up once again, dusting off the relics of this world and gathering them to your heart."

She gasps, her eyes are closed, and I know she finally sees the tangle of threads of her mates connected to her.

"You are never alone, not in your life, not in your power. We are here. We are yours. Let us be that."

I see the moment she fully accepts us, not trying to protect us or love us, but accepts our help. She cracks, breaking in my arms. Her legs give way, and I hold her up, stroking her hair and whispering words in my native tongue. She will tell me what happened when she is ready, but for now she needs my strength.

She can have it.

When she is done, soft and pliant, I turn her and help her wash, scrubbing at the blood and dirt caked onto her beautiful skin until she shines like the most beautiful jewel in the world. She looks up at me when I am done with a soft smile on her mouth.

"There, perfect once again," I murmur.

"Thank you," she whispers, as we put her back together again. When we leave the shower, she is back to her usual, monstrous self. "I have no clothes, it's a good job I don't seem to get cold."

"I would offer you mine..." I lift my shirt up and she snorts. It's basically rags, so I leave it with her shirt, but slip on my trousers after she assures me she doesn't want them.

"I don't mind being naked, it makes me feel stronger...better. Like I know they can't touch me, it's our most vulnerable state yet when I feel the strongest," she tells me as she grabs my hand and twines it with mine. "Let's get our army, Jair."

I love the way she says the name she has given me. Like a pet name, it has a softness in it that the rest of the world doesn't get to see. Our own private sweetness.

We head back out into the corridor and the wolf falls into step next to her other side as we pass cell after cell as we wind around the dungeons. "What are we looking for?"

She stops suddenly, head tilted. Frowning, I listen and then I hear it—crying. It's soft and wispy, definitely feminine and far away. I look to Dawn to see that her eyes are black. They flick to me and I realise I am now holding hands with her monster, not her, so I hold on tight, my own fangs dropping. She turns away and leads me towards the cry. It gets louder and louder until we are outside a cell that looks like all the others.

"Blood," I murmur, sniffing the air and scenting the copper tang. "Human."

Letting go of my hand, she stabs her hand straight forward. I move to intercept, to protect her from hurting herself, but she throws me away with a thought. I hit the wall just as her hand plunges through the metal with a screech. She looks at me as I get to my feet, a look that tells me I need to trust her in this. So I nod and stand behind her, although it is hard. I am used to being the first person through the door, uncaring of my safety, but these protective instincts towards my mate are strong, a continual fight between defending her and letting her do what she needs to.

With a shriek she warps the metal and flings the easily four-hundred-pound door away like it is a feather. We both peer into the dark as the cries suddenly cut off, a small scream coming from a form huddled in the corner.

"No, no, not again, please," comes the soft voice. It's weak and afraid. The whole cell stinks of fear and blood.

My fangs descend farther, and the human woman whimpers, burying her head into her knees and rocking back and forth. We step inside and I glance around to see the bucket in the corner. Ignoring the stench of piss, I spot the rotting food on the tray next to the door. But then something else hits me.

"Two, two heartbeats," I snarl, looking around for the other person as the wolf snarls behind me, drawn by my anger.

"She's pregnant," Dawn says softly, and I look over to see she is right. The woman's belly is rounded, her face raised now, pink and dirty, her tears leaving white tracks down her plump face. Her eyes are a deep brown, her hair a mucky, greasy brunette. She is naked,

I note in a clinical way, and her feet are also bare and covered in dirt.

Blood coats the soles of her feet as well as her thighs. "Dawn."

She nods, crouching down before the woman as I block the wolf to try and help calm her. "Hello," she begins, but the woman cries and jerks away. "I won't hurt you, I'm not here to hurt you. Look at me, I'm not with them."

The woman eventually lifts her eyes, eyeing Dawn with a frown before glancing at me and cringing away. Dawn glances over her shoulder, her eyes smouldering. "Wait outside?" she pleads, and I nod, throwing the woman one last look before standing at the doorway where she can't see me, but I can still hear. I can hear the rustle of them shifting before Dawn's sweet voice comes again. "I'm sorry for what they have done to you. What's your name?"

"I, erm, I'm Kelly," she whispers, voice a bit stronger now.

"Hi, Kelly, how long have you been here?" The woman doesn't respond, and I hear Dawn sigh. "I swear they won't hurt you again, I swear it, Kelly. Look at me, that's it. I know what it feels like to be seen as nothing, to be a punching bag. To be scared of your own shadow. They make you hate your own body, make you feel like it's no longer yours, but it gets better. I promise you, you heal. You don't forget, but you heal and come out stronger. This? This is a blip in your life, you are so much stronger than you will ever know. Look at you, surviving in the midst of such destruction. And you have another to think of now."

"I—he—it," Kelly stutters before lowering her face. "They-they raped me," she cries out before getting a hold of herself. "It's—this thing in me could be a monster."

I stiffen at her admission. They forced their seed into this woman? I will spike them all!

"Look at me, Kelly. We both know human monsters can be so much worse. This baby in your belly, they might have made it, but you will raise it, it's part of you, and trust me, sometimes the monsters are better than those who paint themselves as your saviours."

"I'm tired," Kelly admits. "So tired, I don't think I can fight anymore. I thought when-when that thing came that I would die, but then I didn't. But now I feel it, the baby, moving inside me, and now I don't think I can do this."

It goes quiet and I listen carefully, knowing this woman is on the precipice of giving up, I have seen it in soldiers often. Their will to go on gives out and they die.

"You will go on because you have to. It's never easy to be a woman, Kelly," Dawn starts, her voice strong and commanding, that of a true leader...a queen. "When men are born, they are told the world is theirs for the taking, to dream big and never give up. Us? We are told that the world isn't fair, that our dreams might not come true and to be prepared for that. As I grew up, I was told to bite my tongue, because boys will be boys. I was told not to be too smart. Too loud. Too sexy. Too opinionated or rude. Well, fuck that."

"I was told what I could be while men were told they could be anything. Even when I became an adult, I saw the injustice every day. The men I worked with, dated, they stood before me confused as I got angry, because they have never had to fight just to be heard in a room full of men. To be taken seriously. To have to walk home quickly, clutching your keys out of fear. To cry in the shower as blood runs from my body, because they made it their own. And it's not mine anymore, and no matter how I dress or how I act I will never be good enough.

"I became an object, like you, since birth, raised to be perfect for men. But I never was, even when I was everything they dreamed of. They still hurt me, still pushed me around and treated me as lower than them. Just an object. Fuck that," Dawn spits, her anger palpable.

"If you want to scream, do it. If you want to rage or run naked down the streets, do it. I will do it with you. If you want to get drunk and tell every man they are wrong and womansplain their asses, do it. If you want to murder the people that hurt you, want nothing more than to kill them. I'll help. If you don't want this baby, that's fine. It's your body, your choice. You are not just an object. You are a person. You are stronger than any man because you have faced battles they never could. We are women, and we are stronger than you will ever know."

I suck in a breath, pride at my mate filling me.

"Kelly, it's your life, I will set you free. But you need to be strong enough to take it, can you?" she finishes, and I hold my breath with her. Her speech makes me want to kill all men. Everyone who ever told her to be quiet, who hurt and used her. Who made her afraid.

Maybe this is why I am here.

To help her, because my mate is a fighter. A fighter for everyone who has ever been wronged. She will set it right. She sees the pain and the underdog and understands them, feels for them. Protects them.

Because she was one.

We are just along for the ride.

"I-I want to be free, I want to live," Kelly whispers, then her voice gets stronger. "I want to live!" she yells and then laughs, it sounds choked though. "Even if this baby is a monster, it's mine. But first, how do we get out?"

"Hold on." Dawn goes quiet then sighs. "My friend is coming, he can get you out, okay? I need you to trust me, he is a man, a bit surly, but I promise you he will never hurt you. He won't even touch you, Kelly. Can you do that? You are your own hero here."

"I can, I can do this," she repeats, and then I hear them shuffling. Dawn appears in the door and I just stare at her.

I am beyond lost for words. I do not know how I got so lucky as to be a mate to such an amazing, strong, confident, and smart woman, but I will pray that I am enough to stay by her side. Because I want to be, I want to see where this world takes her, because for someone so strong, so fate touched, things are going to happen.

She must hear my thoughts, a side effect of her understanding the bonds she has weaved I would guess, because a smile covers her face. "You will always be by my side. Griffin is coming, but then he has to get back to work. We better go before he arrives and tries to kill you. I need to get to my minotaur."

"He could try." I shrug and she grins.

"You're hot when you're cocky." She looks at the wolf then. "Stay and protect her? You can find me again, right?"

The wolf whines but nods and sits, looking at the woman whose hand is on her curved belly as she watches the wolf in confusion. Dawn turns to her and takes her hand. "Good luck. If you need anything, find a woman called Victoria, or Victor." She reels off an address and the woman mumbles it back before tears fill her eyes.

"Stupid hormones, thank you," she tells Dawn and takes her hand. "Thank you so much."

"Give them hell." Dawn winks and then takes my hand and leads us away. I glance back to see the woman staring after Dawn with a wondrous look in her eyes. Glancing down at my mate, I smile. She has that effect on people, she drives them to want to be more, to never give up even in the darkest of times. Because she is right there with you.

As are we. The monsters gathered behind her in the dark—horns, fangs, and wings hers to command. We will raze this world and rebuild it in her image. She doesn't even realise it as she walks along next to me, but she is starting something here. Something that will change the world, that will change the fate of our people.

All because of one skinwalker.

CHAPTER 43

LUCIFER

Exiting the dragon's car, I take in a deep breath of fresh air. It has been so long since I have been free, and now I have the world at my feet. I will find the woman who called to me, I will chain her by my side, and we will walk through this world together, my fire trailing in my wake. Chaos, war, and death blooming under my hooves.

She will want for nothing, she will be my very own pet.

Unlike the prideful dragon still arguing on the phone, I know the truth. Love isn't real, it's what humans and supernaturals tell each other to try and make sense in this world, to find someone to ride it out with. So when the darkness gets to be too much, they have something, someone to turn to. True love, mates, it's all a game by the fates, a cruel one. Someone will always end up hurt, betrayed, and left—love isn't real. But lust?

Oh yes, lust is real, and I am very much aware of that.

My little pet will be as well, she will worship at my feet, mine to do with whatever I want. And when I grow bored with her, I might let her free if she has been good.

I met a fate once, a vile woman she was. She possessed a human I was about to kill in a battlefield. Blood had sprayed us from all angles, the cries of the damned rising amongst the field as the war cry came from both sides. And there we had stood in the midst of it all, her soulless eyes locking on me as she dropped her weapon.

Those eyes, they saw everything. In them was the whole universe, the working and turnings of it, a constant stream of past, present, and possible futures.

She had told me, informed me, that one day I would be tested. That when the pull of life outweighed that of death, I had a choice to make. To save this wretched world or burn in it.

I had laughed in her face. I would always choose death, it is what I am.

She had looked at me sadly.

"Then you will all burn. Choose death out of fear, Serpent. Choose it because you dread the very depths of your soul and what you are capable of when faced with the entity of life and change and you doom them all. Humans and supernaturals alike. You alone can turn the tide. Choose wisely."

She gasped and dropped to her knees as the warrior returned. Her silver armour stained red with hers and others' blood, her sword on the ground beside her. Her brown hair was tied back into a plait at her side, her face wild and covered in dirt and blood. Those eyes had locked on mine, tears misting in them as she looked upon me and saw the truth.

In me she saw her death.

I picked up my sword and I took the life like I always do. As I turned and walked away, something bloomed in me. A thread of doubt...burn, she said.

Why would I not choose that?

A slamming of the door brings me back and I shake off the memory, turning to the dragon. "Ready?"

He nods, his chin high in the air. "How does this hop—"

Without letting him question me, I wrap my power around him and tear a hole through space and time and drop us out at the other end. My mist still swirls around us as I laugh. He groans, gagging as he bends forward. "Snake," he hisses. "Warn me next time."

"Fine, we have four more hops," I drawl, bored.

"Four?" he roars as I do it again.

He falls to his knees this time, his eyes pinched in pain. "Four?" he repeats, eyes glassy as he glares at me.

"Yes, I cannot travel around this world in one, not with you in tow, it would drain me too much." I shrug and hop us again.

He snarls this time and gets to his feet when we land and throws himself at me. Laughing, I hop us that last time, throwing him backwards. He lands on his back on the soil near the council's mansion. Groaning, he lies there limply as I stroll over, sucking the mist back in until I am a man once again. He stares up at me.

"Tell me, do the great dragons struggle with riding time?" I taunt.

"Demon," he grumbles, and tries to get to his feet, only to fall on his face. Groaning, he gets to his knees, panting, and waits. Rolling my eyes, I offer him my hand.

"Come, dragon, we have your mate to save, do we not?"

At that he lurches to his feet, his eyes ablaze with purpose and love. Spinning, he turns to take in the mansion from where we stand on the hill next to it. I turn with him, taking it in. "She's in there," he whispers.

"I would hope so, or otherwise this trip was for nothing. Come, let us go kill some beings, it's time they are reminded who is really in charge."

Chapter 44

GRIFFIN

After rescuing the human female, I quickly fly her beyond the council's reach before leaving her at a rest stop. I daren't fly too far in case they notice my absence. That wouldn't work well, they would punish me, and I need to be invisible to investigate who we can kill and who we can trust. I still don't know what Titus is doing, but I know for sure we can't trust Amos. That leaves Derrin and Greta.

I follow her first, making sure to stay out of her deadly, icy grasp.

The only reason she doesn't notice me is because she believes I am beneath her. She struts around the mansion in her flowing white gown, never once checking to see if her nephilim guards, or slaves as she calls them, are who they say they are. She trusts in her power, and in the power of the council, that we will be there to protect her from any threat. Her eyes do not even graze across us.

The icy tendrils of her power pass over us, making us shiver as she enters the breakfast room, which is the size of a house. She sits at the head of the table, sipping on champagne and staring out of the window until her voice suddenly barks out, "Slave."

I spot the nephilim in the corner cringe slightly before he straightens and heads over, getting to his knees beside her and bowing his head. Her hand reaches out and she pets him like a dog. I feel anger on his behalf flowing through me, but I stay pressed to the door like a good little slave.

Not yet, I will not compromise my mate's mission over one nephilim who hates me.

She carries on stroking him, sipping her champagne before leaning back in her throne-like, wingback chair and finally looking at him. She grabs his chin and lifts his head, staring at his face the same way you would cattle. "Not bad looking, have I had you before?"

"Yes, my lady," he replies.

Her lips tilt up at that. "Good. Under the table, slave. Show me why I shouldn't kill you here and now for meeting my eyes."

He stills for a moment before ripping up the tablecloth and slipping under the wood. A moment later she groans, her eyes closing in bliss, her other hand dropping her champagne glass, which causes another nephilim to dash forward and catch it, placing it on the table beyond her reach as slurping, wet noises sound.

Cringing, I slip from the room. No fucking way am I going to stand there watching her get head. Christ, she even made that seem cold. Not like my mate who is all fire, all passion. When she wants, needs, she takes it, but oh fuck, it's so good.

Shaking my head, I decide to try Derrin instead. The incubus tends to rise late, so he should just be waking after his orgies last night, or feeding fest, as the nephilims call it. They wait until morning to dispose of the bodies he drains dry. I've heard them speak of it often, how many sheep he goes through.

I hate sheep, especially the small ones, but he tosses their lives around without thought. Like they are nothing. Maybe I always thought that previously, but my mate was once human, so I can't hate them too much.

They might be destructive, self-serving creatures with a short lifespan, but they are more like us than we want to admit.

I head to Derrin's chambers on the top floor. The doors to his wing are open, so I slide through them, moving into the dark space that smells of blood, sex, and death. I pass his sitting room and kitchen and other rooms until I find his bedchamber. The doors are open and the scent is stronger here.

Some candles are burning, illuminating the area which is covered in satin and silky materials, red and gold everywhere. It looks like an old, French tart's boudoir I saw in a film once.

And there is Derrin, positioned in the middle of the double king-sized bed, with silk draped across his thighs, his arm over his face. His body is naked and covered in...well, fuck, I don't even want to know. Next to him are five women, all spread across the bed. Some face down, some on their backs.

All dead.

All naked.

Derrin's eyes open and he locks his gaze on me. Grinning, he slips from the bed, unashamed of his nakedness as he heads to a bar in the corner and pours himself a drink. "On body duty, fallen?" he asks, his voice infused with the power he drained from those sheep.

He tosses his drink back and looks over at me. "Get to it then, can't have their bodies rotting and stinking up the place."

I spare a glance at the sheep. Fuck, now I'm on body removal? This job sucks, no wonder so many sheep kill their bosses. "Of course," I snap, adding some venom to my voice to make it seem like I'm ordered to be here, not snooping.

I head to the bed, but he stops me. "Fallen?"

"Yes?" I snarl, turning to him and giving him my best pissed off expression, which is my normal face, so it isn't too hard.

"I have a question," he starts, so I wait silently, not replying. He grins, pours himself a drink, and leans back against the bar, watching me. "You see a lot, hear a lot no doubt, any clues on what has Amos so...riled up?" he queries, sipping the clear liquid.

Huh, he doesn't know? My face must say it, because he rolls his eyes.

"No one trusts an incubus, and though people deal secrets for sex, I can't seem to find out, but there is something happening. I can feel it, I'm not stupid. I want to know what so I know where I need to stand."

Well, that crossed this idiot off our list. He's more bothered about getting his dick wet than what's happening right under his nose.

"I don't know." I shrug. "They don't tell me anything."

"But you must suspect something," he snarls, pushing away and stalking towards me. He trails his hands across my chest, a tingling power following. Is he trying to seduce me? What the fuck?

He stops behind me and leans closer, pressing his body against my back as I fight the urge to fling him across the room. Asshole, using his powers to get what he wants. The worst bit is, the power is shooting straight to my cock even though I don't do men and I really don't want him to touch me. I try to pull away, but I can't, he has me locked in place even as I try to fight his control, my body revolting at his touch and his ability to make me want him. Taking what I'm not offering.

His hand traces lower, gripping my hard length through my trousers and flinging more power into it until I'm gasping, nearly spilling in my jeans.

"Tell me, fallen, and I will make all your dreams come true. I will suck your dick better than any woman, I will give you the best sex of your life," he purrs against my ear, licking the shell. Bile rises in my throat. Is this all we are to them?

Puppets to control? To order, to use, even when we don't want it?

If so, how are we any better than the sheep lying dead in his bed?

"Stop," I demand, even as the madness swirls in my head, trying to protect me from what's happening, wanting to lash out. To get his hands off me, his mouth away from my body. Even without having a mate, I wouldn't want him to touch me, but now, with Dawn in my life? Every touch that isn't hers is actually painful, sending a shot of wrongness through me.

It meets his power which is still swirling through me, the pain and the pleasure almost sending me to my knees. I hate his hand, I hate the fact that my cock is reacting to his power, and I hate it even though I know it's what he is.

Lust, pure fucking lust, and he's using it against me like a weapon to get his way. I don't know how to fight this, how to stop it. Panic rushes through me at what he could do to me, at what he could take...

"Why? You like it, I can feel it," he murmurs, and reaches around me, pressing his other hand against my hard cock, both of his hands rubbing me now. I feel disgust from his touch and finally break past his influence, stumbling away as he laughs at me, his eyes bright blue with power as he watches me. "Oh, you're a strong one, no one breaks my spells."

Snarling, I let my madness take over as I slink backwards, my mind blank and uncertain over what just happened. It doesn't happen to men...right?

I smash him back into the wall, my grip on his throat, but all he does is laugh. "Oh, you like it rough? Fine." He flings out his hand and I'm thrown backwards into the wall. I jump to my feet straight-away and point at him.

"Never touch me again or I'll kill you," I snarl, meaning it. I want to kill him right now, right here, but I can't. Desire for revenge wars inside me with my need to stay on our mission. So I do the only thing I can do before I bathe in his vile creature's blood—I leave. "Clear your own bodies," I yell at him, and race from the room.

Once outside, I press my back to the wall, my heart tripping over itself, my stomach in knots. What just happened? The madness recedes and I slump, it was nothing. Just a power play, nothing else. He didn't do anything, nothing happened. Women have offered themselves like that, it was just a joke...a ploy.

Then why do I feel sick?

I hear voices coming this way, so I wipe my face clear and push off from the wall, storming away from the incubus's suite and back downstairs until I'm outside. I can't help it, I need to get away, to feel clean. I leap into the sky and fly as fast and as hard as I can to escape my own thoughts.

The feel of his hand on my body, making it do things I didn't want.

It doesn't help, I can still feel his slimy touch, so I swing back around and land in the forest, rushing to the secret entrance in the nephilim quarters until I enter the dungeon, my heart racing, my stomach still roiling, and my head a mess. I push into the showers and throw my clothes away, wanting to burn them.

The smell of him, feel of his power...

I yank on the water, panting as I scrub my body. When my hand passes over my cock, I turn my head and gag, remembering how his power made it hard. I scrub until I'm red raw and then step out. I feel cleaner, but not better.

I need—I need—

I need Dawn.

Ignoring my clothes, I race through the maze of cells until I find her. She's in the cell with the minotaur, it stinks of sex, but I can't even summon my jealousy. I smash open the door, my eyes wild until I find her.

She sits up, her face concerned.

"Griffin?"

CHAPTER 45

NOS

"You are a believer, fate chosen."

The voice is strong, both male and female. A blending of soft and hard. Velvety and rough. I know what it is—fate. I do not open my eyes, I stay seated, if fate has chosen to appear to me, it is for a reason. But why? And why now?

"You know why, fate chosen. You were brought into this world for a purpose, for a reason. You were quite literally chosen by us to be a protector, a guardian, a mate, and an anchor."

"Dawn," I whisper.

"Yes, the little skinwalker...or is she? You must learn what and who she is, fate chosen, it is how you will all survive what is to come."

"And what is that?"

"Change, it is time for a change, the rule of man is over. We grew tired of their destruction and vile acts. Dawn, your mate, she is the catalyst. Do not fight it, god, embrace it and everything she has to offer. Only then will the future we desire come to fruition. Do your duty, your purpose, and you will be rewarded."

"And if not? If it doesn't transpire?" I question, knowing the likelihood of what this fate is seeing turning to reality is slim, almost non-existent. It is merely a hope.

"Then this world will burn and you will lose her for eternity. You are so close to what you want most, god. Do not let it slip through your grasp now."

I open my eyes to see the room is empty, she is gone. Did she mean I would lose Dawn? That if we do not somehow complete the fate's vision, we will all die? I do not even know what she wants us to do, she told me I had a purpose...to protect Dawn?

Only time will tell, and I can feel it drawing closer. I want to find her, my mate, but I can't. Not yet. Fate keeps me locked in place, Dawn has things she needs to do first, an abundance of choices and actions to complete. One wrong move could send us all tumbling into death, I feel it.

No. This fight is Dawn's. It is her choice.

But you will not do it alone, Little Monster, I am here. Feel me. Soon, we'll be together again.

I pray we can win, that we can please fate, for I want a long life with my mate, not the stolen moments I have had. I want her forever, for eternity.

My little monster.

She is fate chosen.

CHAPTER 46

DAWN

I lead Jair to Dume's cell and slip back inside. He's waiting for me and covers the distance in two strides, pulling me into his arms and kissing me so hard I swoon. He releases me and looks at Jair. "Dume, this is Jair."

Dume smiles. "So you like the name?"

"I do." Jair nods and then bows with an old-style flourish that has lust shooting through me. I can imagine him back then, at a court in a fancy outfit with music playing as he bows before we dance.

Dume bows awkwardly in return and grins at the man. "Nice to meet you, I am Dume of the Labyrinth, another of Dawn's mates."

"How many do you have?" Jair questions, not angry but curious.

"A few." I shrug, not wanting to stir anyone's jealousies. "Are you okay?" I ask Dume, aware I've been gone a while.

"Of course, *Draya*, you?" he rumbles and I sigh, snuggling closer to him, having to crane my neck back to meet his gaze.

"I am now," I answer.

"Do you want me to wait outside?" Jair queries, again not appearing to be jealous—it seems my vamp can share.

"No, it's okay," I tell him, and hold my hand out to him from Dume's embrace. He hesitates before taking it and pressing me between them, making me sigh in happiness. "We are doing it tomorrow morning," I inform Dume. "Tonight we will free all the monsters down here. Let's show them exactly what they have been keeping imprisoned. You can't break or tame a monster."

"I am with you always, *Draya*." Dume nods. "Tomorrow we will head to battle."

"Battle...yeah, I guess we will," I agree, and then it seems to hit me. We will be taking on the council, some of the most powerful members of the supernatural community. Even with my powers and my mates, we might get hurt.

We might die.

But I have to, what they are doing is wrong. I have to stop it because no one else seems to be stepping up to do it, and I have people depending on me. BB, all the girls we rescued. Jair. Griffin. Nos. Kelly. All of them and many, many more.

I feel a sudden rush of panic, of utter need to keep them close. To feel them against me, to know they are okay. I can't lose them, they are my life. All of them. I need them now more than ever.

"Shh, my love, we aren't going anywhere," Jair murmurs, kissing my head.

"*Draya*," Dume rasps, and I look up at him.

"What does that mean?" I finally inquire, trying to distract myself.

"It means goddess, that is what you are." My heart bursts as he cups my cheek and I lean into his touch. "I have lived on my knees for a queen once, Dawn, and I promised myself never again. You don't ask for that, but I would fall to them gladly right now for you, my goddess."

I gasp and he leans down, pressing his lips to mine. "I would live on them, I would die on them if that is what you wanted, just to be close to you. To keep you. *Draya*, my goddess."

"We are here, we are not leaving your side. I have faced death on many occasions, my love, and I will face it again—this time, for you. What more of a noble cause is there?" Jair asks, and I swear if they weren't holding me up, I'd be at their feet. The love, the passion from them wraps around me until I feel so safe and cared for.

Even in the most unlikely of places, who knew you could find such love in darkness?

"Prove it," I demand, my voice strong. "On your knees," I order, and he grins against my lips and falls to them instantly, his head still level with my shoulders as he peers up at me, giving me all the control.

But when faced with death, I find myself wanting to try everything, to be together for once. Fully. Wholly.

Grabbing Jair's hands, I drag them up my body until he covers my breasts. I let go and he groans, his fingers rolling my nipples as I watch Dume. His eyes flash red as he watches the other man's hands on my breasts.

"Let me taste you," he rumbles, my bull asking.

"Open your thighs," Jair murmurs, kissing along my neck before dragging his fangs back along the column of my throat, making me moan as my head drops back to his shoulder, my eyes still on Dume.

"I need—" I groan as Jair flicks my nipples and digs his fang in deeper, but he doesn't break the skin like I wish he would. "I need to test these powers in me, I need to free everyone."

"There's time, my love, but right now we are asking you to let us worship you. To show our mate just what we are fighting for," Jair growls from behind me, his body pressed against my back. I can feel his hardness through his tattered trousers.

"Who am I to stop that?" I tease as I part my thighs. Jair's hands glide down and push them farther open, my slickness already coating my tender flesh.

Dume presses closer, his rough hands gripping my thighs as he sits on his heels. But he's still too big. He grunts and lifts me, pushing me up against Jair, and throws my legs over his shoulders until his face is level with my pussy.

One flick of my bull's clever tongue has me moaning. His thick fingers push against my opening, just pressing as he lashes my clit with sure, harsh strokes. Bucking, I rub myself on his face as Jair continues rolling and tweaking my nipples, his fangs dragging back and forth across my skin.

"More!" I demand.

Dume growls, blowing hot smoke over my pussy, which has me screaming. His fingers slip inside my wet heat, stretching me, the pain is delicious. Jair licks my throbbing vein before sucking it into his mouth, making my eyes close as I shiver, caught between them, unable to move.

Completely at their mercy.

Dume flattens his tongue and presses it to my clit, holding it there as he growls, the tremor of the vibrations making me jerk as I clench around his fingers, panting and twisting in their grasps. More, I need more. I need everything.

They must know, because Jair suddenly strikes, burying his fangs in my throat and drinking as Dume sucks my clit between his lips. The draw of Jair's mouth sends shockwaves of pain and pleasure shooting through my body, meeting the fire already burning low in my belly from Dume. It's the last spark it needs to ignite, I scream as I come, writhing as Jair drains me, drinking my blood while Dume drinks my cream.

It's a circle, around and around, building to something until Jair breaks it by pulling away. Dume sits back and helps me to unsteady feet, but I fall to my knees. Turning my head, I see Jair's chin and mouth sparkling with my red blood, so stark against his pale skin. "What was that?" he pants, licking his lips.

I shake my head, unable to speak, but Dume does. "Power," he rumbles as I turn to see him, his chin and lips glistening with my release. "Power that needs to get out, to be let out. She needs us."

"Then let's not keep her waiting," Jair replies with a smirk and a twinkle in his eyes. "I want her mouth."

I shiver at that...does he mean? Oh, fuck yes! "Yes," I hiss. "Dume, I want you in my pussy." Flipping over, I wiggle my ass at him, ready on all fours, aching for his thick cock to fill me, to stretch me only the way his bull can. To feel him transform behind me to just an animal rutting with his mate. To look into Jair's eyes as it's my turn to drink, to suck him so deeply his essence mingles with mine.

Jair groans at the sight as he grabs his hard cock, stroking the length as he watches me. Crawling towards him, I clutch onto his legs as I roll my eyes back to meet his glowing ones, mine, undoubtedly, doing the same. "Does your cum taste as good as your blood?" I murmur silky, and dart my tongue out to lick the mushroom head of his cock where a bead of precum sits.

"Mmm," I groan, closing my eyes and savouring his taste before blinking them open. I meet his eyes again with a smirk. "Even better, but..." Darting forward, I bite the skin of his stomach, making him yell as his hips jerk forward. I dig my teeth in until the metallic tang of his blood bursts into my mouth, and I release a groan. His hands yank on my hair, not to pull me away, but to drag me closer. Laughing, I pull away, licking my lips as I watch the ruby red of his blood trail down his stomach to his cock, dripping on it. "Better." I laugh.

Just then a large, heavy hand comes down across my ass and exposed pussy. "Stop teasing him, Draya," Dume scolds, and I grin up at Jair. His fangs are hanging down over his lips, his eyes red and wild, his chest heaving.

"But he loves it," I purr as Jair's hands tighten in my hair, dragging me closer to his cock.

Dume growls, grabbing my hips, his grasp denting the bones there with the force of his hold, and it makes me push back, wetness dripping from my pussy. I love their harsh, mean hands, their utter raw, primal need. It reminds me that I'm alive in the midst of such death and destruction.

I feel his monstrous cock press against my pussy, forcing it to stretch around the tip, but then he stills. Fuck that. I wink up at Jair as I slam myself backwards, impaling myself on his giant cock.

He groans, his hands cutting into my skin, the scent of my blood filling the air as he rips through me. Panting, I hang my head, moaning in pain and pleasure—fuck yes. This is what I need.

He doesn't wait, no, he trusts me to know what I can handle. He holds me still for his cock as he pulls out and slams back in, the sound of our skin slapping together loud in the room.

Jair wrenches my head up, snarling, "Suck my cock, mate."

He prods my mouth with it, demanding entrance. I keep my lips closed for a moment to see what he'll do. I like this side of him. He wrenches my head closer, making pain shoot through my scalp, and prods at my lips, painfully so. Almost laughing, I part them, and he surges inside, forcing his cock down my throat.

I swallow him. He bumps the back of my throat and I hollow my cheeks, sucking him down until my lips meet his base. He groans as my throat constricts around his cock. Breathing through my nose, I pull back, scraping me teeth down his length, making him jerk in my mouth and groan above me.

Dume snarls as I clench at the sound, and he loses all restraint, slamming inside of me over and over, forcing me to swallow Jair's cock deeper. I have no choice but to just hold on, my mouth and pussy theirs to fuck. I accept it, knowing I have no way to control this, no way to fight this.

Being dominated.

Whimpering, I push back into Dume's thrusts, loving it. That last edge of always being in control, of always being looked to, falls away. With them I'm nothing more than their mate. There are no expectations. I lose myself in them, in their hands and cocks, just feeling each glide of Jair's cock into my mouth as it matches Dume's punishing thrusts. Their rough hands add the edge of pain I love, the blood and scent of sex filling the air until I'm drunk on it.

Dume's cock drags along those nerves inside me that have me lighting up, screaming around Jair's cock as his blood and my saliva drip down my chin. I feel that same power rise again, and with nothing else to focus on, I watch it swirl inside me before moving to Jair and then back to me and then Dume. Again and again, it washes through us. They feel it. I see it on Jair's face, feel it in the clenching of Dume's hands. In his fast, hard thrusts which are picking up speed. As it gets stronger, we draw closer to our releases. It builds in us, dragging us nearer, nearer, nearer until, with screams, we all explode.

Power and cum.

It surges from us, splintering out like a shockwave. My eyes are locked closed, my body jerking and draining of both power and energy until, finally, it's over. My mouth is filled with Jair's cum and I swallow it as I feel Dume's cock filling my pussy. They both pull away and we collapse.

Holy fuck.

CHAPTER 47

DUME

We all felt the pulse of magic from our union. It flowed between us, dragged from body to body, speeding up until it burst from us with a scream of release. It blasted outwards into the dungeon, and I felt magic bindings snap, chains break, and nets and spells shatter in the wake of our magic.

Her magic.

I look down at Dawn, my *draya*, curled up between me and her vampire. She seems so small, her pale skin dotted with bruises, but there is a giant smile on her face as she wiggles closer to both of us. Popping myself up on my arm, I stare down at her before glancing up to see Jair is doing the same. His eyes run across her face lovingly, a sheen of tears in them as he watches the woman who saved him.

I know the feeling. Like your heart might explode. Even broken, damaged, blackened, and hurt, she put it back together with her own blood and pain and made it beat again. For her.

That's what she does for us, she brings us back to life, gives us a purpose, a reason to live.

All in one small, beautiful, dangerous package.

He meets my eyes, not ashamed by his tears, and in those depths I see a promise. To always protect her, to always be with her. I know because it is in my own. Nothing could make me leave her. When the rest of the world does, even if her other mates do, I never will.

I am hers forever.

I will follow whatever path she takes, fraught with danger and enemies. Even if it leads me to chains again, even if it leads to my death, I would follow. He nods, promising the same, and we have a moment of understanding. It is hard watching another touch and love the woman who is supposed to be mine, but when they love her, when they want nothing but to protect her and be close to her like me, an understanding forms. I only hope the other mates are as accepting.

Because Jair and I aren't going anywhere.

She sighs and we both jerk our heads down to check that she is okay. We are so in sync, waiting, watching, offering whatever she needs, but it's happiness on her face as she presses her palm to my chest and grabs Jair's hand and drags it across her waist, holding us both close like she can't bear to be without us.

Our *draya*, offering and taking. Others might see her as a monster, a feat of evil, but I know the truth. Dawn is an act of God, a true saviour. Come to collect the monsters of this world and save them, to right the wrongs of man.

To some she is a monster, but to us, her mates, she is perfect.

And we will be here to help.

My hooves and horns are hers, and when we get free of this prison, I will kill those who dare to hurt my mate, who dare to make her question herself.

"*Likom, Draya,*" I whisper, leaning down and kissing her head.

I love you, I repeat mentally. She lifts her head, her eyes wide with understanding.

I love you too, my bull.

The whisper floats into my mind, wrapping around it with such love, such obsession and need, that I gasp. My little mate, how does she hold such emotions in such a tiny body?

That makes her giggle and Jair smiles at that as he brushes some hair from her neck and drops a kiss there, making her shiver. I inhale deeply as the musk of her arousal fills the air. Jair's eyes flash red, his fangs descending as smoke curls from my nose, called forth by my mate's need.

My cock hardens, prodding her stomach, and her eyes start to bleed to black again as her breathing picks up, but just then the door is wrenched open. I leap to my feet, dragging her closer as Jair turns, his fangs out as he snarls at the intruder.

Fallen.

CHAPTER 48

DAWN

"Griffin?" I exclaim. I've never seen him like this. His eyes are lost, his body wet and naked, and he looks wild and...scared.

I look to my men. "Leave," I order. I don't have time for niceties, he needs me, I feel it. They nod and get to their feet, but Dume doesn't even tease Griffin. When they go to pass him, he cringes away from them and slides into the room, slamming the door behind him and pressing his head to the metal, muttering to himself under his breath.

Getting to my feet, I step over to him and rest a hand on his back. "Griff—"

He spins, his eyes leaking black. "Dawn," he whispers raggedly. "Help me."

"What-what happened? What can I do?" I almost scream, searching his eyes, knowing something is really wrong. This isn't like my usual teasing or even angry fallen, something is very wrong.

I reach for his mind and see flashes of skin, of a hand before he jerks away, his eyes filling with tears. "Help me," he repeats, and in those words I hear a plea. He's asking for something, something he doesn't even know how to do.

I open my arms and he rushes into them. I fall to my knees, wrapping myself around him. "Shush, it's okay, I'm here, I'm here, I'm here," I chant, holding him close.

His hands convulse on my back as he drags me closer, his head burrowing into my shoulder as a sob racks his body.

I hold him, anger burning in my gut. Whoever did this, whoever hurt him, will die.

I hold him as he cries, as he breaks in my arms. I can feel his mind shying away, he wants to speak, to tell me, but he can't. He feels guilty, wrong, like he shouldn't be reacting like this. Gripping his head, I pull it away until I can stare into those red-rimmed, tear-filled eyes. "Baby, tell me, I'll fix it."

"You can't," he croaks.

"Griff, please, what's wrong?" I beg, gripping his cheeks. He shivers, his eyes closing for a moment in such immense pain and...guilt?

"I can't—"

"Can you show me?" I suggest and he cringes, staring into my eyes. "Show me, baby, let me in."

He takes a deep breath and closes his eyes, tears rolling down his cheeks as his mind opens to me. I dive in, reliving what happened. As I watch, I feel what he felt. The confusion, the horror, the guilt, the utter hopelessness. He feels like he shouldn't care, that he shouldn't be upset. God, my poor boy.

I push away my anger and need to hunt the fucker down—I can do that later. Right now my mate needs me. "Griff," I murmur, and he opens his eyes, beyond hurt, expecting me to invalidate his feelings. "What happened was wrong. You hear me? It was wrong. He should have never touched you. Do not blame yourself or try to explain it away. It was wrong."

"I-It was just a touch, though, and it doesn't happen to boys. It was just a power play," he whispers raggedly.

"Who the fuck says it doesn't happen to boys?" I roar, then calm down. "Baby, look at me, did you want him to touch you? Did you consent?"

"No, but—"

"No buts, then it was wrong. You have every right to feel the way you feel, baby. I can't take it away, God, I wish I could. I wish I could go back so you never have to experience that, but all I can do is offer you my arms. I'm here if you need to rage. To cry or to feel nothing. I'm here, I know what it feels like, baby, and it won't disappear, but you have to let yourself feel it, no matter how hard it is. You need to, don't repress this, it happened, baby. It happened."

Sometimes all you need is someone to believe you. I see the moment he realizes why he feels this way in his eyes, because deep down he knows he was sexually assaulted. He presses himself closer and I hold him, I hold him for as long as his tears fall and then even longer.

Pain is pain, it doesn't discriminate based on gender.

The door opens and he jolts but doesn't pull away. Jair and Dume are there, the wolf too. They regard us before they step inside and shut the door. "Guys, not now," I whisper.

Dume looks at the man in my arms, his face sad and understanding. "I was raped repeatedly by my queen. By a woman others followed and looked to for leadership, she even made me enjoy it. I hated myself for it, hated myself for so long. I still see her face."

Griffin lifts his head and Jair steps closer, anger flashing in his eyes. He doesn't glance at me, but keeps his gaze trained on Griffin, and I can feel his struggle at admitting what he shares. "I was turned by a woman who used my body as easily as she used my fangs. I convinced myself I enjoyed it as we killed and fucked. After, I would even cuddle with her surrounded by their corpses and blood. But inside I hated myself, I lost myself. It twisted me, and only now am I able to look back to see that I never, not once, wanted her. I felt like I owed it to her, that she controlled me, and I was so scared that I had to."

Griffin swallows, his eyes confused at their admissions, at them sharing their deepest, darkest pain for him. "Baby, I was raped, again and again. I was so scared to resist that I used to lie there, that I used to fucking thank him after." Tears fill my eyes, matching his as I stare into those dark depths. "We are here."

He licks his lips and presses his head to mine as Dume and Jair step closer and fall to their knees, wrapping their arms around us. I freeze, unsure how he will react, but he shivers and presses closer, accepting their comfort.

We sit like that, together, a tangle of limbs of understanding and shared pain.

Hours later, I lift my head. Griffin is asleep in our arms, his mind peaceful for a moment. I look to the others to see the same anger, same hate there for our hurting mate...friend. Family.

"It's time and I know whom I'm starting with," I snarl, losing myself to the darkness. I want his pain, his screams. I want him to pay for what he's done to my mate.

No one hurts what is mine.

CHAPTER 49

LUCIFER

I hop right into the council's nest, straight to the dungeons below where the dragon insists we are needed. We end up in a hallway and he whirls to me, his eyes flashing purposefully as he barrels towards me. Laughing, I dodge his outstretched hands. "What about your mate?" I remind him, and he stops, frozen in indecision before turning and storming away.

I follow after him, whistling, when suddenly, I stop. I bend over, gasping. Such power fills me, calls to me, courses through me. Lifting my head, I meet the dragon's gaze. "Your mate, what is she?" I demand.

"A skinwalker," he answers, frowning.

"No, something down here is much stronger, so much stronger." I grab him in a blink and hop us to the location of the power, needing to know.

We arrive in a cell that smells of blood, sex, and pain, all my favourite things. That's when I see her—the woman who called me forth from my slumber, who slipped inside my mind, who restored me. She's so small, her blonde hair wrapped over a bare, pale shoulder, with a curvy body that men would fall to the floor and worship. She seems harmless as I melt into the shadows to watch her, keeping the dragon trapped with me. But then those black eyes turn my way, and in those depths I see the same hate, rage, and need for violence that swirls inside me.

I suck in a breath, aching to reach through the mist to grab her and hop her away. Take her back to my home and lock her there with me as I peel back what makes this little woman affect me so, to see if she tastes as sweet as she looks. Her eyes flicker away and I want to roar, to drag them back to me...only then do I realise there are others in the room. I was so distracted by her, so taken aback, everything else had faded.

There are three.

I sniff the air—a fallen, a vampire, and a...minotaur. Interesting.

Just then the dragon struggles in the mist and somehow breaks through. Panting, he bursts into the room as I stay in the shadows, observing as he strides towards the woman I can't seem to look away from. I actually growl when he grabs her and swings her around in an arc.

She giggles, seeming overjoyed. "Aska! You made it!"

"I told you I would, *Neriso*," he murmurs, and then lets her slide down his body, still holding her in the air as his lips meet hers. I see red, wanting to rip the world apart, to kill the dragon who, a moment ago, had amused me. My nails dig into the wall as I debate ripping him away from her, but then he pulls back and I have never seen such joy, such happiness. "My mate, I finally have you."

Mate?

This is his mate?

I should have killed the dragon when I had the chance. I do not share. Not ever. I will find out what the council is doing, kill them if I must, then I will take her from him. She is mine, I feel it now. The pull, the call. Yes, I'll take her, make her mine. Chain her by my feet as she reveres me, and when I am done or kill her, he can have her body back.

With one last look at them, I hop from the room, intent on killing someone, anyone, to rid myself of this anger, this pure, unlimited chaos raging through me, swirling without purpose and needing to be let out.

Because of her.

ASKA

Dawn grins, resting her forehead against mine. I can feel the others in the room staring, but I do not care. I finally have her in my arms, after everything, we are finally together. She feels so good in my embrace, her lips against mine like the touch of gold against my skin. There is nothing compared to her, our dreamscape was a pale imitation of the beauty of my mate.

"You told me—" She exclaims, kissing me again before pulling away. "That you would tell me what *neriso* means."

"I did, didn't I?" I whisper, staring into those stunning eyes. "Beloved, mine."

She shivers and wraps her legs around my waist, holding me close, need and happiness warring in her eyes. I feel the same. I have waited so long to feel her touch, to feel her close, and now I have her.

"*Draya*," comes a voice, and I growl, tucking her closer as I snarl at the others. A big man with a nose ring holds his hands up and looks from her to me. "I mean no harm, dragon, she is my mate too."

I run my eyes over him and the long-haired man standing next to him, noticing a tired-looking Griffin leaning against the wall. "Wing man." I nod seriously.

He snorts and shakes his head. "Didn't kill you, did they? What a shame. I was hoping they would," he taunts, but his voice is almost flat, his eyes sad.

"They could try, we both know they wouldn't succeed." I puff up. "Where is the god?"

He shrugs. "Upstairs."

Dawn sighs and Griffin's face eases. "*Vasculo*, I will go find clothes for us both and see what havoc you have caused on the other cells, you can...welcome your dragon," he addresses her softly, then looks at me, his eyes narrowed as some life returns to them. "I will still kill you."

He rips open the door and leaves. The other two nod at me and look to Dawn, their gazes softening. "Be back soon, *Draya*," the big man calls, before following Griffin.

"Try not to kill anyone without me," the other man tells her with a wink, before closing the door behind him.

We are finally alone.

She runs to me, her eyes holding questions, but staring into that gaze I am wordless. "You and Griffin seem..."

"He is confused on how to act around a king. It is okay, he is learning, he will make a fine servant," I declare seriously, and she giggles.

"Oh God, you two are going to kill each other." She laughs. "Then I would have to bring you back." She shivers, her eyes locked on mine. "I'm so glad you're here," she whispers.

"Nowhere else I would rather be, *Neriso*," I state, pulling her closer, noting how she fits so perfectly in my arms. "I am betting we do not have long until your other mates come back."

"Then we better make the most of it." She grins, wiggling her eyebrows. I kiss her tenderly before fluttering my lips over each eye.

"*Neriso*, I have waited thousands of years for you, I can wait a bit longer. Our first time together, my first time with my mate, will not be rushed in a dungeon. It will be on silk sheets when I can show you just why dragons are worshipped." I cup her cheek. "I want everything between us to be perfect. You have things you need to do, my dragon and I understand that, we will wait."

"What if I don't want to?" she whispers, searching my eyes. "What if we don't survive and I never get to have you?"

I grin, flashing purple eyes at her. "You do not get to die, my beloved. We will survive this because you are too strong not to, too stubborn to die, and you have a king at your side. A minotaur, a fallen, a vampire, a god, and now Lucifer himself. We can handle this."

"Wait, Lucifer?" She blinks, pulling back, and I roll my eyes.

"Don't scream that, he won't let you live it down, and if he offers to hop you somewhere, say no, he's a mean bastard."

"I mean...he's the devil, right? Kinda makes sense." She huffs and I scowl.

"If he wasn't, I would have killed him," I grumble, and she grins.

"Okay, but after...after?" she asks, intently regarding my expression. "Unless you don't want me anymore?"

"Do not be foolish," I growl, my dragon leaking through, scales flashing across my body. "I want you more than my next breath, more than I have ever wanted anything, including a crown, including my first shift. You're the only thing in this world I want, you are what I woke for, what I searched this whole world for, and I intend to have you until the end of time, but first you have a council to stop."

She groans. "Your fancy talk is hot."

I ruffle at that, almost puffing up. "Then I will talk fancy, as you say, forever."

She giggles and kisses me again, moaning into my mouth as I deepen it. Winding my hand into her hair and duelling my tongue with hers, my dragon growls in satisfaction, wanting me to claim her now, so I rip my mouth away just as my phone rings.

Groaning, I pull it from my pocket to see a strange notification. "What in the world?"

Dawn blinks lust-filled eyes and looks at the phone, laughing as she swipes. "It's called FaceTime, so you can see their face while they talk."

"Why? Why wouldn't I just see them in person if I wanted to?" I grumble just as Jean Paul's face comes on the screen. At this point I am beginning to believe he is doing this on purpose to see my struggle.

"Sir, erm, you are upside down." He laughs and Dawn plucks the phone from my grip and turns it so he is right side up.

"You must be Dawn!" Jean Paul gushes, pushing his face to the screen. "I am so glad he found you! I can't wait to meet you!"

"Thanks?" she replies with a small smile, as Jean Paul looks back at me.

"Did you, erm...get your ride with Satan, sir? I am bringing the car now."

"I did, he was rude." I huff.

"Leave him a bad rating," Jean Paul quips, and Dawn giggles as I frown at them both.

"I don't understand. Rating? As in sexually? I didn't have sexual relations with Satan!" I almost yell, just as the door opens and Griffin strolls in.

"Well, okay, I think the dragon doth protest too much. *Vasculo*, did you let your little pet suck Satan's dick?" He laughs.

I narrow my eyes on a chuckling Jean Paul. "I will talk to you later."

"Yes, sir! Bye, Dawn!" he calls and hangs up, so I pocket the phone.

Dawn slips from my arms and leans against me while her hand reaches for Griffin. He takes it and lets her pull him closer, throwing me a glare which I return.

"I did not suck Satan's...I did not!" I gripe, making them both laugh.

"If you say so, wing boy," Griffin taunts. "I wondered how you got the sleeping council to come, now I know...in more ways than one."

"You two behave, or when this is over, I'll make you share a bed. Griffin, baby, did you find me some clothes?" she asks sweetly.

He ignores me and looks at her, his eyes swirling. "Yes, though I do prefer you naked."

"Shush." She grins and takes the bundle from him. He's dressed now too, in just some leather pants with his wings out behind him. "Where are Jair and Dume?"

"The minotaur probably went to ram into things and got stuck. Your vamp is still checking cells. Looks like whatever power you unleashed knocked loose all the spells and bindings down here, so all the monsters are going to be free."

"Good." She beams as she slips into a dress. It's silky and red, tight on her body and short with spaghetti straps. She glances down at it then fixes her stare on Griffin. "Do I even want to know where you got this?"

He grins, winking at her. "Probably, you like it when I'm bad."

"I do," she agrees and leans up, kissing him. "Thank you, baby, now let's go get the others. It's time, let the monsters be free. The council isn't going to know what hit them." She twines her hand with his and starts to leave, stopping at the door and looking back at me.

I don't know where I fit. The others seem to, they've been with her and my dreamscapes don't appear to count, so I don't know how to fit into her life, but I want to. So badly. When she holds her hand out for me, waiting, I hesitate.

"Take her fucking hand, dragon, or I'll lock you in here," Griffin snarls.

I reach out and take it. She squeezes mine as she laces our fingers together, her eyes understanding. "Our whole lives, Aska, but for now, like you said, we have things to do. And I have someone I want to start with first."

"Who?" I query.

"Someone who touched what wasn't theirs," she snarls, her eyes bleeding black and her power rising. Our hair whips all around as her energy rushes down the corridor in a punch. My mate is power-ful, that is for sure, and it only seems to be growing.

I can't wait. She's the best treasure I have ever found.

CHAPTER 50

DAWN

I march down the corridors with my mates. The dungeon is alive. Banging, yelling, and howling fills the winding passageways with life. Where there was once pain and suffering, now anger and hate bloom. They call for blood, crave it, need it. They want revenge. I know that feeling.

They will get it, my monsters. Those deemed wrong, not perfect enough, rich enough, strong enough. I will free them all and let them fill their aching souls and hearts with the pain and screams of those who hurt them.

For now, I have my own blood to bathe in. We have a few hours until the morning where the meeting will take place, and I know exactly how I will spend those hours. That man, Derrin, he hurt what is mine.

I'm going to show him what real pain feels like, what real hopelessness and panic tastes like. He thought he was the most powerful and smartest being in the room, just using his power to get what he wants, not thinking about the consequences of his actions. I will remind him exactly how wrong he was.

Actions have penalties.

He won't answer in the next life, but will in this one, to me. A monster.

Somewhere between my pain and hate, a need to right wrongs arose, a need to protect those I love and care for. Because I know the pain, the hurt. Griffin is strong, so strong, and has survived things that others would not. He doesn't know how to ask for help, but he came to me when he needed me most. He will never have to ask, I will always protect him. Always hurt those who try to hurt him.

He is mine. He's damaged, broken, mad, and angry and all mine.

I lead them from the dungeons and to the house above, no longer sneaking. I almost wish Amos or his men would find me—let them. I will kill them all right now, fuck the plan. Fuck the meeting. I'm too filled with hate and anger to care.

They need to die.

But lucky for them, no one is about. They are busy preparing for the meeting or sleeping as we head through the hallways and up the stairs until we reach the incubus's suite. I stand at the doors, feeling Griffin's hand shaking in mine, and I look to him with black eyes. "Wait here."

"No," he snaps, his eyes swirling with our madness.

"You do not have to be there," I tell him, giving him a way out.

"No, I need to see it. I need to see him die, and I won't let you near him alone," he growls.

"Baby—" I start, and he slams me into the wall. I hold my hand up to stop the others as Griffin lowers his head, his eyes angry and locked on mine.

"Where you go, I go, no more apart. We do this together, get that through your fucking skull, skinwalker."

I shiver from the violence in his eyes and voice. "Got it, you can pin me to a wall and fuck me later, baby. Let's go."

He blinks, staring down at his hand like he didn't even realise he had me pinned. Releasing me, he takes a small step back, not letting me too go far as I wink at Jair, Dume, and Aska to let them know I'm okay before turning to the door.

"You three wait out here, block the door. Kill anyone who gets too close, we need to do this," I order. I can feel them wanting to come with me, but I look back and something in my eyes stops them.

"Be careful, my love," Jair murmurs, and turns to watch the hallway.

"*Neriso*." Aska nods and copies the vampire, crossing his arms.

Dume meets my eyes and, saying nothing, puts his back to the door, not letting anyone past as we slip in and shut them behind us. To the left is a hallway. It's dark in here with no lights on, and the scent of blood and death wafts towards me, making my heart slam in my chest.

I'm called by it. I follow it down the corridor, Griffin on my heels, both of us silent and racked with a need so strong you can taste it. I reach a room at the end and the door is open slightly, so I push it inwards, cringing at the gaudy decor of silk, red, and gold.

And there, in the middle of the bed draped in fineries and bodies is the incubus himself.

Derrin.

Griffin sucks in a breath so I blast him with waves of love. I hear him groan and press closer as we watch the slumbering incubus who seems unaware that we have even entered his room. I mean, really? How does this man even survive? Is he so reliant on security and his powers he thinks he's untouchable?

Of course he is.

I'm about to show him how wrong he happens to be.

I turn and slam the door, waking him. He jolts upright, his eyes blurry and hair messy as he blinks and runs his hand through his locks. He's beautiful, has ultimate sex appeal, but all I feel when I look at him is hate.

He glances from me to Griffin and a smile tips his lips as he reclines naked in the bed. "Well, well, fallen, brought someone to play with me? I knew you liked it."

I step in front of Griffin, holding him back as well as drawing Derrin's attention to me. "I did come to play, in fact."

"Is that so? And who are you, little bird?" he coos, and slips from the bed, prowling my way. He moves like a panther, graceful and sensual, but it does nothing for me. His cock is at half-mast, and as I look on in disgust, he runs his hand across his chest to cup himself as he stops before me. Griffin's hand darts out and grabs the back of my dress, trying to tug me back from the incubus as he lowers his head and blows power right into my face. "I promise you will love it, *cher*. Why don't you show me what that dress is hiding? Let's put on a little show for the fallen, show him what he ran away from." His eyes pulse with power, it fills the room, slamming into my veins like a drug, trying to create a reaction, but I feel nothing.

This is nothing.

Compared to the pull, the utter lust, need, and magnetism of my mates and their bonds, this is fake, false, and wrong. I scowl at it, pushing it away, and he blinks in shock before stepping back. I take it no one has ever rejected his powers before, I'm happy to be the first.

"What are you, *cher*?" he murmurs, his voice husky, and Griffin growls, making Derrin tut. "I am not talking to you, fallen." He slams power into Griffin who shivers, so I press my back to his chest, offering him my strength. He dips his head onto my shoulder, sucking in my scent as I reach for his mind and share myself with him, blocking out the incubus.

"He is mine. Don't ever look at him again or this will be over before we even start," I warn, my eyes black and my own voice low and velvety with power.

He mistakes it for need, for want, not for the hate and anger it is. He can't fathom someone not wanting him. He winks at me. "As you wish, my beauty." He turns and heads to the bed, sitting on the edge with his legs spread. "Why don't you come over here?"

An image of Griffin ripping off his head flashes into my mind from my surly mate, making me laugh. I pull away from him after sending him a mental kiss and saunter towards the bar instead. I pour myself a drink and sip it as I turn to see Derrin watching me with interest, like I'm a bug under a microscope. Something different, something he isn't used to.

"Tell me, Derrin, has anyone actually ever wanted you without the magic? You're pretty and all, but I can smell your rotten soul from here," I muse, sipping on my drink.

His face clenches in anger as he leaps to his feet, his gaze going to Griffin. "How dare she speak to me like that! Bring her here, now!" he orders.

I flick my fingers and the incubus flies back onto the bed as I step closer. "I told you, he's mine. You do not get to order him around, you do not even get to look at him, understood?" I snarl.

He fights my hold, thrashing on the bed, so I drain my drink and stop at the foot of the mattress, staring down at him. He stops fighting and glares at me. "Who are you?"

"No one to you, just a woman. A woman whose mate you touched," I reply, and he growls, his eyes trying to slide to Griffin. "Yes, him, and I don't take too kindly to what you did." Leaning down, I grip his chin, forcing him to stare into my pitch-black eyes. "You think you can hurt people? Force them to want you? To do whatever you want with no consequences? You think forcing them with your power means they want you because they can't resist or say no? You are a fucking parasite, a fucking rapist wanker hiding behind his title and power. You touched him. You hurt him. You will pay for that."

His eyes widen, even as his bravery and power resurface, his expression wiping clear until I see the reason he's part of the council. He might not be the smartest, but he is powerful. It knocks me back a step as he gets to his knees on the bed, his eyes flaring with it. I laugh in the face of his power and leap at him.

He doesn't expect it, they never do. Not when faced with a small blonde. They don't cower or hide, but they should. I pin him to the bed as he gapes, my legs on either side of his stomach as I lower my head and lick a line across his cheek. "You taste like sex. I wonder if your blood tastes the same...do you still bleed red or is that rotten as well?"

"Get off me! They will kill you for this, I'm a council member!" he yells, making me giggle as I lift my head to meet his eyes.

"Oh, I know, don't worry, you will serve two purposes—a warning to them as well, since they fucked with the wrong monster."

Ignoring his protests and swearing, I look over my shoulder to Griffin who is watching me. I feel his anger and hate towards the man, muddled with his need for me, his lust at seeing my monster come out to play. I extend my hand once again, this is his choice. Either way, Derrin dies, but if he wants revenge, wants to be a part of this, he can, whatever will help him.

He looks at my hand for a moment, indecision warring on his face before he steps forward once, and then again and again until his fingers touch mine. I grip him and pull him closer, and he comes willingly. Turning, we both look down at Derrin. "What do you say, baby? Should we torture him first or just rip him to pieces and fuck in the aftermath?"

"Make it hurt," he growls, his eyes swirling with madness. "I want him to scream."

Purring, I lean down to Derrin whose eyes are wide and flickering between us. He's finally getting it. He's not the predator in this room, I am. "You hear that? I can't wait to see how he makes you scream." I stroke across his face with my nails, cutting him as I go, making him hiss. "When he first met me, he tried to drop me from the sky to kill me and I'm his mate...I wonder what he'll do to you, his enemy?"

He starts to struggle again, emitting feeble attempts at power. "You will pay for this, fallen, the council will finally kill you!"

"They can try." Griffin shrugs, dropping a kiss to my shoulder and making me shiver. "They won't be living past dawn, so I'm not too worried. Before the day is through, I'll be wearing all of your blood for what you did to me and mine," he growls, his madness leaking out. It pushes into my head, infecting me with it. It's addictive, so freeing and yet powerful. They did this, they created us both.

Two abominations, never meant to live, and now we're here to end them.

They birthed their own deaths.

Derrin stops struggling and watches me, his eyes narrowed in anger. "Then get on with it already, you are boring me," he snaps, his voice filled with false bravado.

"Boring you?" I purr, leaning down. "Well, we wouldn't want that, would we?" I murmur, almost pressing my lips to his. I feel the need to consume his power, but I won't. I refuse to drain this man or wear his skin, his power and vile, rotting soul dies with him.

I feel it call to me, the seductive edge, and it only makes me angrier. This man did that to my mate, forced him, and now I will force him to feel every ounce of pain he can before he dies. Slashing my claw-tipped hands down his chest, I watch the blood well as he screams, his eyes slamming shut as he jerks beneath me. Licking my lips, I watch the crimson liquid slither down his side and drop to the sheets below him. They start to stitch together so I drag my nails back down the same wounds, digging them deeper, almost slicing him open.

He howls in pain, bucking and kicking, and between his screams, he swears at me in French. I let him calm until he's still on the bed, his chest heaving as he pants, his eyes narrowed in pain and anger as I look at my handiwork. Tracing one, black-tipped nail down his torso, I stop above his cock. "What do you say, Derrin? They used to cut these off for less, shall we?"

He shakes his head, his eyes wild as blood pumps steadily from his cuts. "Baby, do me a favour," I address Griffin. "Heat me a knife, we wouldn't want him to die before we have had our fun."

Griffin slips away as I keep my hand there, digging into the soft skin of his stomach and making him whimper. "Not so strong now, are you, little incubus?"

"Fuck you!" he screams.

"Real original, no thanks," I purr, just as Griffin comes back, holding a large, glowing knife in his hand. Turning back to Derrin, I know my smile isn't nice as I grab his cock and rip it from his body. He screams and then slumps, passing out as blood squirts across Griffin and me. I take the knife from my fallen and press it to his skin, the sizzle loud as it cauterises the flow. It wakes Derrin back up and he snivels, tears trailing down his face as I regard the bloodied cock still in my other hand.

"I have to say, it's small. I thought as an incubus it would be bigger." I laugh, but Griffin snarls and grabs my wrist, his eyes wild.

"You do not get to look at him, *Vasculo*," he growls possessively.

Grinning, I toss the cock into the fire and turn back to Derrin to see him sobbing big, ugly cries with snot dripping from his nose onto his quivering lips. "Which hand did you touch him with?" I ask.

He shakes his head, whimpering, and I roar, "Which hand?"

He still doesn't answer. "Fine, I'll take both."

Griffin grabs his right arm and presses it to the bed as I switch my grip on the knife. Humming to myself, I begin to cut through his wrist. He screams, the sound echoing around the room as I continue to cut through skin and then muscle, blood squirting at us in an arc before pumping steadily. I feel it dripping down my face and onto my lips, so I lick them clean, stopping for a second as I look at Derrin. "You taste like terror," I inform him, then go back to cutting until his hand only hangs from an tendril of sinew and bone that I can't get through. Sighing, I lean back, sad I couldn't get it off.

"Let me, *Vasculo*." Griffin smirks at me, and with quick moves rips away the hand and throws it behind us.

"That was hot," I murmur, licking my lips again. He follows the movement with his eyes, the man beneath us fading away for a moment as I'm locked under Griffin's possessives and wild gaze. Only the scream of pain from Derrin interrupts us.

Sighing, I turn to look down at him. "Do you mind? You are being very rude."

"Fuck you! He wanted it! He fucking loved it, he was so hard —" I slash my hands across his neck to stop the words, Griffin doesn't need to hear those vile lies.

His eyes widen, tears dripping from his lashes, his mouth dropping open in a gasp. I watch as a bubble of blood forms on his lips as his blood slowly pumps from the wounds. He lifts his good hand to try and stem the flow of blood, so I stab the knife through it, pinning it to his chest as he chokes and struggles. His eyes remain locked on me in terror, true terror, the type you get before you die. I know because I've felt the same way.

As he chokes on his own blood, Griffin tangles his hand in my hair and yanks my head around, his lips coming down on mine. Hard. Groaning into his mouth, I arch into his touch, tasting his need and anger on his lips. He pulls away, eyes dark as the outline of his body shakes, almost misting.

"You are magnificent," he growls. "I feel it, that madness flowing between us, your need, my need. Our need." He moans, his eyes closing for a second as I watch blood drip down his cheek, the ruby red bright against his pale skin.

My chest heaves, my nipples tightening at the utter dominance as he holds me here, taking his time and even sitting on a dying man. He's right. I want him. My pussy is slick, feeling empty as I imagine him throwing me to the bed and fucking me. He must see it in his mind, because his eyes open and catch on me, not blinking. In those depths, I see my life and death. If anyone was ever going to kill me, it would be Griffin, and I know I would deserve it.

"Yes, no one else gets to. Your life is mine, always mine to take, *Vasculo*." He tightens his hand, tugging my hair and making me cry out, but not in pain. He leans close, brushing his lips against mine. "And you would love it, you would come around my cock even as I drained every last drop of blood from your body, as I killed you, my blade in your heart. You would ask for more."

"Griff—" I gasp and he growls, biting down on my lip and drawing blood. "Yes, more," I demand, pulling my lip free and tearing the plump flesh until more blood flows.

He groans at the sight and drags me closer, kissing me with desperate, open-mouthed kisses, the taste of blood and need filling our mouths, and when I pull back, I see my blood coating his chin and lips.

Derrin stops sputtering and I look down to see his eyes are vacant, his mouth open, his lips coated in blood. His neck has started to stitch back together, but his body clearly gave out. I can't feel him or his power anymore.

He's dead.

"Huh, he died quickly, shame." I turn to Griffin. "Guess you will have to entertain me," I purr, and then dive for him. He rolls us backwards and throws me. I spin and land on all fours on the rug, watching him with black eyes as I grin. His wings are out, his chest heaving, his leather pants slung low and bulging at the front.

He wants this.

He needs this.

A fight to prove he is in control. To prove to himself the strength of his power. I'll do it gladly, I'll be his whipping boy for all time, whatever he needs. Even if it's my death, that's the dance of me and my fallen. Always.

I love it.

He comes straight for me and I meet him mid-air. He throws me into the ceiling and I fall downwards, grunting as he catches me mid-flight and flies us up, slamming me back into the ceiling next to the chandelier, which shakes from the impact, the twinkling of diamonds filling the air as cracks fracture around it. Laughing, I grip Griffin's hand which is clutching my throat as he snarls at me.

Darting my head forward, I smash mine into his, and he growls as he falls backwards, blood blooming from a cut on his head as I plummet. I crash into the floor, my stomach flipping, and he's on me in a second.

He grabs my hair and slams my head into the floor. It rings for a moment as I groan, pain flashing through me, meeting the lust in my stomach and igniting. "Stop fighting me," he demands.

"Make me," I taunt, as I crawl forward and grab a decorative vase next to the wall. Turning, I smash it into his skull and roll away laughing as he rears back, clutching his head.

"Dawn," he warns, his voice deadly. I hear my death in it, his anger...and his need. His need for this, to fight, to get it all out, even if he doesn't know it.

"Scared, fallen?" I gibe.

He flies at me, cutting through the air with a yell. I roll away from where he lands, but his hand catches my hair and drags me back to him. My spine smashes against his chest as his hand slides around my throat to try and still my thrashing body. "Behave," he shouts.

"Or what?" I laugh and then I let myself fall forward. He releases my neck to try and stop the fall, and I wiggle from beneath him, grinning even as I pant. This fighting is turning me on like nothing else, and I can feel his desire as well, mounting, wanting. "You will have to catch me if you want to fuck me, Griff."

He lifts his head, crouched on the floor with his wings behind him, his eyes alight with power. He looks like a god and I catch my breath. "Then you better run, *Vasculo*," he advises, his tone low and gravelly.

I stare at him for a moment longer before leaping up and racing towards the door, my feet slipping on the polished wood. I'm moving quickly, but it still isn't fast enough. I hear the beat of his wings, the air crashing into me before he's there.

I'm thrown into the door and it closes with a bang as he rips up my dress and presses my face to the gold surface. He kicks my legs apart while I laugh, his hands rough and mean. I hear the hiss of his zipper, loud in the room, as he frees his cock and I start to struggle —I need this too. I need to forget about my fear of what is to come, the dive into the unknown and the odds we're taking on in just a few hours.

I need him, I need him to control me. To force me, to make me into nothing but a living, breathing pleasure vessel, his to do with as he wishes. This started all about him, but I guess what one needs...the other needs too.

We are twisted together that way.

I push back, using my hands on the door, my muscles straining, and he slams me forward again, making my breath whoosh from me as his mouth meets my ear. "Stop," he snarls.

"Never," I pant, and push back again, this time adding some power to it. He goes flying backwards, and I turn with a grin to see him getting to his feet. "That all you got, fallen? Going to let one little girl beat you?"

Sauntering towards him, I run my hand down my thigh, and he watches the movement. "Can't even dominate your own mate?"

It unleashes something inside him. I see the moment he stops being Griffin, stops being worried about hurting me. He lets everything go until he's just a feral fallen, his madness leaking into the room and infecting everything. It even sends a spike of fear through me for just a moment. He senses it, his nostrils flaring as he smirks —it only seems to spur him on.

I don't see him move, he turns to mist and is gone. Turning, I gaze around the room, but I can't see him.

"Boo," he whispers in my ear, and when I spin he's gone again.

Suddenly, I'm launched at the bed. I fly through the air and land on the soft edge of the silk and slip to the floor. I grunt as I'm pressed to the flooring, mist covering my entire body, and in that mist I spot his eyes. Moaning, I look down to see almost ghostly fingers tracing up my thighs and pushing them apart.

He wrenches them wide, sending pain through me as those ghostly fingers glide across my wet pussy, making me still as I stare into those floating orbs. "What were you saying?" he asks, his voice coming from everywhere and nowhere.

"That you can't even—" I end on a scream as those fingers suddenly turn corporeal and plunge into my pussy, stretching me around them as he fucks me with them with sharp, mean thrusts. He twists them, which has me bucking and lifting my hips. Needing more, needing him.

"Still, can't," I pant, mocking him.

He snarls and then his weight comes down on me, his body turning solid as those lips I love turn up into a snarl and he yanks his fingers free, wrapping them around my throat. He squeezes, harder than he ever has before, and for a moment, I see the flash of death written in his eyes—he will kill me.

He keeps me on that edge, my vision blurring, my ears ringing as my chest screams for air. I can't even fight him, the energy is sucked from my body as he grabs my leg and throws it over his shoulder, and with one hard thrust, spears my pussy.

My mouth opens on a wordless scream as he stretches my channel, the pain and pleasure of him filling me mixing with my body's natural panic at feeling myself slip away. He fucks me through it, pulls out and slams back inside me, filling me, fucking me, each thrust painful and oh so fucking good.

Leaning down, he grins against my lips. "Like I said, I could kill you and still make you come as you die," he utters, his voice flat, emotionless, and so opposite to the harsh, angry hand around my throat as his hard cock slips through my clenching pussy. He's right, my own cream is dripping down my thighs, even as I feel myself die.

I bring my hand up and scratch at his, trying to loosen his grip, but he just laughs. It's a cruel sound, all while those powerful thrusts jerk my body beneath him as he drags on my nerves, setting off fireworks through my body, ones I can see as my eyes go black. Bright orange and red lights flash before me, my body clenching and tightening, already on the brink of release as I ride the knife's edge of death.

He keeps me there, controls it, showing me exactly who is in charge. Just how much he has been holding back. This isn't Griffin, this is his madness. This is the monster who hides so deep within he doesn't even know it, the one that craves death and blood, pain and pleasure, who needs it to survive.

I feel my body slump, the pounding of my blood in my ears as my heartbeat slows, turning sluggish even as he fucks me. Then, suddenly, I don't feel him anymore. I'm floating in the dark. Ropes surround me, twisting me, keeping me attached, dragging me back, and abruptly with a snap I'm back in my body.

I rear up, sucking in lungfuls of air, my eyes wide and locked on Griffin's smirking face as he pushes me down and continues to fuck me, even though my body won't respond. My throat aches, my lungs scream, and my eyes are dry and yet, yet with one press of his finger to my clit, I come with a silent, ragged, raw scream, my pussy clenching around him and milking his cock. He roars, filling me with his cum just as the door smashes open behind him. I peer over his shoulder, still panting and shaking from the most intense orgasm I've ever had.

There, in the doorway, is my forest god. Dume and Jair are behind him, but all I can see is Nos. His head is covered in his skull, his eyes black in those sockets, his body tall, almost touching the ceiling, and I feel his panic, his utter hopelessness, but when he sees me alive he stills, staring at me from those black holes as that panic recedes and a burst of relief and love flow to me.

"You have been busy, Little Monster."

GRIFFIN ROLLS from me as I sit up, staring at Nos as tears well in my eyes. All this time I've been so strong, but looking at my first mate now, I'm weak, needing his embrace even though I was just in Griffin's. It's been too long, too fucking long without him.

Griffin brushes a kiss across my cheek, tasting my tears. "Go to him, *Vasculo*," he says softly, his voice filled with love.

He might have just killed me—well, partly—and then brought me back, but he knows I need Nos right now.

A cry slips from my throat and then I'm on my feet. I stumble, my body still recovering from almost dying, and fly across the room. Nos storms towards me and meets me halfway, scooping me into his arms and pressing his skull to mine, those black eyes flickering white for a second as I shiver in his grasp.

This is home.

With them, all of them.

"I missed you," I whisper raggedly.

"I missed you so much, Little Monster, so very much. I felt you —I thought you had died," he rasps, the end filled with pain, and I shake my head.

"You know me, no one can kill me," I tease, even as I bring my lips to his, my nose crashing against the skull. His big hand comes up and covers the back of my head, holding me softly as he brushes sweet kisses along my fumbling lips.

"Shh, I'm here, Little Monster. I promised, did I not? I will always come for you, no one will ever stop that. Not death itself," he reminds me, lending me his strength.

I nod, shivering and shaking in his arms. With him, I always feel so small, so weak, but when he holds me, I feel his strength bolstering me, his love filling me up. I didn't even notice the hole where he should have been, but now that he's here, I feel it and it hurts until it's replete, like a piece clicking back into place so I can breathe again.

"Where have you been?" I question.

"Here. I spoke to a fate and gathered others, they are outside waiting for orders. And you, Little Monster, you've been busy." He lifts his head and looks around, noting the bodies and destruction.

"Yes, so much has happened I don't even know where to—"

"Shh," he hushes me, and the skull melts to reveal his human face, his eyes white and hair flowing over his shoulder. "Show me if you wish. Just reach for my mind and I will look."

I nod and close my eyes, focusing on his link, his pull. I follow that line and throw open the door to my mind. I feel him rush in, his warmth and the fragrance of nature that follows him filling my head and relaxing me. He flickers through everything, I can almost see it, and then pulls back, leaving a trace of his love in its wake.

Opening my eyes, I meet his gaze as he smiles sadly. "Do not believe him, my little monster. They might have made you, but you are so much more. You choose what you are and what you will become. You are the strongest of us all, and not because of magic or science, but because it was willed. You are special, not just to the world, but to us. To me."

I shiver. How did he know I needed that? I was so worried about what I could be, what they might have made me, that I didn't even think about asking for reassurance, yet he knew. He always does.

Just then a pop sounds and we all turn just as a panting Aska skids to the doorway, his eyes going to me as he slumps in relief. My wolf trots behind him with a snarl on his lips as he growls at the others, coming towards me and only stopping when I reach down and pet his silky fur on his head.

Together, we are all together.

It feels so right, I feel so full that I could burst.

But a voice interrupts my happy thoughts, a low, velvety, rough one. Like whisky on rocks that flows through me with a promise of pain and chaos.

"Well, that was interesting. Got to say, you are a lot crazier than I thought you would be. Do you enjoy being killed, walker? I'd be happy to oblige those fantasies."

We all turn to the voice, and Aska groans as he hesitates in the doorway. "Dawn, meet...Lucifer."

The man smirks at me, his full, plump lips curling up dangerously. His red eyes flare, his cheekbones are high and arched, and a shadow of horns on his head interrupts the rich darkness of his black hair. He bows, his eyes still on me, ancient and knowing, which sends my heart pounding for some reason. "A pleasure, I can assure you."

Lucifer...as in the devil?

Oh fuck.

CHAPTER 51

LUCIFER

I can't take my eyes off the magnificent creature held in a forest god's arms. I scan the others and note I am the strongest...apart from her. Her power feels wild, uncontrolled, and unknown. I can see a link between them as power flows between her and the men, and I don't think she even realises she is pulling it. Interesting.

I straighten and she watches me, her teeth digging into her plump lower lip. The skinwalker likes what she sees, good, this body was created to tempt weak mortals and supernaturals alike. It is good she is attracted to it, it will make stealing her and taking her for my own that much easier.

"Lucifer?" she repeats, and turns her head, seeming to communicate telepathically with the man holding her before she kisses him and he puts her down. I almost feel the buzz of their minds as they speak. Interesting, that will make it more difficult, but not impossible.

I watch her walk forward, unafraid of me even as I relax against the wall, not worried even when faced with all her monsters...mates. Indeed, she must be powerful to call all of these creatures.

After growing tired of watching the council prepare for yet another pompous meeting, I had been unable to help myself. I had hoped to find her, following that pull she seems to have over me. Only when I did, she had been dying at the hands of a fallen, but she enjoyed it. I had watched, ready to intervene. He doesn't get to kill her, only I do when I have had enough of her. But then she came back, snapped right back like she was unable to die, and screamed with release.

Oh yes, the little skinwalker is perfect. Craving power, blood, and death, she will crave what I offer. Will beg at my feet for it, and for scraps of my attention.

They did not know I was here of course. I had blended in, waiting, watching, and learning, but I couldn't handle it anymore, I had to introduce myself. I had to meet her.

"In the flesh, walker." I grin and she shivers as my power hits her, washing through her. Hmm, she's so responsive. I wonder if she will be the same when she is on her knees sucking my cock, chains around her neck and ankles.

Her eyes narrow like she heard the thought—impossible.

"Well, that won't work for me. I'm not calling you that stupid name. How about Lucy?" she suggests, hands on her hips, her eyes spitting venom at me. Oh yes, she heard my thoughts.

"Lucy?" I echo, scoffing. "Snake, Serpent, Oh Great One. Take your pick, walker, but remember who you are talking to."

"Oh, and who is that?" she taunts, eyebrow raised. I can see the others looking between us, no doubt they know who and what I am, yet they don't try to stop her, don't try to control her as she angers me, so instead, I laugh.

"Your little dragon fetched me, precious. I am the sleeping council," I inform her, and she just stares, the declaration falling flat. Normally people cower, cry, or beg for forgiveness, some even scream.

"So?" is what she says, unimpressed.

"I am the big bad, precious, so watch your tone. I am here to right the wrongs, after all, and you wouldn't want to be caught in the crossfire," I snap, my voice leaking power. How dare she question me.

"See, that's where you're wrong. Aska woke you, brought you here to stop me from being killed when I—as you call it—get caught in the crossfire." She steps closer then, her eyes leaking to black, and my cock jerks in my pants, wanting to be buried in her warm, wet heat like the fallen was as she screams for me, her nails clawing through my back, flaying me open. "'Cause, Lucy? I'm the crossfire. You might be some big bad, but I'm the fucking worst. Nobody's walking out of that council alive, with or without you there. Kill me if you want, kill us all, but it won't stop what's happening, what's started. We have had enough, and a price has to be paid. A blood debt is owed for what they have done. You can either be a part of it or against it." She shrugs, as if everything is that easy.

How dare she.

One little woman questioning me? Telling me, *me*, what to do?

Attraction or not, pull or not, she does not get to speak to me like that. I have killed for less, and she will be no exception. She will fear me, she will obey me. Or she will die.

Anger flows through me as I start to change. I shall show this little skinwalker exactly why I am on the sleeping council. Why the world fears me, why they locked me away to keep themselves safe, and why they barely breathe my name at night in case it calls to me.

Why they hate me.

Why they cringe in terror.

She watches as I grow, my eyes flaming as I transform into my true form. The others step closer to her, trying to protect her from me as my hooves burn through the floor, my mist swirling with power and swarming the room. "You will show respect and address me correctly!" I boom.

She laughs, actually laughs, and steps closer to me. I watch her approaching in confusion. Why isn't she running? Throwing herself at my feet and asking for forgiveness? "And you will stop having a tantrum. If you are here to right the wrongs, you might want to come with us, since the meeting is about to start and I would hate to be late, Lucy," she declares, and then ignoring my anger, she turns and starts to saunter away.

"Skinwalker," I fume, my voice shaking the room. She stops at the door. "You will not call me Lucy, or else."

She grins, winking at me over her shoulder—such bravery. "Are you coming, Lucy, or are you going to stand around here stroking your cock and telling yourself how powerful you are?"

Then she leaves, and I blink in shock as the others laugh and follow after her...I do not understand. How could one little woman, a skinwalker, face me down. Even Xaph is hesitant to...yet she was not.

What just happened?

Most importantly, if people start to call me Lucy, I am going to kill that little woman.

CHAPTER 52

DUME

I think my mate, my goddess, has a death wish. She walked right up to that demon and faced him down, almost reprimanding him like you would a child. It was clear he didn't even know what to do, but she must have felt his power, his age. The ancient demon is stronger than any of us.

Something, someone to fear.

Yet she didn't. Does she know something we don't, or is she simply past caring?

We can all feel it, her need, her bloodlust flowing through her. A pull draws her from the room, a tie leading her to the council as if she must be there. As if she is destined to be there. She can feel it too, the urgency. Her feet speed up, her little legs blurring as we leave the suite and storm through the mansion.

We are all surprised when the demon appears right next to her, watching her out of the corner of his eye like he is unsure how to respond or act around her. "What is your plan, walker?" he snaps. "To just storm in there, you and your men?"

She grins, not even glancing at him. "Why don't you wait and see, Lucy?" I know she's calling him that on purpose now. His face contorts in a sneer and I think he is debating throttling her, so I slip between them and grab her hand, holding it as we head back to the top of the dungeons. She stops at that door and looks at Nos. "Get them ready, it's time."

She looks at us then, her face softening. "Now's your chance to turn back, you don't have to do this, they might kill us."

"We do this together," Griffin snarls.

"Together." I nod.

"I'm not going anywhere," Jair adds.

"Little Monster, it's time to put our actions into words, we will follow you anywhere."

She sighs as the wolf inserts his bark to the chorus of agreements, wearing a brilliant smile on her face as she looks around at us. "Then let's kill the council."

She turns and swings open the dungeon doors. I pull her back as the monsters from below boil upwards and out, their claws, teeth, and anger filling the air. They want revenge, they want blood.

They will get it.

CHAPTER 53

DAWN

I send a whisper to Griffin's mind and watch as he breaks away to do as I ask. I watch the outpouring of monsters from the dungeons, more than I even knew existed, never mind know how to name.

There are wolves, snakes, witches, nymphs, vampires, and so many more. All angry, all looking for blood. It's chaos at first. I hear screams farther down the hall, and I know they have found some guards. Laughing, I feel my mates press closer, but I'm not afraid.

Not of these monsters. No, the council should be terrified, not me.

They are lost. They are like us, like me. They are mine.

I gather my power and direct it to them in a surge. Every eye turns to me, all waiting, watching—they know I set them free. They don't know why, but if left alone they would fracture and fight each other, maybe even be captured again, and I can't let that happen. I need every single monster here if I am to get to the council. Even now, I can feel them calling upon their nephilim, and when Griffin returns with the information I requested, he nods at me.

"As you thought, they are closing the doors, and the nephilim are lining up before them like lambs to slaughter," he snarls, mad at his own people for letting themselves be used.

"If they wish to die for the council, we will oblige." I grin and he smirks.

Looking back at the gathered monsters, I raise my voice and infuse it with the power inside me that seems to know what to do. "They stole you! They mistreated you, tortured you, and locked you away! They left you in the dark!" I yell, and roars, howls, and shouts go up among the monsters, making me grin evilly. "Let's show them how wrong they were, let's show them why they should be afraid of the dark!"

Looking them over, I carry on, "Anyone who wants to leave, do so, anyone who wants blood and to get even, follow me." With that, I look at Nos. "When we get inside the council room, when they think these are the only people we have, you will know...bring in your army. Let's not show all our cards at once, this will be a war, not just a battle."

Done with waiting, I push through the masses, and they part for me. Hands, paws, tails, and... tentacles reach for me, running across my body, across my power. I feel their solidarity in their touches. Monsters are seen as creatures to fear. To lock away and forget, and they are tired of it, they are tired of being hurt for just being themselves. In me they see their future, they see a hope.

I feel it.

I reach out to as many as I can as I pass, touching them, letting them feel my intent and power—I know they could turn on me just as easily. They are a deadly, faceless horde, but they won't attack me. Not yet.

I have to prove to them that I'm worthy of their loyalty first.

When I reach the end of the hallway with my men, I spot some dead guards on the floor, so I step over them, my bare feet squishing in their blood as I leave gory footprints behind me. Blood is still dripping down my face and chest, drying in places and flaking, and in my hand I have a surprise for them.

Grinning, I head to the chambers, up the stairs, and into the entryway where hundreds, if not thousands of nephilim are waiting, all still, all holding weapons, their eyes empty and cold. They move as one as they step forward, nothing but hollow soldiers. How they can differ so much from my feeling fallen, I have no idea.

They are nothing but toys, tools even. Griffin's a tool for sure, but a different kind.

I heard that, don't make me kill you again.

Laughing out loud, I smirk at the army. "Well then, shall we begin?" I suggest, before turning to Lucy and passing him my surprise. "Hold this, won't you?"

He narrows his eyes and I wink. "There will be plenty of people for you to kill."

He takes it as I spin to face the nephilim, my eyes flashing black as my voice goes deadly and saturates with power. "I will bathe in your blood."

We surge forward, not as one, but as a boiling mass of anger and hate. We rip through their masses, screams of anger and pain ringing out. Blood rains from all angles, drenching us, and the nephilim take to the ceiling to fight. I spot Griffin tearing through them while he laughs. Nos rips out their hearts and tosses them away. My wolf is here and severing limbs from them. Jair slashes throats and breaks necks as I search for Dume.

Suddenly, a mighty roar shakes the whole building and we all freeze, even the monsters as we turn, fear swelling inside us at that sound. It's the call of a bigger monster, a bigger predator, but when I see who it is, I laugh.

Dume.

Fully changed.

He stands from his bent position, and I pant as I watch him.

His head almost reaches the ceiling, and his body wider than the doorway, so when he steps forward, he crashes through the walls on either side. His horns are curved and scarred, his bull coming out to play. He's bigger and meaner, and those red eyes lock on me amidst the fighting. He smashes his hooves into the floor as I hear another voice.

"Oh, we are changing. Watch this then." Aska snorts and I spin to see him there one second, with intestines in his hands, and then suddenly his dragon takes his place. Its jaw opens, flashing purple as he snarls at everyone. His tail whips out and smashes into nephilim, sending them flying backwards. Those serpent eyes blink as he looks around before meeting my gaze, then he lumbers closer on four taloned feet, which carve grooves into the floor.

Little Monster.

Change, show them who we are.

So he does. Nos shifts into the creature he thought I would fear —into my forest god. I turn back to the guards, and for the first time I see fear flicker in their eyes. They know they are going to lose. Faced with my monsters, they are terrified, but they still follow orders. They dive back into the fray as the noise of screams and fighting begins again.

I watch Aska rip the souls from people, cutting them like strings. A nephilim lands on his back, but he flaps his wings and impales him on his spikes by smashing him into the ceiling. Looking around, blood covering my hands and claws, I meet Lucy's eyes where he's standing, watching it all go down with a smile on his face. He feels me and turns his head, his red gaze meeting mine.

If I joined in, little walker, they would be dead in a blink. Where is the fun in that? Bathe in their blood like you wanted.

Just then someone slices across my back. I feel my skin split as pain thunders through me. Spinning, I snarl at the nephilim and tackle him, slashing with my claws again and again. Blood and skin soar as he tries to fend me off, but it's no use. I lean down and rip out his throat with my teeth, spitting it on his dying face before throwing myself at one who's stabbing at a whimpering wolf.

He is surrounded, his brown pelt covered in blood, still snarling as he lunges and retreats. Tearing the head off one guard, I slide between another's legs and punch him in the junk. As he falls, I leap onto his face and tear off his nose before slashing his throat. Glancing at the others, I see the wolf is eating one as another sneaks up on him.

Oh no you don't, I think, but a nephilim grabs me from behind just as I'm about to take him down. Fuck. But then my wolf bounds over, knocking over anyone in his way, and picks up the nephilim like a toy, dragging him around as he screams and tries to stab at his muzzle. My wolf is bigger, really big actually. Wow.

I watch in awe, just hanging in this guy's grip, but then the nephilim stabs into my wolf's muzzle, making him cry out in pain as he drops him. Oh hell no. Lurching forward, I throw myself on the guy, but I land on the floor, so I grab his ankles and pull him down, grunting as he lands on the nephilim already piled on me.

Fuck.

But then the weight lifts, and Lucy stares down at me, holding both fighting nephilim, one in each hand like they are nothing more than a nuisance. "Okay, walker?"

I nod and he smashes the nephilim together. I hear their skulls crack and then burst like melons, gore raining down on me. Lucy crouches, wiping some brain matter off my face. "Then continue, I enjoy watching you fight. It is...erotic."

"You're messed up, you know that, right, Lucy?" I laugh.

"Devil, darling, what more do you expect?" He winks before helping me to my feet and then disappears as soon as he arrived, leaning back against his wall, his eyes on me. He waves me on to continue, making me giggle as I turn to take in how we are doing.

Monsters are everywhere, and the walls are red with blood. Nephilim are being pushed back, but they are still fighting hard, still trying to follow orders, even to their deaths. I'm done with this, I want to see the council.

Stepping back, I feel for the power that waits inside me, and it draws from the floor, racing towards me from the blood and corpses scattered around—both ours and theirs. More and more comes to me until, with a scream, it bursts. My arms fling out as I'm thrown into the air. My mouth and eyes are open, and I can see them lighting up, swirling with visible power. It grows stronger and stronger until I know if I don't get rid of it, it will kill me.

I do the only thing I can do—I send it outwards, trying to aim it at the nephilim. I feel each person it hits. Friends are strengthened, while enemies explode in a shower of muscle, bone, and blood until there is nothing left. Just a massacre with me in the middle, floating above the ground like some great big glow worm.

The power drains, heading back deep within me, still there but not as much as before as my feet touch the ground. Blinking my eyes to clear them, I shut my mouth and look around at what I've done.

They are dead, all of them. I wiped out a species with one move. I should be sad, disgusted, and scared, but I'm not. Especially when every eye turns to me in reverence and gratefulness.

I step over fallen bodies as a laugh reaches me, then Lucy pops up in front of me. "What are you, little walker?" he murmurs, watching me as he runs a finger across my blood-covered cheek. He pulls it back and sucks it into his mouth, his red eyes focused on me. "I will find out, until then, it's my turn to play." He offers me his arm and I accept it, pressing my hand to the crook of his elbow as he returns my surprise to me. "Shall we?"

"Let's not keep them waiting anymore." I grin.

My monsters open the doors for me, and they bang against the wall from the force, causing every eye within the chamber to turn to me. Those in the seats scream and gasp, while some get up to escape. I feel my men behind me, their minds touching mine, and it strengthens me to do what comes next.

I'm no one, just an abomination. Yet today they will see what that no one is capable of.

"Enough, sit down!" Amos thunders, and his people do as they are told. He's standing at the front before his throne. The other council members are there also, all apart from Derrin. They watch us with disgust like we are something to squish, to be disposed of. How wrong they are.

Gripping Lucy tighter, I stroll down the aisle with him, straight towards the council.

Every eye follows me as I saunter into their masses with Derrin's bleeding head clutched in my hand, my surprise for them. "What is the meaning of this?" Amos shrieks, but I see the worry in his eyes. I'm supposed to be dead, how did I get free? Where are his guards? His questions almost reach me telepathically, his mind whirling faster and faster.

I don't want to play games, I just want them dead. I refuse to offer pretty words or appeal to the people here. I don't want their support or even their respect. I just want these bastards scared...and then dead. Throwing the head, I laugh when it splatters on the desk before their thrones. "This is what happens to those who hurt people who are mine, and you, Assmos, and your lackeys, they hurt mine."

"We did—"

"You hurt women! And children! And humans! You stole our people!" I scream, and then settle down, sauntering closer. "Today is your reaping, Assmos, any last words?"

"You are crazy!"

"That I am, I put the bat in batshit insane." I giggle and turn to see the gathered creatures—only the richest and strongest are within the council chambers, the others are outside, ready. "But everyone else agrees. I don't mean the rich pricks you select, but your actual people. The ones you stole and betrayed. They are angry, they see you for who you really are. You have been judged, sentenced, and now I will execute you," I inform him.

"You and your band of...of—" He snarls, and I interrupt.

"Monsters." I grin.

"Monsters! You are nothing! They are nothing! Just mistakes!" he shrieks, and I hear Nos mentally reach to the people outside, letting them see and hear everything as they head indoors. "So what? We took some women, there are plenty. We are trying to stop the death of our races, to make ourselves stronger to stop those sheep from taking over this world. It is ours! We deserve it, natural selection."

"But what you are doing isn't natural, Assmos," I taunt. "You raped women and men, you made them have your super soldier babies, and you changed those babies. You experimented on your own people. You broke so many laws to what...get more power? Get off your fucking high horse, you are nothing more than what you hate most—a monster." I laugh. I'm surprised he hasn't said anything about Lucy yet, but maybe he's too distracted.

He can't see me, not yet, I am waiting. I needed proof before I kill him. The rules of my tiresome job. I just want to see him dig himself deeper into that grave.

Ah, makes sense. Just then I feel the others surge from outside, all the different races, every single one they stole from. They heard everything. Their voices rise in a cacophony, demanding the council answers for what they have done. The room breaks into chaos as I laugh. Amos looks around, his expression shocked and unsure for the first time ever before his eyes zero in on me and turn dark.

"You...you did this. You ruined everything!" he screams, and I see the moment he flings his power at me.

I don't try to stop it, I wait, hoping I'm strong enough to survive it. But it never hits. I blink and there is Lucy, right in front of me. He stops the power mid-air and tuts. "Oh, Amos, you and your little council are so stupid. Did you think we would never find out? That we would let this stand? You are not above the law, you are to uphold and protect our people. You are just like everyone else. And now you must pay that price." He flings the power back and it smacks into Amos, making him fall backwards.

A woman on the council tries to flee, and suddenly Lucy is behind her, his hand protruding from her chest. Her mouth opens and closes in shock as she slowly looks down in dawning horror. With a squelch, he pulls his hand back, holding up her heart for everyone to see. He smirks as he sets it on fire, letting it burn until only ashes coat his palm. She tumbles down the steps, her body broken at the bottom as he turns to the other council members. "One blood debt paid. I, Lucifer, the great snake, the eternal flame with the power and authority of the sleeping council, hereby strip you of all titles and responsibilities. You are sentenced to death for your crimes against our people. Do you accept the charges levied against you?" Lucy asks calmly.

"I do not! I am the head of this council! These people are mine, you are nothing but relics!" Amos yells.

Wow, what a drama queen. Can't he die with dignity?

He turns then, his eyes alighting on me. "And you! I gave you everything, power, opportunity, and what did you do? You threw it all away! Well, I don't need you! We don't need you!"

"We who?" I roll my eyes.

Veyo sniggers, and I glare at him as Griffin snarls, "He's mine, he touched you."

"We? Oh my, did I not tell you who made you?" Amos cackles, seeming very calm all of a sudden. "No use hiding anymore, why don't you come out?" he calls.

A door behind the throne opens, but I can't see the person yet. "You saw his laboratory and work, Dawn, one of many, I assure you. This man has been doing this for years. I, of course, had to hide it and kill a few people who condemned his actions, but I recognised what he was doing for what it was—genius."

The man steps from behind the thrones and I hear Griffin suck in breath, "Da—Gabriel?" he whispers.

My eyes dart from Griffin back to the man, the angel, waiting there. He looks like Griffin, I can see the resemblance. This is the man behind it all? The very same man who made all the nephilim....and my mate? Who supposedly died for his crimes?

Fuck.

CHAPTER 54

GRIFFIN

Dad...Gabriel.

He's alive.

He's alive...it keeps repeating in my head. All this time, I thought he was dead, killed for his crimes, and here he is. Alive and well, and not only that, but thriving and making more of his experiments, one that includes my mate. He stands tall, proud, and cold. He looks the same, but it all feels so wrong. How did I never notice the utter callousness behind his eyes, the cool way he would watch us, even back then? Because I was a child, wanting my dad's love. I can see the real him now, but did he ever love me...love us?

God, Mum. He let her die, he let it happen and didn't even try to stop it! He could have! He could have stopped it, why didn't he?

"Because she was a means to an end, boy, nothing more," he retorts, watching me with those golden eyes I used to wish I had.

He never loved us.

"No, you were amusing. I will give you that, and once I felt something akin to kindness towards you and your human mother, but then I realised that sentiment was holding me back. If I wanted to complete my mission, to make the strongest soldiers, I could not afford such luxuries and weaknesses."

I flinch and he steps forward, his eyes on me, driving each word home, flaying me open until I stand before him broken, damaged, and unloved. I start to spiral, my madness rushing through me...

"You were not the perfect soldier, too driven by emotions. And those others could not even think for themselves. I realised where I went wrong. I needed to start with babies with souls and minds of their own. Take the strongest of our kind and mate them, breed them until we had soldiers. Raise them as ours to follow us." He looks at Dawn then and I slump when not under his gaze. "But you...you were a hope. A daydream. I did not think it would actually work, but here you stand. And how magnificent you are!" He grins, pride on his face. "You are what I was searching for all those years. They were all failed experiments, but you? You are true power, I filled you with it. Enough to kill any man, human or otherwise. Pulled directly from the oldest of us, the gods, and injected into you as an embryo. You bonded with it—" He shakes his head, staring down at my mate like she's his world...he used to watch us like that.

It was all a lie.

"Gods?" she repeats, confused and angry, her fists clenched at her sides.

"Old relics of a world past, creatures best forgotten. They turned their backs on this world and retreated. The very first of us. I found a few of the first seven, the original gods. I took their power, harvested it!"

"And put it in me," she whispers, watching him in horror. "What am I?"

"I don't know!" He laughs. "Nothing we have ever seen before! You have the exact untrained and unknown magic that made them...but now it's more. So much more, and you are magnificent!"

he cries, and steps towards her. "Think of everything we could do! We do not need the council, any council, they can't rule us."

"You mean me," she spits. "You are nothing, just an angel. You call your son fallen, an experiment, an abomination, but you are the same. You're fucked up, so fucked up." She shakes her head. "Even if I didn't hate you for what you did to me, I would loathe you for what you did to my mate!" she screams at him, and power launches through the room, tossing everyone back as it spins faster and faster with her at the center of the storm.

"Mate? Interesting," Gabriel mutters. "What else can you do?" he questions, looking around at the evident power.

"You want to know?" she queries, her tone deadly, quiet, and I know she's going to explode. "I'll show you!" she roars. "You will never hurt him or anyone again!"

I know she means me. She's angry on my behalf, and love for her fills me at that, pushing back some of the darkness. The woman who loves me despite everything, who wants to protect me from my own father, from my own mind.

With her last word, pure, unfiltered power flows from her, like she's a conduit, to do her bidding, but it's too much. Too powerful. "Dawn!" I yell as she screams in agony. I can feel it searing her, killing her. "*Vasculo*, stop it!"

Everyone else fades away—my anger, my betrayal, Gabriel, Amos. Nothing matters but my mate.

Dawn.

"Little Monster, that's enough, they will pay!" Nos tries to gain her attention, laying his hand on her arm, and I watch it start to burn. He winces in pain but holds on. "I am here, Little Monster, I can feel you, so lost, so alone...you never are." He looks at me then and I know.

She needs me.

Stepping forward, I struggle against the power, but when I get close enough, I lay my hand on her too. My knees almost buckle from the pain, not just my own at the fire racing across my hand

that's touching her, but at the pain inside her. Coming from her...
she *is* lost. Alone in the middle of all that power. It's controlling
her, not the other way around, wanting to do her bidding, but it's
too much for her alone. She's curled into a ball inside, cut off from
everyone, unable to even feel our minds.

Locked away.

This is what she feared even if she never voiced it. She feared
that the power was too strong. That she couldn't control what she
was and one day would hurt someone, but she should have realised
that she's never alone, we are here. We are hers, made for this. For
her. We can handle it together, control it together.

"She needs us!" I scream to the others, as the chairs and decor
in the room are picked up by the storm. The windows blow open,
and glass shatters everywhere, yet still I hold on.

Dume takes hold of her shoulder and the power lessens. Jair
clutches her other shoulder and I can almost touch her inside now,
so close. Aska wraps his tail around her leg and I feel her look up at
us from the bottom of that storm, searching for us, so close... It has
to work... Why isn't it?

No, I can't lose her.

Not another person I love, this has to work!

But then the wolf presses his head against her leg and her hand
reaches for him, so close...we are so close. Her fingers brush us,
feeling us, and the storm stops for a moment, but it's not enough.

We are not enough.

She screams, and it fills the room as the storm rages on. She's in
the middle, the tempest called by her rage and hate. Fuelled by it.
She needs love to break it, us, her mates...

Then he's there—Lucifer. He presses his forehead to hers, his
red eyes locked on her unseeing gaze. "I am here, come back. Let it
go, feel us, we are here. Find us, touch us, release it into us...let it
wash through us and out again, let us help. Let us anchor you."

She reaches for us again, fighting so hard to get to us, and then
she's there. Her hand grips ours, her mind mixing with ours, our

bindings surrounding her, anchoring her to this world and our arms.

The power stutters and then redirects, flowing through us. At first it hurts, there is too much. Fuck, how did she survive this? How did she have all this inside her and not go mad?

But then it lessens to a trickle instead of a tsunami and I can breathe again. Opening my eyes, I look to my mate, my *vasculo*.

She slumps in our grasp as all that power finally leaves her, flowing within us, filtered through us until she can handle it, then it drifts back to her. Her eyes close for a moment before they flicker open, and I let out a breath I didn't know I was holding. I was so scared. So scared I had lost her forever. I would have died with her here, in this storm, because there is no life without my love.

My love.

Our love.

"You saved me," she whispers, looking around at us. "I couldn't feel you anymore, I was so scared...and then you were there, a light in the dark...I could feel each and every one of you. How deeply you cared, how sure you were I could do this..." She shivers in our grasps. "Feel your love."

"Even monsters need love, Little Monster, you know that. You always have ours."

She nods and we hold her. Here, in the middle of her destruction, we hold her. Eventually she nods and pulls back, looking towards Gabriel and Amos. "You were right, I don't know what I'm capable of. I'm powerful, uncontrolled, and untrained. A threat, a monster. But with my men, with my monsters at my side, I can conquer it."

She steps forward.

"We fight death. I survived the worst of humanity and your world. I can survive anything with them at my side. That's what you didn't count on. You thought I would need you, but I don't. I need them, the ones you feared and tossed away. My monsters. And I'm the biggest one yet."

Pride fills me, such pride and love. Never before have I wanted to follow anyone, but this woman...Nos was right. I would follow her anywhere.

"As one, we are more than you could have ever imagined, and now those you created will be the ones who kill you. Poetic." She grins and lifts her hand.

She's going to save us all.

CHAPTER 55

NOS

"I can't let you kill him." Titus sighs, stepping from among the crowd. He looks to Gabriel. "He created me, after all."

Griffin's mouth drops open as I step closer to Dawn. She frowns, glancing between them. Titus watches her with a smile. "I guess that makes us related in a weird way, all of Gabriel's creations in one room...well, most of them." He winks as he steps up to Gabriel who nods at him.

"You did your job well."

"Y-You are with him!" Amos sputters, answering the question I was just thinking—who knew who it was...no one, I would say.

Titus looks at him. "It was imperative I was on the council. I fed you information that would help you find him so you would see his greatness once again. We knew you would see the possibilities and hire him, then I made sure to gain your confidence and trust with my position, to stop any threats to his life while using you."

"This is better than any Jeremy Kyle," Aska mutters.

Dawn shrugs. "Fine, you die too."

Titus shakes his head. "I'm afraid I can't let you do that. You see, you might be powerful, maybe even more so than me...but I have been around a long time. And I plan to be around for a lot longer, at least until our mission is complete."

"I knew you would not allow this." Gabriel smirks, looking at Dawn. "Kill her."

Titus sighs and pushes up the sleeves of his shirt. "Apologies, I would have liked to have gotten to know another like myself, but I must do my duty."

"You're a puppet," she hisses.

I glance from him to her and step in front of her. She can protect herself, my little monster, that is true, but he is not touching a hair on her head. He isn't even getting near her. Just because she can defend herself doesn't mean she has to, we are here too. I look to Griffin and he nods, then we move as a unit, as one.

He aims for Veyo, I for Titus. I hear a scream and glance over to see Griffin ripping the council lackey to pieces. Titus is more difficult, he's powerful and sees me coming.

We clash in a flurry of fists and power, but I have something more I am fighting for—not duty, but love.

And love, with a bit of hate peppered in, always wins.

He flings his power at me, trying to throw me off guard, but he should have known I am stronger.

I block his desperate hit and twirl behind him, breaking his neck. He drops to the floor, dead. Gabriel stumbles back, gaping at his now dead creation. "You killed him! You killed him!"

I shrug and step over the body. "He threatened my little monster, council member or not, he dies." I look to the crowd. "No one, no matter of their station or power, touches my mate. Don't so much as look at her wrong! Do we have that clear? She is mine!" I roar, letting my power blast through the room, every inch of it. It knocks them to their knees, and their eyes widen. Even those who thought they knew me, who have never felt it before, I let them see every trick I have, everything I will use to protect her.

"And mine," Griffin snarls, passing over Veyo's bloodied stump of a hand to Dawn. "The one he touched you with, *Vasculo*."

"And mine," Aska adds, tilting his chin back as he allows his magic to leak from him. In the shadow behind him, I see a dragon with a crown on its head.

"Mine," Jair and Dume declare in unison, stepping closer to her.

"Touching," Lucifer drawls and looks around. "This woman is under the sleeping court's protection for now, death will be swifter for those who think of breaking that rule."

Dawn grins at us with tears in her eyes before she blinks and gazes over my shoulder. I turn in time to see Gabriel picking up a sword and rushing me. Before I can move to intercept him, Dawn is there.

The sword plunges into her stomach and we all freeze. She looks down slowly at the glowing, golden blade as Gabriel steps back with a triumphant expression. Time freezes for a moment as everything in my body stops. No.

No.

Little Monster!

Eyebrow arched, she reaches for the handle and unhurriedly pulls the sword free of her body. My heart stops at the blood there.

Little Monster—

She holds the sword up to the light, her blood coating the blade, and we all stare as her stomach mends. The hole closes, allowing me to breathe again. A fear like I had never experienced before recedes to anger. She looks at Gabriel and tuts. "That was a bad move, angel." Then she plunges that same sword into his gut while he is gaping at her.

She doesn't stop there. She pops up behind him and rips both wings off, the sound screeching and loud. He screams as he drops to his knees. She grips either side of his head, her eyes locked on mine as she leans down to whisper in his ear. "They are mine, no one touches what is mine. Angel, god, divine, no one."

She twists, ripping his head clean off. Clutching it in her hand, she looks around at the other gathered council members. "Assmos, I've wanted to do this for a while."

"You can't—you—" He starts, but no one dares stop her as she saunters up to the terrified man as he tries to back away, only to run into Lucifer. He squeaks and turns as Lucifer laughs.

"Boo," Lucifer says with a wild, wicked smile.

Dawn taps Amos on the shoulder and he spins, his feathers ruffling as he attempts to change, undoubtedly to fly away. "Oh, just fucking die," she snaps, then plunges her hand into his chest and pries open his ribcage. She wrenches his heart free and drops it to the floor to join Gabriel's head.

She looks to Lucifer then. "Care to burn them for me? I want to make sure they are really fucking dead, can't have them coming back and hurting anyone again."

"My pleasure, walker," he murmurs, and raises his hands. Two fireballs form in each palm and he drops them on the corpses, head, and heart. They ignite, burning nothing else until only ash remains, and then they wink out of existence.

It's done.

It's over.

She is safe.

She turns and smiles at me. "Let's go home."

"As you wish, Little Monster," I reply, and take her hand, pulling her closer. The others step near as we begin to walk away, but Lucifer calls after us.

"The others?"

"Your problem, they are your council," she answers without looking.

Suddenly screams fill the air, and I glance over my shoulder to see the rest of the council's bodies draped around him on the floor, dead. "For ignoring your duty and allowing this to happen, I offered you a quick death," he tells them, before looking up and meeting my stare.

I incline my head. We both know that is only partially true. He did it so they would never seek revenge over the woman who exposed their secrets—Dawn.

"You cannot leave, walker," he shouts.

"Watch me!" She giggles as the crowd parts for us. Everyone gathered drops their eyes and bows their heads as we pass.

A murmur of 'thank yous' goes up to the woman who stopped the people who were hurting them. They look at her with fear and respect.

When we reach the door, I stop just as Lucifer pops up there. He stares only at Dawn. "You cannot leave, walker. There is no council, there must always be a council, I cannot sit on it. Conflict of interest, plus, you killed them. This is your job now."

"What? No!" Dawn exclaims in horror, looking to me.

But Lucifer raises his voice. "Who here wishes to vote in Dawn, the skinwalker, as temporary council head until others can be found to help her lead?"

Numerous hands and voices agree, nearly every single person in attendance. She blinks in shock, looking at her mates. "I-I can't lead."

"*Draya*," Dume rumbles. "I will follow you anywhere. You lead us, and now they are asking you to lead them."

"*Neriso*, it is both a burden and an honour to lead your people. Choose wisely. Whatever you decide, we are here."

She stares at me in confusion. "Your choice, Little Monster, your choice." I know this is what fate meant. I can't decide for her, she must choose her path. It won't be easy, it will be fraught with those trying to stop the change she signifies, and she knows this.

The whole world seems to hold its breath as she deliberates. She looks at Lucifer who smirks at her. "I cannot allow you to leave, walker, the people have spoken. They trust you."

"And you?" she questions.

"I will do my duty. The council needs replacing. Attraction or not, you must be worthy, or you will die."

"You will kill me if I fail these people?" she clarifies, a smile on her face.

"Yes," he retorts. "It's time for new leadership, for a change, what do you say?"

"Yes," she whispers, and then blinks in shock like she can't believe she said that.

And I know this is why I never wanted to sit on the previous council. Because I was waiting for her, for her council. For her change.

"Then take your chair, tomorrow we make it official. For now, let us calm the people and sort through the rabble. The world will feel the effects of their betrayal long after tonight, let us learn the full extent of it. Together." He offers her his hand.

A choice.

The world is made of them.

We made ours—her.

Now she must make hers.

If she runs, I will run with her. If she stays, I will lead with her. Whatever my little monster wants, I will be there. We will never be apart again, not even the fates themselves could stop us now.

ASKA

She places her hand in Lucifer's, who nods knowingly. A wind blows through the room, one of change, as he turns her and guides her back through her people.

Her people.

Ours now.

Where she goes, I will too.

I once walked away from the throne, the crown, for her.

Knowing she was coming and she needed me, and now I am willingly walking back towards it. Not to wear myself, but to support the one wearing it.

We can all feel it, the tug of destiny guiding her to take the throne. No one else deserves it, no one else could lead us. Monsters will follow her. These people will fear and love her, and the humans will be protected by her.

She isn't a hero, not the good guy coming out on top like one is taught when learning good versus evil as a child. But she is what the world needs, someone willing to bloody their hands to protect theirs, someone willing to give up everything they are, everything they have, to protect those weaker than them.

She is a true leader.

A true queen.

CHAPTER 56

DAWN

I don't know what this means. I don't know how to lead. My mind is jumbled, my emotions out of whack. I just wanted to save those people, to protect my mates, and all the women and men hurt by Gabriel and his schemes. How did I end up being led to the council's throne?

Why me? I am no one, just a monster.

Yet the people in this room watch me with something akin to worship, why? They should stare at Nos like that, he led them there. Or Dume, who waded into the nephilim and killed them. Or Aska, for bringing the sleeping council back when no one else could. Or Griffin, who underwent torture, pain, madness, and now betrayal to stop the men responsible. Or even Jair, who stayed strong through the worst thirst to try and stop them. To free the people who willingly helped me.

They deserve this. Not me. I never wanted to lead anybody, I just wanted revenge.

Actions have consequences, my child. These are yours, your chance to make a difference. Do not fail or all will be lost, seek those who hold the key. Those of the old world. Make them new again and help them defeat the darkness. Only when the bloodlines are filled will your people be safe.

The voice floats to my mind and I whip my head around, searching for the person responsible, examining the sea of people, but no one stands out and it's clear no one else heard it. So, who was it?

And what did she mean?

You will learn in time. Until then, unlock the secrets of your mates' past, for they hold the truth. We will be watching, fate chosen.

I'm so distracted by the voice that I don't even realise we have reached the golden throne. It's not my style, too...over the top. If I sit, I know I'm making a promise. To help these people, to protect them even with my life if needed. It's a lot of pressure and responsibility, but when I look back to my mates, they are there.

Every single one of them is watching me, waiting. Willing to follow me into this new test. I'm not alone. Never again, not even now. Turning back to the throne, I lower my voice so only Lucy can hear me.

"Is this forever?" I whisper.

"No, they chose you, but it's a democracy. There will be other council members, there are laws and traditions to follow, but I always hated those, so I'm fast-tracking this," he murmurs.

"Why?" I ask, looking to the devil beside me.

"Because today you did more than any ever has, including me. I've been walking this world for a long time, sleeping and then awakening to cause chaos and bloodshed. I was warned once to make the right choice, and this feels right. Little walker, you are the future. I feel it now. It's time the old is tossed aside and new blood leads. I will be there throughout it all."

"Waiting to see if I fail so you can kill me?" I grin.

"Yes," he replies with no remorse. "My duty."

"You don't seem like a person who follows that a lot," I counter, glancing back at the throne.

"Only when it suits my needs, like now."

"And what's your need now?" I whisper, swallowing hard.

"To keep you close." He takes that last step to the throne and helps me sit. Once there, he bows, his red eyes on me as he kisses my hand. "We have much to do, little walker, enemies to stop and monsters to kill. After that...let's just say you might have wished you had walked away when you had the chance."

He steps to my left side then, and views the faces before us, all waiting for explanations, for help. For me. I look to my mates and they surround me and the throne. Their hands touch me as much as they can, offering their silent support and aid as I swallow and tilt my chin up.

I wonder if Amos saw what he had created when he looked at me, a chance for change, but not in the way he wanted...did he hate me because of that or because he couldn't control me?

I suppose it's no good delving into the past now, since all I have left is the future. The hope that I can do better, help these people any way I can.

In that moment, watching their faces as they look at me...I feel my hate tapering away, replaced by something else. Something so much stronger. Something so much more filling and beautiful.

Love.

Rage often blends with hate, but love? Love can so easily bloom from the darkness, or the other way around. I guess it's time to see where it can take me.

CHAPTER 57

JAIR

After everything that happened, Lucy instructs everyone to
search the castle for their people. Anyone they can't find is
to be reported to us, and we will either find them or determine
what happened to them. We have Amos and Gabriel's lab, and
Titus's room to go over. We will split it between us, since Dawn
doesn't trust anyone else. We also need some new guards and, well,
the rest of the council. Lucy asked Dawn for her opinion as head of
the council. She looked to Nos and grinned, mentioning she had
some ideas, but not who as of yet.

All the bloodshed, power, and death has tired everyone out,
and with the decree that the crowning ceremony will happen
tomorrow and then work to solve everything will commence the

following day, Lucy dismisses everyone. There is some grumbling, but Nos works to assure them and speaks with the leaders of the groups.

Dawn talks to the women and the monsters she found in the dungeon, offering to let them stay at the mansion if they have nowhere to go. A few chose to leave to head back to their old lives, but more than half chose to stay. Their old lives are gone, and they don't have anywhere to go—plus, like myself, they seem to be drawn to Dawn. They recognise a leader and the understanding in her, she is like them. She bled and almost died for them, which creates a whole lot of loyalty, more than any crown ever could.

She doesn't even realise it, but she already has an army under her roof, ready to die to protect her.

Once the room is cleared, she slumps against me. I wrap my arms around her and hold her up. The once gold room is coated in blood, bodies, and death. I look around and she does the same, a startled laugh bursting from her lips.

Griffin glances over at the sound, spots what she's looking at, and winks. "I always thought this room needed redecorating. Love what you did with the place, *Vasculo*."

She grins and then sighs, snuggling closer. "Tired, my love?"

She yawns. "I guess a revolution can take it out of a person."

"There are plenty of bedrooms, Little Monster," Nos offers, as he bids the last person goodbye and heads her way.

"Ugh, yes, but what did they do in them? If I could, I would burn this whole place to the ground," she mutters.

"You could." Lucifer shrugs as he strolls around, seeming to enjoy all the blood and death. "Pricey though, but if you wish to sleep somewhere this council never touched, there is the sleeping court's wing. They were unable to even access it, so rest assured nothing will have happened there...well, not by them anyway. I know I personally turned one room into a massacre a couple hundred years ago." His eyes go far away as he smiles. "Ah, so much blood, that was a good day."

"You know what? That actually sounds good." She sighs.

He blinks and looks over at her with a grin. "I also happen to have a torture room in that wing, in case you would ever like to play with my toys," he rumbles, and she shivers against me.

I look to Dume to see him watching them too. We are all wondering if they are mates. I mean, I thought they were with the way she needed his touch, but then he seems aloof. I guess only time will tell.

"Follow me. I will grant you access, then I will prepare for tomorrow. I do have to complete the ceremony according to our laws, or others will have grounds to challenge you. That doesn't mean they won't, but they will have to do it by other means..." He shrugs. "Then we can discuss putting an acceptable council in place."

"Why me?" She sighs and he looks over his shoulder.

"I have a feeling if you did not, the other monsters would revolt and simply kill them. You, Dawn, have shown them they do not need to follow someone just because they are told to. You have to accept the change you wrought."

Dawn keeps hold of my arm as Lucifer leads us up the stairs, ignoring the corpses of the fallen outside, and then up another set of stairs before he turns left. He carries on walking, taking twisting, turning corridors until we come upon a large black double door blocking the path. I can feel the magic pulsing from it from here. It's warded, like he said.

The actual door is decorated with skulls and bloody handprints and Dawn grins. "Now that's more my style."

Lucifer presses his hand to the door above one of the handprints and looks back at her, his eyes blazing like a fire. "Thought you might like it, little walker."

The door hisses and then swings inwards, the interior dark and gloomy. Lucifer steps through, whistling as he goes, and I follow after with Dawn still holding onto me. I would go anywhere at the moment if she kept touching me. She feels so good, so warm.

Looking down at her, I can't help but soften inside. This woman is incredible, a true leader. So strong and brave and she doesn't even see it.

She's a true warrior.

"There are numerous bedrooms, but my favourite one is at the base of the tower. There is also a kitchen, a living area, a place to fight. Make yourselves at home." He sweeps his arms out to encompass it all. I gaze around, noting the walls are covered in an old-style paper with wood at the bottom. Large candelabras are attached to the wall with candle chandeliers above. Lucifer snaps his fingers and they all light with a sizzle, illuminating more of the hallway.

It's so different from the rest of the mansion, I actually settle a little. It feels more real and reminds me slightly of home.

"Lead the way," I tell Dawn. She reaches up and kisses my cheek before exploring further as we all follow along behind.

"Hurry up, *Vasculo*, I'm tired and want to wash this blood off," Griffin snarls.

"Poor angel, too harsh for your delicate sensibilities?" Aska taunts.

"Carry on, lizard, and I will—"

"Do nothing!" Dawn shouts, and then storms into their midst, her eyes narrowed and black. "You will not hurt each other. If you do, then I will kill you myself. Mate or not. I need you all, and I know it will be hard, but for me? Please? I've had enough fighting and hate in my life, and there's so much more to come, but in here...with us, can we not? Please?" she implores, and seems to slump.

Nos glares at everyone and sweeps her into his arms. "Any infighting and you will be kicked out. You heard our mate. Now let us find somewhere for her to rest. You can finish butting heads out here like children while the rest of us take care of our mate," he growls, each word filled with power that almost bows us backwards.

We wander the corridor until Nos finds the room under the tower. We step inside the door, looking around. It is certainly big, with a bed upon a pedestal large enough to accommodate most of us. I'm not leaving her side, even to sleep.

She must hear my thoughts, because her mind brushes mine. *Good, I'm not letting any of you go.*

I grin at that, my little warrior. So fierce. I can't wait to see where this life takes me. Maybe this time I will get it right, not my second chance...but third. The final one with the woman destined to be mine.

Her vampire.

CHAPTER 58

LUCIFER

I watch the little walker be carried into the room, my old room. Well, the place I stayed whenever I felt like staying here to scare the council and cause chaos. I knew if I let her walk out that door downstairs, this little blood thirsty woman would have disappeared. I had to keep her close while I figured out why she seemed so important, and why I had been dragged into her circle of power.

So I had made her stay. The people seemed to support the idea of her leading. That won't always be so, and when it settles, they will question why this outsider is leading, then they will try to kill her. Overthrow her. They will use mind games and verbal trickery. It will be interesting to see how she handles it.

"Tomorrow, the ceremony will be conducted early to settle the power disruption and unrest, be prepared." I nod and then turn to leave. There is a shuffle, and suddenly a small hand lands on my arm. I look down at the pale, dainty thing and follow it up to those big eyes.

"Thank you," she whispers.

"I did nothing." I smirk.

"Thank you," she repeats, searching my eyes until she nods and turns away. I have the strangest urge to grab her and pull her back, to make her look at me again. To make her touch me. But I don't.

I turn away as well and leave her to her mates, no doubt they have a lot of...making up to do. I ignore the fact that it fills me with jealousy and the fires of hell at the thought and leave the room.

As I shut the door behind me, I feel a tug, a pull in my stomach to go back, but I ignore it and head farther down the corridor to the double doors at the end, pushing them open onto the stone balcony. I ignore the gargoyles and stare out into the night sky. From here you can see the world laid out below. So small and distant.

People have fought battles over less—the view I mean...not Dawn.

Why is she under my skin so?

I am used to doing what I want, when I want, without concern for the consequences, simply living in the moment, spreading death and bloodshed wherever I go. But when I thought about killing her, it didn't feel right. In fact, it made me sick to my stomach just at the idea.

Fool. She has clearly done something to me, the question is what?

All these years, all these millenniums, kings, queens, and Xaph have tried to get me to take my place, to take my role seriously and care for someone other than myself. They used their bodies, riches, words, and laws, but I still didn't fall in line. I revolted, I burned the world and walked through battles I started with joy, relishing it.

But now?

As I debate leaving Dawn to the chaos she has sowed, I find myself unable to move from this balcony. I am split in two, my need for blood, for death, wanting to leave this place and seek it out in the world, start another war, anything. But the other half...it wants me to stay, to keep her close.

Why?

To kill her? No, that can't be it.

Maybe to toy with her?

It's infuriating to say the least, and putting a damper on my world burning plans. So, I will stay. I will get rid of these pesky feelings and do my duty for once, maybe then Xaph will leave me alone for a couple hundred years and I can go and find a war somewhere. Wash with the blood of my enemies and sleep surrounded by the most beautiful creations this world has to offer.

But even that image feels empty and cold, and the black eyes of the woman sleeping down the hall burns that vision away, mocking me.

Under it all is fear, fear because I know what she is...who she is.

My mate.

She represents change, she represents restriction, and...fondness. That scares me. Change is the ultimate sacrifice. I was made into this creature of darkness, to burn and kill. To cause chaos, but...but if I choose Dawn and turn away from that, who knows what I will become?

Is that what the woman meant all those millennia ago? The choice is mine, to burn or love?

How foolish she thought I would be to choose one small, black-eyed woman...

Dawn

The bed fits us all. There is some chafing and butting heads, and I have to smack both Aska and Griffin and separate them, placing them on either side of the bed. It's so large that my mates can lie comfortably without touching. For once I simply sprawl in their midst, in the middle of this huge...huge monster pile.

Their hands seek me out in the dark, stroking my skin, touching and holding, and each caress sparks with power and love.

Even my wolf is here, lying on the floor by the bed, his eyes watching me as if guarding, as if memorising. It's strange. When this is over, I need to learn more about him somehow. It feels important, but first I must survive tomorrow, something that fills me with dread.

I'm not a leader. I could barely keep myself alive, so what sort of example do I set? I kill anyone who annoys me, which is surely not a good fit. But Lucy seems to think so, and everyone was adamant.

Maybe I could do it for a while and just see how it goes while they put all the other council members in place, and once they are there I could resign. I guess only time will tell, but for now I push all that away, just enjoying being lost in my mates.

We have never all been in the same room.

It feels so right. I know we can't spend every day like this. They would kill each other, but for tonight, one night, there's a truce. I feel it.

Staring up at the large, ornate ceiling decorated in murals of battles, blood, and death, I let myself relax for the first time since before all this began. Since before I was taken, before I was killed. Before I met that ass monkey ex. There was never a time I felt this...complete, though, this happy. This right, as if I was always going to end up here.

"Thank you for coming for me, for staying, for fighting with me," I whisper into the dark. Their hands contract on my body, and I feel their eyes looking to me. "You didn't have to, so thank you."

"I told you, Little Monster, I'll always come for you. We all feel the same, we could never walk away from you," Nos murmurs, and I turn my head and meet his white eyes. The fact he's relaxed in this form tells me he at least feels comfortable with everyone, if nothing else.

"But why? And don't say because we're mates, there has to be something else. A way to resist that if you wanted to."

"Why would we want to?" Jair inquires.

"*Draya*, we search our whole lives for a place to call home, a family. Happiness. You are all of that. Why would we ever walk away when we find love in your arms?"

"And fucking great sex," Griffin adds, and then I hear a yelp as someone kicks or smacks him.

"A chance to be what we want, to not follow the path spread out for us, but to make our own. *Neriso*, we stay, we came for you not because destiny told us we had to, but because if we didn't...we would never be happy again. Our moon rises and sets with you." Aska croons.

"Get that from one of your shows?" Griffin snorts.

Their back and forth makes me smile. So they aren't here just because of destiny or because they had to. But because they wanted to.

"Of course we did, Little Monster. We choose to mate you, to follow you, because we love you," Nos insists, and pulls me closer. Sighing, I lay my head on his chest as Griffin snuggles closer to my back. Aska picks up my feet and drapes them over his chest, one hand locked around my ankle. Jair rubs against my legs as Dume's arm stretches across him to touch my thigh.

I let their warmth fill me, replacing all those dark parts with shades of grey until I start to feel more whole, even if something inside me reaches out beyond these walls and down the hallway to someone else.

Lucy.

I shake my head, that man...that demon will decide his own rules. Always will, I can tell. He's not like my other mates, he never wanted a family or a home...or love. If he chooses to walk away, I have no choice but to let him, even if a tiny part of me cracks at that thought, feeling like he should be here, with us.

"Sleep, Little Monster, tomorrow is a big day. We will watch, we will protect you, just sleep," Nos murmurs, as he drops a kiss on the top of my head.

I missed you so much, my little monster, never leave my side again. There is no me without you.

Smiling, I snuggle closer and close my eyes, sleeping with my mates surrounding me. For tonight this is all that matters.

SOMETHING WAKES ME, and once it does, I can't go back to sleep. I lie in a pile of snoring males, cringing. Guess I didn't think about the practical side of having so many mates. God, I hope they are better than human men when it comes to the bathroom and cleaning.

Hands slide across my skin, making me gasp. They are all asleep, just reaching for me, but each touch sets me alight. A fire burning in my gut.

Fuck.

Great, I'm horny and all my monsters are asleep.

Lying here, I try to distract myself or go back to sleep, but one of their hands slides between my thighs and their face snuggles into my hip. Fuck.

Well, that's not fair, all these dicks and no one to ride. I wonder if they would be annoyed if I woke them up...I bet if it was sucking them off they wouldn't complain. Before I can roll over and try to wake one of them, a hand slips over my mouth and lips meet my ear. "Shh, don't wake them."

I settle at Nos's velvety voice as he gently scoops me up and slides me away from them before silently leaping from the bed and landing on quiet feet. Wrapping myself around him, I let him carry me from the room.

He brings me out the door and down the corridor. I spot two open doors behind us at the very end and see Lucy standing there, staring out into the night. He looks so lost, so alone. I ache to go to him, but I don't think he would accept it, so I snuggle closer to my forest god.

He takes me to the next room a couple of rooms down and opens the door, kicking it shut behind us. I don't get to look around except to see there is dust and cobwebs covering most of the room, and sheets over what looks like sofas to the left and a bed to the right.

Nos doesn't stop, he leads me right to the double balcony doors at the back, past the bed, and pushes them open. They swing with a squeak and remain open behind us as he heads out into the night air.

Smiling, I suck in a deep breath as he places me down on the wooden table waiting out here, and steps between my thighs. How did he know I needed air before I did? That I needed to be outside, to be held, and touched...

Because my forest gods know everything about me, even before I do.

He tilts his head down, his hands braced on the table on either side of me. "Your need woke me."

I grin at that, leaning back. "I guess I should be sorry, but I'm not. This is the most I've seen you in a while."

"So it is, Little Monster. I'm sorry I wasn't there. I knew you needed time to finish what you needed. If I interrupted, it might not have gone down like that and we wouldn't be here. I stayed away to protect you, do you believe me, Little Monster?"

"Always." I nod. If he says there was a reason, that it was important, I believe him. I just missed him is all.

"I missed you too, so much." He grabs me and pulls me closer, leaning his head against mine, his eyes bleeding to white. "Life is boring without you, it makes me miss when we first met. Chasing you across the city, now chasing you here. It seems like you're always busy or running," he murmurs.

"No more chasing, no more running, baby. It's us now," I

soothe, as I reach up and stroke along his horns. He growls, his eyes flashing.

"Whoops, I forgot about that," I say innocently, blinking at him.

His eyes narrow as I continue to stroke his antlers. "Little Monster, behave."

"And when have I ever behaved, god? Tell me that." Leaning closer, I lick his lips. "And when do you not like it when I don't?"

"Little Monster," he growls.

"What are you waiting for, forest god...every time you catch me you have me...is this going to be the exception?" I purr, tracing my nails down his back, adding an edge of pain to my touch, knowing my god likes it when we push boundaries. Flashes of the last time we were together, of the blood, the pleasure, fills my head. God, I want that.

I want him.

So badly.

His hands trail along my thighs before gliding upwards, delicately crossing my chest, and brushing across my taut nipples before he cups my chin. "I feel your need, it's so strong, Little Monster. You never have to ask. I always want you, always need you. Never worry about waking us or disturbing us, you are our world, Little Monster. It's time you realised you can trust us to always take care of you."

"What—" I start, but he covers my lips.

I groan into his mouth as he tangles his tongue with mine, playing with me, his hands trailing back down. He flicks my nipples, tweaking them, his touches alternating between hard and soft until I'm moaning into his mouth. I'm so wet I bet it's dripping onto the table, imagining all the ways my forest god is going to fuck me.

He pushes my thighs apart and strokes across my wet pussy, the caress more teasing than anything, back and forth, back and forth, at the same rhythm of his kiss until I'm panting and rocking against him. Needing more.

Ripping my mouth away, I snarl, "More!"

He chuckles breathlessly, keeping up the movement. "Trust me, Little Monster."

Groaning, I drop back to the table and he leisurely kisses across my chest, sucking my nipple into his mouth before rolling it around. I feel his tongue change around me, becoming forked as he lashes me. Yes, now this is what I was talking about!

But then he pulls away and blows cool air over me before giving the other breast the same treatment. Fuck control, fuck patience and trust. "Nos!" I snarl in warning.

He growls, lifting his head as the change comes over him, the skull forming over his face until his eye sockets are black. "I wanted you, Little Monster, you will trust us."

He picks me up as I struggle in his grip. The scent of his blood fills the air, but he ignores it as he drops me onto the balcony. I tumble backwards and his hands catch me around the waist as I dangle halfway off the edge.

Squirming, I try to get up as one of his hands releases its hold and goes back to stroking my pussy.

"Trust, Little Monster, it is hard for you. But we will learn, I will prove it repeatedly, starting now."

"Trust! Let me down," I growl, fighting his grip even as pleasure rockets through me, drawn by his touch. He ignores me, kissing along my side and legs as I struggle, my hips rolling to meet his fingers as he finally dips one inside me, but when I start to fight to get up again he pulls them free.

Fuck.

I still and he slips his fingers back inside me, this thumb brushing my clit as he plunges deep. Groaning, I bite my lip as I writhe in his grasp, the pleasure fighting against my panic to move, to get up.

The top half of me is weightless, this is more than a power play. This is about trust, me letting go and expecting him to protect me, to save me and keep me safe. To give me everything I need.

I release the bannister and trust him, and when I do, immense pleasure and love fills me from our connection.

This was never about him, but about me. About letting go, living in the moment, and trusting. Right here and now he's showing me that I can always depend on my forest god, even during very hard times.

God, I love him.

My hair cascades over the world below, my eyes closing as the wind blows across my naked body, the night sky surrounding me. The stars shine down on me as he rubs his cock across my pussy.

"I will always catch you, Little Monster. This isn't about sex or fucking. This is about love. Our love. It's stronger than you will ever know, but I will spend every day showing you, reminding you."

"Fucking me, I hope," I tease, my lips curling into a smile as I let him do whatever he wants to me.

"Always," he murmurs, dropping a soft kiss on my clit before his forked tongue darts out and lashes it, making me moan. "You asked once what else I could do, want to see?"

"What—hell yes," I exclaim, almost sitting up before remembering, and I relax again, a decision he rewards with a kiss.

He laughs as he pulls away, taking his fingers with him, but then his cock suddenly replaces them. Spearing my pussy in one hard, quick thrust, he fills me. I scream into the night as he stretches me around his hard length. He waits for me to stop squirming and then lifts my hips, exposing me further until I feel the cool air blow over my ass.

He's holding me up with two hands, dangling me above a fifty-foot drop. Fuck, why is that so hot?

Then he starts to move with quick, sure thrusts. It feels good, really good, and I let myself go, relaxing with each one, allowing him to use my body, driving my higher and higher towards that peak.

Only when I've given myself over to him completely does he speak again.

"Did you know snakes have two penises?" he murmurs almost matter-of-factly.

"Wait—what—holy fuck!" I scream, as something soft yet strangely hard—almost reminding me of a tentacle—slides down my pussy before gliding back up and pressing against my clit as he drives in and out of my tight channel. Fuck, fuck, fuck. My eyes roll into the back of my head, but then the extra appendage slides farther down and slips inside me, right alongside his other cock.

He's fucking me with two cocks.

It stretches me to the point of pain, and that extra appendage presses against my nerves, hard, until I'm squirming and crying out as a sudden wave of pleasure washes over me, dragging me with it. I shout his name into the night as I come. But he doesn't stop. Fighting my clenching pussy, he pulls his second cock free and, wet with my cream, presses it down to my ass.

"Fuck, fuck, fuck," I chant, knowing I don't have a choice. He's going to do whatever he wants to me, I'm just along for the ride, completely at his mercy, and the thought is hot. Imagining whatever that second cock looks like, slipping and slithering into my other hole, has me clenching on his cock again.

"Is that what you want, my little monster? Me to fill every hole you have, until there is no space between us at all? Until you are consumed by me? Filled so completely you will always feel empty without us inside you?" he murmurs as he fucks me.

God, yes.

"No need to pray to me, Little Monster, never," he snarls, his hands tightening on my hips, cutting into the skin there. The fragrance of my blood fills the air, even as he slithers into my other hole. That snaking cock slips through my muscles, and when it fills me, it seems to expand.

Still slithering, jerking like a tentacle, it feels so wrong, so different, that I can't help but wriggle. He drives into me with his other cock, stretching me so completely that I scream, letting it all out into the night.

Letting him replace my emptiness all with him. He's correct, nothing will ever feel right after this.

His other cock slinks inside me, reaching so deep I swear my eyes cross. I chant his name, meaningless words falling from my mouth. I'm nothing but a living, breathing ball of pleasure, driven higher and higher into that night sky with each thrust, each slither, each breath.

"Mine, you are mine!" he roars, as he picks up speed.

His hand comes out and slaps my clit, adding pain to the mix until I can't hold back, I can't stop it. It's a deluge, a tidal wave of pleasure. It rolls through me, wrecking everything in its path and rebuilding it again and again.

I come so hard I don't think it will ever end, my pussy and ass clenching so tight he can't fight me. He roars as he fills me, shooting his release into my pussy. I jerk beneath him, my stomach rolling and lungs tightening.

When it's over I feel boneless, and so full and satisfied beneath him, I can't move. I lie there, hanging over the edge, trusting him completely.

He gathers me closer, softly now as he slips from my ass and pussy, and I catch a glimpse of a long, slightly purple tentacle-like cock before it disappears. His face shifts to human, his eyes still white as he lifts me back up until I face him.

I stare into those white orbs, my mouth dry and throat sore from screaming. No doubt my other mates heard that or even felt it, but I don't care. They can try and make me scream harder, it's going to be a fucking hot competition.

"Next time, Little Monster, I'll show you knotting." He grins as he strokes my face so softly and tenderly, I nearly cry. This man, this god, undoes me in the best way. He shows me the best of myself, and accepts the worst, never judging. Understanding and knowing what I need and giving it to me without a thought for himself.

"Knotting?" I echo quietly, my eyes wide as he pulls me into his chest.

"We have so many animals to go through, little one." He chuckles.

"Fuck, you're going to kill me." I giggle as I snuggle closer, relaxing in his arms.

"And you will love every second of it." He grins. "Me and you, Little Monster, forever."

Forever is a long time. I can't wait for it to start.

CHAPTER 59

NOS

After we made love on the balcony, she fell asleep in my arms. I pulled her closer and took us back inside. There, in the shadow of the room, was Lucifer—Lucy, as she calls him. I don't think she even knows she was calling her mates as she came, that she was pulling them closer, and here he is, waiting and watching from the dark like he can't break free of these shadows to reach her.

I hope he does. She needs him and it's clear he needs her. He needs to allow himself to understand and feel that, otherwise it will break both of them a little. Maybe a lot.

My poor little monster, nothing is ever easy for her, it never will be. She has had a hard path in life, to be a fighter, a leader, to never give up. I hope I—we can lessen that burden for her and give her shoulders to lean on when it gets too hard. Like tonight.

She needed that, I needed that. To prove to both of us she doesn't always have to be in control. Doesn't always need to be strong and dominant, that she can trust us to give her what she needs, even when she doesn't know it. It will be a long road to break down those barriers she still has, the ones built on pain and betrayal from the many people in her life who hurt her. Sometimes we will cut ourselves on those bricks, but we will still keep going until we get inside.

Because she is ours.

And we are hers.

And that is what you do for those you love. You love them so completely, so fully, even when it's hard or it hurts, especially then. It's when they need you the most. It's not always easy or pretty, but I'm learning that love is both selfish and selfless. You can't love without both.

"You should let her in, you might be surprised what she can do," I whisper to him, not wanting to wake her.

"Is that right, forest god? Or maybe she would destroy me," he rumbles from the dark, his eyes glowing.

"She could, but to burn in her flames would be better than to burn alone. Think on that before you break whatever bond is between you," I advise as I walk by.

"And if I chose to walk away?" he calls.

Sighing, I look down at the precious woman in my arms. I never thought I would be here. Offering another man my love's heart, but she needs him and what she needs, I give her. Always.

Selfless.

It doesn't mean I won't kill him.

Selfish.

Got to have both.

I leave him to think on my words and what he will do as I head back to the room. We will need to make it home if this is where we plan on staying, I want her comfortable here. She is the leader, after all, she needs a place she can come to when it gets to be too much.

We all need a home, it's what we searched for.

I wonder if this could be it.

Laying her back on the bed, I climb in beside her. As I position her, the others reach for her, awake and aware of what happened. Jealousy and anger fill our bonds, but they settle as soon as they touch her. Yes, a hard road. Let us hope we are strong enough to traverse it.

Together.

BRUSHING HER HAIR BACK, I curl a silky lock and stick it in place with deft fingers until her hair is styled in a style suited to a queen. Who knew having to do Isla's hair when she was little would come in handy with my mate.

Dawn slept so long we had to wake her, and the ceremony is soon. Somehow, Jair and Dume found her something to wear. Griffin helped her bathe, and Aska aided in dressing her, adding jewels and treasures to her frame that someone called Jean Paul delivered. Each one had a story, a tale, and he had to tell her each as he placed them on her body. It took a long time, but we understood. After, he regarded her and declared her the best treasure he has ever found, then he bowed and left her to me to finish off the look and make sure she is ready.

They all seem to defer to me in that way, and I wonder why. I never wanted to lead anyone or for anyone to look to me, yet they do, as does my mate. I hope I am enough. That's when I realise she must be feeling the same way, and right now she needs me to support her, to comfort her. To be her rock, the man standing behind her.

Every great woman has one. But a woman like this? She has a number of them.

"You are ready, and beautiful."

She sighs and turns to look at herself in the mirror. This brings back some memories for her, so I wrap my arms around her waist and press my head to her shoulder. "You okay, Little Monster?"

"What if I can't do it?" she whispers, meeting my gaze in the mirror. "What if I'm not good enough?"

"Dawn, look at me. No one, I mean no one, could have done what you did. You brought this world together, all its monsters and misfits, and got them to not only listen to you, but to fight for you. Look at your mates. They are some of the fiercest, most rare creatures in the world, and you got them to get along and sleep in the same room. You can do whatever you put your mind to. I promise you. And we will be here, behind you, ready for whatever you need. When those stares and stressors become too much, we will block them. We will stop them and give you time to rebuild."

Tears fill her eyes as she watches me, showing such weakness from such a strong creature. The fact she shares them with me only solidifies my love for her.

"Nos—"

"Always, Little Monster. Now, let's show this world and your new people just why we love you. It is time you took your place in history."

"Together," she whispers.

"Together," I agree, and take her hand. I kiss her knuckles and raise my eyes to the beauty who is my mate.

The dress they chose is stunning, highlighting the magnificence of her. It's black, pitch-black like her eyes, but the top of the bodice twinkles with gems, white like my eyes. It's low cut and skin-tight, bisected right down to her navel where it flows out into a silky gown, which trails behind her on the floor, sparkling with yet more gems.

Her pale skin peeks through the lacy long sleeves, which cut off at her wrists. The lace is not a normal lace, no, it has trees, vines, skulls, and such sown into the fabric. It's delicate, yet deadly. Like her. The dress is backless, only showing off her perfect, unblemished skin. I want to rip it from her and sink into her wet heat, but I don't.

Not yet.

Jewels adorn her neck. Black stones with purple highlights, Aska's touch. There is a choker at the top with one, giant stone in the center, but smaller ones trail down her cheek and between her cleavage.

Her fingers are filled with rings they chose, some red like her mates' eyes, some golden like her other mates' features. We dotted more gems, red, black, white, gold, and silver, in her hair. And on her forehead is something incredible.

I don't know how he found it, but he said he felt the pull of it years ago. Its black beads trail to her forehead where a silver, iridescent crescent moon hangs, matching her wolf's.

It was meant for her, brought by her dragon.

Her black eyes are kohl lined, only highlighting their starry beauty, with red and purple makeup delicately swirled around them. Her lips are painted ruby, like blood.

She looks regal and monstrous.

Perfect.

"I'm ready," she declares, her voice strong and confident as she tilts her chin up, a lesson from her dragon.

Yes, yes she is.

CHAPTER 60

MAGNUS

I watch the radiant creature that is Dawn head my way. They seem to forget I am here and happily believe they have privacy with her despite my presence—apart from her, she never forgets. Her eyes are always going to me with a private smile, her confusion clear in her gaze as she watches me trying to figure her out.

If I was a man right now, I would gasp at her splendour.

She is stunning when covered in blood and gore, naked and draped in power.

But in a gown? Cleaned up? She is a regal beauty.

I can't decide which I like more. One calls to my man, who's used to dining with gods in riches, and one calls to my wolf, who wants to take her under a full moon. The forest god grasps her hand and tries to lead her from the room, but she stills, watching me. Turning to him, she kisses his cheek, leaving a red stamp of her lips. I wish I had that on me to prove I was hers. Strange.

"One minute, wait for me outside?" she requests, and he nods, his eyes sliding to me.

He also looks contemplative when staring at me, but he abides by her wishes and leaves, the door shutting behind him, giving us privacy. She kneels before me, watching me, those eyes meeting mine. "I don't know if you can understand me, but I think you can. Something tells me you're more than can I imagine...but thank you. For staying, for fighting at our side. One day, I will discover what you are—" Her eyes go far away for a moment. "Somehow, it seems important, but until then, join us. It would make me feel better having you at my side today."

I press my nose into her hand in affirmation. Where else would I be? I need to ensure she is safe before I leave. She smiles and pats my head before brushing her fingers through my fur. A rumble of pleasure escapes me as my wolf stretches under her touch, brushing himself along her body. But he's too big and she falls backwards from his strength, laughing as she lands on her bum.

Whining, he lowers his muzzle in apology, and she leans forward, kissing his nose. "It's okay, thank you."

He preens at that as she gets to her feet, her hand tangling in his fur, almost like she is holding his hand as we walk out the door. We catch a glimpse of ourselves in the mirror, and I realise I have a red lipstick stain on my muzzle. The sight makes my wolf way too happy and he preens, trotting from the room at her side, pleased to show it off.

That his mate marked him.

Mate.

It echoes through my head.

No, I can't be.

I can't stay, to do so guarantees all of our destruction. I have a path I must walk, and it leads me away from her. Even as the thought settles in my stomach like a lead weight. I have the present, that is all.

I stay pressed against her side, even as the male they call Lucy bows to her, his red eyes locked on her with fierce intensity, as if he cannot look away. "Ready, *Regina?*"

"As ready as I will ever be." She smiles and he shivers under her gaze before straightening.

He steps back and runs his eyes across her, seeming unable to speak, which is understandable. As a man, I would be the same. She is simply too much to behold. Like a flawless diamond. Finally, he meets her gaze again. "A true leader, you look the part, little walker."

"Yeah? It's okay?" she asks, teasing him, but he doesn't seem to notice.

He steps forward, mist flaring around him. "Okay? Who told you that you just look okay? You look magnificent, even the angels would weep. Perfection in a dangerous, beautiful package, *Regina*, that is what you are," he snarls defensively.

She giggles, the sound tinkling and making me press closer. "Nice to know what you think. Come on then, Lucy. Lead the way."

His eyes narrow as he tugs her closer, his expression closing down to something dangerous, but despite that, my hackles don't rise, so I stay still. "Do. Not. Call. Me. That," he snarls, sounding deadly.

She pats his chest. "Sure, Lucy, let's not keep them waiting."

He stills, stops moving completely as if he's frozen. His eyes flicker like flames and then he lets out a breath. Eyes narrowed, he cups her hand and leads her away, his back straight.

I stay next to them and the others follow behind us. It feels right to be at her side, but I know that won't last forever. Nothing does, not even when you wish it would...

Everything ends. Everything dies. Everything destructs.

And I will be the key.

Chapter 61

Dawn

Lucy leads me downstairs and towards the throne room. The bodies and blood from yesterday are gone, it looks spotless apart from some holes in the walls and doors. It makes me wonder who cleaned it all up, but I guess I better get used to that type of thing now.

He stops in front of the closed double doors where we can hear the muffled voices of the crowd gathered beyond. "They voted for this, show them why," he murmurs to me, and then blows open the doors without even touching them.

He's right, I might not understand why they think I can lead, but they chose this. I have to show them I can be what they need, at least right now. Give me a battle or someone to kill and I'm your girl, but when faced with a room full of expectant supernaturals all looking to me, I hesitate.

But I can't afford to.

Every eye swings my way and the crowd slowly quiets, then they all get to their feet. There are thousands of faces, some I recognise, some I don't. But they all know me. Some, most, bow their heads. Some stare, waiting, watching, analysing. They are all expecting me to mess up, to prove I'm like Amos and his men. It won't happen. I'm not.

I raise my chin and step into the room, and as Lucy leads me through their masses, murmurs go up. People shuffle to see, to get closer, but my mates keep them from stampeding or getting hurt, and when I view the thrones, I have a brief flash of panic.

You can do this, little regina, no one but you. Look at their faces, you give them hope. Hope for change, for the future. Embrace it, embrace your past. Let it guide you, let it build you into the queen they see...that I see.

I glance at Lucy as his voice floats through my head, but he doesn't look at me. I swallow, his confidence filling me so when we reach the throne, I turn with him, in sync, until we face our people. I don't know what to expect, there wasn't a lot of time to explain, but I do know Lucy isn't one for traditions and laws, so I'm betting it's going to be a quick, no frills ceremony.

Good.

Just my style.

Standing on the podium before the gaudy thrones, I let Lucy take the reins for now. "Today we are gathered to crown our new council head. The rest will follow. This moment is about stability and structure. We will keep this short, since everyone is anxious for what is to come. Change is...change is always hard, even if it is for the better. But this woman, Dawn, she has the backing of the sleeping council, and more so—you."

He turns to me then, watching me closely, so I give him a small nod. I'm ready for whatever the future brings. I'm scared, that's true, but some of the best things in life are scary. Without fear, how can we truly appreciate something?

"Dawn—" He cuts off, blinking in confusion. *What's your last name?*

Smirking, I let the answer drift to him. *My mother's last name was Agana, it means blood.*

Fitting. He smirks.

"Dawn Agana, do you accept this role? Do you swear on your life to uphold our laws and to protect those who may not be able to protect themselves? Do you, as an extension of our council, vow to represent our races with dignity, strength, and understanding? Do you promise to exact swift justice on those who deserve it, and accept the role of judge, jury, and executioner?"

"I do," I vow, my voice strong, and something wraps around me —a rightness. It's warm and caring, it pulses around me, pride filling...it.

"Kneel," he orders, and I do so before him, bowing my head. He places his hand there, his power encasing me, sinking through my skin, coating my veins. I gasp as I feel it lock around me, chaining me to not only him...but this role.

"Then as a representative of the sleeping council and those who govern the races, I hereby proclaim you head of the council. You are to do your duty without fear or prejudice. You are the new protector of all our people, called upon to service by need and trust. Dawn Agana, you may now rise and take in your people." The scent of blood fills the air and then his blood-covered hand is at my mouth. "Drink, let our power fill you, let our people be yours now."

Gripping his hand, I raise my eyes to his, meeting those red depths as I lap at the blood he's offering. He grinds his teeth as I watch, and I can't help the clenching of my pussy at the taste...at the ultimate power. He observes me darkly, his eyes firing with each lick of my tongue until he yanks his hand away and steps back.

At first nothing changes, but then I feel it moving through me, setting me ablaze. Then all at once, lights start to turn on in my head. Like fireflies in the dark, growing brighter and brighter. More and more appear until I'm almost blind. I nearly fall to the side with the force, with the vastness of it. My mind expands, white-hot pokers stabbing into my brain.

"Rise," Lucy demands. I blink to try and push the lights away and concentrate on what's happening. I can't mess this first thing up, I can't.

Lifting my head, I let him assist me to my feet. A roar of applause and screams go up among my men and the gathered crowd. The room shakes with their stampede of approval. Pride fills my mind from all my mate bonds, true pride filled with love, and I almost stumble. The belief they have in me is astounding, and as I turn and smile at them, their eyes reflect the truth I felt in our connection.

Whatever this role entails, wherever it takes me...they will be there. That's when I realise these people need the same promise. They need the truth. They are staring at me like I stare at my mates, for help and assurance...for strength.

Turning, I face the crowd again, scanning them as they slowly become quiet. All eyes are on me, waiting to see what I'll say or do.

I stand, knowing they are waiting for a speech, some reassurance. Taking a deep breath, I gather my mates' and my strength. "I know you wonder who I am, and the truth is, I am nothing. No one. But I have been through hell and back to get here. I have fought every day of my life. I know what it means to be beaten, tortured, and thought of as nothing." I look around, meeting each and every gaze that I can. "I never gave up, not once, and I never will. This was a big step, razing the council, but their reach, their rot, is still pervasive, and we, together, need to get rid of it. They thought we were nothing but pawns." I shake my head. "They were wrong. Even the youngest, even the least powerful of us have a place, a reason...a destiny. I'm finding mine, and I don't know if I belong here, but I want to help, and I hope that's enough."

Sucking in a breath, I hold my head high. "I will try my best, that's all I can do. I might make mistakes, I might fumble, but I promise you I'll never give up. To those who followed me into battle, you are up here with me. I may be the voice, but I'm fighting for you. For everyone who ever felt mistreated or unseen, who was sick of the power plays. The games and the injustices. We are all one people. Despite our differences, they are what make us strong. Together we can stop everything, this is our—your choice. We can live as they did, nothing can change, or we can fight and never give up, and maybe, just maybe we can be great again. Maybe we can find our destiny together."

Cheers go up and my heart slams in my chest at the hope, at the pride, and fierce devotion in all their faces...and my mates' minds. When they start to calm, I look about once more. The lights are drawing closer, so I know I need to end it soon before it overwhelms me. "It starts now, no empty promises. I'm not better than you, not above you. I'm one of you. You are one of us. Together, as one. So let me begin with the truth. The human hunters are still out there, as are some of the witches who helped Amos. Titus also made it clear he has other experiments. We start with them. I will have others combing through the wreckage the council left behind, scouring their notes and plans to see what else we are unaware of, but until then, I ask this—who here will help me? Who here wants to change this world? I can't do this alone. This is a war, not a battle."

For a moment, nothing happens, then a woman steps forward. "You saved my life, I'm with you, whatever you need."

Then another and another until a cascade of voices fills the room. It shocks me to my core, I never expected it. They want to help, they want change. I look to Lucy who steps up beside me. "We will start with guards."

"Griffin, is my head guard, he will be taking applications," I announce.

Lucy looks at me with a raised eyebrow but nods.

"Nos will be in charge of liaisons with the old council and the new changes. Go to him if you have issues and can't get to me. That's all we know for now, everything else will be decided, but my first priority is you. Ensuring we are all safe and well. No more lies, no more experiments. We are one!" I roar.

"One!" they scream in response, as my men step closer to my back, ready for what we'll face. We have an uncertain future, but up here, looking out at those expectant, ready faces, I know.

I made the right choice.

This is my destiny.

AFTERWARDS, I'm led through the crowd. Questions are fired at me, but I ignore them for now, slightly overwhelmed. It's as if I can feel every member of this country. Every power, every person. Their lights fill my head until it feels like it might explode. There are so many, so fucking many, and now they are all looking to me.

Once we are past the door, Lucy yanks me into the closest room and cups my cheeks, forcing me to look at him with blind eyes. It hurts, it hurts so badly, there are so many...the more I think about it, the more I feel it.

"Breathe, let them pass, don't focus on them. Push them backwards, that's it. They are still there but block them, build a wall, you only need to reach for them in dire emergencies, good girl, that's it. Breathe."

I still can't see, but I let his touch anchor me. "What is that?" I whisper.

"Your people, every single one. You will feel their lights extinguish when they die, you can call them, you can master the connection and use it to monitor and control your people," he murmurs.

"God, so many..." I gasp.

"Yes, now imagine seeing the whole world like that."

Blinking, I meet those red eyes, my head not hurting any longer. "You see all the supernaturals around the world?"

He nods. "All day, every day. It's exhausting. It's one of the main reasons only one of the sleeping council ever rules at any given time, and not for too long, to stop us from going crazy. Feeling better?"

I nod silently. Fuck, I can't imagine the chaos, the pain in his head at all the lights, all the people. Never truly being alone even in your brain. No wonder they pulled away from the world. I would as well.

Looking around, I realise we are in a cupboard. "Where are we?" I snort.

"Closest room, I think it's a cleaning cupboard." Lucy laughs. "Your mates are blocking the door, making sure we have the time you need to rebuild. They could feel the pressure in your head...I could."

"Thank you." I sigh, and then we both seem to realise he's still touching me at the same time. I expect him to jerk away or make some nasty or dirty statement, but he stays quiet, his hands still cradling my cheeks. Those red eyes watch me closely. "Lucy—"

"Don't call me that," he murmurs, but it's an offhand comment, like an automatic response as his eyes dip down to my lips and seem to trace them. Shivering under his gaze, I dart my tongue out and wet them, making him groan.

"You love it, Lucy," I tease, pushing him, wanting to see what he'll do. The world is waiting right outside this door, but in here, I feel suddenly very far away...very alone with this powerful demon.

"I'm warning you..."

"Yeah, you keep doing that. I'm wondering what the warning turns into...Lucy," I press.

He's still for a moment, then he snaps. He shoves me backwards, and my back hits the shelves with a bang, making me grunt. It's dark in here, and small, and there isn't much room for me, never mind a demon. He presses his body against mine, his hand tugging my chin up before he covers my lips with his.

He's warm, really warm, like touching a candle or an open flame. His lips taste like burnt embers and blood...it's addicting. Groaning, he grips me tighter, pressing harder against me until there is no space between us. He bites down on my lower lip and I open my mouth, the taste of my blood apparent as our tongues tangle in a deep, harsh kiss.

His hands are mean, painful, his lips soft, yet harsh. I want more.

My hand darts out and grips his shirt, twisting it in my fist as I pull him closer, then, using my strength, push him away. I start to walk us backwards, still kissing. He grunts into my mouth as he crashes into the shelves behind him.

If he thought I was just going to be a good girl and sit there and take it, he doesn't know me very well.

His hands reach down and cup my ass, lifting me higher until our eyes are level. His gaze is so bright, it's almost blinding as I toss my head back. Fires burn and twist in those depths. "You want to play games?" he snaps, as I laugh.

Then we're gone. My stomach flips, and there is a feeling of movement, and then we appear outside. Blinking, I look around. I don't even know where we are, it doesn't look familiar. There is a castle behind Lucy, a big, towering structure. The moon is high, and mist creeps along the grass to where we stand at the edge of the property.

Spinning me, he slams me into a tree, but I snarl and shove him away. "Where are we?"

"Somewhere we can't be found." He smirks.

"Lucy!" I yell.

"Just a little place where they still worship me. Want to see?" he offers, and before I can respond, he moves us again. I'm not prepared and bile rises in my throat, but I swallow it back and look around.

We are in a clearing in the woods—the same woods, I can feel it. There is an altar made of stone with bowls of blood and bones surrounding it. The stone is etched with carvings depicting what looks like a great demon...Lucy.

Half burnt candles with wax dripping down them circle the

large altar, and with a snap of Lucy's fingers, they come to life, illuminating everything. "The people of this world still beg for me, worship me. I am their god...they fall to their knees before me. They ask for boons and assistance, but they dare not look in my eyes...yet you, brave little walker, do," he murmurs behind me, his breath blowing over my hair. "Are you afraid?"

"No," I reply, and it's true. I'm not. He can try to kill me if he wants. He might even succeed, but I'm betting he won't. I intrigue him, and like it or not we are linked somehow. Oh, he wants to kill me, that's for sure, at least half of him...but he won't because the other half wants me.

Like I want him.

Spinning, I smirk at him. "They worship you here?"

He nods, his eyes alight, and in the smoke behind him I see his demon emerging—big, twisting horns, fire eyes, and bulging body. A terrifying sight...also a hot one. "Then how about we change that? You think you are untouchable. Above it all. You laugh at their sacrifices, you bathe in their blood, and appear on altars of lost souls and bones...how about you worship me on it, demon? Let us see if you are worth all that...loyalty." I smirk and then turn, leaping onto the altar. I sit and swing my legs back and forth as I watch him from the circle of flames.

He's smoking, this is probably sacrilege and he doesn't like to be tested. His body changes until he towers above me, those horns ablaze with an internal fire, his mouth twisted in a snarl, and eyes black like the pits of hell. Grinning, I spread my legs wider, letting the dress part to show a glimpse of my white skin under the moon.

He circles the altar behind the ring of fire, watching me as he stalks around it. Power fills the clearing. It's dark and twisted and so fucking delicious. He calls it, and the night silences in fear. Eyes of the people and animals across the forest turn away, downcast. People hide, feeling it.

Me? I revel in it.

Falling backwards, I arch my back into the air as it skims across my body, touching me.

"I am the one they fear in the dark. Not you, little walker. You do not command me, you do not know me, *you do not disrespect me!*" he yells, and the world trembles.

"But I did, Lucy. So tell me, oh great demon, what are you going to do?" I laugh breathlessly, my body writhing on the altar as his power increases, seeming to slip inside me like fingers, an actual touch.

Suddenly, he's there inside the ring of candles, and as soon as he steps across them, they burst into flame. Stronger, higher, until a circle of fire surrounds us, so tall and fierce we can't see out.

We can't escape.

The thought makes me moan. Yes. Fuck.

He thinks he's trapped me in here with him, but in reality he's imprisoned himself with me...the one thing he can't control. I wonder if either of us will come out alive.

"I could kill you, *Regina*. So easily. Slit your throat and watch the blood run across that pale skin, rip your soul from your body...so fucking effortlessly," he whispers.

"Then do it, I dare you," I taunt.

Never, ever dare a demon...or Lucifer.

His face looms above me, then he grips my arms and yanks them over my head, restraining them to the stone until I'm stretched out below him like a sacrifice. Maybe that's what I am.

"Killing you would be too easy, little walker, it's much more fun to watch you live..."

"Lucy, you pussy," I goad right in his face, even as I'm pinned, unable to move below him. Really, I'm asking for it at this point, but I can't seem to stop. My life is spiralling out of control, everything is changing, so maybe this is me laughing in the face of death, daring him to try and take me.

"Pussy?" he rumbles, as one of his hands trails down my body, making me gasp. He shoves open my thighs, and one claw-tipped nail slides down my wet heat. "Like this one? You see, I can smell your arousal, little walker, how much you want me. So tell me, do you want to make a deal with the devil?"

"No, but I'll fuck him." I giggle, and then press my lips to his.

He freezes, shocked by my actions. I'm betting about now all those girls, even the dark ones who thought they could handle him, backed away, ran off scared. I can almost see it in his mind, how often they thought they wanted this, him, they believed they could handle him. But his darkness was too much from them and they ultimately feared him.

Not me.

Never me. His darkness? I crave it. I want him to paint it across my skin on his altar. I want everything this demon has to offer. I want to consume him until nothing is left.

He rumbles against me, those claws dangerously close to my most vulnerable areas as he returns my kiss, dominating it, changing it until he's draining me. Taking everything from me. And I let him. I let him lead, helpless beneath him, craving his harsh, mean touch.

One finger presses inside me and I gasp into his mouth. The edge of danger is making this so much hotter, but then he pauses. I open my eyes to see his gaze has gone far away until he blinks.

"We need to go back," he snarls, but he doesn't seem happy about it, nor does he move away or stop touching me.

"Let's go then...and demon? There might be hope for you yet. I can see why they worship you, why they pray to you. But I never will, you have to earn that, if you dare." His eyes go red again while I grin. "Better take us home, Lucy, they will be looking for us."

His hand grips my chin, no doubt leaving a mark. "One day I will fuck you on this altar, *Regina*. I will take you and everything you have to offer. I will drain that magic from you as your blood runs over the stone and soaks into the ground. And there is nothing you can do about it."

I can't wait.

CHAPTER 62

DAWN

He brings us back and we appear in the cupboard just as the door is flung open. They must have felt us leave, but Aska, who opened the door, seems to know what happened. He throws Lucy a glare and takes my hand, leading me out, and then keeps hold of it as he brushes some hair behind my ear. "*Neriso*, my jewel, you were so far away," he murmurs.

"Sorry," I reply, and lean up and kiss him. He nips my lips in punishment. "Did you need me?"

"Always," he rumbles, his eyes flashing, and Griffin fake gags.

"Fucking hell, let's go see what your visitor wants, *Vasculo*, before you two fuck each other right here."

That has me pulling back and looking away from my dragon, even though I'm tempted to do what Griffin just threatened. "Visitor?"

Lucy sniffs and then groans. "Xaph."

Aska's eyebrows rise. "The angel from the volcano...the sleeping court?"

"Angel? Well, this should be fun." I look at Lucy. "You know what he wants?"

"Probably to be killed again." He smirks.

Rolling my eyes, I head back to the throne room. This time we enter through a backdoor that Lucy guides us to and step right out onto the dais. There is a man there, staring out at the room, his back to his. But yeah, he looks like an angel. Halo and all.

He turns as we enter, his gaze clashing with mine for a moment before going to Lucy. "Serpent," he snaps. "You kill me once more and I will banish you! Now, what has been happening here? I have been hearing whispers that you...you killed the council and put some, some woman child in charge."

"I guess that's me." I laugh.

He dismisses me with a disgusted glance and a snort and looks to Lucy. "You abandoned your position. I have been too busy to chase you down! This is not a game, Serpent, you are mocking our laws!"

"Oh shut up for once," Lucy retorts. "Why are you here? Left your little mountain, did you, to look down on the peasants below?"

Xaph narrows his eyes and tilts his head high in such a heavenly way I nearly laugh. What a pretentious asshole. No wonder Lucy killed him.

Tried, he regenerates, very inconvenient if you ask me.

"I am here to lead, since you clearly cannot. This, this can't stand. I am here to remove her from power." He sniffs.

"No, you're not," Lucy counters.

"Sorry, not going anywhere." I grin.

"You cannot lead, you know nothing of our laws! Our ways! You're a child...you're a—" He stumbles.

"Woman?" I offer and raise my eyebrow. "It seems to me if there were less dick measuring contests and power games, we wouldn't be in this mess in the first place, angel. I am a leader now, so suck it up and start acting like one yourself. If you did your job, we wouldn't be this lost. Your lack of leadership is the problem."

"She makes a good point, Xaph. This happened under your watch." Lucy smirks.

The angel's face turns red. "You know how hard it is to monitor all these creatures, they are always killing or doing something. I simply do what I can, under his grace." He looks back to me and glares, his eyes flashing gold as he growls, "You are to be removed from your position."

Yeah, Lucy isn't allowed to kill him...but I can.

So I do.

As he turns to argue with Lucy, I take him by surprise. He turns just as I appear before him, his eyes widening as he stumbles back, but he doesn't make a move to defend himself as I grip his head and twist, snapping his neck with a self-satisfying crack. His body tumbles to the floor as I dust off my hands and saunter back to my men.

Looking at Lucy, I shrug. "He was annoying me."

I find myself very turned on right now.

"Too much information, Lucy." Griffin snorts.

Lucy turns to him with narrowed eyes. "Only she calls me that," he roars, just as a click sounds. We all turn to see Xaph's neck straighten as gold shimmers across his body, and then he's on his feet, blinking.

When he realises what happened, his mouth drops open. "You-you killed me! That is punishable by death!"

"I saw nothing." Lucy shrugs.

"Me neither," my men chorus behind me, and I wink at Xaph.

"Serpent, you can't seriously expect us to let her lead. She clearly is not mature enough to uphold a prestigious position and seat such as this!"

"She is and can," Lucy responds, yawning.

"Serpent!" Xaph protests. "She knows nothing! How will she

lead? No, it cannot be allowed, she would need too much guidance and help."

"I'll help," Lucy declares, and everyone gapes.

Xaph stares at him. "You will help?"

"Why not?" he asks, voice clipped.

Slowly, a smile covers Xaph's face. "You are finally taking your place. It is good to see, even if your first stand is with this child. Fine, you wish her to be your responsibility, you shall have your way, but if she fails it will be on your head. Your position and life lie with her now. If she fails, you both die. Understood?"

"Understood. Now, you are boring me, so if that is every-thing..." Lucy drawls and turns to walk away, but Xaph stops him.

"It is not, in fact. She was not the only reason I sought you out. We have a problem, a big one, with the dragons," he informs us.

"Dragons?" Aska echoes, stepping forward. "What kind?"

"They are breaking through, I saw it myself. Eight of them flew from the entrance to Klasfor and into the world."

"But—" I stumble and look at Aska. "Why? Aren't they trapped there?"

"Voluntarily. They didn't want to be a part of this world." He frowns, appearing confused. "If they wanted to come through...they can. I found a dead male, one from my childhood, not too far south of here. He had been killed in a challenge with another dragon, which is not uncommon, but if it is spilling into this world..." He shakes his head.

"Aska, what does this mean?" I inquire, getting a really bad feeling.

"Eight dragons," he whispers, and looks to Xaph. "Did they go in all directions?"

Xaph nods.

"They are scouts," Aska rumbles. "Here to scout the world."

"Scouts?" I say with a frown. "What? Why?"

"*Neriso*, scouts come before a war...an invasion," Aska explains.

"But why now?" Xaph snaps. "You are a dragon, you must

know. They withdrew from this world several millennia ago, happy to die and breed in your own world. Why now?"

"I don't know. I haven't been home since they closed the gates. If they are sending scouts...coming here, it's for a reason. We need to find out why and fast. Dragons aren't known for making friends. They will burn this world if they want to do so."

"Great," I growl. "So first the council and now a dragon invasion, anything else?"

"We still need to deal with the rogue humans and witches," Dume supplies.

Fuck.

The whole world is going to shit. Why now? What's happening? Do they feel the unbalance of power? No, Aska would have mentioned it, but when I look at my dragon's face, he seems worried, very worried. And something that concerns my untouchable dragon downright terrifies me.

"Okay, well, we will have to—"

"You, not we, child. You wanted the role, then you have the responsibilities associated with your position. Most of the dragons are heading this way, into your territory, and the door is closest to you. This is your problem." Xaph smirks and looks to Lucy. "Try not to destroy the world." Then, he disappears as swiftly as he arrived.

"What the fuck? The whole world is in danger and he's all like 'okay, bye, hold my beer?'" I snap, throwing my hands in the air.

Lucy snorts. "*Regina*, you will learn over the years there is always a war, a plan to destroy the world. It is so common it is boring. He knows it will not happen, we have seen it time and time again. He is giving us a challenge to prove ourselves or fail."

"And if we fail, we die," I conclude. "Brilliant, no pressure."

"That is tomorrow's problem, you will learn that soon enough. Until then, let us sort some of the council's issues, clean up this house, and begin planning." Lucy sighs. "I guess I'm going into teaching mode."

"Yeah, I'm betting you didn't listen a lot during council laws and proper leadership studies." I snort and he smirks at me, proving me right.

All of our lives are hanging in Lucifer's hands...that's okay...right?

WE RETURN to the sleeping court's quarters, but go into a living room this time. It's a little dusty, but still beautiful and definitely to my taste. It has large, charcoal, button sofas around the space with black accents, very little gold, and a huge fireplace. It looks homey, as much as a giant living room in a mansion can.

My mates sit down throughout the room as Lucy leans against the wall, his eyes far away. "We could do with a guard we trust for your door," he suggests randomly.

"I have all these mates, not to mention myself."

He raises his eyebrow as Griffin stands with a, "Need to pee," and leaves the room.

"Not enough, I have an idea."

Just then a pop sounds, and at Lucy's side is a dog...well, more like a skeleton, but it's dog-shaped for sure. I can't help but melt. It's so cute with little red eyes and flaming feet. I want to touch it.

So I do. I drop to my knees and reach for him. "Oh my God, you are so adorable!" I squeal.

"He is fierce, a killer, a—" Lucy stops, his mouth hanging open as I stroke his fur, cooing to him.

"Oh my gosh, who's a little cutie, yes you are! Look at those sweet little flames, who's a good boy with flames? Yes you are, yes you are." The dog barks happily and rubs against my hands.

"Stop, woman, that is a fierce hellhound! Death itself, he—"

"Yes, you're a good boy," I gush, scratching his head.

"Woman!" Lucy screams, throwing his hands in the air as the dog flops onto his back and I scratch his tummy. "You have turned my hellhound into a slobbering puppy!" he protests, staring at his hellhound in disgust. "Get up, Hades, act like the demon you are!"

Hades ignores him and curls around me, rumbling happily. Just then, Griffin comes back into the room and spots the dog. His eyes widen and his nostrils flare. "Oh, hell no! Nope, we already have a wolf and a fucking minotaur, we have no more room for pets! None!"

"Oooh, I could get you a little bandana with skulls on it. Oh my God, we could get your daddy a matching one, yes we could," I tell Hades.

"*Vasculo!*" Griffin roars. "I'm serious, no more pets!"

I blink at him. "He stays, problem?" I challenge, raising my eyebrow.

Griffin tosses his hands in the air as well—I have that effect on people—and leaves the room, grumbling about dog piss and stupid women. I look to Lucy. "Is this your guard?"

Lucy watches the dog in disgust as he crosses his arms. "Yes, he is a fierce, loyal beast...usually. He burns souls and eats them."

"Oh my gosh, how cute, you are adorable," I tell Hades.

I hear laughing behind me as Lucy glares at me. "Let's sort the rest of the roles and go through what needs to happen now. *Regina*, please don't tickle the hellhound."

Grinning, I carry on with my ministrations. "Shouldn't have brought him then! Okay, so what's first?"

Lucy takes one more pained look at his dog before diving into what the people and council now expect. By the end my head is spinning. So many rules, so many expectations...so much to do, and fighting and killing won't be the solution this time. Words and power games will be.

And we are only just beginning.

CHAPTER 63

ASKA

"Tell me everything I need to know about dragons and what this means," Dawn requests over breakfast the next day. After Lucy's lessons, she had fallen into a deep sleep. They went on until the early morning and she woke up exhausted. I can see it, it's getting to be too much for her.

"I will, but first you need a break. You went from hunting your ex to stopping the council without a pause. We can have a few hours off, my love," I tell her, my hand gliding up and down her thigh. She is sitting beside me on the sofa, and I can't stop myself from touching her, from being close. I am not ashamed to admit I tackled Griffin to get the seat next to her.

"A break?" she questions, tilting her head and blinking at me as she eats her sausage. Which is very distracting when she is in a room full of horny supernaturals. All eyes are locked on her. She either doesn't notice or doesn't care, but the slight smirk around her lips tells me she's noticed and is doing it on purpose now.

She takes another bite and moans, her eyes fluttering closed.

My cock jerks in my pants and I shift uncomfortably. Looking around, I can see the rest of her mates are in the same predicament. Nos laughs at her. "Little Monster, be nice or be prepared to run."

She blinks open her eyes and they bleed to black. "Only if you promise to chase me."

"Focus, *Vasculo*." Griffin snorts.

"Fine." She huffs. "What kind of break?"

I look at the other guys. I had asked them earlier when she was asleep. They agreed she needed to rest, although Nos had to smack Griffin on the back of his head when he tried to kill me for, and I quote, 'stepping on his territory' with her. He also told me we couldn't fuck or he would chop off my 'tiny dragon balls.'

"You'll see. Put on trousers, *Neriso*, and meet me out back," I instruct her, then lean down and lick the sauce from the corner of her mouth, making her shudder against me. I hop up before any of her other mates can kill me and stroll from the room. I glance back at the door to see my mate's eyes on my arse.

I wink at her and Griffin rolls his eyes at me. Laughing, I head downstairs and prepare for our break. This is the first time I will be alone with my mate and not in the dreamscape. A part of me is nervous about what I want to show her, but it's better to do this now instead of later. She didn't flinch when she saw me shift in battle, but this is different. My dragon is aching to meet her, to wrap around her and protect her.

They need to meet.

If she will let us, I want her to meet my dragon and then take her flying. Let her soar above the sky with me and get her away for a bit. Get her to relax so she is ready to face what is coming, because if I am right, if the dragons are preparing for an attack...we have a war approaching.

She doesn't keep me waiting long. She hops down from the second floor balcony and lands before me, grinning on the grass. Her legs are encased in leather pants, which look painted on, with a tank top tucked in, showing off her bare, pale shoulders and arms. I debate keeping her to myself, but then shake it away.

"So what are we doing, dragon?" she queries, seeming excited.

"We are going for a ride." I smile and then, without warning, I change.

My wings sprout from my back as scales take over my expanding body, the ground and air around me swirls with power, and through it all I see her eyes locked on my transformation in wonder. Then, my dragon stands before her.

Her mouth drops open. "Aska...you're beautiful," she whispers.

Huffing, I lower my head and she steps closer, pressing her hand to my snout, unafraid, even as my purple magic seeps through my black, spiny leather skin. She stares into my eyes, looking so tiny against my curled body.

My dragon hesitates, not wanting to hurt her since she is so little. *Want to climb on? We will go for a ride.*

"You want me to ride you?" She beams, still stroking my snout like she cannot stop.

You can ride me anytime, Neriso.

She giggles and looks at my body. "You are huge, how do I even...ride you?"

Tilting my head to the side, I sink my body to the ground as low as it goes. *There are some spikes behind my head, use them, don't worry about gripping too hard, my skin is very thick. You couldn't even shoot an arrow through my hide.*

She nods with a wide grin, and without hesitating, grabs onto my spikes and throws herself up onto my neck. Huffing with a smirk, I rise up and she gasps.

"That felt so wrong, rumbling between my legs."

So, of course, I do it again and she gasps. I feel her warm body against the skin of my neck and turn my head, blinking at her as I blow smoke right in her face, making her laugh.

"Come on then, big guy, let's fly!" she shouts, almost squealing.

Taking her word that she is ready, I push from the ground and soar into the sky, flapping my wings. I allow her to get settled and hold on before I dive towards the ground, sweeping low before tucking in my wings and spiralling higher until we break through the clouds.

She whoops, squealing as we move faster. Once through the clouds, I open my wings and we glide. I turn my head and watch her arms spread on either side, reaching out to touch the clouds, her eyes closed. She looks so peaceful, so happy with her mouth curved in a relaxed smile and the wind blowing through her blonde hair.

She is beautiful.

Her eyes open and lock on me. *So are you. Now, how fast can you go, big guy? Let's take this dragon for a real ride.*

Oh, she wants to go fast?

Hold on, Neriso, *if you fall they will kill me.*

She screams in delight as I stop my wings and tuck them close, letting us plunge through the clouds and spiral closer to earth. I streamline my body as much as I can, letting us go faster and faster, and then I start to spin. I hear her screaming, the wind taking the sound away, but I feel the excitement and thrill in her mind. I make sure to keep an eye on her, not wanting to hurt her or push her too far, but my mate wants more.

Everything.

She wants this.

Before we hit the ground, I spread my wings and take us higher, then I loop over the city and farther out, doing tricks and spins, flying fast and slow. It's like being a youngling again. We did this to show off, to test how fast we could go. It was exciting, a thrill, and I get that feeling now, sharing this with my mate. It's incredible, I've never felt more alive, more connected to another person.

I slow down on the way back and she drapes her body across my neck, her hand reaching out as far as it can go and stroking my scales. *Thank you, my dragon, that was amazing, I needed that...*

Always, Neriso. *You can fly with me anytime. It has become a function to me, but you reminded me of the joy in it.*

I spot a waterfall below, cascading into an azure blue pond, and glide towards it, landing on the edge. It's hidden by the trees, not far from the city. I change back after she slips from my neck and lays on the ground with a smile on her face. Back in human form, I lie next to her, my arm under my head as I stare up at the clouds, the sun shining down on us.

"It's so beautiful," she whispers.

"It is," I agree. "Though the beauty this world has to offer in no way matches the beauty of you, *Neriso*."

She laughs and rolls over, sprawling on my chest, her head on my heart. "Cheesy, but I like it. Want to go for a swim?" she asks, and leaps to her feet, her hand outstretched to me.

I accept it and stand, pulling her closer as we walk down to the pond, the rush of the waterfall loud and relaxing. It reminds me faintly of home, but this is so much better, because now I have Dawn.

She dips her toe into the blue water and sighs. "It's warm." She looks over at me and grins before releasing my hand and diving in.

Smirking, I follow after her, splashing her as she surfaces. She laughs and splashes me back. I can't seem to stop smiling, even as she dives under the water to escape me. I follow her, cutting through the pool until I can pull her close under the blue water. The world above seems far away.

Her eyes grin at me as she leans closer and presses her lips to mine. Gripping the back of her hair, I push us to the surface, our heads breaking the water. She sucks in a breath and slicks back her hair, her legs wrapping around my waist as I hold us both up, kicking my legs.

"Aska," she murmurs, her gaze going to my lips. "Tell me, are you ever going to fuck me, my dragon?"

Grinding my teeth, I ignore the jerking of my cock. "I didn't want to pressure you and a lot has—"

She giggles and covers my lips with her finger. "Aska, I have been waiting for you. Now you are finally here, and you're worried about not pressuring me? I want you so fucking much it hurts. And today, soaring through the sky with you, feeling all that power between my legs...it's only made me want you more. So tell me, my dragon king, do you feel like consummating our mating?"

There is no need for any more words. I growl, my eyes lighting up as they lock on her. She isn't getting away from me now, she made this choice, she wants me...she's going to have me.

Gripping her head, I twine my fingers through her wet locks and yank her closer, covering her ruby lips with mine. She groans into my mouth as I lick and nip, teasing her before she opens her mouth to me. Tangling tongues, I swim until I can stand. Not breaking our desperate kiss, I hoist her from the water, which flows from our joined bodies as I walk her backwards until we meet the rocks surrounding the pond. One is like a shelf—half in the water, half out. I drop her onto it and step between her parted thighs, still keeping our lips locked in a desperate battle of wills.

She tastes like water and sex. Images of silken sheets and pale thighs flash in my mind, making me rumble with lust as I press closer still. She's addictive, and the sensation of her wet, silky body pressed against mine sends my heart racing and my cock jerking from desire, wishing I was buried inside her.

Tipping her backwards until her back rests against the rock barrier, I tear my lips away from her and kiss down her neck, leaving a trail of open-mouthed kisses as she gasps. Her hands grip my shoulders, digging in as her nails pierce the skin, and I smirk.

"Feeling needy?" I murmur, as I kneel between her thighs. My head is level with her heaving chest, her ruby nipples hard and taut, her breasts floating in the water as she pants, her eyes black and locked on mine.

Grinning, I reach out and cup her breasts, squeezing them in my palms until her eyes close and she gives herself to me, her body pliant and soft as little moans escape her lips, driving me crazy. I wonder if she will make them when I'm pounding into her pussy.

Leaning down, I suck one of her nipples into my mouth and roll it around before moving to the other, switching back and forth until she is scratching at my shoulders, pulling me closer. The scent of her arousal fills the air, the fragrance heady and addictive.

My cock is throbbing, swollen from the need to be inside my mate, but I'm not rushing this. I have been waiting a millennium to feel my mate, to taste her, fuck her, and make her mine. I want her to scream like she did in the air, this time while she rides my mouth and fingers.

I want those black eyes locked on me as I bring her to the edge again and again.

She moans my name, her eyes flashing dangerously as she drags me closer still, trying to get me to do what she wants, but I ignore her nails buried in my shoulders and lower my head, blowing warm smoke across her nipples, making her shudder and moan. Her body seems to melt into the water, nothing but the stones and my hands holding her up.

Stroking along her thighs, I part them further and run my hands up the silky inside until I meet her wet center. She groans, her teeth biting down on her bottom lip as I glide my finger down her lips before spreading them. Keeping my eyes on her face, I analyse each change and nuance, storing away what she likes and what she loves. What gives her the most pleasure.

Circling around her throbbing nub, I lower my mouth to her nipple and suck it into my mouth, biting down gently as I press on her clit. She jerks closer with a silent scream, her eyes wild and begging.

"Aska," she growls, as I release her nipple with a smirk.

"*Neriso?*" I rumble, as I trace my finger down her slit and press inside her pussy, my eyes locked on hers.

They flutter shut as her head drops back when I curl my long fingers inside her, dragging along her nerves that have her lighting up like a firework. With my other hand, I wrap it around my cock and squeeze the tip, trying to ignore my own need and stop myself from just pounding into her.

"Yes, yes, God," she moans, as I rub her clit and fuck her with my fingers.

Her chest glistens with droplets of water and I lap them from her skin, tasting the saltiness of her sweat and the sweet, fresh flavour of the water. Her pussy clenches around me at the rough texture of my tongue, making me smirk. Dropping lower in the water, I take a deep breath before diving under, looking at her pink, raw, wet pussy. Her clit is engorged and begging for my mouth. I watch my fingers dip in and out, coated in her cream, her tight hold squeezing around me. Fuck, I bet she will feel amazing wrapped around my cock.

So responsive, so needy.

Perfect.

Darting out my tongue, I wrap it around her clit before lashing her with it. Her moans get louder, my name escaping her lips on a prayer that has me feeling mighty and powerful. Fucking her harder with my fingers, I suck her clit into my mouth, biting down slightly before I start to rumble the way I did in my dragon form.

She comes apart with a scream, her hands searching for me in the water and pressing my face closer to her pussy as she rocks her hips through her release. Her pussy clamps around my fingers, massaging until I can't wait anymore.

Ripping them free, I surge up through the water, droplets falling from my lashes and lips as I lick her cream from my digits. I grab her hips and drag her farther down the rock, pressing my cock to her still fluttering channel.

Her eyes flare open and meet mine as in one, long thrust I bury myself inside her. I almost roar from the feel of her, so tight and wet. Clenching around my cock, trying to stop me from pushing deeper. Grinding my teeth, I dig my fingers into her hips, denting her skin as I pull free and work myself back in again and again until I am balls deep, my hilt meeting her core.

Her chest arches, her nipples pointing to the sky as she takes all of me, her curvy little body fitting mine perfectly. "Aska," she moans. "God, move, or, or—"

I do as my mate demands, I move, pulling free from her clinging body and driving back in. She reaches up and grips her breasts, swaying from my thrusts. Tweaking her nipples, she rolls them between her small fingers, making me grunt.

That's a beautiful sight. My cock jerks inside her, my balls aching as I watch her body beneath me. So beautiful, so perfect. Her tight little cunt taking me, her lips raw and bruised from my kiss, teeth marks around one nipple.

Shit.

I have to close my eyes at the onslaught, the image of her accepting my cock is too much, I need this to last...

But she doesn't let me. She dives forward as soon as I close my eyes and her lips meet mine as we fall backwards. I manage to stay inside her as we tumble into the water, the blue closing above us.

Gripping her head, I kiss her back desperately, hard, showing her just how beautiful, how perfect she is.

More.

Her voice floats in my head and I growl into her mouth as I draw my cock out of her and pound back in as we sink to the bottom of the pond. I hope she can hold her breath. Flipping us, I press her back to the sandy floor and use the leverage to fuck her for real.

She bites at my mouth as I drive into her with hard, pounding thrusts, the sand kicking up around us, obscuring everything but us as I take my mate. Hiking her legs higher, I angle her hips until I am hitting those nerves with each thrust. She screams into my mouth as she comes, her pussy clenching around me again.

I can't hold back. The feel of her lips, her body, is too much. I roar into her mouth as I pound into her once more before stilling, my cock jerking with the force of my release. It's never-ending, filling her as I gasp into her mouth. My lungs scream at me, needing air, but we can't move.

Something snaps into place between us, making the thread that was once there seem almost grey and frayed compared to this strong one. Like the strongest wire, wrapping around us, linking us together forever. Her mind rushes into mine and I push us off the bottom, breaking through the surface of the water. We both drag in long, deep breaths as I flip onto my back and float with her spread against my chest. She's so tiny compared to my huge body.

"Fucking hell," she gasps, not moving, and I feel the utter pleasure still coursing through her, the same one going through me, making my legs weak and stomach clench.

And that was only our first time, the edge taken off...what will it be like day after day with my mate? Better, though I don't see how. Her body fits so perfectly against my hard one, her softness a contrast as we float in the water under the sun, relearning how to breathe.

"I love you, my dragon," she whispers, and presses her lips to my chest that she can reach.

"I love you, *Neriso*. My greatest treasure, I can't wait to start our life together."

AFTER I COULD WALK AGAIN, I helped her clean up under the waterfall before carrying her to land and laying her down on the sofa grass so we could lie in the sun to dry.

"So, tell me everything I need to know about dragons." She sighs wearily. Dragging her closer, I kiss the top of her head, unable to help myself. I need her pressed against me all the time, touching me, feeling her. It's the only time my dragon settles and is quiet, almost purring beside her.

"Dragons are old, powerful creatures. Once we walked this earth as gods. We were worshiped, this was before my time. There were so many of us, but we started to die out from our own pride mixed with hunters. Dragons." I shake my head. "Our pride is our downfall. We were only allowed to mate with pure bloods, which meant our bloodlines started dying, wasting away. When two of the strongest were completely wiped out, we decided to pull back from this world, to bring everyone home to Klasfor."

"Where is that?" she asks.

"It is hard to explain, *Neriso*," I murmur as I kiss her head, her warmth settling me as I tell the tale of our people. "It is both alongside this world and not, similar to the fae. We have our own lands, linked through doorways, but all except one was destroyed. The only link to this world, guarded at all times. No one but dragons can enter or leave. Our lands are vast, built into the sky. Golden palaces filled with treasures and jewels this world has never seen. Palaces in the sky...dragons sweeping through the clouds. A vast and rich land, but our people..." I shake my head. "They are greedy and proud. That land was mined until there were no more precious jewels and gold became scarce, until the rich became richer and those weaker died trying to elevate their station."

"Same story everywhere." She snorts and I nod. "What happened when you went back?"

"We stayed there. It was our own choice to be locked away from the humans and others. We were untouchable, but the killing didn't stop. Our lands might have been vast, but pride and strength led to a lot of battles between our own. So a king was chosen to lead us, to set down laws. The king had to fight, to prove his own strength, the only way they would accept him. When I was born, I was different. Some saw it as a sign of change, of the future of our race...others not so much. I was so strong, so fierce, it wasn't long before I was crowned king, defeating the other in battle. I, of course, let him live, which many took as a weakness, but he was a friend, a mentor, he helped me learn the way. And for years it worked. I led, I ruled...but I always felt so empty, so alone, like I did not belong there. I yearned to leave, my dragon pulling me from that world. So I did. I put laws and a new leader in place, one I trusted, and I left. I just left, Dawn. I searched this world for the reason I needed to be here, but could not find anything. Tired, I retreated to my mountain and slept...until you woke me."

She sucks in a breath. "What do you think happened to the dragon you put in charge?"

"He is probably dead. The dragon I found was someone he took under his wing, a good kid, so if he was allowed to be killed, then the king is undoubtedly dead."

I clench my fists before sighing and pulling her closer.

"So...who's in charge now...who's king?" she inquires, her eyes confused.

"That's the question, isn't it...and why does he or she want to finally leave Klasfor and enter this world after all these years?"

CHAPTER 64

GRIFFIN

Dawn returns with her dragon hours later, almost night time. She looks happy but her eyes are calculating. He probably answered all of her questions about the dragons. Dawn isn't the type to ignore a threat against us. But when she sees me waiting, she grins and skips my way. I grab her and kiss her hard. She groans into my mouth and smiles as I pull away. The madness that swirls in my mind like always slows with her presence.

"Where is everyone?" she questions.

"Did you have a good day?" I query, as Aska strides past with a nod.

"I did. Griff, where is everyone?" she repeats, as I take her hand and lead her inside, it's not safe outside with just me now.

"Nos is working with Lucy on laws and possible council members, on who they can trust. Dume is with Jair, checking the armoury, house, and dungeons. Your wolf is somewhere in the woods hunting, left not long after you," I inform her, trying to remember if that's all her men.

"Oh," she offers, but she seems sad. Narrowing my eyes, I throw her into the closest wall and glare down at her, my body pressed to hers, vibrating with madness and anger.

"Disappointed to be with your fucked up experiment?" I snarl in her face.

She arches her eyebrow, her hands threading through my hair and massaging. "Never, I just missed them is all, all of you, and yes, even you, Griff, before you start. Now, what's wrong?"

"Nothing," I snap, and try to pull away, but she drags me back until my fist presses to the wall next to her.

"Liar," she retorts, kissing me. "Tell me, Griff, what's wrong? Who do I need to kill?"

Sighing, I grin at her. "You can't solve everything by killing someone."

"Huh, coming from you?" she teases. "Now stop avoiding the question."

"I—" Looking away, I grind my teeth before forcing the words out. "I wanted to know if you still wanted me, still felt the same after meeting my dad and all the others...I'm not exactly a mythical creature like them."

It hurts to admit, hurts to ask, and I'm terrified she might agree, making my worst fears true, but she laughs.

Right in my face.

Snarling, I smash my fist into the wall and push away, storming off, leaving her there. "Griffin, you get your fucking ass back here right now," she yells, angry now.

I turn and stride back to her where she is waiting in the corridor, towering above her as I press my hand to her throat. "Or what, your fucking majesty? Going to kill me? No, you'll just give the order now, no need to get bloody yourself."

Her eyes bleed to black, her anger clashing with mine. "I did this for all of you, Griff, so don't you dare look down on me because you have a problem with the council. I did, and that's why I fucking killed them. You do not get to treat me like shit because you're scared. I'm scared too, and no, to answer your question. You aren't a mythical being, you're not fate chosen or any of that shit. You're Griffin, you're an experiment, like me. We are two fucked up experiments in this powerful, dark world. You're my home, so yes, I still want you. I don't know how you could think anything else, Griffin. Even when you're mean, even when you're filled with hate, I still want you. I want everything you have, I want to fly with you through the skies again, I want to lie in bed with you. I want your cock, mouth, and body, I want you. All of you."

Searching her eyes and face, I see the truth written there and I relax a bit, stroking her throat lovingly. "Even with all the others you have now?" I murmur.

She smiles at me. "They don't understand. Not all of them get the pain of just being alive, of wondering if you're enough. Of questioning if you're an abomination, pondering if you will go mad like the man who made you. You do, Griffin, you understand me in a way they never will. Our rage, our hate is the same...and so is our love. Don't ever doubt that. You are mine, Griffin. Until the end...you are never getting away from me. So get it through your head, and next time you need reassuring, just ask, don't storm away."

"I did ask." I roll my eyes and she laughs as I press a lingering kiss to her lips. "You want to fly with me, even after being with your dragon?" I murmur.

"Always! No one flies and fucks like you, baby." She snorts and then pulls away with a mischievous look on her face. "Why don't you catch me if you can?" she challenges, and then she's gone.

Whirling, I see her racing away and up the stairs, giggling as her hair blows behind her. So fast, so quick. But I'm quicker, and she is never getting away from me.

Racing to the front entrance, I see her climbing the stairs two at a time. I leap up onto the second floor, landing in her path. She squeals and turns, running the other way.

Smirking, I feel my mist leaking around me, my body lighting up with power as my wings burst from my back. She twists and turns, panting as she tries to outrun me. I match her pace, my hand catching her hair every now and again to remind her I'm there, but wanting to see where this goes.

She laughs harder and I know, I just know what she's going to do.

There, at the end of the hallway, is a window. She grins over her shoulder. "Catch me, Griff," she yells, and throws herself through it.

Glass shatters as air rushes in and I throw myself through it, diving after her, tumbling from the third floor of the mansion. The air whizzes past me and there, like before, she is. Her eyes locked on me, her arms held out at her side, and no fear in her body. Just trust that I will always catch her and love.

Plunging, I manage to wrap my arms around her before we meet the rapidly approaching ground, and flap my wings hard to get us back into the sky. She pants between laughs as she watches me. "*Vasculo*," I warn, wanting to chastise her but I can't, I love her.

So much, even when she's crazy...like me.

"Always." She grins and presses her lips to mine as she wraps her arms around me. "Now how about we try that fucking while we fly thing again?"

Fuck, how did I get so lucky?

Looking down, I grumble, "Why the fuck are you wearing leather pants?" She laughs, keeping her legs around me but trusting me to keep her up as I soar, flying us higher. Her hands reach down and undo the leather pants, and she tries to wiggle them off but they are too tight. She sighs. "You're going to cut them away, aren't you?" She pouts.

"I'll buy you more." I smirk as I pull a blade free, holding her with one arm as I cut down the leg and across her arse before switching her to the other hand and cutting the other side. With one yank, the tattered leather falls away, leaving her bare. "Fuck, you're not wearing panties."

Gripping the back of her shirt, I tear that away as well, exposing the pale globes of her breasts to the setting sun, which is throwing orange and pink across the sky we are hovering in.

She's so stunning, held against my darkness, her pale skin lighting up the sky like the moon. She tips her head back, exposing more of her chest and throat as her arms hang down, her body bending backwards as I trace my eyes across her unblemished skin.

I watch her, my heart stopping for a moment. It's like touching an otherworldly creature. My arms and hands are not perfect enough to hold this being, but then she lifts her head. Her black eyes focus on me, her red lips parting on a whisper.

My name.

Fuck not being good enough to touch her, it's never stopped me before and never will. Gripping her arse, I hold her close and slope her back, splitting my concentration between her body and flying. It wouldn't do good to fly into a plane or some shit, that's how much she distracts me.

Shifting her higher, I free my cock, which is already hard and throbbing for her, knowing what's going to happen. She bites her lower lip when I press my cock to her wetness and coat myself in it. She is already soaked, ready for me like always, no doubt our argument made her wet.

Fuck.

There is no time for teasing or niceties, I need her too much. Looking into those black eyes, I take a deep breath and tuck my wings in, letting us descend as I surge into her pussy in one smooth thrust.

She screams, her head falling back as the wind whooshes around us. Holding her tighter, I fuck her with deep, hard thrusts. She's so tight, so wet, so perfect that I almost forget to fly.

Flapping my wings desperately, my back straining from it, I

swoop back into the sky as she gasps, her hips rocking against me to meet my thrusts, her fingers trailing through the darkening sky.

Surging in and out of her, the clenching of her pussy gets to be too much. The weight of her in my arms...I need more. I need her mouth, her screams. I can't concentrate on flying anymore, not with her wrapped around me.

"Griffin," she begs, her hips moving furiously to match my rhythm, her lips parted on constant moans.

I can't fly anymore, so I aim for earth, not looking where. As soon as my feet touch the ground, I whip my head around frantically, spotting the trees. Perfect. Picking the closest one, I slam her into the bark as I fuck her. My cock pounds in and out of her. Her head tilts back, her chest bowing as she pulls me closer. Kissing her breasts over and over, I show her just how much I love her.

She clenches around me. "Griff, God, I'm so close—"

Growling, I press her back into the tree and the scent of her blood fills the air as I rip through her quivering heat, forcing her higher until, with a scream, she comes with my name on her lips. It undoes me. I fuck her harder, faster, until I can't anymore. My balls are drawing up, my stomach rippling as my cock jerks and I come. Filling her with my release.

We still and I lean against her, unable to move, my legs quivering until I'm afraid I might drop her. Fuck, I came so hard I saw stars, and when I lift my head slightly, I see blood on her chest...I must have bitten her. But she doesn't care.

"I'll buy you lots more leather pants," I pant, and she laughs breathlessly.

"Fuck, I love you, Griff. Always, I'll remind you of it whenever you forget," she whispers, pulling me closer. I lean against her, the tree holding us both up after that, and my darkest fear surfaces...the one I've been trying to outrun.

"I'm scared I'll hurt you."

"What?" she asks, confused, so I lift my head, meeting her gaze.

Swallowing hard, I stare into those eyes and in the silence of the woods I reach for her, showing her my deepest, darkest fear. "That man, my dad, you saw him, *Vasculo*. He hurt my mother, not always physically, but his hate...his drive. He hurt her and he hurt all those women. I'm part of him, his legacy, and blood, baby. What if I hurt you, not...not the way we play, but actually hurt you?" I explain, willing her to understand. "I'm terrified I will...that I'll become him."

She grips my cheeks hard. "Blood doesn't mean shit, Griff. You have the most strength of anyone I have ever met. If anyone can beat that bastard's fucked up genes, it's you. You fight even when others would give up, when you get dark sometimes, lost in that madness. But I'll always be there to hold you through it, to let you get it out on me. So bring it, baby, hurt me. Give me the best you got, I can handle it. You and me, Griff. Take it all out on me when-ever you need to. Whenever you feel scared, angry, or mad. Get me. Fuck me. Kill me. Whatever you need. You can never hurt me too much, haven't you learned that by now? Maybe that means I'm as fucked up as you, some might say the pain that prick put me through tainted me. I don't give a fuck, as long as you don't. So what? We're crazy, we are angry. Who fucking cares? Being sane is boring anyway. So, to it all, baby...I say bring it."

With each word that fear falls away, that man's words...my father's words, leaving me. Filled with Dawn, always Dawn. She is my world now, my center, she's right. She can take whatever I deal out, always could, always will. She will meet me in the dark, just as mad as me. Ready to take me down until I feel better. He might have messed me up, but maybe, just maybe, there was a reason for that.

I had to suffer.

I had to become mad, angry, and hateful for her.

For Dawn...because she is too, and she needs someone in the dark with her. I'll be it, always. She will never suffer alone again.

"I love you, *Vasculo*," I whisper, unable to say everything in my head, but I shouldn't have worried because she sees it, knows it, even when I can't speak the poetic words like her other mates can.

"I love you too, Griff. Now let's feed me, huh? I'm starving and for more than just cock." She grins, making me laugh.

"Come on. It's time, no more hiding. We've got shit to do," I declare, and she snickers.

"I couldn't have said it better." She takes my hand and we leave the forest together, my father and my fears left behind where she ripped them free from me, the poison gone even if the effects remain.

We've got shit to do.

CHAPTER 65

DUME

Dawn arrives for food with Griffin, who seems calmer now. He lets her go and she slides in next to me, not even tasting her food as she eats, a yawn splitting her lips. Nos and Lucy are still busy, so it's just Griffin, Jair, and me. Griffin eats quickly, and with a kiss on her lips, leaves us with her. We are all trying to be considerate, to make an effort. For her.

"Want to lie down?" I offer when she is finished eating. She looks at Jair who smiles at her.

"My love, go. I will be by your side tonight, we have the rest of our lives. Right now, Dume needs you. Go," he murmurs, and leans over to kiss her solidly before going back to eating. How did he know I needed her? That man is an enigma, and an honourable warrior.

She smiles and grabs my hand. We wander around the house for a while until we find a room with a giant fireplace. I rush upstairs, grab wood, and hurry back, lighting the fire for her before lying down and pulling her into my arms.

This is what I need, just a reminder. Just her.

She cuddles against me, the flames dancing over her pale skin clad in nothing but Griffin's shirt. She wraps a leg around me and sighs in happiness, finding solace in my arms as do I in hers. I don't always need to feel her desire or feed it, sometimes I just need my mate.

To remind me why I fight when the pain of my memories gets to be too much. When I feel the chains wrapping around me again and my bull snorts and fights in my head.

"Will you show me more? Take me away from here for a moment. I always wanted to see the world...wondered what it was like in different eras. Will you show me?" she requests.

Lifting my head, I look down at her. "A lot of my memories are bad until I met you, *Draya*."

"There must be one," she whispers. "Please, my bull, today is all about escaping. We all know what's coming, can feel it bearing down on us. I might never get to do this again."

"Anything for you, *Draya*, you know that," I murmur, and search my memories for something not tainted by bloodshed and death, or hurt and pain. I blink when I find one I had forgotten about. I had pushed away my past, so angry and hate filled at what happened, that I had suppressed that one night.

The only night I felt free.

Alive in the splendour of my home surrounded by my people. And she's right, I want to share it with her, to have our own secrets, to show her my soul the way she shows me hers. Taking a deep breath, I dive into that memory, opening my mind so she can see it with me.

The fire roars before me, the gold and amber flames dancing, reaching for the sky within the labyrinth walls. The stone, plant-covered walls curve around where we camp.

Laughter and talking fills the air as the others dance and drink. Mead and the scent of sex saturates the air and my nostrils. Here, I am free to change and be who I want. With them. My people.

Tomorrow I will be taken back, returned to my cell. Tonight is my prize for my fifth victory, yet more proof of how powerful my queen is. My people are imprisoned here, yet they don't see it. Don't see how she controls the walls coated in magic. The mist directing them back and forcing helpless humans in here to be killed. Her enemies.

My people are happy, thriving...but kept here like animals. The walkers of the maze, the killers. Yet, they laugh. They mate. They die and live here, never seeming to realise it is wrong. It's possible I know this because I have left the maze, I can see past the magic, but they cannot.

Yet every time I am allowed back here, I take it, because it fills me with a sense of kinship, that loneliness fading away from just being in their presence even though I sit apart from them with my back to the maze wall, the palace of my queen visible behind me. Only I sit at this fire. The others before me.

Together yet apart.

Until a child breaks from the gathering and heads my way. She's small, so small, her brown hair brushed back in warrior braids, the lower half of her face covered in a red hand mark. Horns, small ones, protrude from her head, which shows she is a high blood. Only the high blood—descendants of the original monsters of the maze—can change into human form. Or shift features.

She stops before me, her head tilting adorably, that small arm outstretched towards me with a skin of mead. "You should drink."

"Why?" I rumble.

"You look sad, and whenever they look sad, the drink makes them happy again," she states matter-of-factly, and thrusts the skin at me again.

A small smile curves my lips as I accept the skin and draw a long drink. "Can I have some?" she inquires, her voice small but strong. She plops herself down next to me, her feet kicking near the fire. She's unafraid in my presence...not like the others who look at me with fear and pity.

"No," I tell her, and look at the fire, dismissing her. She shouldn't be around me. I'm a killer.

"Why?" she questions.

"You're too young," I grumble, and she seems to consider the answer before leaning forward.

"I'm thirteen tomorrow," she whispers, and I suck in a breath.

Thirteen, only three years until she is forced to walk the path...to find her own way in the maze. A barbaric act, but one given to every child of the labyrinth.

"Still too young," I tell her, and she sighs, the sound older than her time.

"My daddy says the same." She pouts.

"Where is your dad?" I ask, looking around, but no one pays attention to the child.

"He left me here, said he heard something in there." She looks at the dark opening of the maze, fear and wonder in her eyes. "That was two weeks ago, I hope he comes back soon. I can never fall asleep at night without him singing to me," she murmurs in fear.

"The screams?" I query, and she nods solemnly.

"I hear them all the time, they are scary," she replies sadly.

The screams of the lost souls, the dying. If her father is out there...he's responsible for the screams in her nightmares...but two rotations. That's a long time to be gone. Usually they do one sun turn, not two whole rotations. That means he's overdue to come back to his baby girl. I hope he is okay.

"Will you sing to me?" she whispers. "I-I want to sleep."

"Child—"

"Please?" she implores, her big eyes pleading with me, leaving me unable to say no.

Sighing, I throw back the skin and drain it before wiping my mouth on my arm. Focusing on the moon, I begin to sing. A tale of a pale goddess, the moon, coming to earth. She walks among us, through the maze, and frees us. Breaks the chains of the monsters and releases us, her heart so big that she loves us all. But she has to *go home, she has to leave. She returns to the sky without her monsters.*

As my voice croons into the night the girl shifts closer until her head is on my lap, her eyes closed. I don't move, dare not disturb her as I feel her small body relax. When I look away from her, still singing, I see the others gathered around my fire.

Their voices slowly join in, tales woven together through time. Tales of sorrow, of love, of hope, and pain. A shared destiny, a shared understanding. And here, next to the flames and before the palace of my oppressor, I find my people.

They no longer look at me with fear...but with understanding.
With hope.
I am one of them, a beast of the labyrinth.

I pull back from the memory and look at Dawn. "It was the first time I felt at home. I heard they all died when I escaped, whatever was left of them."

"Thank you, my bull," she says, tears in her eyes.

I wipe them away and kiss her softly. I want my life to be like this forever, and I will learn from the past. I won't let my hate ruin this, and when I look back, I will remember all the good that came with the bad.

Because of her.

Draya, my goddess.

Our saviour.

I made a deal. We all had our time with her today apart from Lucy and Nos. Nos agreed to spend time with her tomorrow, and Lucy... well, who knows about him. So tonight, she is mine. All mine. I pull her closer. Dume dropped her off where I had been waiting, laying in the silk, four-poster bed with candles around the room. I prefer them to real lights, as Griffin called them.

She jumped on the bed and crawled straight into my arms. I turned us and pulled her back to my chest, our legs locked together. This is what I missed most, holding someone when the night dawns and the cool comes. When the dark blocks out the light, I missed holding someone through it, to not be alone when the nightmares rear their ugly heads and those skeletal fingers of death and the souls I have taken reach for me.

"Jair, do you wish you had longer with your family?"

I debate her question, not wanting to offer her false information. "Yes and no. I can never forget the time I had with them, it is precious because of everything that happened. Yes, I wish they had a longer life that never had to end that way. But everything happens for a reason. I wish...I wish for a great many things, my love. But wishes are not reality, what happened, happened, and I cannot change that. All I can do is learn from the past and do my best to treasure the time we had together, even if it feels like they existed with and loved another man. They were happy, we were a family. Now that time is over, now my time is with you. I have learned, I have lost, and now I have love again. A love so strong I feel like a new man. I feel all those shadows and grey areas becoming whole again. Why?"

"For everything that's coming, I'm afraid. Afraid to lose those I love. I never had much to lose before, just me, and now I'm scared I'm going to regret this. Regret not spending more time with you guys, not finding us a way out that means we don't have to face what's to come," she admits, her voice wrapping around me.

"That would make you a coward, my love, and you are no

coward. You are a general, a leader, a warrior. You head into fights without thoughts for your own safety, but that of victory. Do not change now, you would never run from this. You will always do what you think is right, even if it means the worst. I, for one, will live every second with you like it is our last, never wanting to miss one moment," I whisper, and drop a kiss on her shoulder, nudging the shirt away until I can place another over her drumming pulse.

She moans in my arms and then gasps. "Do you need to feed? How long has it been?" She struggles in my arms and I laugh, pulling her closer.

"My love, I only usually feed once a month, the other was for pleasure. It comes with age, the space between feedings, and your blood...your blood is filled with power. I could probably go a long while, longer than a month. I am fine."

She sighs and settles back down, but there is yearning there, a need, one I feel too. To feel love, to lose ourselves for an instant. "My love, do you want me to bite you?"

She shivers as I croon into her ear, her arse pushing back against my hardening cock. "I want to feel your fangs in me, feel the power passing between us...to feel our connection," she murmurs huskily.

Pressing closer at her declaration, I feel my fangs drop and I run them across her neck, making her shiver against me. "I always want you, whatever way I can get you, fangs, cock, emotional-ly...never doubt that, and to feed on you is an opportunity I will never pass up."

"Then feed," she snaps, making me laugh against her skin.

"So demanding," I murmur, as I lick her pulse, the vein throb-bing under her pale skin. Dragging my fangs back and forth, I wind her up until she jerks to try and turn around and I strike.

Burying my fangs in her neck, her blood bursts into my mouth. Heady and addictive, I swallow it. It flows through my body and veins, lighting up every nerve, filling me with her power.

She moans loudly, pressing back and rubbing herself against my cock, back and forth, back and forth. Reaching over, I grip her neck and pull her closer, releasing my fangs from her neck before slamming them in again, just to let her feel the pleasure and pain of the bite.

She screams, her body writhing against me, and I groan into the bite, my cock twitching in my pants as I reach my peak as well. All without touching her with anything other than my fangs. The scent of her cream fills the air as she collapses to the bed, breathing heavily.

Pulling my fangs back, I lick at the bite, cleaning the blood and healing the holes. I cringe at the wet mess in my trousers and drop a kiss on her neck. "Be right back, my love." I leap from the bed and clean up in the adjoining bathroom and then bring a towel back. Spreading her willing thighs, I clean her up and then get back into bed, pulling her into my arms.

She giggles. "Damn, that bite is addictive. Next time you can bite me all over."

"It's a promise, my love. I will decorate every inch of your skin with my fangs...including that sweet pussy of yours. You will come so much you won't be able to move," I murmur, and she groans.

"Promise?"

"Yes." I laugh.

She goes quiet for a while, but she isn't asleep, then suddenly her voice fills the air. "You never told me much about the woman who turned you."

I freeze at the memories crowding my head and push them away. "I will, but not now, I'm not ready and you are tired. This wouldn't be a short conversation. We have our whole lives, my love. Sleep, I will hold you through it. Tomorrow is the start of the rest of our lives. Of a new time. One filled with something so much more than the past ever had to offer."

She sighs, her mind brushing against mine filled with such love and understanding, it astounds me. "Goodnight, Jair, love you," she murmurs sleepily. Her breathing evens out and her body relaxes as I kiss her throat.

"I love you too, in this life and the next. My undead heart is yours," I vow.

CHAPTER 66

NOS

My little monster is sound asleep. I told the others to leave her. This time is mine with her anyway, and she needs to rest. She has been through a lot. And her body has too, not to mention the workout her other mates have put her through. I watch her sleep from the chair at the base of the bed.

She is so beautiful. Her hair is thrown across the pillow, her ruby lips parted in a slight snore, and her lashes creating dark crescents across her cheeks. Her body is bare apart from a t-shirt bunched up around her stomach.

So beautiful, I can't bear to look away. We were apart for too long, I felt it. Now she is back and all I want to do is crawl into bed next to her, but she has things she needs to do. Things I have held off for as long as I could, but people are demanding answers and she will want to be part of it.

I can't protect her from this, even as much as I wish I could. I can't protect her from everything, but I can be with her through it. Holding her hand, offering her my support. She will never be alone, that's what the fates wanted.

We have a lot to discuss, a lot has happened. But for now, she can sleep. A few more minutes stolen away won't make a difference. She rolls over and those lashes blink open, her hand coming up to shield her eyes from the sunlight.

She sits up slowly and spots me, a wide smile gracing those lips. Without speaking, she holds out her hand and I accept it, climbing onto the bed with her. Stolen moments, yes, they can have her later.

For now, she is mine.

Leaning against the bed, she presses against my side, both of us happy just to be with each other after all this time apart. I know she has worries, worries about not being good enough, about not having enough experience. That all this is...wrong.

I wait, letting her think through her thoughts, letting her lean on me and ask anything if she needs it—this is the calm before the storm.

"Nos, I—" She sighs. "What if I can't do this? I've spent so many hours debating reasons why I shouldn't, not if I couldn't. This wasn't what I wanted, I just wanted to stop them," she whispers.

"I know, my little monster, I know, but sometimes our lives are out of our hands, and you made a choice to save people, to help them. The world rewards those types of choices. Holding its breath for people who can help stop the destruction of this realm."

"But why me?" She lifts her head, searching my eyes. "Why me?" It's a question I have no answer for, all I can offer her is what I know. The reasons I love her.

"I don't know, little monster, all I know is I love you. So much. As for why...only the fates know that. You are fate chosen, so am I. Two souls meant to find each other. Whatever the future holds, we do it together. No more apart. My little monster, love is our future, don't forget that even when it gets dark and bloody. Before this change is through, we are going to face our biggest test yet, I know it. But we are here, all of us for a reason. With you. Use it, use us. Use what they perceive as our weakness. Love, my little monster. Use it."

It's time.

Lucy's voice floats into my mind, so I take a moment, cupping Dawn's face as I drop a soft kiss on her lips. "You can do this, little monster. Now, it's time, time to go back into that world. Are you ready?"

She sucks in a breath, looking into my eyes. "Yes, I'm ready, are you?"

"If you are, so am I. Let's go change the world, little monster, and start our lives."

CHAPTER 67

DAWN

Nos helps me change into a simple, flowing black dress. No court business today, just more talking, like sorting through the dragon problem, discussing who we are considering for the council, and assigning my men roles. I had a break like Aska said, time away to sort my thoughts and prepare, but now I need to be all in.

Choice or not, this isn't the future I would have ever thought I'd have, but that doesn't matter now. It's my future and I have more than most. I have the power and station to change things, to protect people. People once like me. I have a duty to accept that. It's time to take my place.

I don't know what's going to happen, nor does everyone else, but anyone who stands in our way should be scared, very scared. I have some of the biggest, baddest monsters behind me. Change is coming whether they like it or not. They either get on board or they die.

By my hands.

I've faced down human monsters, men who've tried to kill me. I've met a mob boss and been stolen. I've been killed, experimented on, trapped, and locked away. Hurt, raped, and tossed out like trash. I've seen the worst of this world, but also the best...in those men waiting for me.

Nos kisses me and leaves, allowing me to have a moment to myself, and I smile into the mirror. The good makes the bad all worth it. Every inch of pain, every brutal touch or punch. I would endure it again and so much more to find the happiness and love I have now.

But...these enemies are new, and I have a feeling before this is through, I will see a lot more bad. I'm hoping the good still outweighs it. My hate for the council and what they did is gone, and in its place is a fierce burning of love and strength.

They need me.

The way I once needed them.

It's time.

A noise startles me from my reveries and I turn as I see a flash in the mirror behind me. I have a split second to see the blade coming towards me. But it's enough.

I catch the dagger, and it cuts through the skin on my hand, my blood filling the air and only making me act faster. The man's eyes widen as I jerk on the blade, wounding myself further and yanking it from his hold. I twirl it around and imbed it in his stomach. He falls backwards, his eyes wide as he cups the blade protruding from his body.

He looks down and falls to his knees, blood pouring from the wound. It's a killing blow, I know. He tumbles to the side, his eyes blinking in shock as I stroll closer.

"What...are you?" he wheezes.

"A monster, baby," I purr, as I crush my foot into his windpipe.

He would have died anyway, and I know he wouldn't tell us anything. But one thing is for sure—someone wants me dead...how exciting.

Just then the door bursts open, my monsters filling the frame with a snarl. "What happened?" Griffin demands, coming over and yanking me away from the dead man as Nos and Jair kneel at his side.

"He tried to kill me." I shrug, my grin growing. "I guess someone wants me dead." A rumble goes through the room, only widening my smile. "Looks like we have a killer to hunt."

"Why is she smiling like that?" Aska whispers to Dume, who snorts. "It's both terrifying and a turn on."

"You have no idea. Just you wait, dragon." Griffin laughs. "Our mate just realised that she can get her hands bloody, ain't nothing getting in her way."

I guess we have more threats to deal with than we thought. The human hunters are still out there, some witches managed to escape, and now someone is trying to kill me...isn't this going to be fun?

Once a monster, always a monster...just with a crown now.

I hope they run far and fast, and aren't afraid of the dark...because that's where I live and I'm coming for them.

They should be afraid, very afraid.

EPILOGUE

ALDROS, LORD OF FLAMES

DEEP IN KLASFOR...

The healer winces as he covers the talon gash with ruebc paste. "My king," he whispers, bowing his head, his frail frame shuddering under my gaze as I swivel to stare at him from atop my golden throne, my subjects observing me from around the room. "This is healing nicely."

"Good, leave," I order, and turn back to watch my people. That foolish child had tried to defy me. To stop my plans, to defend his former king who left without a care for his people. Who forsook us, for them. For the humans. It was all too easy to kill him. I did not expect him to escape Klasfor and travel into their world as a warning though...never mind. It has happened and now they know we are coming.

"It is time the world remembers who we are!" I roar as I get to my feet, and every dragon's gaze turns to me, my crown glowing under the fires of our home. "We hid away, afraid to anger them, afraid to kill. To get bloody. We hid and we waited, forgetting who we are. Under his rule and his family's, we became weak!"

Growls sound around the room as I watch them with a smirk. "No more, we are not weak! We are dragons! We are the great riders! They will tremble when they see us coming, they will scream when they hear our roars, and when we take their world, they will fall to their knees before me. Your king!"

Chanting emanates from the crowd as they tip their heads back and fire escapes their mouths. Just then, the great doors at the end of the hall open and my unrest, my guards, drag in three women.

Three witches.

They come willingly, not even fighting the restraining grasps, their eyes cold and knowing. I gesture for them to be let through as I sit back down on my throne. The unrest throws them before my feet, they kneel there, heads unbowed. Disrespect! How dare they! I am a king!

"False king," one of them sneers with a laugh.

"No tricks, witch," I snarl, leaning forward, the throne creaking under my weight. "You are here for a reason."

"We know why we are here, false king, it will not change what is to come. You think to weaken them, to stop their sources. It will not matter," another argues.

"You cannot stop fate," the other concludes, and then they all smile at the same time. I hate witches.

"Fate? Oh, my little witches, fate has no hold on me, it cannot control or order me to do its bidding." My people laugh with me and I glare at them. "But your fate rests here," I state.

Standing, I step down the ruby-encrusted stairs, my bare chest glistening under the fires above, highlighting my scars from the many battles I have been in and won. Leaning down, I bend to look into their eyes as I speak, so they will not mistake my words or intent.

It is time.

What I have been waiting for, planning for centuries. It is finally here...

"It is time for Askaliarian to return home and take his place in my army. Their world will become ours, it will burn under our feet as I rule from high. War, little witches. We are going to war, and you are to be the first casualties."

Turning away, I smile at my unrest. "Burn them," I order, as I head back to my throne, and the sound of flames fills the sacred temple, their screams soon following.

As they shriek, their skin melting and bones scorching, I chuckle.

Askaliarian, I am coming for you. You and your world. They will both be mine...

Acknowledgments

First of all, I want to thank you, the readers. For loving my monsters as much as I do, I hope I have done them justice for you. Dawn is always so much fun to write because I can be totally insane with her and it is never too much (ha) So thank you for always sticking with me, and standing in that dark alongside me.

To Mal and Court, I couldn't have done this without you. Thank you for listening to hours of rambling and incoherent messages while keeping me sane!

To my three-way, for letting me bounce my monsters off them and always giving me the motivation to carry on!
And to my betas, who rode this crazy train with me.

Without them, this wouldn't exist. Thank you for always going along with my ideas and laughing with me during the crazy parts.
I love you all.
Thank you.

About the Author

K.A Knight is an indie author trying to get all of the stories and characters out of her head. She loves reading and devours every book she can get her hands on, she also has a worrying caffeine addiction.

She leads her double life in a sleepy English town, where she spends her days writing like a crazy person.

Read more at K.A Knight's website or join her Facebook Reader Group.

Also by K.A. Knight

THEIR CHAMPION SERIES

- The Wasteland
- The Summit
- The Cities

- The Forgotten
- The Lost

DAWNBREAKER SERIES

- Voyage to Ayama
- Dreaming of Ayama

THE LOST COVEN SERIES

- Aurora's Coven
- Aurora's Betrayal

HER MONSTERS SERIES

- Rage
- Hate

THE FALLEN GODS SERIES

- *Pretty Painful (Coming soon!)*

STANDALONES

- Scarlett Limerence
- Nadia's Salvation
- The Standby
- *Den of Vipers (Coming soon!)*

CO-AUTHOR PROJECTS

- Circus Save Me
- Taming The Ringmaster
- Dark Temptations Volume One (contains One Night Only and Circus Saves Christmas)
- The Wild Interview
- The Hero Complex
- Shipwreck Souls
- The Horror Emporium
- Capturing Carmen
- Stealing Shiloh
- *Harbouring Harlow (Coming soon!)*

THE FALLEN GODS SERIES

TURN THE PAGE FOR A SNEAK PEEK INTO PRETTY
PAINFUL, THE FALLEN GODS BOOK ONE.

YOU CAN PRE-ORDER HERE >
https://books2read.com/PrettyPainful

Excerpt

PRETTY PAINFUL

"Team three in position," I whisper into my mic.

I hear my men moving into place behind me, the rustle of their tactical gear the only sound as we surround the old church. It's supposed to be an easy job, get in, get the package, and get out. We are being paid handsomely for our time, not that we know who ordered this job, but it doesn't matter. We need all the money we can get at the moment to keep our hunting going.

"Team two in position," Gio rumbles into my ear.

"Team one in position. All clear, boss."

"Moving in. Team two, take the back. Team one, you're on lookout. Team three, with me," I order, hopping up from my prone position and into a crouch. Waving my hand, I watch the others cross the grassy, open area and wait on either side of the door. We don't know what to expect in there, only that what we have come for is dangerous. I'm planning to take every precaution to ensure my team makes it home, and we deliver the package on time as requested.

"Move in, take the door," I hiss.

They yank the door open and my team surges in, with me on their heels as they secure the inside of the church.

"Clear!"

"Clear!"

I get shouts from around the room and I nod, switching on my light and swinging it around the space. Cobwebs hang from the ceiling and pillows running along each aisle of the church. Forgotten, wooden pews are tossed carelessly around the room, and the carpet under my feet crunches from lack of care. A big, stained glass window stands at the end of the church under an archway, and a table with a large, wooden cross takes up the middle section.

It looks like nothing has even been stolen from here—gold and silver litter the area like forgotten relics. Why would no one steal it? The fact that it's a church wouldn't stop people...maybe it's whatever we are hunting? I wave them forward, all of us on high alert. I don't like this, something seems off. While everything is expanding and being built around it, this church stands forgotten in the middle of nowhere. An uneasy feeling takes root as I head for the table at the front of the church. I nod at my men, and they quickly shove it out of the way, revealing the hidden hatch our mysterious employer described.

Pulling out my bolt cutters, I try to ignore the fact this thing has been secured from the outside. Whatever they wanted to keep in, they *really* never wanted it to get out again. The chain is old and rusted but still strong, and it takes three cuts before the chain gives way. Yanking on the hatch, I cough as dust and dirt flies into my face, like the air has finally been let into that room after hundreds of years. Taking a light from the man next to me, I throw it down into the darkness and wait. I hear it finally hit the floor, and when I look down, I can spot it, but it looks far away.

"Rope," I command, and as my men work on getting us a way down there, I crouch and take a closer look.

Something moves in the dark, shooting across the light's rays before the glow disappears altogether, sending the room into complete darkness.

"Shh!" I hold up my hand, frowning at the sound of slithering and breathing coming from below...

What the—

Two golden lights flicker on, moving higher towards the opening quickly, until they burst from the hatch, taking the stone floor with them as my men yell and fire at the black shape that busts from the floor.

Holy fuck, what is that thing?

"Hold your fire! We need it alive!" I shout, trying to cut through the chaos of my men's yells and panic.

A scream sounds to my left, and I spin, only to watch as one of my men is picked up in the dark and thrown across the room.

"What is that?" someone screams.

I hear a gurgle before blood sprays us, and more screaming starts from somewhere in the room, our lights swinging wildly as we try to find the thing.

I spot movement out of the corner of my eye and quickly spin there, aiming through my tranq gun. "Gotcha," I whisper with a grin as I take aim and fire. When it hits its target, a roar like a lion cuts through the night, shaking the very foundation of the building. "Hit it with everything you got!" I order.

The blur moves towards me and I keep shooting, with sweat dripping down my face and back as it gets closer and closer. At the last possible second, it falls from the air, dropping to the floor of the church and crushing the pews, a dark blob in the night.

A monster.

Printed in Great Britain
by Amazon

19871422R00246